Praise f

Blue Deer

"Her strong suits include witty prose [and] bone-dry humor . . . *Blue Deer Thaw* is a delight." —*The Seattle Times*

"Harrison demonstrates once again that she's among the most talented writers to grace the genre in recent years."
—*Publishers Weekly* (starred review)

"Lively, hilarious . . . Not to be missed by devotees of good writers with an exquisite sense of humor." —*Kirkus Reviews*

ALSO BY JAMIE HARRISON

The Center of Everything
The Widow Nash
An Unfortunate Prairie Occurrence
Going Local
The Edge of the Crazies

BLUE *DEER* THAW

A Jules Clement Novel

JAMIE HARRISON

COUNTERPOINT
CALIFORNIA

BLUE DEER THAW

First published in the United States by Hyperion Books in 2000

First Counterpoint edition: 2024

Library of Congress Cataloging-in-Publication Data
Names: Harrison, Jamie, 1960- author.
Title: Blue deer thaw / Jamie Harrison.
Description: First Counterpoint edition. | Los Angeles : Counterpoint California, 2024. | Series: A Jules Clement Myster
Identifiers: LCCN 2024010041 | ISBN 9781640093003 (trade paperback) | ISBN 9781640093010 (ebook)
Subjects: LCSH: Clement, Jules (Fictitious character)—Fiction. | Blue Deer (Mont. : Imaginary place)—Fiction. | Sheriffs—Fiction. | Montana—Fiction. | LCGFT: Detective and mystery fiction. | Novels.
Classification: LCC PS3558.A6712 B58 2024 | DDC 813/.54—dc23/eng/20240301
LC record available at https://lccn.loc.gov/2024010041

Cover design by Jaya Miceli
Cover design by Victoria Maxfield
Cover images: statue © Shutterstock / macondo; footprints © Shutterstock / BigTunaOnline; clouds © Alamy / Aloysius Patrimonio
Book design by Laura Berry

COUNTERPOINT
Los Angeles and San Francisco, CA
www.counterpointpress.com

Printed in the United States of America

10 9 8 7 6 5 4 3 2 1

To John and Karin

Remind me to tell you about when
I looked into the heart of an artichoke.

—BETTE DAVIS IN *All About Eve*,
BY JOSEPH L. MANKIEWICZ

I hate people who are not serious
about their meals.

—OSCAR WILDE

CONTENTS

BLUE *DEER* THAW

1 *Snow Dreams*

PEOPLE FREEZE TO DEATH ALL WINTER LONG ACROSS the northern tier of the United States. In Buffalo and Boston the dead tend to be homeless, and in Montana and the Dakotas they tend to be drunks, but alcohol is almost always involved to some degree, especially given such human habits as driving drunk and walking when the car breaks down, hunting drunk and getting lost, fishing drunk and falling through the ice, and napping drunk on a toasty highway. As an added grace note, the warm, spinning, melting sense of paralysis that comes with intoxication is hard to separate from the warm, spinning, melting sense of paralysis that comes with acute hypothermia. At the very end, giving in is almost a relief.

The call came at 1:00 a.m. "I need you to check on someone," said the woman in a chilly, tight voice.

"Call the station," snapped Jules Clement, squinting at his clock.

"I saw a lady heading out of the Bachelor bar two hours ago," said the voice, "and I'm worried she didn't make it home."

"Which way was she going?"

"South, I think. Cross-country."

"Why didn't you offer her a ride?" he asked.

The line went dead.

Jules replaced it slowly and lay still. Gradually the air temperature sank in, and he brought his right leg and the arm that had answered the phone under the goosedown comforter. It was March 22, and spring had theoretically begun an hour earlier in the midst of a huge snowstorm. He reached for the phone again, dialed the station, and asked the night dispatcher to send Jonathan Auber down the valley to the Bachelor bar, where he should keep an eye out for an errant female drunk. Then Jules fell back to sleep, just like the woman in the snow.

2 *The Bachelor*

BLUE DEER BULLETIN

SHERIFF'S REPORT, WEEK OF MARCH 13–19

March 13—A collision was reported, between two out-of-state vehicles in the hospital parking lot. A citizen reported that a young man was aiming at geese with his pickup near the Clement Park playground.

March 15—A woman reported a robbery, stating that someone had stolen all of her husband's shoes.

March 16—A La-Z-Boy chair was found half submerged in the lagoon. Officers decided to wait for the ice to melt.

March 18—A caller notified an officer that someone had set his car on fire. The officer determined that the car had not been driven since the previous morning, and found a discarded can of lighter fluid nearby. The incident is under investigation.

March 19—A number of balloons filled with red paint have been thrown on sidewalks downtown.

ABSAROKA COUNTY, MONTANA, WAS AS HABITABLE and lovely as a place with a nasty climate and vertiginous terrain could be. Not every county in America could claim four man-killing species (grizzlies, rattlesnakes, mountain lions, and the deer mice that had given a hunter hantavirus the fall before); not every county boasted both methamphetamine factories and wolves, floods and avalanches, and hot springs and poisonous mushrooms. There were more cows in the county than people or tall trees, and many of those who didn't make a living in agriculture settled for America's most dangerous profession, logging, or toiled at the federally subsidized local lumber mill, processing trees that took fifty years to reach toothpick grade.

The weather in southwestern Montana was famously variable and offered a 160-degree temperature spread—record high, 112; record low, minus 48—which helped to account for Absaroka County's sparse population. The sparse population in turn accounted for its popularity as a vacation destination. The county marked the top boundary of Yellowstone National Park, and odds were high that if a person didn't work with animals or wood they worked with tourists, though no one quite knew where this last fit on the risk scale. The county had nineteen bars, and the heaviest drinkers were people in this trade, be they real estate agents, doctors, lawyers, fishing guides, or writers.

Visitors, especially the Yellowstone-bound summer hordes, could never understand why more people didn't live in the area. Many locals did their best to steer these earnest beauty-seekers toward Jackson, Wyoming, or Whitefish, Montana. Some visitors persisted, actually tried to move in, and their survival rate—the ratio of people who stayed at least five years to those who left after a second or third winter—approximated that of a new restaurant in New York City. Which was why the population (twelve thousand people in four thousand square miles) was about the same as it had been in 1900, despite constant immigration.

When Jules Clement, the county sheriff, had first climbed into bed on Tuesday night, a sixty-mile-an-hour chinook still kept the air warm. Within an hour the chinook had stopped, the temperature plummeted, and fresh, dry snow had begun to cover the now crunchy layer of thaw slush. By morning the air near the ground was foggy with ice crystals, the sky clear and blue and disarmingly sweet above. The March thaw had come to a screeching halt, and if you listened closely you could almost hear Blue Deer's gardeners wail.

Jules was thirty-six, tall and skinny with chocolate-colored hair, matching brown eyes, and a crooked, angular face, an interesting face but only handsome to the fondest eyes. Wednesday was the morning he and Axel Scotti, the county attorney, regularly met for a greasy breakfast and a midweek appraisal of the state of justice in Blue Deer, the county seat. They did not often agree, but food somehow muffled the acrimony: meetings that might have ended with screams in an office often reached a truce at the diner. Possibly they each felt compelled to finish chewing before responding to annoying comments, smiling for the benefit of other diners, who did their best to listen in to the two legal wheels of the area, who happened to be cousins-in-law. This coincidence was compounded by the fact that Jules's father had been sheriff, too, which explained a good deal: not many liberals with doctorates in archaeology turn to law enforcement in their mid-thirties. The career switch hadn't made much sense three years earlier, and it made less and less as time went by.

Jules didn't reach the station until nine, by which time the deputy who'd been on duty the night before, Jonathan Auber, was long gone. In truth Jonathan, only twenty-four, was never fully there; Jules read through his reports with the usual mix of despair and glee. Part of the reason Jonathan was on night duty was that it was the quietest possible shift, at least in March. The deputy had still managed to plow up a few pearls: a transient sleeping in the middle of Park Street, a possible burglary that turned out to be a stowaway cat hidden in a child's closet, and a post–bar closing father-son argument over a dented car.

This last had taken Jonathan until 2:10, when he had finally responded to Jules's walking woman phone call. By the time Jonathan reached the Bachelor, twenty miles south of Blue Deer in the defunct town of Paris, the bar was locked and dark and snow had dusted into the last car tracks in the parking lot. Jonathan didn't say this, but Jules imagined it. What Jonathan said was that he'd played his spotlight over the surrounding fields, seen nothing but snowflakes and a billboard for Yellowstone Park, and driven back to Blue Deer.

Jules weighed the options. The odds that anyone had come to harm the night before were minuscule, but not making sure would leave him worried and edgy. Not checking the call also meant a morning mired in the bottom line of the job. Grace Marble, the station manager, was humming ominously while arranging stacks of paper for his inspection. One of the tasks for the day involved trimming the jail food budget and another was setting the staff schedule for the next month, more of keeping mankind as safe from Jonathan as possible and vice versa.

Jules ran for it as soon as Grace began her morning phone call with her daughter, leaving a brief note for her on top of one of the paper towers and slipping a little in the doorway on melting ice from his own boots. The car had already lost all its warmth, but a temperature of eight didn't matter so much when the sun was out and the option was totaling columns of numbers under fluorescent light and acoustic tiles.

He saw seven other cars in the twenty-minute drive. The Bachelor, which doubled as a secondhand store, was halfway to Gardiner and the border of Yellowstone Park, and in the summer he'd have seen hundreds of cars, dozens of RVs and motorcycles. Paris had been founded on a pretty bend of the river in 1890, and named without irony: Montana also had a Manhattan, a Belgrade, and a Glasgow. Now the population stood at eight, and not one of these people was French. Paris had once been served by the Yellowstone branch line, had been the best place to dance for the poor Irish and Italians in the now defunct mining towns of Aldridge and Electric. The dance hall had been gone for decades, and no one had ever used the Bachelor, a pile of logs that had served as Paris's gas station, post office, and grocery, as a destination resort. It sat alone just off the road, a few scraggly willows marking what had once been an irrigation ditch. The building was tucked against a long bench, a ridge that was itself tucked against the mountains; in a vertical land, many of the loveliest lines were horizontal. There wasn't much to break the view. An old ranch house was nestled against the same line of hills almost a mile to the north, and to the south stood a tidy eyesore of a chalet and a doublewide trailer, gutted from a fire that February.

Jules made a third set of tracks in the fresh snow of the lot and parked at the back door, near an old Chevy and a new Range Rover, not a car you saw often in Absaroka County despite the fitting terrain. The Chevy belonged to Leon Baden, the manager of the Bachelor and the owner of both the chalet and the trailer. The Rover made sense a minute later.

Jules didn't bother to knock. A woman in a long-sleeved

leotard and jeans leaned against the bar, reading a newspaper and drinking a beer. It was Merry Maier, Halsey Meriwether's niece; Halsey owned the Bachelor as well as a hotel named the Sacajawea, and for the last few months had also been Jules's part-time employer.

"I didn't know you were working here," said Jules.

"Well, I am," she said, frowning as she tucked the newspaper under the counter. "It's not like I picked the job."

"Did Halsey ask you to help out?"

"I don't know," she said. "Does Halsey ask?"

Jules eyed her, judging her mood. When he'd run away from the station he hadn't bargained on dealing with Merry.

"Usually," he said.

"Be glad you're not family." She tossed a coaster on the bar top. "What can I get for you?"

This was their usual conversation, her usual style of complaint. The world owed her, and the world hadn't delivered adequately. Merry had moved into the Sacajawea at the beginning of February, two weeks after Jules had started sorting Halsey's messy collection of antiquities, some two dozen crates and a list that hadn't been updated since the fifties. Jules had just finished stuffing everything into the music room when Halsey informed him that his niece would be moving into the third-story tower room above, and could Jules help? Jules liked Halsey, and there was always the possibility he'd like Halsey's niece. He gave the idea up the same afternoon, after she critiqued the way he handled her belongings. It had been years since anyone had called Jules "boy" in quite that way. Finding out he was the county sheriff didn't shame her; a cop was a servant, too.

"Nothing," said Jules. "I'm here because you called in a welfare check on a woman last night."

There was a long pause. Merry's expression was absolutely blank. She was plush; solid but curvy, with pink, sun-blasted skin and droopy, dark eyes, spaniel eyes that could have been gorgeous if they showed a hint of life. From a distance she looked twenty-five, but close up, on certain mornings, she seemed closer to fifty.

"No I didn't."

"I recognized your voice. Take the credit."

"I don't know what you're talking about."

Her voice was nasal, clipped but edged with a bit of a little girl's whine. Jules tried again. "Were you working last night?"

"Yes."

"Maybe someone else called about her from here."

"No one used the phone."

Jules threw his hands up. "Look," he said, "I'm not trying to make up a problem. I'm just here to follow up. I'll ask Leon Baden."

"He's in the shop next door. He'd prefer not to be bothered."

He drummed his fingers on the bar and watched her. She'd washed the same glass three times, and not very gracefully. Dottie Cope, Halsey's manager at the Sacajawea, refused to allow Merry near anything breakable.

"You don't want Leon to know about the call," he said.

"I don't know what you're talking about."

"Tough shit," said Jules. "You should have thought of that last night, before you did the right thing."

"Fine," she snapped, flicking water from her hands and spinning out from behind the bar.

She said it with all the charm of a cornered terrier. Merry wasn't fat, but there was somehow so much of her physically and so little mentally that even standing next to her was cloying. All that hair, wide cheekbones, the obviously bobbed nose with a fine network of alcoholic's veins, lips that were full but lacked subtlety. She was almost six feet, and probably stronger than Jules, with a tiny waist but huge, wayward breasts, a high ass, and surprisingly fine-boned knees and ankles and feet. Nothing seemed to go together, and her mind was so acrid, mean-spirited, and paranoid that Jules had begun to think of her as a meat-eating plant, one of the terrors of a fifties B movie.

Jules followed her through the doorway into the used furniture store and threaded through mounds of junk—chairs and lamps, bedframes and bits of wrought iron fence, and enough bad art to support a sidewalk in New York. Leon had managed the Bachelor and this sideshow for three years, ever since he'd retired as the local high school's history teacher, and during that time the piles hadn't seemed to change, partly because Leon spent more time refinishing other people's furniture than selling his own.

Leon was in the back, peering into a bureau mirror with a rag in his hand, looking at his own reflection rather than working on the woodwork. He watched them approach in the mirror.

"Leon, this is Jules Clement, the man who puts the broken stuff together for Uncle Halsey."

She acted flirty but deferential, and her description would have worked for either of his jobs. "Leon and I know each other," said Jules. "I'm sure you've noticed people don't always drink gracefully. We come out every month or so." They answered calls from the Bachelor in double time, usually to protect the drunk from Leon rather than vice versa.

"I told him you were busy," said Merry.

"Shoo," said Leon. "Try not to break any glasses."

She surged off, and Jules wondered how long she and Leon would last in the same building.

Leon had gone back to rubbing the frame. "She's supposed to be a present from Halsey until the Sack opens," he said. "Thank him for me. The girl is a complete pain in the ass."

"Yes," said Jules.

"You're a pain in the ass, too," said Leon. "I didn't call about trouble this morning. Isn't it a little early to be here for a drink? Even if you never wear your uniform anymore?"

"We got a welfare call last night about a drunk woman who left here on foot," said Jules. "We didn't find anyone last night, and I'm just following up."

"A drunken woman." Leon looked amused. Jules supposed he couldn't blame him. He lifted his head and really looked at Jules. "Is she the one who called?"

"Yes, but she won't admit it."

Leon smiled. It wasn't very pleasant. "That's because of me. I have to tell her to keep out of people's business."

"You shouldn't mind a welfare call." Jules eyed a stack of three chairs, topped by two ugly porcelain soup tureens. "That stuff from the Sack?"

"Fred dropped it off yesterday," said Leon. "I keep waiting for Halsey to get rid of something I can sell."

Jules shrugged. The Sacajawea was in the midst of renovation and had a basement full of unusable crap. Leon, who took the stuff Halsey didn't keep on consignment, would be waiting a long time. "So who was in the bar last night?"

"I was home with a cold," Leon said mildly, pointing to his cherry-red nose. "I wouldn't know. You'll have to spend more time with charm girl."

"Did you hear anyone outside your house?" asked Jules. "This woman supposedly headed south cross-country."

"No. I went to bed early. I try to do that when I get a night off."

Beauty rest, undoubtedly. Leon had a bizarre resemblance to Robert Plant, bandy-legged, with curly gold locks and a graven, arrogant face. Despite reactionary politics, on days off he did not dress or act his age, which had to be nearing on sixty, and in the summer he had a fondness for muscle shirts. He'd served as the high school wrestling coach until rumors circulated that he'd been too liberal in dispensing steroids.

"Did Anne hear anything?"

"Not to my knowledge."

Leon was usually more talkative, but except for the February trailer fire this was probably the first time Jules had seen him before cocktail hour. He walked to the door and stared to the south across the soft, bumpy snow, wondering how deep it was. "Is Anne home?"

"I don't know." Leon snapped on rubber gloves and poured some stripper on a cloth.

The yard looked empty, though it was possible a car was on the far side of the chalet, or completely covered with snow. "What's she driving?"

"Jackshit. The Nissan's in for brake work."

Jules sorted this out, started to ask for clarification and decided not to bother. "I'll just walk over," he said.

Leon sneezed. "You could always try calling," he said, pointing to the grubby beige phone in the bar.

"I feel like a walk," said Jules.

It was all bravado. He swung a leg over the entirely symbolic hitching post at the edge of the porch and sank in to his knee in the snow. He floundered off stubbornly, aiming for the bumps that signified frozen hummocks of grass and saved him a few inches of depth. He knew Leon was watching, and found the thought maddening: halfway to the A-frame he felt sweat trickle down his sides. Leon was almost always an asshole, but today he seemed to have extra reasons: a bad head cold, bad attitude, bad help. Jules had apparently gone from escaping his job for the morning to intruding on an ugly marriage; he no more wanted to talk to Anne Baden, a woman who rarely opened her mouth anyway, than he'd wanted to do the staff schedule. And it was so cold that within two minutes he lost contact with his nose.

Jules knew as soon as he dragged himself up the steps that no one was home. He pounded on the door anyway and yelled for Anne, not particularly eager to begin the return journey. He opened the door a crack and started to call for her a second time, then focused on the wet nose of a silent rottweiler waiting patiently for him six inches inside.

He slammed the door hard and jumped backward down the steps so abruptly that the porch hopped. Leon's failure to mention the dog was completely in character. Jules looked mournfully at his zigzag tracks from the bar, found a hat in one pocket, and struck off on a more efficient return course. He was rummaging through his other pockets for a pair of gloves when one foot hit something hard and he swam through the air, landing on his chest in an explosion of white.

Jules rolled onto his back, wiped the powdery snow from his face, and screamed a filthy imprecation at the clear blue sky. Then he sat up to see what he'd tripped over and screamed again. He'd found Anne Baden, and she was looking right at him.

LEON HADN'T ACTUALLY lied, but he'd certainly misled. The semantics didn't matter much, because now he was sobbing, soaking a dishrag with tears and snot. Merry, who'd cleared the drifts with alarming ease to see what Jules was yelling about, was in the bathroom throwing up.

"So you just didn't know where she was," said Jules, panting a little. He'd charged back across the snowy field to radio Harvey Meyers for the coroner and a van. Anne Baden didn't need the county's only ambulance.

Leon shook his head, eyes closed and face maroon.

"You must have been worried about her."

The man shrugged, then covered his face and let out another wail.

"You didn't want to admit to me that you didn't know where she was?"

A nod behind the dishrag. Jules found the phone book and dialed the closest neighbor, a man he knew had been friendly with Leon and his wife. Meanwhile, Leon suddenly quieted and stuck his head under the gooseneck faucet of the bar sink. Jules hung up and watched.

"We haven't been getting along," whispered Leon.

"She hasn't been living at home?"

No reaction. Jules tried again. "Do you know where she was staying?" He shook his head.

"Someone had to bring her here, if she didn't have her own car. You don't know who?"

Another shake.

"Did Merry call you when she called me?" He'd have to ask her the same thing, but he could still hear her retching in the background.

"I take the phone off the hook when I sleep," said Leon. "I've got some back problems, and sometimes I take pain meds."

"You lock your door?"

"Shit, yes."

"Anne still have a key?"

"'Course." Some life worked back into his eyes. "She still stayed on the couch most nights. What are you saying?"

It figured that Leon would keep the bed. "I'm just trying to figure out what she had in mind when she started off across that field."

"Nothing, probably," said Leon. "She'd been drinking a lot lately. Our problems and all. I'm not sure which came first."

Jules nodded. It was hard to tell intoxication from a literally frozen expression, the contorted mouth, bad color, glazed eyes locked on a pleasant daydream. Anne's face had been pearl gray in the snow, her lips a shade lighter, and her hair a peculiar blond, the color of the manila folder into which Jules would eventually stuff her particulars.

Leon had moved to the window. "Can I see her?"

"Wait till we get her to town."

"There's magpies out there."

"The birds aren't going to bother her, Leon. I'll go back out in a sec to keep an eye on her."

Jules tapped on the bathroom door. Merry didn't answer and he turned the knob. Her cheek rested on the toilet seat, and her face was covered with tears, but her voice was still mean.

"Leave me alone."

Jules let the door swing shut and walked back slowly to the bar's main room. Leon was staring into space. "Anne got any family to phone?" asked Jules.

"Not that cared." Leon wandered down the bar and made himself a very tall whiskey.

"Still," said Jules. "I'll contact them if you're not on good terms."

"Name of Peralski, in Orlando. Parents, and there used to be a brother down there, too." He drummed his fingers bitterly on the bar. "They'll probably try to claim half the house and business."

Sadly, such behavior was average in Jules's line of work. "Halsey owns this building, right?"

"Right," said Leon, taking a swig.

"He'll help with the business," said Jules, standing up. "You sure you can't think of who Anne might have been with?"

The front door opened and Harvey Meyers, Jules's tiny deputy, stood in the glow of the snow light.

"Her fucking boyfriend," screamed Leon, suddenly galvanized. "Her fucking boyfriend dumped her and let her freeze to death."

Harvey and Jules both jumped. "What's his name?" asked Jules.

"I don't know," said Leon. He started to cry again and threw his highball glass across the room.

THE COUNTY CORONER was at a seminar in Spokane and Horace Bolan, the reluctant medical examiner, wasn't due back from a golfing vacation in Phoenix until that evening. Of the other two doctors who might have answered the call, one was delivering a baby and the second had bronchitis; the neighboring county examiner to the west was in the Bahamas for his twentieth anniversary and the Billings examiner was mired in a fatal fire. So Jules and Harvey took photos, measured, recorded an external skin temperature (12 degrees, a degree or two cooler than the warming air; they despaired of attempting an internal temperature while in the field), checked the dead woman's coat pockets (they found $2.83, a lipstick, and some tissues). Her jeans pockets were too tight to pry into, given that Anne herself was hard as a rock.

There was no way of telling how close she might have come to the house. The fresh snow was eight inches deep, and the old layer, the one Anne had walked across, had been reduced to slush in the sunny field before it had crystallized under the new stuff. This old, solid underlayer of ice soon proved to be a problem: Anne had curled into a ball and frozen into it, and Jules sent Harvey off in search of an ax.

When Caroline Fair pulled up in a patrol car and waded across the field, Jules had almost finished chopping around the perimeter of the dead woman.

"Jesus," she said, her cheeks apple red and her eyes watering in the cold wind.

Jules and Harvey tried to lift the body, but the ice was still rooted to the ground by stalks of alfalfa. Caroline lay on her stomach and slashed at the grass with a pocketknife until the whole mass was free. They heaved Anne and her bed of ice onto a dropcloth.

All three of them were red-faced and panting, haloed by their own steam. Jules looked up and tried to catch his breath. The wind was boiling overhead, a cold stew of real snow and tiny ice particles. Looking up was even lonelier than looking at the dead woman. "Get the van, Harvey," he wheezed. "Bring it around to Leon's driveway and we'll only have to carry her twenty yards or so."

Harvey staggered to the road, too winded to complain. He took a shortcut past the burned trailer. Leon had rented it out to a man named Robert Raphael Frame, who'd exited town just before the fire. In the aftermath, his wife had wandered through Blue Deer's bars, muttering about dark plots and how her husband talked to her from Heaven. Jules and Divvy Ott, the fire chief, had been close to sifting the trailer for shin bones and teeth before it came to light that Mrs. Frame was a former tenant of Warm Springs, the state's asylum for women, and needed another state-funded rest. In hindsight Jules decided that at best Robert Frame had simply run out on his dotty wife, and at worst had tried to kill her by torching the trailer.

Leon concurred with the first theory, happy to collect insurance and be rid of the couple; Anne Baden, as usual, had had no opinion. Even when she'd called Jules to rid the Bachelor of bad drunks she'd been muted: this man "might have had a little too much," another "seemed upset." This didn't mean she was compassionate, simply wary to the point of shutting down completely. Jules had always believed that Leon beat her, though he'd never seen a bruise to prove it. If Leon hadn't beaten her, someone in her past had.

Rarely had a woman had so little to say, alive or dead. Jules's eyes veered away from her mouth. Caroline's fingers were red and stiff, and Jules watched her struggle to close the knife for a moment before he took it and handed her a glove.

"I left mine in the car," said Caroline. "I was finishing up a fender bender at the bottom of McDonald Creek when I heard the radio. I gather you think this is alcohol."

"Yeah," said Jules. "I do." He flexed his fingers and tried to pry ice from Anne's back jeans pocket to see what was inside, then straightened and stuffed his hands in his coat.

"I thought you said it didn't get cold after February," said Caroline. "You said snow, but nothing this miserable."

"I lied," said Jules. "It probably won't be the first time."

JULES, CAROLINE, AND Harvey took Anne Baden to the hospital morgue and found themselves at a loss for what to do next. If they refrigerated her, she might take days to soften up. Caroline pointed out that even a twenty-pound turkey took forty-eight hours. If they left Anne out, surface tissues might degrade, fouling all sorts of tests, and the hospital staff would protest. Jules called the crime lab in Missoula and listened, amused, while several specialists argued among themselves on the far end of the line.

"So what happens when you freeze to death?" asked Caroline. She was eating a chocolate bar, apparently unperturbed by the dead woman a few feet away. "They don't bother spelling it out if you train in Baltimore."

Jules parroted a text. "'Ethanol abuse, which is strongly associated with hypothermia, results in vasodilation and interferes with peripheral vasoconstriction, an important physiologic mechanism of defense against the cold.'"

"Fine," said Caroline. "But what do you think it feels like? Does it help or hurt if you have a mile-high blood alcohol level?"

"You go into shock faster if you're drunk," said Jules. "You die a little faster, but some people panic just as badly. The shivering response doesn't work anymore, and you flail around."

"Grace was telling me about some hunters a couple of falls ago who died about a hundred feet from their truck."

"That was a bad storm," said Jules. "A very fast one. Those men were a hard thing to find."

"She said they walked for miles, all in the same two-acre patch, and that when you guys were following the tracks you came within a few feet of their bodies several times."

"Yes."

"She said they were probably drunk."

She offered him a last bite. Jules shook his head and she

polished it off and balled the wrapper. “They were sober,” he said.

Caroline raised an eyebrow. “Grace specifically mentioned whiskey.”

Jules could put that argument to rest: it had been his first search and rescue mission, and they’d been his first frozen people. The men had pulled most of their clothes off and clawed at their toes before they finally gave up. The unopened whiskey bottle had been located in the hunters’ truck, parked only a hundred yards from where they gave up, and after the rescuers strapped the frozen bodies on sleds they each took a single long pull.

“Most people do that at the end. Maybe Anne was too drunk to bother with the last step.” He was still on hold with the scientists in Missoula. “It probably didn’t matter,” said Caroline. He’d managed to finally kill her curiosity.

“Probably not,” said Jules.

The phone squawked. The Missoula consensus was fifty degrees and a sealed body bag, which was somehow along the lines of “take two aspirin and call me tomorrow.”

Jules’s mother, Olive, had taken a part-time job at the hospital the year before, and as Jules followed Caroline to the door she raised an innately sarcastic eyebrow.

“They want to know how long you need to keep Ms. Baden here.”

They was one of Olive’s favorite words; Jules even remembered her using it before his father died. “Tell them I don’t have a clue.”

“I hate to admit that,” said Olive.

Outside in the cold parking lot, Caroline wound her long dark hair back under her hat and headed for her car.

"I don't care if you stop patrol for the day," said Jules. "Find something warm to do."

"I like driving," said Caroline. "It'll keep me from seeing that poor woman's face. But I might not bother pulling anyone over."

"Are you going out tonight?"

"I think so," said Caroline. "The final war session. Alice is having trouble accepting the truth. Are you coming?"

"Not at gunpoint."

"But you'll help?"

"Of course I'll help. You three tell me what to do and I'll slave away. I just don't want to have to talk about it."

"I like the idea of you slaving away," said Caroline. "I'll let them know."

She walked away and he watched. She wasn't particularly tall, but she had long legs and a surprising sashay. Just before she opened the car door she turned back, but Jules was making a show of checking his pockets for his keys.

She hadn't caught him looking yet.

JULES HAD PARED down his appetites that winter, though it would be more accurate to say that the appetite remained and he'd simply buried the follow-through. He ate, drank, and slept with apparent normalcy, and managed to sleepwalk through nine-tenths of each day without thinking too much. Really waking up would be a ruinous booby trap. He'd made it through most of one more winter without trying antidepressants, which some people—his friends Alice Wahlgren and Peter Johansen especially—regarded as a Pyrrhic victory. But Jules didn't think of himself as depressed; it was just that his major reaction to winter was silence. He'd read somewhere that the hallmark of a mild depression was actually a greater realism: you realized that no one got out alive, that suffering was inevitable, joy rare, inequity the rule. And there was no point to love if you couldn't have what you wanted. Though he'd never been averse to personal misbehavior, he'd become lonely, yet often happier alone, a sensualist with a bullying Protestant core.

Jules was possibly farther left politically than any other cop in the state, though in and of itself this didn't say much. He was a bona fide bleeding heart, but one who believed in gradations of right and wrong, and one who was not endlessly forgiving. He was equally unpopular with the county commissioners and the people he'd arrested, so persistent that most people had forgotten or would never guess he'd only been a cop for a few years. Jules had rolled around the world for fifteen years after high school before he'd fallen into his current trap, rolled right through college and graduate school, rolled through stints as a cook and a social worker and an archaeologist, rolled through countries and love affairs without forgetting them but without sticking around. When he'd come back to Montana at thirty-three, he'd been wiser but possibly not wise enough for a career as a pillar of the community.

He bought a paper and read it after he ordered a huge platter of old-fashioned Chinese food. Every few weeks he might deal with something that made him want to run away, but he understood his good fortune in this regard: if he lived in a larger city, he might see such things every few hours. Jules never had to deal with gangs, bad heroin, or tornadoes, and rarely with traffic jams or prostitution. Most other places had more of what Blue Deer had too much of—child abuse, spouse abuse, theft, juvenile turmoil, car accidents—though with only six officers Absaroka County's cop to citizen rate was little better than Dade County's. The county's neat and tidy shape ignored the geographic reality of mountain ranges and rivers and national parks: a trip from its northwest to southeast boundaries took hours.

But Jules had no right to whine. Over hot and sour soup and Mongolian beef and potstickers he read of all sorts of things that hadn't yet happened in his neck of the woods. A woman hadn't fallen from the sky and split in two over a garden wall; a pregnant woman hadn't been blown to bits by a car bomb; no Absaroka County house had slid down a cliff, killing the sleeping family inside; no father had forgotten his baby in a car overnight.

As usual, the news excised enough self-pity for him to carry on. At the station, Grace floated toward him at high speed despite chubby legs. "Did you think if you didn't call in for the news it would go away?"

"We already had the news of the day," said Jules. "Let's not try to outdo it."

"I don't spend my life trying to think up ways to make you miserable," said Grace testily. "I often try not to think of you at all. You received nine calls that I couldn't pass on to someone else." She held a sheaf of pink messages up like a hand of cards. "Two from the mayor, two from Scotti, one from Peter Johansen, one from the owner of that dog, one from Alice, one from Stiltson about three juveniles throwing dead gophers at cars, and one from Divvy about that barn fire."

"That's not so bad," said Jules, relieved. "What did Divvy say?"

"He thinks the fire was natural."

Jules liked natural: it made him happy in conjunction with fire, death, birth, and many though not all foods. "You don't happen to know Anne Baden's parents, a couple named Peralski, do you?" he asked.

"Awful people," said Grace. "Nasty s.o.b.'s."

Grace was sixty, a bridge player and a churchgoer, a combination that somehow led her to imply bad words rather than doing without them entirely. She constantly corrected Jules's often floral vocabulary, even though the fact that he used such words gave her obvious delight.

"Leon didn't volunteer to call them."

"There's one thing I can't blame the man for."

"Well," said Jules. "Since you know them, you can call them."

She slammed a fat pile of paper onto his lap. "Sort your own reports," she said.

"Okay," said Jules. "Don't fret. Anything but the parents. What did Alice want?"

"She's worried about Peter. She thinks he's working too hard." Grace looked smug. "It's a bad idea, people living together right up to a wedding. They need some time apart."

Jules increasingly agreed, despite the fact that Peter and Alice had shared a house for ten years. "What did Peter want?"

"A ride up to Halsey's. He's supposed to meet with him, and Alice needs the car, and he thought you'd be working up there, especially if you found a body today."

Over the years, Peter had done a better job of anticipating Jules's moods than Alice's, a talent that had been especially useful when Peter had been a reporter for the *Bulletin*. He was a lawyer again, and they both had had dealings with Halsey Meriwether and his numerous possessions—part of the reason Halsey wanted Jules to organize what he called his "treasures" was so that Peter would have an accurate list for drawing up a will. Since Halsey was constantly coming up with more crates, treats hidden in storage units across the West during any of his many divorce proceedings, these tasks weren't simple. Jules was in no danger of losing his escape anytime soon. Peter's concerns were more complicated. Halsey was in the habit of announcing that his death was imminent and that his bequests had to be finished as soon as possible. This distracted Halsey from his other big project, the renovation of the Sacajawea, where Peter and Alice hoped to be married in two and a half weeks.

Jules looked up at the clock. It was four twenty, almost cocktail time. "I better haul Peter up there, then talk to Halsey about Anne."

"You know," said Grace, "I can tell you're not planning to run for reelection."

3 *The Sacajawea*

Inventory, crate 12:

(recent acquisitions, rcvd from S Francisco; Polaroids sent 3/15 to Soth. for tent. confirmation)

2 ashtrays, supp Monet, prob fake.

Bronze spray of wheat, probably Celtic 50BC +/− 100. Est val 3500-5000

tiles

coins

3 Coptic funeral plaques

bronze griffin, 19th c casting. No idea.

Venetian glass flagon, 6" high, shell pink. Est val 12-15K.

Tapestry strip, prob 1400-1500 Dutch, 12" x 4'. No idea.

Inventory, crate 13:

(in storage since approx 5/61, Denver; pictures sent 3/2)

barometer, Swiss 1840s. No idea.

device to measure alcohol level in wine, 1860s, French. No idea.

Attic vase—copy. SELL.

Small marble Roman nude of woman on pedestal. Prob. copy.

Phoenician weights, 200BC +/− 200. Est val 750.

Five Playboy magazines. (To Halsey)

2 lapis monkeys, Old Kingdom. No idea.

Gold 3-headed dragon amulet, 10 cm high, poss Thracian.

Silver phial decorated with lotus leaves, 4th-6th c, Thracian.

PETER JOHANSEN WAS JULES'S CLOSEST FRIEND. They'd known each other since college and stayed friends through years in New York. In their late twenties, after Jules had left for archaeological digs in southern Europe, North Africa, and the Caucasus, Peter and Alice Wahlgren soon gave up on the city in favor of Jules's hometown. By the time Jules returned, they'd settled in for good. Peter had worked as a prosecutor for the city, then as a reporter for the *Bulletin*, and now he split a small office with another lawyer and strenuously avoided divorce work. Alice, a caterer in New York, had gradually realized she didn't have the patience to turn a profit in a town where the hamburger was king. Now she made a small salary as the curator of the Absaroka County Historical Museum, whose members—fifteen women whose average age was seventy—were known as the Aches.

Jules's mother liked to spout a truism about old friends, usually after bitter bridge games: the older and the better friends they were, the more you had to disagree about. But Peter and Alice and Jules hadn't argued about much beyond Peter and Alice's treatment of each other and Jules's handling of various fourth-female parties. Even Alice and Peter didn't disagree with each other about the usual things, things like religion or who might care for prospective children or whether those children might exist (which was good, since Alice was due to have a baby in mid-September). They didn't wrangle over social habits or laundry or the wedding guest list or what used couch to buy. They had forgiven each other's infidelities, put these problems so far away that they hadn't come up in years. They had enjoyed each other's families for over a decade, with nary a patch of stress, and mostly agreed on how to raise the dogs (more good news for the baby).

They'd decided on a ceremony, a time, a place, and other sometimes troublesome particulars. In defiance of the time of year, Alice would carry delphinium and old roses (she'd found a place in Texas that would send specific types, and dithered for weeks between varieties named Cardinal de Richelieu and Madame Isaac Perriere). In acceptance of her ever-evolving figure, she'd wear an off-white, low-cut silk dress with an empire waist. And in complete rebellion against financial reality she insisted that the wedding would be served, and haute: a caviar toast, followed by a seated procession of courses that, at the very least, would include a bisque, preferably lobster, and something involving foie gras and truffles. And even though she wouldn't be having more than a sip, each course would be served with an appropriate fine wine.

This was the problem. Peter wanted the food and wine they ate and enjoyed on a daily basis, which wasn't to say he wanted pigs in blankets or Cold Duck. He'd suggested a buffet with plenty of appetizers and three loose main course choices: a daube of some sort, roast quail, pork loin, or a baron of beef; and sides of salmon, either poached or grilled, with several sauces.

The eighty-dollar-a-head differential on these two visions was only part of the problem, though no one involved was rich. The quarrel over the menu was so vicious and childish that Jules decided Peter and Alice had boiled down every small wrong they'd inflicted or endured since they met, and now the mess had foamed out of control. Some women start dreaming of weddings as young girls, usually focusing on dresses, flowers, guests, and the groom. Alice had skipped this stage in favor of plastic horses and a *Wuthering Heights* vision of romance, and when the daydreams came home at age thirty-five they all centered on the ultimate dinner, to be followed five months later by an infant. She loved Peter more now than she had a decade earlier, but he was reality. Food was to dream about.

Peter thought she was being pretentious. She thought he was being cheap and mean-spirited. This offended him deeply, and he looked to Jules several times for reassurance on this point. No, said Jules; I can't say I've seen you cut many corners. In the deepest, darkest depths of impoverished Montana winters, with no savings and pending power bills, he'd seen Peter and Alice mail-order Parmesan from New York, then live for weeks on noodles and rice, game, and endless green beans from the freezer.

As the war became more entrenched, other problems arose. The renovation of the Sacajawea had fallen far behind, and when Alice panicked and tried to move the ceremony and thirty of the guests to Blue Deer and a hotel called the Baird, she discovered the place had been booked by the National Association of Independent Panners and Miners, who'd scheduled their big party and a polka band for the same night. It was also increasingly clear that Halsey didn't have a clue about how to find a chef who could cook either menu. The man he'd hired in December had ordered the equipment and ten grand in comestibles before decamping in January, maddened by renovation delays and boredom, enraged by the reprehensible eating habits of the local population. Two more candidates had failed Alice's acid test, which was to come up with an edible fish soup. Both had produced a kind of glue, and been sent packing.

In late February, Alice agreed to drop the caviar and the more expensive Domaine du Tempier vintages, and asked Peter to consider crab cakes in lieu of quenelles. Peter said no to anything more complex than chilled shrimp and oysters on the half shell. It was his way or the highway. Alice, ten weeks pregnant, packed and left, and it took Jules and the rest of Blue Deer's finest a full two days to track her down at a fleabag in Bozeman. Caroline found her eating potato chips and drinking chocolate milk while she watched a stack of Masterpiece Theater videos.

Everyone agreed that Peter and Alice should no longer handle their own wedding, and Jules asked Arnie Wildason to fill in. He was another ex-roommate—a tough, wiry guy from North Dakota who was on a sort of sabbatical between three- and four-star Manhattan jobs; Jules had had to bribe him with promises of lifetime shipments of venison, morels, and chanterelles. Arnie looked over both menus and said he'd come up with a compromise and have supplies shipped out wholesale. He refused to discuss the menu and told Jules he'd need a cook staff of six and a wait staff of eight. He would expect Jules to help prep in the week before the wedding, and he'd expect Jules to keep Peter and Alice away from the hotel.

Peter and Alice, now beatific and peaceful, thanked Jules profusely and promised to take care of his own wedding if he ever got his butt in gear. Jules said that if he got lucky, he'd elope.

PETER WAS OUT on the sidewalk when Jules pulled up, yelling over the fence at his own dogs, sibling mutts named Earl and Pearl who listened attentively. The names had been a bad idea; when called, Pearl assumed Earl was the one in demand and vice versa, and neither ever came unless they imagined food was involved.

"They got into the garbage again," said Peter. "Alice made stock and forgot to take the bag out. The whole back room is pasted with shank bones."

"Is or was?"

"Is. I didn't forget the bag."

"Oh come on," said Jules. "I'll help you. Let's keep things peaceful."

But Peter was already in the car. "She won't mind," he said. "She might not even notice. I'm just worried she'll forget something important, like the stove or which lane she's supposed to drive in."

"I thought that was a cliche about pregnant women."

"Alice has never entirely been in the here and now."

This was true.

Halfway to the Sacajawea they passed the renovation crew heading back to town. Everyone waved. The mood darkened on Peter's side of the car. With a matter of days to go until the first guests arrived, only the main room of the bar was completed. Not the kitchen, or dining room, or any of the twenty-odd reserved guest rooms. It was a good thing Alice had settled into a happy hormonal fog; Peter, on the other hand, seemed to have absorbed all her usual anxiety and squared it.

"I think Fred was going to finish the wiring in the long wing today," said Jules. "That's just next door to drywall."

"I hope it's just next door to made beds. I don't want my family sleeping on your floor."

They left the interstate at Honeywater and Jules stopped to wait for sixty cows to cross the road. Three men on horses watched without trying to hurry them. Peter gestured and one man flipped them the bird.

"Give him a ticket."

"Nah," said Jules, revving his old truck. "What's the rush with Halsey today anyway?"

"New complications."

Peter had been struggling for half a year with Halsey's complex holdings and bequests. One of Peter's many Halsey-related problems was the elderly man's tendency to reveal his possessions gradually, and that these possessions were varied and rare was enough to make valuing them a nightmare. It was a huge estate, and fairly complicated; Peter stood to make a bundle, but he was actually earning every penny of it, sorting and locating possessions, putting some property in trust, covenants on stray acreage. Every week held a new revelation, a forgotten patch of land on the Oregon coast, part ownership in a golf course near San Diego. Peter had begun to suspect that Halsey kept coming up with complications for the sake of company, and lately the older man had been driving him batty with a net of interrelated small bequests, mostly to friends and ex-bartenders. Halsey insisted on paying Peter for every phone call and edit, not a typical desire; he paid Jules a fortune to daydream while he sorted pottery shards.

"He's getting married again?"

"Nope. He's inheriting for a change. One of his wives died and left him more art. We're trying to figure out how to slide it through, taxwise."

"Wasn't that up to her?"

"None of the stuff s inventoried or insured, except for one Turner oil. The other stuff doesn't technically exist."

"Christ," said Jules, accelerating and clearing the last cow's hind leg by inches. "Halsey doesn't need more art. Why doesn't someone die and leave us art?"

Peter smiled. "He has twenty pages of bequests. I'm sure someone will."

THE TOWN OF Honeywater, an easy twenty-mile drive from Blue Deer on the county's eastern border in the foothills of the Crazy Mountains, had a population of fifty and its own post office for the area's ranchers and grade school for their children. The Sacajawea Hotel was a mile north, on the far side of the river, and a shocking sight in comparison to Honeywater's tiny buildings: it was three stories of stone and log built over a period of seventy years, fiddled at by a dozen owners; it seemed to have landed in Montana via Constantinople, northern Scandinavia, and Veracruz. Even the bar was a strange mix of time and styles, more Parisian than Montanan: an eighteen-foot ceiling, faded green silk wallpaper, and a spare, Art Deco back bar of paned glass and almost black mahogany. The public rooms had ceilings of coffered fir, and the hotel entry and the bar boasted stained-glass domes of creamy gray-green, ribbed by a brass pattern of leaves. In classic western fashion the lobby had stairs leading up to an open, wrap-around landing and a half dozen rooms, stacked in a three-story, copper-roofed tower. It was one of the odder constructions Jules had seen in his life, and he'd seen what were now coyly termed "socialist building crimes" on the far side of the Berlin Wall. This was far prettier, joyously weird.

In its heyday the Sack had seen thousands of visitors a year, wealthy adventurers bent on a leisurely stay near Yellowstone, or a cure for tuberculosis, or dude training, or brain surgery. The resort had been dying since the late twenties, a long, slow slide that was actually only skin deep: the first two versions had burned down, in 1883 and 1905, but what remained of the last structure was essentially sound, despite a winter fire in 1944 that had taken off one wing (there'd been talk of balloon-borne Japanese incendiary bombs when the glow in the sky became visible in town). The Sack had afterward functioned only as a bar and a highly informal inn, which meant that until the sixties three or four prostitutes could usually be found living in the tower rooms.

Halsey Meriwether, a diehard optimist, liked to point out that at least no one had muddled things with a bad renovation and claimed the place only needed a face-lift. In the South, thirty years of having been boarded up would have caused animal and vegetable problems, but killer vines and invading reptiles weren't a problem in inhospitable Montana. There were only a few mice, some spider nests, bats in the belfry, and a willow that had managed to split the Moroccan tiles and grow out of the bottom of one of three empty hot springs pools.

Six months after Halsey had hired a contractor named Fred Bottomore to begin renovation, the face-lift had come to include new plumbing, new wiring, new supporting walls, and some foundation work. None of the original plaster was worth saving, and the tile and wood floors needed extensive repair. The roof and most windows needed to be replaced. Beyond the essentials, there was the variable of Halsey's taste: he moved doorways and changed his mind on windowsills and baseboards and bathroom fixtures. The cost of renovation didn't seem to slow him, and he liked to point out that he'd gotten the place almost free, acquired in his first divorce settlement in exchange for a house in Berkeley.

It seemed that this was the wife who'd just died and left Halsey more art. Her name had been Muriel Zilpha Zirn Vinnecombe Meriwether Gagnaire, and Halsey had been the only ex-husband she'd chosen to honor. One of the many items she'd left him was the same house in Berkeley.

"Maybe Merry would like the place," said Dottie Cope, a tall woman with curly dark hair who was Halsey's manager in most things. "The air out here doesn't seem to agree with her."

"Stop trying to get rid of her, Dot. She needs to be with family." Halsey turned back to Jules and Peter. "Poor

Muriel's grandparents built this place. We stayed here off and on during our marriage."

"'Poor Muriel,'" said Dottie with a snort. "'Poor Muriel' died in her sleep at eighty-two without ever having more than a head cold, according to you."

"An older woman," said Peter.

"Yes," said Halsey, seventy-something. "She was quite a piece of work. We kept up with each other over the years."

"As opposed to your other wives," said Dottie.

"No reason to burn your bridges if you can just get a divorce," said Halsey with a small smile.

This good nature wasn't entirely genuine. Halsey actually kept a huge empty frame on his apartment wall, and told Jules it symbolized the way he'd been left after each divorce; he kept it up to remind himself. It seemed just as likely that he kept it up as a cheap excuse for future acquisitions. Jules couldn't imagine what the collection would look like if he hadn't been forced to part with a chunk every decade or so. On the other hand, the divorces were certainly the reason so much was hidden in warehouses across the country.

"This stuff of Muriel's should be a little strange, Jules. I'm expecting it this weekend."

"I promised Fred I'd finish the dining room with him," said Jules.

"I'd like to know what Muriel's given me as soon as possible," said Halsey, trying to look haughty.

"Seventeen days to the wedding," said Jules. "Is that Fred back there, making progress?" The hammering came in short bursts; Fred was probably finishing the wainscoting in the hall and the bathroom. "Maybe Peter and Alice should just reschedule for the Fourth of July."

"That's not funny," snapped Dottie.

"That's not funny at all," said Peter, in his underwater voice.

Halsey, the oldest person in the room, had a more elastic sense of time, and laughed. He was relatively quiet that afternoon, muted by the news about his first wife and Anne Baden. He had pale green eyes, a huge jaw, and the skinny butt and long legs of a young man. He was wearing bright red high-tops with his overalls and T-shirt and managed to look oddly angelic despite his age, five marriages, and a bout with cancer. The first two times Jules had seen him, Halsey had been indulging in his favorite sport, driving between his two local establishments—the Bachelor and the Sacajawea—down the center line at approximately thirty-eight miles an hour. Jules had been close, on the second sighting, to slamming him with a DUI, but when Halsey had rolled down the window, his bad chemo wig and gray skin and swollen abdomen had made anything but a simple hello impossible. Halsey had later confided that he'd been a bad driver long before he started to drink or die, and according to Peter he wasn't doing either anymore, was in fact in full remission.

Halsey liked drama, even on his quieter days, though he sometimes lost track of the last version of the story. Jules had heard several different versions of wives number two and four (had they been Jewish, Hispanic, or Holy Rollers?), and a half dozen explanations for why a million-dollar renovation of a hotel in one of Montana's smallest towns made sense. Now Dottie filled their glasses again, and Halsey launched into the private life of the county inspector, who'd come by that morning to critique the Sacajawea's electrical renovation.

"Back when I was in grade school, his father screwed his cousin."

"You knew this in grade school?" asked Jules.

"Of course," said Halsey, who'd left the county in 1950 for forty years of city luxury. "Everyone knew. We're dealing with a family tree without branches, which is why the man sees tiny wires instead of the big picture."

Dottie met Jules's eyes and raised an eyebrow. She was two thirds skinny legs and her top was mostly bosom, with blue Irish eyes that spun a little when she was angry or confused or drinking, possibly due to a youthful love of hallucinogens. She had long black curly hair, now streaked with gray, and a deep laugh that sometimes sounded evil but was almost always based on affection. Jules had met her twenty years ago, before he left town and she'd moved to northern California, where she'd first hooked up with Halsey. She loved to talk and drink and wear strange clothes, go on road trips to Las Vegas and Los Angeles. When the mood took her she screwed herself silly with an always temporary object of fancy. She'd told Jules once that she could never understand a man who dared to hold her hand on the way to breakfast the next morning: that was a far greater intimacy. She preferred long-term affairs with men who lived elsewhere.

She behaved, in short, exactly in the way women are often disgusted with men for behaving. As a bartender she was absolutely unforgiving, but that was another story. And she never let Halsey digress for long.

"Let's get this out in the air," she said. "What you're saying is that Halsey's little girl didn't call for a check for two hours after Anne left the bar."

"She called," said Jules. Dottie's dislike for Merry was so strong that even he sometimes had to defend her. "That's more than she had to do."

Halsey looked miserable. "It's awful, you know, but it's hard for me to see Anne's face already. She simply wasn't distinct. I never really thought about her, and now I already can't remember her, so I don't know what I can come up with that might help."

Jules nodded. During the course of the day he'd begun to realize this was a standard reaction to hearing Anne Baden's name, and even he had trouble remembering the way she sounded or had looked alive. When some people ceased to exist, they disappeared faster than others. But the look of her dead would be with him forever.

Leon was another matter. "When you first started to give me the bad news, I assumed she'd finally shot the asshole while he slept," said Halsey.

Jules stared at him. "Why? Leon told me she was having an affair."

Halsey snorted in disbelief. "He browbeat her, and I'm not sure it was always just the brows, if you take my drift. And she was the type who just goes *pffft* one day. Kind of like my third wife." Halsey gestured to his glass, and Dottie filled it with milk. She looked tired; he was already edging away from the topic of dead Anne again.

"Your wife tried to kill you?" Peter finished his burgundy and rubbed his head.

"Just one of them. I figure one out of five isn't bad."

"What did she do?"

Halsey smiled. Dottie filled in. "Stuck a gun in his mouth while he was sleeping, snoring away. It was right after I started working for him."

"She wanted to kill you because you snored?" Peter was alarmed, for good reason. Alice was the only person who'd share a room with him.

Dottie leaned over the bar and patted his hand. She was wearing a tight, low-cut striped sweater as she sorted glasses, and every minute or so would dip forward and provide an eye-popping view. Last week she'd worn overalls and sweatpants. Jules assumed she was warming up for a visit from one of her absentee boyfriends, or perhaps intending to acquire a new one. She smiled at Peter, then Jules, then turned back to Peter. Jules shook his head.

"She wanted to kill me because I was snoring next to her good friend, and my fourth wife." Halsey smiled, happy in the past. "I gagged on the gun, started retching, and for some reason this alarmed her and she pulled the thing out."

They all stared. "Then what?" asked Jules.

"Horrible stuff," said Halsey. "Never mind."

Jules nodded. Dottie slammed down a wine bottle. Halsey eyed Jules over the top of his milk. "Even if Anne had a boyfriend, where does it get you?"

"I'm just looking for why she wanted to curl up in a snowbank and freeze to death."

Dottie filled Peter's glass, looking a little pale. Halsey was quiet for a long moment. "Wouldn't you, if you were married to Leon?" he asked. "I bet you a hundred bucks he never would have let her leave."

JULES WORKED IN the long narrow room that faced the front of the hotel on the second floor. Halsey and Dottie each had deeper apartments across the hall, facing the back, and Merry had taken over the habitable part of the third-floor tower. Fred Bottomore had a small shop off the kitchen on the ground floor.

Jules's room had originally been the music room, then a private lounge in the forties. The room had windows on three sides facing south, and he could see the whole sweep of the Absarokas, from the Boulder divide to the smaller mountains near Blue Deer. Beneath the windows he'd built a desk of plywood balanced on top of a dozen two-drawer file cabinets, all of them full of things he'd identified and cataloged that Halsey wanted to keep. The interior wall was stacked with more file cabinets and twenty-some crates holding everything from medieval manuscript pages to Egyptian bowls, the spoils of a lifelong appetite for beauty and esoterica, wheeling and dealing. The center of the room held a grand piano and a pool table, leftovers, along with an Art Deco couch and a long mirror, from the room's lounge days. Jules had no idea how they'd gotten into the room—he used the dumbwaiter to move the smaller crates; anything larger than a television was a nightmare to handle on the cramped upper stairs. Both were now stacked high with papers and folios, and canvases were arranged like dominoes on the pool table, propped up against a statue of Aphrodite.

Halsey's uncle had been one of the higher-ups with British Customs in the twenties and thirties, the glory days of archaeological pillage. The man had absorbed graft from the Sinai, Constantinople, Naples, Athens, the Crimea, and Alexandria; some of the crates he'd left to Halsey had never been opened. Jules had been stunned to find his archaeology degree good for side money, and three months into the project it was common knowledge among friends and coworkers that he preferred cataloging Halsey's strange possessions to his real job of cataloging Blue Deer's strange inhabitants. Halsey paid better, and sculpture fragments didn't talk back. No one realized that Jules's sudden, out-of-character interest in making money had to do with an escape plan.

Halsey's stuff could have filled the hotel: it was worthy

of a museum, and it was a joke to have one man sorting it. But Halsey didn't want to sell any of it yet, only wanted to know what he had roughly enough to be able to insure it and add it to his will. Dottie had put her foot down on this: the hotel had already burned three times in its history, and, anyway, if he really cared about the stuff, he'd put it someplace safe. Halsey's response was to hire Jules and insist that Fred install a state-of-the-art sprinkler system throughout the hotel. This detail tallied up to another two-week delay. No one mentioned it to Alice and Peter, and Fred accelerated from double time to triple time.

Jules, as a cop with a PhD in archaeology, was a strange creature to find in Montana; Fred Bottomore, a carpenter with an art history master's, was only slightly more likely. Fred had aspired to be a painter, an ambition that had been whittled to nothing by drink and odd jobs before he was twenty-five. He had never quite finished his doctorate, just like he had never quite become an artist, just like he'd never gotten a rock-solid handle on a drinking problem or a marriage or the simple passage of time. He would turn forty that spring, poor and talented and handsome and alone except for those few nights when he hunted, always successfully, for company. No one really thought they knew him, but everyone liked him.

Fred hadn't had a drink in two years. He'd repaired most of the bridges he'd burned with a series of perfect, inspired jobs as a finish carpenter, and now Halsey had given him the Sack renovation, plus a sideline in helping Jules identify paintings and prints. In total it meant a year of pleasant work and very good money, and Fred made no bones about loving it, even though he and Dottie occasionally came near to blows and Halsey, polite and soothing to everyone else, was given to petulance, indecision, and impatience with his contractor, who as usual was the last man working.

Jules found him on the hall floor, installing baseboards and blinking through the layer of fine sawdust that covered his hair. Fred had light blue eyes, dirty blond hair, and creamy freckled skin. His coloring was delicate but he was in fact substantial, about six feet and two hundred pounds.

"So, how bad has it been?"

"Christ," said Fred. "Alice is going to come looking for me soon with a shotgun. It does no good to explain to her that everything would have been done by now if Halsey didn't keep changing his mind."

"What now?"

"He wanted deeper sills in the dining room, and I told him I'd quit. We compromised on a darker stain for the room trim. The Nitwits will work on it tomorrow, after I finally get them to clean out the basement and haul the crap to Leon."

The Nitwits were Fred's crew. "What do you think of Leon Baden anyway?"

"He's an asshole," said Fred pleasantly. "But if he weren't around we'd have to haul our trash farther. And he's a good refinisher, especially with metal. He just cleaned up all the doorknobs."

"Do you know his wife at all?"

"Not since she kicked me out of the bar the last time. I know she's dead. Merry showed up more bent out of shape than I've ever seen her."

Jules watched Fred hammer, fascinated by his grace. There wasn't a single dimple on the woodwork in the length of the hall. "That's saying a lot."

"Jesus," said Fred, straightening. "May I survive. Poor twerp. I felt like I'd been hit by a swarm."

Merry had a crush on Fred. There was no other way to put it, even if the phrase seemed odd on non-teenagers. She constantly came up with small chores for him, tried to get him to work on her apartment even though none of the private tower rooms would be touched until the rest of the hotel was finished.

"Do you know where she is now?" asked Jules.

Fred shrugged and blew sawdust off his table saw. "Off drinking, I'm sure. I'm surprised she even tried to call about Anne. Halsey's trying to keep her busy."

"By giving her a job in one bar and sticking her in a tower over another?"

"I know, I know," said Fred. "But he means well."

THE TRUTH THAT Alice Wahlgren was having difficulty accepting was brought home to her for the umpteenth time that evening.

"You have 102 acceptances," said Edie Linders. "Three people declined."

Alice chugged her cranberry juice. "It doesn't seem fair."

"You invited them. Everyone's bought their tickets. It's final."

"I meant the wine."

"You should have postponed the wedding until after the baby was born," said Caroline.

"We've postponed it for ten years," said Alice. "It's just as well I have to do it sober. Peter and I don't even fight anymore, at least since the food thing."

"Do a lot of these people think it'll be spring when they get here?" asked Edie, sorting through response cards. "They're all planning to stay awhile, and some mention camping."

"April? In Montana?" Alice tied a knot in her straw, looking more tired than annoyed. "How stupid can people be?"

"A lot of them are from the East," said Caroline. "They'd be hazy on geography. I know I was."

"You don't count, Caroline. You were running away. You wanted to move here."

Alice had no one to blame but herself: she had wanted a tiny wedding followed by a huge party, but she didn't want to offend anyone by not sending an invitation to the ceremony. She'd reasoned that hardly anyone would want to make the trip during a season when snow was more likely than not and the plains were brown, with buds still invisible on the cottonwoods. April was too late for skiing, too early to rely on the fishing. She and Peter had hinted broadly: don't worry about coming, we know it's a huge inconvenience.

Alice had also chosen the date with future escapes in mind, so that she and Peter would have an excuse to get warm every year. A later honeymoon would interfere with gardening time, something that was completely out of the question.

"We should have done this in Arizona," she groused. "If I'd known everyone would come anyway, we could have had the ceremony at the mission in Drum, and shooed everyone off to Tucson or Mexico for the rest of the time."

"Yes," said Caroline. "You should have given us an excuse to leave. My eyes are tearing up just thinking of it."

"Peter's parents would have loved it," said Edie sarcastically.

"They wouldn't have minded," said Alice. Peter's parents had owned a restaurant in Drum, Arizona, for years. "At least Jules isn't complaining."

"How's the work going on the Sack?" asked Caroline.

"I'll lose my mind if everyone ends up in a town motel," said Alice bleakly.

They watched her. Though Alice was no longer subject to sudden snits, she had recently begun to cry when the going got tough, which was unnerving to those who knew her well. The old Alice, the woman who'd hopped up and down and broken telephones against walls, hadn't howled in weeks.

"Try bribery," said Edie.

"I have," said Alice. "I'm running out of things Fred cares about, now that he's sober and thinking clearly."

Edie, still tan from a honeymoon in Mexico, was ready to leave. She tapped the list with a pencil. "So all of Peter's family are making it."

"Every last one."

Caroline scribbled.

"How about the New York contingent?"

"All but Bob. He's going to Nice with someone instead."

"Can't blame him. Your family?"

"Everyone but my cousin Louie."

"The one in Moscow?"

She nodded and gnawed a fingernail. "I'm going to try to sleep through this."

"No, no, no," said Edie. "Not to jump the gun, but how many people will need chairs? I've got to finish up the rental order."

Alice looked over the list. "Fourteen, plus all the Aches. Let's get thirty."

"Cicely won't sit," said Caroline. Cicely was her aunt and a member of the Absaroka County Historical Society, of which Alice was the youngest and only paid member. "She'll be offended if you try to make her."

"I know," said Alice. "But she'll remember if I don't have one waiting for her precious ass, just in case."

"Who'll make the airport trips?"

"Jules and Peter and I, mostly. If you'd like to volunteer for one, let me know."

"At least you're getting the bachelor party out of the way early."

"Peter doesn't want anyone calling it that." She tried to humor him, but Alice wondered what else you called a dozen men on a tour of a half dozen county bars. "I'm making sure Jules doesn't drink and keeps the keys out of Peter's hands."

"Jules is the sanest one of the bunch?"

"I think so," said Alice. "Scary, isn't it?"

Edie stood to go. "I can't wait to figure out the seating chart. Where are you going to put him?"

Alice sighed. "He can sit next to Caroline. He hasn't slept with her."

Caroline jumped and they both stared, suddenly alarmed. "Has he?"

4 *Broken Stuff*

Dear Dora:

Is there any historical or scientific proof that mankind is meant to be monogamous? Geese seem to take to it more naturally than we do.

Best, Bert

Dear Bert:

I asked my resident expert, and he points out we've always seemed to try, though with limited success. Much of what he had to say would get me in Dutch with many members of our community, but he mentioned such ancient institutions as eunuchs and harems, chastity belts and the stoning to death of unfaithful wives, as evidence that fidelity has always been a struggle. Also, recent research yields the news that some twenty percent of each man's sperm are created to simply keep an eye out for and kill another man's sperm. Such worker bees probably wouldn't exist if this hadn't been a problem for much of the past.

Still, I think it's best to be an optimist, don't you?

Yours, Dora

NOT EVERYONE PROVIDED GRACE WITH BOTH A QUESTION and an answer. Jules didn't think she was appropriately thankful.

"They'll never print it," said Grace.

"The editor told you they wanted spicy stuff before tourist season," said Jules. "Something to keep people awake."

That fall, Grace had begun an anonymous advice column in the Blue Deer *Bulletin*, "Dear Dora," and spent most weeks dispensing wisdom to the lovelorn. Friends and family and coworkers took turns when there were lapses in viable real letters. Jules had been an eighty-year-old who coveted his neighbor's wife and a mother of four who wanted her husband to get a vasectomy. Ed Winton had written in posing as a woman whose elderly mother-in-law had taken over her house; the situation had the ring of autobiography. Caroline Fair had donated a letter from a woman whose old boyfriend wanted to follow her across the country, uninvited. (Jules had studied it, searching for more truth between the lines.) And Jonathan Auber had penned a deeply earnest question about what to do if a woman wanted to have sex before he did. He desired her but felt it wasn't right to move too quickly.

The rest of them had dithered for days over the response. "I've never heard of such a thing," said Caroline. "At least not since Methodist youth group. What on earth does he have in mind?"

"If he'd grown up when I did, he wouldn't take such things for granted," said Ed. "You get a chance, you make a swan dive."

"Maybe he was abused as a child," said Harvey.

"Maybe he's one of those people who just doesn't care that much," said Wesley Tenn. "I've heard rumors they exist."

"Maybe he's a virgin," said Jules. "And he's scared."

That was a showstopper. They stared; he lifted his eyebrows. "He confessed," said Jules. "It's that college girl, and I'm sure his secret will remain safe."

That had been last week's letter, and they'd talked about it at the monthly staff meeting while Jonathan was out buying the doughnuts.

"Alice left another message," said Grace. "She says thanks for not calling her back, and she needs to know how the renovation's going because Peter seems upset and won't explain. But she knows you don't care, even though she's worried about you."

"Jesus," said Jules. He kept sorting reports. A possibly deranged woman had reported a burglary three times the night before, and Wesley had taken a stepfather into custody for locking a nine-year-old outside at midnight. Someone was setting cars on fire. To be specific, only elderly foreign cars parked in alleys, and only on weekend nights. This was based on three cases; Jules was happy he didn't have to discern similar patterns in murders.

"She says she'll probably miscarry from the stress of it all."

"Actually, she's been pretty relaxed lately."

"Hormones," said Grace. "I got like that every time." She slammed a drawer. "I wonder if you'd talk to Jonathan."

"Wonder away."

"He's upset about something, and you know it'll just get worse. He won't tell me, and he's on his third cup of cocoa in the kitchen."

"Okay," said Jules.

"And when you're done we still need that schedule."

Not just cocoa, but bad instant cocoa. Jonathan was the kind of guy who believed convenience equaled quality. Jules poured himself a cup of coffee and watched the young man out of the corner of his eye. Jonathan normally looked as fresh as a happy peach with a buzz cut, but today he was gray around the edges.

"It's not good to drink that shit when you're going off-duty and need to sleep," said Jules. "So what's up?"

"Nothing," said Jonathan.

He said it the way a twelve-year-old might, a whole dank world stuffed in one word.

"Problems with romance?"

"Ho, ho, ho," said Jonathan.

Jules had never before heard the deputy attempt sarcasm. He perked up. "Did you talk to your friend about your misgivings?"

"She's not talking to me."

"Ah," said Jules, after a heavy pause.

"Someone's coming by my house," said Jonathan. "And calling, and hanging up the phone. It's making me nervous."

"Make any special enemies on the job?"

"No, no," said Jonathan. "I think someone is following me, but it's nothing to do with work."

As if he'd notice, thought Jules. Jonathan could be terribly righteous, which was why Jules tried to keep him away from young mothers on drugs, young men with guns, potential suicides. The list of safe pastimes was short. Jonathan's lectures possibly bored minor criminals into better behavior, and he was remarkably efficient, in a scorched earth fashion, with drunks, but Jules would rather dance naked at the Blue Bat, something he hadn't done in fifteen or so years, than take Jonathan on a violent domestic call. Jonathan's utter lack of experience (years as a grocery bagger and a degree from a North Dakota community college before police training) or observation meant that he believed in the letter of the law because he lacked the imagination to grasp its spirit. The discovery of a joint in a pocket was as important as finding a straight razor or a basement of mail-order kiddie porn. The concept that the police might sometimes be wrong or that justice might not always be just passed him by faster than a television commercial. He was only gradually acquiring a life, a sense of humor, saving knowledge of a wide world. His childhood had been a diet of sitcoms and Baptist Sundays. And despite all of this he was sweet, freckled, and milk-fed inside and out.

Jonathan had affirmed Jules's suspicion of people who were always sure of themselves, moved through life with a plan they expected others to accommodate and applaud. They were people who lacked the curiosity necessary to believe other people truly existed, and they were people who became cops for all the wrong reasons. They tended to either be dim or psychotic in the simplest sense of the word, not necessarily criminal but certainly not empathetic. Jonathan was different only because of his sweetness, though he'd become unpredictable during the last year, due to a late-blooming interest in reading instilled by the ardent coed. Jonathan believed everything he read, good or bad, and the coed had given him upsetting stuff. After "The Lottery" he'd dreamed no one had real eyes, and after "The Bear," in great confusion, he'd dreamed of being buried in a swamp, reaching out of it to try to touch still-visible air (Jules thought that winter's avalanche victims might have been behind this). These were stories he should have read in high school, but why quibble when someone's only read *Sports Illustrated* (Jonathan had confessed to Ed he'd never so much as touched a *Playboy*, and Ed had ever since tortured him with centerfolds taped inside his locker).

The week before Jonathan had finished *The Collector*, which explained why he was letting a little thing like harassment bother him.

"A man or a woman?"

"A woman."

"How many times has she shown up?"

"Two, maybe three."

"What does she say?"

"Not much."

"What does she look like?"

"I don't know."

It figured that Jonathan would be harder to interview than the average bar drunk. "Then how do you know it's a woman?"

Jonathan looked miserable. "She stands on my porch and talks."

"What does she say?" asked Jules for the second time.

Jonathan shook his head.

"The lady's crazy," said Jules. "It shouldn't embarrass you."

"She wants to do things to me. I won't say any more than that. Really, really dirty things."

Jules sighed, not really caring to know whether his idea of dirty coincided with Jonathan's. "What does she do once you see her?"

"When I open the door, she runs down the sidewalk."

"You haven't followed her?"

Jonathan looked shocked. "Well, I don't want to catch her."

Jules had never heard him say something so practical.

FIVE DEPUTIES, UP from last year's three, was still a sparse contingent for an area half the size of Connecticut. Each year the sheriff's department handled about 250 major arrests—mostly thefts, domestic abuse, drugs, and DUIs—and 5,000 minor problems. The county had gone for years without a murder or stranger rape, but during Jules's tenure he'd seen several of each, and the mayor seemed to find him somehow responsible.

Each of the deputies had their own strengths, though their weaknesses were even more distinctive: Ed, for instance, was large and unwieldy, his lower body a paradigm example of patrolman's spread, though he had the arms of a construction worker. He'd kill a horse or himself on a mountain trek, and so avoided search and rescue calls. He disdained any research that required more than three phone calls, and was miserable at citing bad hunters and overly enthusiastic drunks—he just didn't bother. At fifty-six he never had, and Jules saw no point in trying to make changes. But Jules tended to lose his temper on domestic abuse calls, a definite no-no in such situations, while Ed was a pro at putting on a soothing attitude while standing in a bloodied living room, then making the man wish he'd never been born by the time they reached the jail and convincing his spouse to stick with charges in later house calls. Harvey Meyers was Jules's age and terrifically lazy, but once roused—rousted—was good at almost everything: pissy teenagers, medical emergencies, violent assholes on methamphetamine, forlorn owners of trapped cats.

Jonathan was the reason that Jules had chosen Caroline and Wesley, the new deputies, over a host of more earnest candidates the previous spring, mostly kids who thought life as a small-town deputy would be a hoot or career-oriented city cops who thought it would be a breeze, and were a little too weathered for comfort. Caroline and Wesley had had less law enforcement experience but more of a life—Caroline had been a lab biologist, Wesley spent years chained to a computer, tracking hate groups for Alcohol, Tobacco and Firearms. Jules didn't know if they were innately better humans, but they'd at least given themselves a chance to become so. Both were intelligent, compassionate, and funny. Both sought the job and the town because they wanted, in so many words, to work with people they'd see more than once.

Jules, having come from a profession with the same essential disconnection, couldn't find it in his heart to argue. In interviews, he had pointed out that there was a downside to knowing everyone you dealt with if you found them dead behind a wheel or stuffing their child's head in a toilet. They'd get to sit in a doctor's lobby with an abusive husband, both of them pretending to read *Newsweek*; they'd overhear enough to learn he was dying of colon cancer. At the grocery they'd wait in line behind a young mother of three whom they knew was dealing crank; at the hardware they'd have to ask for a hinge from someone they'd busted for a third DUI. Another drunk might fail to recognize them at one of the local bars and ask them out on a date, or maybe he would recognize them and wait in the alley with a baseball bat. The job meant ticketing, paperwork, telling the same man to stop beating the same girlfriend, the same drunk to stop drinking too much of the same liquid at the same time night after night. It was grim and numbing, boring even compared to an archaeological dig, taking a camel's-hair brush to the same patch of dirt for weeks.

Wesley nodded and smiled. Boredom was relative when you'd spent years with a federal agency. One of Caroline's previous jobs had involved building amniocentesis profiles, several a day, thousands before she quit. At the end of the procedure she'd sometimes understand that the person whose DNA she'd parsed was headless, or lacking a colon, or doomed to die at six months from a lack of a certain protein, but she never met that person's parents, never even met the doctor who would talk to them.

The first day Jules had met Caroline, after he'd said all this and she still seemed to want the job, she stood to go, then turned and asked him a question. "Then why do you do it?"

Jules shrugged. "Archaeology can be slow, and I did some social work in my twenties."

She waited, watching him, and Jules had the first inkling that he might have trouble being near her day after day. "My father was sheriff."

"Your father was shot to death. That's not much of a job incentive."

"True," said Jules. "How'd you know that anyway?"

She shrugged.

"Why do you want the job?" he asked.

"I have an uncle in Baltimore who's a cop," she said. "And I was sick of being indoors."

They had both lied. Jules had wanted to come home, period, and his father, dead before Jules started high school, had left him with the misconception that being a cop was something that would come naturally. He didn't have a clue as to why he'd been stupid enough to run for sheriff. Caroline had been working with abstractions and living in Maryland with a man who had suddenly revolted her. She had run for cover, connecting a great aunt who lived in Blue Deer with a stage of life that had been filled with ease and curiosity. But she didn't tell Jules about the man, or that her aunt was Cicely Tobagga, one of the Aches he'd known since childhood. It had taken Jules several months to figure that out.

People rarely did things for the right reasons, and sometimes there were no right reasons. By the time Jules thought of prying into what had really made her come, he only cared that she didn't leave again.

JULES DROVE NORTH at noon after a morning pushing paper, having accumulated weeks of overtime with no money to pay himself for it. He let himself in the Sacajawea's kitchen door and climbed the rickety back stairs to his second-floor den. The place was swarming with carpenters, buzzing with saws; from down the hall in the dining room he could hear Dottie riding herd and Fred barking back. She ran the place with decision and efficiency, and though Halsey's constant whims were trying, she usually managed patience.

If Jules ran into anyone, they'd ask him to help. Today he made it to the music room without being seen, unlocked the French doors, dropped the Yale lock and his keys on the big couch, and continued up the stairs to the tower. He knocked to no response, then knocked again.

Merry Maier said, "Leave me alone," exactly the way she'd said it the day before in the Bachelor.

Jules stood in the hall and thought over how to handle an extra-large toddler, especially a toddler related to an employer. "Sorry," he yelled. "But I can't do that."

She opened it slowly. "I didn't know it would be you."

"Who did you think it'd be?"

She peered at him intently. "I am so sorry about yesterday. I'd never seen a dead person before, outside of a funeral."

He entered warily. He hadn't been in the room since he'd helped her move a month earlier, and it didn't look like she'd spent much time at home. When Merry wasn't making a show of working she was a blur, a complete gear freak, what used to be quaintly referred to as a fitness buff. Between chores performed with aching slowness, her day included fifty requisite stomach crunches, a jog in the morning, and rowing or biking in the afternoon, unless she took to actual mountains or rivers. According to her uncle, she also surfed,

Rollerbladed, and excelled in beach volleyball, at least when beaches and surf were available.

"Does she ever not exercise?" Jules had asked, after the first week.

"Only when she's drinking," said Halsey. "Then she goes in for other sports."

At the far end of the room he saw a kayak, an exercise bike, and various weights. The center was mounded with shopping bags and skis, and the perimeter was stacked with strange collections of things. A half dozen needlepoint stools, topped by at least a dozen picnic baskets; open boxes of Bakelite, boxes of tin toys and Depression-era radios and telephones and a shelf of egg cups. He counted fourteen clocks on one wall, all with faces advertising citrus companies.

"I collect, too," said Merry. "But not Leon's kind of garbage."

"Ah," said Jules.

"Otherwise I still haven't really unpacked. Thank you so much for helping to carry all of this upstairs." She smiled. "I don't know what I would have done without you and Fred."

This, for Merry, was a massive social effort, and Jules realized she was drunk, maybe still drunk from whatever she'd been up to the night before. She'd come to her uncle's hotel after a long stay in a California "spa," but she veered off course at least twice a week.

His whole professional life, no matter the specific profession, Jules had been trained to scan particulars, weigh them, and come up with a whole. He was good at patterns, even when paying only halfhearted attention, and over the course of working at the Sacajawea he'd come up with Merry's m.o. She wasn't the typical female alcoholic, didn't tend toward subtlety and increasingly early and numerous glasses of white wine. She'd start with beer at 11:00 a.m. and have at least a six-pack before she moved on to scotch at cocktail hour. By three she'd be jolly and effusive. At seven her eyes would begin to move in different directions, and she'd become very, very friendly. On such nights, when Fred wasn't shepherding, Dottie was under standing orders from Halsey to shake her head at the man of the hour. Merry would keep it up for two or three days, then go clean for three or four. She had the constitution of a twenty-year-old boy or an Australian. On mornings and the clean days in between she completely ignored Jules's presence (and Dottie and Halsey's, when possible, but never Fred's), and in the beginning he enjoyed following her around, talking at her.

"You know, Merry, I was thinking about what you said last night, about men's nipples and metaphysics."

She'd sneer at him, or tell him to go away, or pretend she hadn't heard, but twice now she'd completely lost it and begun to scream, saying she was persecuted, saying everyone but Fred was evil, saying they'd all be sorry when she was dead, saying they'd all be sorry when *they* were dead. Midway through the second outburst Jules finally, belatedly, realized that she was mentally ill. Now he avoided her all the time, instead of nine tenths of it.

Today he already wanted to run for the door. She gestured vaguely, as if he should sit, but the only place to sit would have been the unmade bed. The whole place smelled of morning breath.

"So," he said. "Tell me what happened at the Bachelor that night before you called me."

"Not much," she said, fiddling with a box of CDs. "But it was only my second week, so I don't know what's normal. Let me pour you some tea," she said, moving to the hotplate near the exercise equipment.

"No thanks," he said. But she didn't seem to hear him, and he looked down at the CDs. Techno pop, New Age pseudo-soulfulness. Pre-rehab, Merry had lived in Los Angeles, where she'd spent several years as a music publicist. This amused Dottie, who pointed out that Merry didn't like good people or good music; Merry had changed jobs every eight months after her bad days had added up. Dottie had many theories about what was wrong with Merry, whom she'd disliked intensely throughout the fifteen years she'd worked for Halsey. She would aim at Merry's childhood in Palm Springs, her parents, dead of cirrhosis and pills, an early boyfriend who'd committed suicide with a heroin overdose, shock therapy gone wrong, gynecological damage. None of it was stuff Jules wanted to know; he'd heard enough of such stories at his other job.

Now Merry was handing him some very herbal-looking liquid. "How many people came in?" asked Jules.

"A dozen or so. Mostly my skiing friends."

"Did Anne talk to anyone?"

"Not really. There was a man sitting near her," said Merry.

"Do you know the man's name?"

"No."

"Was he with anyone you recognized?"

"I think he was alone, but I'm pretty sure he bought one of Anne's drinks."

"What did he look like?"

For some reason, this brought her up short. Her mouth opened and closed and they had another awkward moment. She'd put on bright pink lipstick with a shaky hand, and it made her skin look sallow. "He had dark brown hair, short but messy," said Merry with an effort. "Brown eyes. He was tall and skinny. Six-two or six-three."

"How old?"

"Maybe thirty-five or forty."

"That's funny," said Jules. "You could be describing me."

Merry's eyes widened and filled.

"If you don't remember, just say so," said Jules gently. "What were they talking about?"

During the next pause, he guessed she was deciding whether or not to go haywire, and he stiffened as he waited. Merry rallied. "I don't remember what he looked like, not a bit. But they were talking about good places to go on vacation, Mexico, places like that."

"Places to go together?"

"No, just places they'd been in their lives."

Standard bar chatter for a blizzard at the end of March. Jules would have talked about Mexico, too, if his option was walking home drunk to Leon. "Did this man leave with her?"

"No. He left before she left."

"Leon says she had a lover. Did you ever see him?"

"No."

"Do you know if Leon has a lover?"

She made a face. "No."

Jules tapped his pencil on his knee. "A devoted couple?"

She laughed out loud, but he sensed he'd almost used up her fragile patience. Jules sighed. "How many drinks did she have?"

"Two or three screwdrivers."

Jules looked dubious. "She was already lit when she came through the door," said Merry defensively. "What am I going to do, not serve Leon's wife? And anyway, she probably wanted to wind down without him around. When she started sliding off her stool I told her to go in the back, rest on the cot, and I'd get her home when I closed up, if that was what she wanted."

"But she left instead?"

"I saw her walk toward the back and thought she'd find the cot. But she must have left by the kitchen door, because when I checked an hour later she was gone."

"And you called me?"

"First I tried Leon's number, but no one answered. I figured she'd made it home, but I worried, so I finally called you, maybe an hour later when I was closing."

He held his tongue, not entirely believing her but not wanting to challenge her. Since Merry had come to the Sack she'd been adept at excuses, at blame, at rewriting simple messes, like who had left the lid off the wallpaper paste or who had forgotten to clean a paintbrush or who had left the bar door open in the middle of the night.

"What time do you think you saw her last?"

"Eleven, eleven thirty."

"Why did you call me at home rather than calling the station?"

"Anne always said to call you rather than the other jerk-offs," she said, giving him a smile that didn't quite work. She was trying to be flirtatious, and Jules had no problem seeing why Fred Bottomore steered clear. "She had your number by the phone."

"Was she in the habit of drinking like that?"

"I hadn't been there long enough to know."

"Had you ever seen her that drunk?"

"No."

"Huh," said Jules. "If you remember anything, let me know."

"Freezing isn't supposed to be a bad way to go," said Merry, still trying to maintain a breezy conversation.

Jules wanted out of the cluttered room, the sense that her misery was catching. "Hard to know unless you've done it," he said.

Merry looked like he'd slapped her. "How could you say that? Why do you hate me?"

"I don't hate you," said Jules. "It has nothing to do with you."

She started crying hard, big liquid hiccups. She rocked back and forth for a minute, then ran into her bathroom.

Jules stood for a minute, weighing options. He knocked tentatively on the bathroom door.

"Leave me alone."

Jules left, slamming the door just for fun. He took the back stairs all the way down to the kitchen for a snack, but when he got there the old refrigerator was gone and Dottie Cope was sitting on the only remaining freestanding object in the room, an old prep table, surrounded by a sea of new tile, blank wall, and unfinished counters. She didn't look happy.

"What's wrong?"

"The equipment just arrived and none of it fits through the back door."

She didn't elaborate and Jules heard the sound of men swearing coming from the front of the building. He opened the back door to eye the width of the frame and saw Leon's pickup skidding away, laden with more junk.

"What's he doing here?"

"He grabbed the broken lamps in the basement and the box of frames you left in the hall, plus the old fridge and stove."

"I meant what's he doing working the day after his wife died?"

"Leon's a prick," said Dottie. "It's simple. When we had to work together I wanted to shoot him after just a few nights. It's a blessing Halsey keeps him at the Bachelor, and it hardly matters if a few receipts or some doodahs are missing."

Fred wandered in looking troubled, stared at the back door, and wandered out again.

"Leon's stealing from Halsey?" asked Jules.

"He skims," said Dottie. "And he's compulsive. I heard you up there making Princess cry. If your door was open I bet Leon would've walked out with something from your table, something small."

Jules filled a coffee cup and headed upstairs. He returned two minutes later, despite the threat of being drafted by Fred's crew.

"A weight. He took a Phoenician weight."

"Petty thievery," said Dottie, scribbling notes on a list.

"What do you mean, petty? Petty's a six-pack of beer or a lipstick. This is a three-thousand-year-old thing of beauty."

She shrugged. "It's nothing compared to what he put that woman through."

"What'd he put that woman through? Shit or get off the pot and stop dropping hints."

But when Jules pressed her she only admitted to vague rumors. He'd started to turn back toward the stairs when Halsey, surprisingly quiet for an old man, slammed a hand on his shoulder. "You're helping, now."

TWO HOURS LATER Jules sat down to work on a box of amulets, some five dozen from a variety of worlds and times, amber and stone bears and wolves from Scandinavia, Scythian honeybees, a bronze Cretan bull. Most of the amber came from the same Baltic source, even though the pieces had been carved over a thousand-year span, as far apart as Spain and the Russian steppes. Halsey had collected mostly by looks, rather than provenance: if he liked it he bought it, at garage sales as often as in tony galleries. Once a week they sat down to appraise the week's toys. Halsey would read through what Sotheby's had had to say about the most recent batch, and they'd decide what would be kept, what donated, what sold outright through dealers. Junk statuary and fakes had always gone to Leon, but now they simply went to one side; Leon had told Dottie he'd lost his "fine arts" contact and now only wanted furniture.

To say Halsey's taste was eclectic was to do the man an immense disservice. One box held almost a hundred combs, two of them Roman and one carved from a kangaroo jaw; it sat next to a row of framed mirrors, one of which was Haitian and showed pigs and mangos. Another box was filled with pieces of armor; a third, labeled "bestiary fragments," held an opal ladybug, a brass mask of a dragon, a lead giraffe's neck that had once been the handle of an amphora, a coil of malachite that had once been the tail of a Persian tiger.

Jules still wasn't used to doing something he actually felt competent at—if he couldn't identify an object, he knew who to ask, which was most of the battle. These sources, old friends and friends of friends, had asked if he was getting back into the business, and now, instead of simply saying no, he said not yet, inching away; the week before, working on the Baltic amber, he'd asked a friend in New York to let him know if she heard of anything interesting.

Outside it was cold but clear, and the sun through the window baked him pleasantly and made him sleepy. He stood to stretch, and looked down at Fred standing in the long empty pool below, out of the wind and surrounded by pots of

Miami color, repairing the circa 1921 mural. He was singing but intent, a lonely man doing something close to what he'd wanted to spend his life doing. Painting anything was Fred's way of relaxing after dealing with a walk-in refrigerator, three sinks, a deep-fat fryer, and a two-thousand-pound stove. He was dabbing at a jade green train, one of four that chased fish from one mountain range to another at each end of the pool, from night into day. Jules particularly liked the night train at the deep, cool end, indigos, golds, and white, moon above and snow below. It ran under a rendering of the Crazy Mountains, while the day train had the Absarokas, the mountains Jules looked out on over Fred's head.

It wasn't so bad sitting in a sunny window above this, looking out at the same very real mountains as they thawed, the sun warming his chest as he leaned back. Jules was past master of the twenty-minute chair nap and he polished this talent now. When he roused himself and looked out the window again, Fred was still painting, moving toward the dark end of the pool, but Merry was there, too, ostensibly helping. While Jules watched she wrapped one arm around Fred's shoulder and kissed him on the cheek. Jules thought Fred jumped, but maybe it was his imagination.

An hour later he was searching his room for the keys and the Yale lock when Fred showed up in the hallway. "You coming back tomorrow?" asked Fred.

"Saturday. I'm all yours."

"We could get that stove in and finish the dining room."

"We could," said Jules. "Whatever."

"What's wrong?"

"I can't find my lock."

Fred smiled. "Halsey probably took it," he said. "You know how weird he's been about me having anything installed."

This particular neuroticism drove Dottie wild; locks were something Halsey would have to get used to if he wanted to run a hotel.

"My keys, too," said Jules doubtfully. He'd bought the Yale himself, even though the French doors to the music room were curtained glass, and someone could obviously take anything if they wanted it bad enough. The key ring didn't include anything from the station or jail, and he had an extra truck key in the bumper, but it was still a pain in the ass.

"Dottie's got a couple of extra padlocks hidden downstairs," said Fred. "I'll give you one."

They started down the stairs. "Why does she hide them?" asked Jules.

Fred paused, trying to be careful with his response. "She says Merry made a copy of her keys without asking."

"What did Merry say?"

"That Halsey asked her to."

"What does Halsey say?"

"Nothing." Fred smiled. "Naturally. But he was extra nice to Dottie after that."

They saw Dottie through the bar window, yelling at a man in a bulldozer who was widening the drive and making a hill in the wrong place. Halsey's landscaping plans were just as baroque as his architectural goals. Everyone hoped he'd hire someone who knew what they were doing; Alice was currently giving him bids, considering yet another career change. Fred reached under the bar and slid open a small drawer, one Jules had never noticed. He pulled out one lock and gave Jules both keys.

"Will she mind?" asked Jules.

"Nah," said Fred. "She trusts you."

"Why does she hate Merry so much anyway?"

Fred shrugged and watched Dottie gesture at the man in the hardhat, who looked like he wanted to cry. "I'd guess it's the will. Wouldn't you?"

"Never mind," said Jules. "I don't think I really want to know."

JULES MADE IT back to the station by four thirty, and found a message to call Horace Bolan, MD.

"What's with the extra-stiff lady downstairs?"

"Has she softened up at all?"

"Compared to what?"

"I need an autopsy," said Jules. "Do you have time this evening?" He blew on his coffee and watched Caroline and Grace gesture in their customary end-of-the-day wrangle over loose ends.

"I haven't finished unpacking. Send her to Missoula."

"We don't have the money," said Jules, sitting up and putting down his coffee. "Please, please. Just a few samples and a once-over. I can be there now."

"Now means ten minutes and I'll be out of this bin in five. I'm not cutting her."

"She got drunk and froze to death. I don't want an autopsy. I just want to make sure we don't need one."

"I can hear you running for the door," said the doctor, hanging up.

Jules stood and groped for his coat. "Caroline, we have to go now," said Jules.

"Now what?" She looked harassed; Grace was probably telling her she couldn't read her writing again.

"A quick look at Anne Baden."

"Why?"

"What do you mean, 'Why?' A forty-six-year-old woman ends up dead in a field, and we're not going to check her out?"

Caroline raised an eyebrow and looked at the piles on her desk rather than his face.

"Did you have something to do tonight?" he asked. "It's not that big of a deal, and I know your shift's almost over."

"I never have anything to do at night," said Caroline, pulling on her coat.

A HALF HOUR later she was hunched over on a stool with a pad on her knee, staring morosely at a naked Anne Baden. Jules's fingers were stiff with cold from helping Horace undress the body, bagging each item for Caroline to number and label. They'd had to cut the too-tight jeans from the body.

"What the hell do you want anyway?" muttered Horace, peering into orifices. "She froze to death, just like you said on the phone."

"I want her blood alcohol," said Jules. "And a full tox report."

"I'm not cutting her up," said Horace again. "You want urine, you can send her to Missoula."

"I just want you to look for obvious things," said Jules. "She was with a man in the bar earlier, and I need to be sure that's the end of the story."

"No sign of sexual assault."

"There's a start," said Jules. "Can you can get a sample of her blood?"

Horace looked dubious.

"How about her eyes?" asked Jules.

"Might work," muttered the doctor, gazing at a tray of syringes.

"Try," said Jules, looking away before he saw a needle enter an eye. He picked up Anne's wet, flimsy shirt and frayed underwear and bagged them. Her front jeans pocket was empty, but in the back one she had a five and a folded page from a steno notebook, a reminder to buy toilet paper, soda pop, and apples. At the bottom of the page she'd written three town names, each followed by a question mark: Bisbee, Silver City, and Nogales.

"Looking to move," said Caroline, reading over his shoulder.

"Wouldn't you?"

"Absolutely. I can't blame her for the boyfriend."

"What did Leon's old bartender say?"

"No love lost between husband and wife. No idea about a lover, and Anne wasn't a habitual drinker, but this guy did say she'd been depressed lately." She pointed to the log by the door. "Leon hasn't been to see her yet."

"I noticed," said Jules.

"Okay," said the doctor. "We have vitreous humor. We have blood. We have no obvious anomalies."

"You sure?" asked Jules.

Horace was writing. "Yes."

"Look, Horace."

"I did look, before I even called you, before I realized she was still frozen. I didn't notice a thing." He kept scribbling.

Jules walked back to the gurney and peered at Anne's scalp. "It might be worth an X-ray."

"They'll love that upstairs," said Horace. "It's bound to make the people in the waiting room happy. Her scalp is blotchy because her blood's pooling as she thaws."

"Her legs are bruised," said Jules.

"People who drink a lot run into things," said Horace.

"She didn't have that rep," said Jules. "Is she one of your patients?"

"She had some back problems," said Horace. "Though I don't recall her being pushy about refills. The blood test will tell. Add a barbiturate to alcohol and anyone might think a snowdrift looked like a pillow."

"She went down in slush," said Jules.

"I'm just saying she had access."

"Everyone has access."

Horace sighed. "Anyway, as far as the bruises go, it's that time of year. This morning one of the nurses walked into a wall and needed four stitches. We're weak, blind, light-deprived animals. Old people die in the early spring, people kill themselves in the spring. Chaucer had it right about April being the cruelest month."

Jules and Caroline considered this in silence, neither bothering to argue that it was not yet April, or that Horace had just returned from a tropical vacation. Caroline pointed to Anne's right hand. "How do you think she did this?"

The tips of her thumb and first two fingers were scraped raw and the nails broken down. The left hand was in the same condition. "Harvey took samples," said Jules, "but we only saw ice."

"Ice is sharp," said Horace. "Sometimes when people die this way they try to dig a hole, make a shelter. We should all be allowed to hibernate until May Day."

Jules decided to send the body to Missoula after all.

BY FRIDAY, THEY'D talked to everyone who'd been to the Bachelor that night and knew all there was to know about Anne Baden, pending the Missoula autopsy. She'd walked through the door at nine, alone, and left at eleven, alone.

She'd talked to Bert Sypes, a welder, and Betty Dillinger, one of Merry Maier's preppy friends. It was clear to Betty, who seemed smarter than most, that the welder (who was short and dumpy but had brown eyes, and remembered talking about Mexico) and Anne Baden didn't know each other well and could not possibly know each other biblically. She hadn't seen anything resembling the boyfriend Leon had screamed about, and she'd been there from eight until closing.

Jules pointed out that this was a long time to sit in a bar and remain observant. Betty said she'd been reading papers and a mystery. This begged the question of why she'd been there at all.

They were at the Sack, having coffee. Merry marched in and out of the room carrying buckets and rolls of wallpaper; wallpaper was her specialty, her only known talent. Betty leaned forward. "Merry asked me to come. Leon makes her nervous, and she didn't want to be left alone with him."

Fair enough. "Is that why she didn't check on Anne right away?"

Betty looked pained. "I made her try Leon, and I made her call you. I went out looking and I made her look and we didn't see anything, but that doesn't mean much. I couldn't see the cars in the lot until I was five feet from them."

The problem, he thought, was that after delaying the call Merry had exhibited no conscience whatsoever past locking herself into bathrooms. She was defensive without being guilty, as mystified and embarrassed with the failure of her token effort as a rich nineteenth-century woman who couldn't understand how a beggar might starve after she'd tossed a penny in his direction. Which brought him to the real crux of the matter: Merry had always been rich, and in her case this had kept her from deigning to comprehend the other 99 percent of the world. One day, when she'd returned from an eight-hour hike in the Crazies, Jules had asked her what birds she'd seen, and she'd told him she'd been working too hard to notice. She'd had every chance to roam and think, see and do, and she'd responded by padding a dog bed of self-satisfaction and neuroticism. He'd heard that Betty's family had founded the company that made the tires on his truck, but she and Merry might have come from different planets.

Jules rubbed his head. "I know she's hard to take," said Betty. "She has bad days, and you just have to avoid them."

"You've known her a long time?"

"Since school."

Boarding school, naturally.

All signs pointed to the idea that Anne Baden's love life was imaginary. Leon admitted that he didn't know the boyfriend's name and had never seen such a man; Anne had consistently denied a lover existed and in fact had never spent a whole night away from home until the night she'd died.

"Then what were you doing, talking about a boyfriend?" asked Jules.

"My imagination gets the better of me from time to time," said Leon. "She just didn't care anymore, and I thought something was up."

What had been up, probably, had been Anne Baden's gradual decision that life as she knew it was no longer worth living. Jules had wasted money, asking for an autopsy, and learned soon after that he might be stuck with a burial, as well. "The bastard says he won't bury her when we get her back from the lab," said Caroline. "I asked him about funeral homes so they could send her direct, and he won't do it. And her parents left on a Caribbean cruise right after they got the news and aren't due home for ten days. I found two siblings, one housewife in Orlando and a seedy asshole in Tampa who didn't volunteer what he did for a living. Neither of them will claim the body."

"Leon'll pay," said Jules. "I'll sue the fucker if I have to."

"How long can she stay at the hospital?" asked Caroline.

"There's not a lot of competition for that spot," said Jules. "We can wait for her parents to come back and then hash it out."

JULES REPORTED TO Fred for duty at nine on Saturday morning. "Kitchen first," said Fred. "Do you mind?"

Jules didn't mind a bit. He'd logged years in restaurant kitchens, could have used psychotherapy just to handle nightmares about miscounting orders on the line, but he'd had a long enough break to find the equipment, the space, the stainless steel and plate warmers and quickly blackened sauté pans lovable again. When you had a bad day in the kitchen you could scream obscenities, move from bursts of adrenaline to the soothing bubble of a sauce to draining the better wine bottles while you cleaned up at the end of the night. When you had a bad day as a cop, standing over a car wreck or just a five-year-old's stolen, ruined bicycle, outbursts were frowned upon and no pleasure intruded.

He'd never seen such equipment new before. These days, he noticed, you didn't have to nearly blow your face off to light a Garland range, and it no longer seemed possible for a fellow employee to lock you into a walk-in refrigerator, as Alice had once done to him. Halsey's deep-fat fryer could have come from a Museum of Modern Art catalog, and it was hard to imagine it ever being covered with yellow gum. Everything promised to work wonderfully, if he and Fred didn't screw up.

By noon they'd finished with the deep-fat fryer and the Garlands. He and Fred were both on their backs, struggling with pipes and hoses under a cut-out stainless counter, when a black high heel toed Jules gently in the stomach. Jules looked up and said, "Eeep."

Fred looked up, too, but didn't seem as surprised. Dottie stood directly above him in a short black skirt. "Herbie can come Monday to check on the gas hookup and the man from Icehouse left his home number in case you have trouble with the freezer."

"Thanks," said Fred.

"Don't mention it," said Dottie. "And then there's Muriel's crates." She bent down to make eye contact with Jules. "They came Thursday, but Fred said we should wait to open them until you were around."

"Don't wait for me," said Jules.

"Halsey's got an edge on," said Fred. "He says stuff's missing from his room, and I got the feeling he had me in mind. I don't want to give him ammunition by not having a witness."

"Well," said Dottie. "We can all guess who's getting into his room."

Fred and Jules both looked up at her. "She insisted on having her own set of keys," said Dottie. "And Halsey went along with it. Now he wants you to unpack some of the stuff before the party tonight. Muriel told him to expect a few surprises and got him all hyped up.

"No," said Fred.

"What do you want me to tell Halsey?"

"Whatever you want," said Fred. "He doesn't believe anything I say anyway, and you're the final authority."

She pursed her lips and kissed the air. "You know flattery won't get you anywhere."

"I know," said Fred, kissing the air back.

Dottie tapped her foot. Jules decided to sit up and sort some nuts and bolts. "Halsey hasn't seen most of the stuff in years. Maybe Jules should do it by himself."

Fred was surprisingly stoic. "I need him. Tomorrow afternoon, if we get everything in place here. The Nits are Sheetrocking today, and I want to tape tomorrow so we can start painting Monday."

"Pretty paintings, Fred. You don't care about paintings anymore?"

"I always care," said Fred. "Even if they belong to Halsey."

She started to walk away, then turned and crouched down. "Hey, Jules. You know any rich people in the state who'd want to buy some ancient erotica?"

"Not offhand," said Jules.

She laughed and walked away. Jules wondered how many times the word *erotica* had been used in a Montana restaurant kitchen. "I'm feeling used," he said to Fred. "Like she wants you to squirm."

"Some days more than others," Fred said. A sink came down through the opening so abruptly that Jules hit his head on a pipe as he recoiled.

JULES DROVE BACK to town and checked in at the station. Caroline was making a very halfhearted stab at cleaning her desk.

"Just out of curiosity," asked Jules, "did your aunt Cicely happen to know Halsey's ex-wife?"

"Which one?" asked Caroline, dumping a large stack of paper into the trash.

"His first," said Jules. "Muriel Zirn, I think. She just died in San Francisco, but her family used to own the Sacajawea."

"I'll ask," said Caroline. "Why?"

Jules didn't want to get into details with Caroline. "She died and left him some art."

"As if he needed more." Caroline put on her coat. "What time are you picking up Peter for the shindig?"

"Six." He smiled. "Wish me luck."

"Good luck," she said. "Just thinking about it makes me want to take two aspirin and crawl into bed. Call me for a ride if you get in trouble."

"I'm supposed to drive."

"I love it when you're an optimist."

Jules spent the next few minutes considering easy ways to sabotage his own car.

5 *Strange Rituals*

If a husband stands alone in a forest,
and no one can hear him,
and he makes a statement—
is he still wrong?

BACHELOR PARTIES WERE MYSTERIOUS, THOUGH NOT mystical, events. It was as if the goal were to ritually kill the groom and his attendants, so that what was left the next morning would be properly newborn, denuded. How else to explain the pageant of intelligent, mature, open-minded men, the most sensitive sliver of their sex on the planet, behaving like brain-dead fraternity jocks, the Serbian army on a winning day. At bachelor parties, even men who managed to remain sane on St. Patrick's Day, New Year's, birthdays, and funerals could be found under tables, sucking the lees of red wine and honking with despair like underfed pigs when they reached the last drops.

In the past, Jules had been known to mull such things over with most of his face pressed into a pillow, one eye open a crack to regard actual red-wine stains. But to his great relief, Peter was avoiding as much craven behavior as possible, partly by having the thing early to prevent his crazed brothers from foisting imported dancing girls upon him. He didn't even want wine or fine food. The people who came could be as stupid as they wanted to be, but he, Peter, would have two beers and eat fried food and play pool and tour the county safely. Jules was assigned to keep an eye on him, and Soren Rue, the *Bulletin*'s teetotaling photographer, would chauffeur the rest in one of the newspaper's delivery vans. The *Bulletin* didn't bother to publish on weekends.

As an afterthought they split some freeze-dried mushrooms, psilocybin so old that Jules joked that the fungi looked like a tomb offering, or maybe a prehistoric coprolite.

"What's a coprolite?" asked Divvy.

"Fossilized shit. You find a lot of it."

"Funny," said Peter, grimacing at the flavor.

"You sure you'll be able to drive?" asked Alice.

"I always used to manage it," said Jules.

"More or less," said Alice. "I'm not sure if I was much of a judge."

Nothing happened after twenty minutes, and Peter and Jules admitted to relief. Divvy Ott, whose idea it had been, sulked. He and Jules had been friends since grade school, and the idea that the two of them were collectively responsible for county safety—Divvy was the fire chief—was a standing joke among certain segments of the population. He and Jules were so good these days that when Divvy did gear up for misbehavior, he was relentless.

They started at the Blue Bat, and Delly Bane, the bartender, pulled out a dart board for the occasion. It was fun for ten minutes. Axel Scotti, who'd had a long day in court, was a little too vehement with the darts and Divvy was too interested in talking with Scotti, who'd recently filed charges against one of Divvy's firemen. Jules was relieved that Axel was the fall guy, as it was Jules who'd arrested Divvy's employee in the act of burgling a residence while wearing the lady of the house's underwear. Jules and Peter decided to skip on ahead to the Sacajawea.

"I have a few questions for you," Jules asked Peter as they headed east. "Things that have been making me wonder."

"About what?"

"Halsey's will."

"You know I can't talk about that."

"I know," said Jules. They passed a goshawk on a fence post, and when it took off it seemed to be in slow motion. Jules slowed down to fifty-five. "Dottie and the niece don't get along, and Fred's led me to believe the will has something to do with it."

"Merry's a pain in my ass," said Peter. "She's trouble."

"Yes," said Jules.

"I can't believe the way they all talk up there. Let's go somewhere else."

"No," said Jules. "We're sticking to the goddamn schedule. So does Dottie actually inherit the hotel?"

Peter sighed. "Not just the hotel."

"The hotel and the art?"

"And enough cash to take care of both."

A southbound car passed at what felt like ninety. Jules flinched and shaved another five miles an hour off his pace. "I'd feel a little pissy, too, if I were Merry."

"She gets most of the rest," said Peter. "She has nothing to complain about."

"Still."

"Do you have any idea of what Halsey's worth?"

Jules didn't, not really. "A couple million?"

Peter snorted.

"Five? Ten?"

"Dottie has been working for Halsey since 1980," said Peter. "He dusted her off after her own divorce and she's kept him in one piece and unmarried ever since. You knew her back then, didn't you?"

Jules saw no reason to volunteer the whole truth. "She was friends with my sister."

"One source of tension is that Dottie will get the art, but Merry will get the cash from most of what Halsey decides to sell. Anything you or Fred recommend he sells. Dottie likes it when you find something valuable and recommend that Halsey keep it, but Merry hates it, gets all in a tizzy. They both drop hints with me and Fred instead of mentioning it to you or Halsey." Peter paused and stared fixedly at a herd of sheep. "Now he's expecting something extra from Muriel, something really valuable, and he'll really be on the fence."

"Halsey's going to have to either change things or get them nailed down," said Jules. "Before he has a real mess."

"He's trying," said Peter. "That's why he wants you to work all the time. But it might be too late."

HALSEY HAD PUT on the dog, as it were: when they walked in, Mozart blared from the new sound system and Dottie, in a very short black and white waitress uniform, was on a high ladder taping streamers to the stained-glass ceiling light.

She looked confused. "Aren't you a little early? Aren't you traveling in a pack?"

"Yes and sometimes," said Peter.

"How soon are the others coming?"

They didn't know. Jules was having trouble with depth perception.

Dottie sized them up. "Would one of you mind holding the ladder?"

Jules turned to Peter, who seemed unnaturally happy, then back at Dottie. "I don't think it's appropriate that the bridegroom stand there," he said, walking forward.

"Fine," said Dottie. "You'll do in a pinch."

Halsey was busy arranging silver trays along the bar, each with a green bottle, several glasses, and a pitcher of what looked like ice water. Jules eyed the items suspiciously, in between pretending to take bites out of Dottie's slender black-stockinged knees. He also saw silver spoons and what looked like raw sugar cubes. He squinted at the bottle labels, bringing his head down slightly, and Dottie kneed him in the jaw.

"Ah," said Jules.

"Sorry. I thought you were going to tickle me."

At least his tongue hadn't been sticking out. Dottie climbed down and Jules approached the bar, reading "Absenta."

Moderation was a pipe dream. Halsey was serving Spanish absinthe, not exactly a legal import. Jules tried to imagine what his blood test might read by the end of the night.

"Halsey," he said. "Don't do this to us."

"It's a special occasion," he said. "I went through considerable trouble to get these bottles here. I remembered Peter saying he enjoyed it when he was in Europe."

"Peter was in Europe ten years ago, when he was young."

Halsey arched an eyebrow. "You think he's old?"

"It's a bad idea. A real crummy idea. You give it to all the yahoos on their way up here and you might not have a hotel left."

"Well," said Peter. "What the hell. It was meant to be."

"Your wife is going to kill me," said Jules.

"She isn't my wife yet," said Peter.

AN HOUR LATER everyone was starting on a second glass. Jules had relaxed about Alice and most other things, even though Axel and Divvy were still sniping at each other. It seemed that Halsey had read up on the topic at hand extensively, using Barnaby Conrad as a modern source to lead him back to the letters of van Gogh and Gauguin, Oscar Wilde and Verlaine. Jules remembered being fascinated by all of this when he was in college, but wasn't sure how it applied to a seventy-five-year-old beset by cancer and ungrateful relatives. "The first glass makes you see things as they wish they were," said Halsey. "The second as they are not."

"You didn't make this up," said Peter.

"Nope. Can't remember who did."

"How about the third?"

"The third makes you see things as they really are, and it's a horrible thing."

Fred was smiling at all of them. "Does this mean you're going to stop?"

"I dunno," said Halsey. "The quote could apply to marriages, too, and I never quite knew better." He stole a look at Peter. "The first is the way to go."

"I wish it were over," said Peter, looking tired suddenly.

"Aren't you his best man?" said Halsey to Jules.

"Yes," said Jules. "Whatever that means."

"It means you have a heavy responsibility," said Halsey.

"To see him to the chapel on time, in fair condition? Do you think you're really helping by serving this stuff?"

"To lessen the potential trauma and suffering of the event, and somehow transform it into happy memories."

"I want to be married," said Peter, with a small smile.

"Of course you do. It's the in-between stage that'll have you bleeding from the eyes by this time next week."

Jules didn't disagree; he'd taken a double dose of vitamins that morning, with just such a future in mind. But Peter was a dozen years older than Halsey had been his first time in, and before he'd ever met Alice he'd mown through much of a Big Ten campus and a good chunk of New York's varied female population. Now he was a dope-smoking small-town lawyer, relatively relaxed and at peace with the world and his place in it, and Jules intended to keep him that way for the duration, even if it meant stealing from the evidence locker. Peter had to be mellow when everyone arrived, lest he argue with in-laws or college friends who'd gone right-wing, start thinking about how much all of it was going to cost, or become melancholy for all the women who would now go unknown.

"Well," said Halsey. "Here's to loving not wisely but too well, or however the damn line goes. Instead of Jules, who's decided to store his dick in an ostrich hole."

Dottie loved that one, and started to giggle so hard that her mascara ran. Jules lowered his glass and placed it carefully on the bar. "I'll leave if you keep it up."

Halsey smiled. Thirty years in northern California had made him a great believer in psychotherapy, but he'd come to realize that Jules would have no such conversations in the winter. In the summer, of course, he didn't need them. "We'll find you a nice girl."

"I have my own ideas," said Jules. "Piss off."

Halsey began lecturing Fred about the progress on the second floor. Dottie poured Divvy and Scotti and Peter a third glass, seconds for everyone else but Fred. "Get away," said Jules.

Dottie tapped her finger on his knuckle. "Halsey says absinthe makes the tart grow fonder."

"Someone said it before Halsey," said Jules.

"Well, I'm saying it now."

Jules blinked. She moved down the bar to clean ashtrays and he turned away and met Fred's eyes.

They both looked down. Halsey continued his harangue. "I told you I'd pay overtime. Where the fuck is the crew anyway?"

"They worked ten hours on a Saturday and went home. They worked twelve-hour days all week. They have lives."

"Well, you don't. So why are you sitting here?"

Jules could feel Peter stiffen to his left. "Lay off," said Fred, still sounding relaxed. "I said I'd open the crates tomorrow for you, after my friend's party."

"You don't drink anyway. What's the point in sitting here?"

Jules looked to Dottie for help, but she shrugged and he spoke up. "Halsey, stop being a shit."

Halsey wheeled around and after a long moment turned away and addressed the bar mirror. "Fred said he'd have the job done on time."

"I will," said Fred. He rummaged in his shirt pocket and pulled out a half dozen paint chips. "Why don't you pick out a color for the bathrooms while we're both sitting here."

Halsey looked down at the chips, up at Fred, and changed gears, sorting through the chips with a happy expression. Fred's jaw was tense, and his cheeks were a little pink. Jules understood suddenly that something had finally snapped—even though he seemed calm, Fred had stopped liking Halsey. Jules marveled at his equanimity; any other contractor would have quit or taken a swing at the old man.

Peter avoided it all by talking to Patrick Ankeny about how they should start a regular poker game again. Everyone was operating on the tacit understanding that Jules, who'd spent two years with Edie Linders, had no hard feelings about Ankeny having married her a month earlier. Farther down the bar, Divvy and Axel were hissing at each other like pissed-off Canada geese, and Soren Rue, despite being sober, was drenching the rest of the men with tales of his daring assignments for the *Bulletin*, the last of which had involved an angry llama.

Dottie was back in front of him, eyes glittering. "You use one of those Garland ranges in your former life?"

"Yes," said Jules.

"Come back to the kitchen and tell me a couple of things about this one. I'd like to be able to heat a can of soup."

"It's hooked up right," he said. "We checked."

"I'm sure it's hooked up fine," said Dottie. "I just need operating instructions."

He didn't want to move; he had an obscure bad feeling, and even though he refused to think it through, he felt the weight of Fred's eyes.

"Now," said Dottie.

The stoves were double-oven Garlands, huge and shiny and black. Jules found some matches and turned a knob. "Soup," he said. "Presto. And this is how you turn on the broiler."

"Come here, you've got something on your chin, some ink or something."

Jules wiped at his chin.

"Bend down," said Dottie. "I think it's where I kneed you."

He lowered his face toward her. She licked a finger and rubbed at the corner of his mouth. "I've been meaning to remind you," she said.

"Remind me of what?" Dottie was holding on to the back of his neck, still looking at the mysterious mark.

"That you need to have more fun. You haven't had fun in the longest time. That's a shame."

"I'll say," said Jules.

"A waste," said Dottie.

"Well, gee," he said, straightening and staring at her in a last moment of self-preservation. "I wouldn't go that far."

"I would," said Dottie, reaching down and touching him. "And I'd know. So how's life?"

"So so," he whispered.

She smiled and took a firmer hold. "Things will look up soon."

"Gaah," said Jules.

"Hmm?"

Years later, it was all coming back. "For Christ's sake, they'll come looking for us."

"Not for a few minutes," said Dottie, pulling him toward the bathroom without removing her hand. "I'm in a good mood, and good moods don't hit me often anymore."

One minute Jules was thinking of Garland ranges and the next nothing at all. His pants never made it down to his ankles. Dottie unwrapped herself gracefully and rubbed a crease out of her skirt. She was actually wearing a garter belt, which had proved his final undoing. "I just love fucking with your brain," she said. "You're just as goofy as you were at twenty."

"What brain?" muttered Jules.

"Say thank you."

"Thank you."

She waltzed off with an evil giggle, leaving Jules standing at a slant in the tiny bathroom, his forehead pressed against the chipped mirror, heavy-limbed and dizzy with nothing much to look at but the used condom in the trash can. After a few minutes he backed up, hauled up his jeans, stared into the mirror, and started daubing lipstick off his face.

He wasn't sure if he should feel smug or traumatized. Out in what passed for the real world, Divvy and Axel were now arguing about whether or not the pool table was level, Dottie innocently scrubbing glasses. Merry was behind the bar near Fred, peering at the color chips, but Halsey had left the room.

Jules had just reclaimed his bar stool, resisting the urge to check his fly, when he realized that Fred was studying him. "You ever have a sense that life isn't fair?"

"Yes," said Jules. "Don't work tonight. I'll help tomorrow."

"I'm not talking about work," said Fred stiffly. He was flushed. "You ever get tired of knowing that virtue should be its own reward?"

Jules stared at him in dawning horror. "I've never been able to stick to virtue long enough to deserve being tired of it," he said carefully. It took tremendous effort to put together a full sentence.

Fred sighed and seemed to pull himself together. But then he and Jules both looked at Dottie, who was unrepentant and smiling as she wiped down the bar.

"Why'd you do it, Dot?" asked Fred.

She looked at him calmly. "Because I felt like it, Fred."

"You know," said Fred. "I think I'll have a real drink, just for a change of pace."

The dozen men in the room fell silent. Merry scanned their faces, not seeming to comprehend what was happening.

"Fred, I didn't know," said Jules. "I'm so sorry."

"Someone knew," said Fred. "Give me a whiskey, Dot."

"Please don't," said Jules.

"Please shut up," said Fred.

He drained it and bolted from the room. A minute later Merry followed him at a run. Divvy and Scotti went back to their argument, which was waxing political.

"Well," said Dottie, her voice a little shaky. "Some people have no sense of humor."

Jules and Peter left soon after, saying they were going to drive extra slowly to the next destination, a restaurant in Clyde City owned by Divvy's cousin Bob. They'd come in through the kitchen door but both of them had forgotten this and headed out the front. Peter surged toward the pool, completely forgetting the funk he'd fallen into when Fred, renovator of Peter's wedding site, had started drinking again. "It's full!" shrieked Peter. "It's beautiful!"

He was teetering on the edge of the plunge, which was really only half full; it had been filled as a test run that morning, and the leaks were numerous. Jules lay down at the edge and stretched to touch the water. It was a perfect temperature, a dream bath, and the trains and mountains shimmered under the water.

Peter gave him a playful boot in the ass. "Try it out."

"I probably will," said Jules mournfully. "He's asking for trouble, filling this before the wedding."

DIVVY'S COUSIN BOB, chef and owner of the Big Tomato in Clyde City, believed in basics. The steak was massive, obscene: forty ounces, according to the menu, accompanied by a deep-fried onion, open and crispy on the tips like a tired zinnia, and potato wedges soaked in buttermilk, breaded, and similarly fried. Axel Scotti ate so fast and hard he bent his fork. Jules, never the food snob he should have been, would have done the same if he could have remembered how to chew for more than thirty seconds at a time. He stuck to water, and so did Peter. Most of the others ate like Scotti, even though they were taking in food too late to save themselves. Jaws were a little slack and political arguments had begun to sprout; Soren Rue, chauffeur, would be the hero of the night.

After the onion and before the iceberg salad with blue cheese dressing Jules walked into the backyard with Peter, who needed another cigarette.

“Do absent and absinthe come from the same root?” asked Peter.

“Good question,” said Jules.

Under the vapor lamp they were mesmerized by the massive kitchen fan. A dark stain ran down the wall beneath it, and Jules thought the stain looked liquid, as if still in motion. Gradually he realized that the stain really was moving, that it was fat from the fan above the stove dripping down the wall to the roof and into the eaves troughs, the grease running down the gutters onto and under the building foundation.

“Divvy says Bob has a raccoon problem,” said Jules.

“Huh,” said Peter, staring up at the sky from a packing crate.

“Pretty high calorie place.”

“Do friend and fried come from the same root?”

“No,” said Jules decisively.

“Friend, find, fend, fed, rend, end,” muttered Peter.

“Fiend,” said Jules. “Fred.”

They were quiet for the next few minutes. “We’re not in any shape for word games,” said Peter. “Anyway, he’s been so good for so long.”

"You know what happens when he falls off the wagon," said Jules.

"This isn't necessarily fatal. People change."

A waitress came out, lit a cigarette, and smiled at them. In the unworldly lighting it came off as a monkey's grimace, and they started to giggle nervously. She frowned and walked around the corner of the building, somehow managing not to slide in the grease slick.

"I just want to go home," said Peter.

"You can't. You're the star of the show."

"I want to sit on my own couch and watch a stupid movie with Alice."

"Ask again in an hour," said Jules.

As if they'd be able to read a clock.

They went back inside, where Axel and Divvy were arguing about the finer points of each other's earliest girlfriends. There weren't many secrets in Blue Deer, and only recent citizenship or advanced age protected you. Peter, who'd lived in Blue Deer for five quiet years, was safe from everyone but Jules, his old college roommate. A few other attendees, like Patrick Ankeny and Soren Rue, had led literally blameless lives. Jules was screwed if his name came up: almost everyone at the party remembered the time he'd been caught naked in an alley with a barrel racer or awakened in a puddle of vomit in the church parking lot or been confronted by three girlfriends at once in the Blue Bat Bar, and beaten rather badly. They could only remember his checkered youth because he'd left for good at twenty-two, and returned to a more law-abiding existence ten years later. He was thankful that not many people had witnessed the in-between.

Jules was fidgety and left the table. Peter followed him up to the bar.

"Axel's going to hit Divvy," said Peter.

"Yes," said Jules, ordering a soda.

They turned in unison, just as the county attorney threw his empty plate (his second; he'd had two steaks) at the fire chief. The fire chief ducked and the plate hit a large middle-aged man in the side of the head just as he was taking his first bite of twice-baked potato.

"Can I go home now?" said Peter.

"Yes," said Jules.

They moved at a fast trot. Outside, the moon was bright enough to let them see the mountains. Five miles south of town, a squad car approached with lights and sirens, the whole shebang.

"Don't think of it," said Peter.

"Okay," said Jules.

Twenty minutes later he found himself pulling up in front of Peter's house without having remembered a moment of the drive. The thought was chilling, though thirty seconds later he'd forgotten it, too.

It was only eleven o'clock. "We're all through," said Jules.

"You got that right," said Peter.

6 *The Gift Horse*

BLUE DEER BULLETIN

SHERIFF'S REPORT, WEEK OF MARCH 20–26

March 20—A possibly intoxicated man was reported to have fallen several times off a bicycle. An officer gave him a ride home.

March 22—Two separate calls were received about a man who was driving with a suspended license.

Two hundred sheep were reported out of pasture and heading for the county airport runway. The owner was notified.

March 23—Several reports were received of power outages and downed trees.

A woman was stranded on some rocks in the middle of the Yellowstone River. Search and Rescue responded.

March 24—A three-legged llama was reported on Cokedale Road. Animal Control responded when no owner could be located.

March 25—A teenager called to report his concern about his girlfriend's father, who was violently angry with the couple after seeing them in a compromising situation. Officers arrived to find the family peacefully eating dinner.

Officers responded to a disagreement at a drinking establishment. An arrest was made.

March 26—Several reports have been received of egg throwing. Some perpetrators have reportedly used slingshots.

WHEN JULES LIFTED A SINGLE EYELID AT 7:00 A.M., his first thought was one of deep, almost religious thanks: he hadn't drunk more than two absinthes, and he didn't have a hangover. His second was of looming trouble, brought on by the memory of Scotti flinging his plate and the size of the man he'd hit with it. Even if Jules didn't have a hangover, he'd still have to deal professionally with others who did.

He tried to avoid it all with a Caroline daydream, but that brought back the episode at the Sacajawea, which ended any drowsiness entirely. He'd had or been had by Dottie on a bathroom counter, and Fred Bottomore had fallen off the wagon. Jules slumped down the stairs and turned on the coffee grinder.

Before he'd quit for the last long period, Fred had not been just any drunk, and Jules's guilt was no minor thing. Fred had made drinking himself to death an almost daily challenge, and every other month or so he'd become murderous to others. On these occasions he'd been by far the worst live, ambulatory drunk Jules had ever dealt with, so bad that the fact that he hadn't been shot or crippled before he quit was one of Blue Deer's largest miracles. Fred moved awkwardly when he was sober, as if he were a teenager whose frame had expanded too quickly, and only seemed coordinated when he had a tool in his hand. But when he was drunk he glided, skimmed through bars and down streets like a large, assertive, elegant lizard. It was a disquieting change, especially because this poise lasted until the bitter end, when he'd pitch off his bar stool in a profound stupor or pound his neighbor to a pulp.

But the real problem was that each time he'd fallen off the wagon, Fred's immediate response, usually within hours, had been to try to kill himself. This had happened three times since Jules had come home to Blue Deer, and he'd heard vague rumors of one other time before that. Personal recollection was enough: in the first incident, at dawn after a binge, Fred had aimed for some spruce in his truck but been thrown off track by roadside boulders and ended upside-down in a snowy field; somewhat poignantly, he'd worn his seat belt. The second time Fred had pulled out a pistol while still in the bar and Delly had whacked it out of his hand. Fred had lost the top of his ear, and his friends in the Blue Bat had taken up a collection for a stay in a private clinic. The third time he'd taken all of an erstwhile girlfriend's collection of painkillers, and the girlfriend's teenaged daughter had skipped school to find him vomiting and dying on the kitchen floor. This time was the charm, and Fred had stayed on the wagon since. He was fundamentally decent, horrified when sober to have worried others.

Jules called the Sack before his coffee finished dripping. "He's alive," snapped Dottie. "Merry just hauled him out to breakfast. Maybe she's found her role in life."

"Ah," said Jules.

"They were up late," said Dottie. "Making funny noises together. For some reason, Halsey thinks this is good news."

"Ah," said Jules again, feeling foolish.

Dottie did not whisper endearments, which was a relief. Jules crept into work at nine, having forgotten for the first time ever who was on shift. He was very happy to see

Harvey, even though the deputy had his eyes closed and his feet on his desk.

"I thought you were on last night."

"I was," said Harvey, opening one pink eye.

Now that Jules brought his mighty brain to bear on the scene, he could see that there'd been trouble. Harvey was covered in dried mud and exhausted. He also had one shiny red cheekbone and a tic in the corner of his mouth that usually started only when he was enraged.

"Okay," said Jules. "Tell me."

Harvey thought this was funny, and gave a little bark.

"We got a call from the Tomato, and found out that Axel had thrown a plate at Divvy, then broken his nose with a wine bottle. Axel tried to get in a car to leave—I don't know whose car—and we pulled him out. Jonathan tried to give Axel a portable breath test, and Axel told Jonathan to give him a blow job and kicked the PBT out of Jonathan's hands. When Jonathan bent down to get it, Axel kneed him in the face."

Jules didn't say anything. Harvey picked up a coffee cup, realized it was empty, and put it back down again. "I told Axel that was no way to behave. Axel repeated the sexual request. I told him to do it to himself. He hit me."

Jules sat down, but only on the edge of a chair. "That's not usually a good thing to do."

"I beat the piss out of him. I was working on a letter of resignation, but maybe I could just tell you now and write it later."

"Whatever you want is fine, Harvey, but I'd prefer you get some sleep before you put things in writing."

"What, like you?"

They eyed each other. "Who's supposed to be in?"

"Wesley. He's helping Al and Bean with a cardiac case."

Jules reached out and read Harvey's rough arrest notes. "Oh my," he said. "What got into him?"

"Divvy was talking about some kind of weird brandy. I believe Axel's having some marital troubles."

Axel's marital troubles were richly deserved. "Go home," said Jules.

"I'll stay until Wesley makes it back."

"You going to let Scotti out?"

"I'm not going near him. I'll ask Wesley to do it when I'm ten miles out of town."

HALSEY'S SWAN SONG the night before, his last absinthe quote, had been "The only way to get rid of a temptation is to yield to it." Oscar Wilde had been given another lease on life in an unlikely place. But if temptations were multiple, they had to be ranked, and Jules had finally pushed himself far enough to make some necessary decisions. It was Easter, a good day to rise above his own little mud patch. On the drive north he attempted, as a counselor would put it, to prioritize. The clear winner was his nonexistent love life, not a very religious notion. Five minutes with Dottie didn't really count as a change; five minutes with Dottie and the resultant mess with Fred never would have happened if Jules had liked the rest of his life. Something had to be done.

On his way toward the kitchen door, a red-tailed hawk swooped out of the bell tower above Merry's hideout, casting a shadow across the gravel and the small tile pool near the back entrance. Halsey now wanted Alice to plant some pear trees and roses back here as soon as possible; he had big plans.

"Hi, Fred," said Jules.

"Hi, Jules," said Fred.

They leaned against the new stainless-steel counters in the kitchen, waiting for another pot of coffee to drip. Jules made a show of reading the paper, and Fred scribbled lists. He looked fine, but against the bright light of the sunny window, Jules could see his hands shake.

"You want me to help you tape drywall this morning? Paint the dining room?"

"No," said Fred. "I'm not a complete idiot. I finished the dining room before the party and I'll tape the guest rooms tomorrow. The crew can start painting them Tuesday."

"Well," said Jules. "Should I do my own work or can I help you?"

Fred regarded him calmly.

"I feel that I should help you."

"Why?" said Fred.

Jules couldn't think of anything to say.

Merry walked in, six feet of scary happiness. "Hi, sweetie," she said, kissing Fred on the cheek and dragging a finger down his thigh.

"We'll open Muriel's crates," said Fred. "Let's not give Halsey a reason to start bitching again."

Fred opened all the dining room windows to clear the smell of paint. Jules slid on the drop cloth and gave a little puff of fatigue. He'd managed to forget how much work might be involved: one crate was monumental, eight by six feet and at least two feet deep, and the other five seemed to bulge. "You've opened them," he said suddenly.

Fred was trying to insert a bit in his drill, a task that seemed harder than usual. "No," he said.

"We painted yesterday and last night," said Merry brightly. "I helped."

Jules walked closer. The screws were still buried in the

wood; what was different was once again entirely in his mind. Halsey walked through the door, followed by Dottie. She checked out the paint job on the trim, not so much avoiding Jules as pretending that nothing had ever happened.

Halsey rubbed his hands together. "We're in for a treat," he said. "A real treat. We'll look in the smaller flat crate first, please."

"Remember, when you're playing with those power tools, none of this is insured," said Dottie. "None of it even exists on paper."

The first painting Fred unwrapped was a Maynard Dixon, showing rain falling on a high New Mexico plateau. The second was a Turner watercolor, showing rain falling on an orchard. They were the same size, a strange but apt pair and possibly worth a hundred grand apiece.

Fred's eyes were swimming and he sighed several times, as if the paintings on top of the previous night might finish him off. "We'll put them on either side of your cabinet," said Halsey. "Open the biggest crate next," he said. "The canvas in there can hang across the room."

Fred and Jules had to get chairs to lift out the frame inside. It was at least three by five, thick and heavy. They unwrapped bubble wrap and brown paper and stared at an oil showing a nineteenth-century parlor with a young father, mother, and two toddlers. The mother was bending to tend the fireplace, the father reading the newspaper just behind her. The plate centered on the bottom of the frame read DOMESTIC BLISS.

"What's the signature?" asked Dottie.

"There is no signature," said Halsey. He looked confused.

"It looks like Charlie Russell," said Dottie.

"In your dreams," said Fred sharply, peering at the painting.

"Why the insets?"

They all leaned closer. The painting had two planes, cut-out portions, with a sturdy silk tassel in the lower-right corner.

"I've heard of these," said Jules, leaning closer. "I've seen something like this in a bar somewhere."

"Imagine that," said Merry.

Jules gently pulled the tassel and the planes of the painting shifted. The children turned into wine bottles and the parents were suddenly naked, the father whacking his transported spouse on her bare bottom with the rolled-up paper.

By the time he could look at the others Jules had tears of glee streaming down his face. Dottie turned to Halsey and said, "You want to put it in the *dining* room?" Merry was fire-engine red and Fred kept saying, of all things, "Wow. I had no idea."

But Halsey looked troubled and only slightly amused. "I remember this piece of shit," he said. "It was hanging here long before I met Muriel. It got her on the road to Catholic taste when she was just a kid. This would be a little joke on her part."

"I thought you were on good terms," said Merry, frowning at the scene. Jules pulled the tassel again out of spite and the frown deepened.

"I still think it looks like a Russell," said Dottie stubbornly. "What's it worth?"

"I don't know," said Jules. "It's too weird not to be worth something, but I'm not sure it would buy you a car."

Since you could buy a reliable car in Blue Deer for $700, this wasn't saying much. "I still think we should have it appraised," she said. "You were expecting something big, Halsey, and if this were a Russell it would be worth half a million."

"I do not give a shit about Charles Russell," said Halsey.

He looked like an eight-year-old who's been stiffed at Christmas.

"Let's sell it to Leon," said Merry. "Let's get it out of here. None of us want to argue."

The comment was so out of character they all turned to stare, even Fred. Jules tapped the frame. "What's that on the back?"

Fred swiveled the frame, so reinforced and thick that it was heavy enough to make the veins stand out on his arms. Jules helped him steady it and peered down.

A big blob of a landscape was mounted on the back of the western scene, something Jules had never seen done before. The back canvas showed a long dark hill with the suggestion of mountains behind. Someone had covered this background with a papier-mâché wash, then dabbed orange and red jungle animals and emerald baobab trees at intervals across the bottom. A big silver moon hung in the gray sky to the left and a huge gold sun on the right. A gold silk cloth, like a theater curtain, had been glued to each top edge.

Halsey was speechless, and no one spoke for some seconds.

"Why would this be here?" asked Jules finally.

"I gather it's another joke," said Halsey.

"Same guy practicing, maybe," said Merry. "Or maybe Muriel was trying to learn."

Jules tried to look more closely without letting go of the frame. The thing had several layers, but there was something familiar about the shape of the landscape. "It looks familiar," he said. "Like someone was goofing on something well known, but I can't place it. Do you recognize it, Fred?"

"No," said Fred.

"I kinda like it," said Jules. He ran his fingers along the

frame. At some point someone had tried to separate the back painting from the panel painting and been stymied by long thin nails and tongue and groove.

"I can't hold it anymore," said Fred. He swung it toward the wall with *Domestic Bliss* facing out.

"You must be tired from working so late last night," said Dottie.

"Was it late?" asked Fred, turning away from her.

"I heard you clanking around at two. Thank goodness you had help."

Fred turned pink, but Jules was watching Halsey, who looked stricken. It wasn't an expression he would have associated with someone who's just inherited two fine paintings and two funny ones.

"What's wrong?" he asked.

Halsey shook his head. "Just thinking of Muriel. She was a real pistol."

"I've heard you say that about all your wives," said Dottie.

"No note in the crate?"

Merry peered in. "No note."

She had a compulsion to be the final authority. Jules reached in and pulled out one more canvas, much lighter and thinner than the first. The paper wrapping was faded, and it was strapped closed with string instead of tape. He carried it to the work table, pulled it all away, and they stared at a very beautiful, very naked brunette with dark green eyes, fine-boned except for apple cheeks and equally generous breasts. She lay in the same pose as Goya's *Maja* but she was set farther back, and looked at an equally naked man who stood in the right foreground and ran off the edge of the canvas. No face, just the left arm and torso, part of a buttock and leg and the back of a dark head. He was holding his clothes.

"Jesus," said Jules. "Who did this?"

"A friend who tried to paint like Edward Hopper and shot himself when he figured out he couldn't. That's Muriel and me, circa 1947," said Halsey. "Like I've said, the lady was quite something."

"Is the dirty stuff in the other crates?" asked Dottie.

"I imagine," Halsey said. "We can look at that later."

"I really think we need an appraisal on that funny painting," said Dottie. "And you've said Jules might have trouble pricing the rest."

"I can send photos to Sotheby's or other galleries," said Jules. "I don't think they'll have a problem."

"This is a real *collection*," said Dottie, with a hop. "Not a little weirdness, a lot."

She was rarely so emphatic, and Fred and Jules and Merry looked uncomfortable. "An appraisal is expensive," said Merry. "I'm sure Jules can handle it."

"Jules won't know where to begin," said Dottie, rummaging into a crate. "And he doesn't know jack shit about paintings, right?"

"Right," said Jules quietly. "But Fred does. What do you think?"

Fred was staring at Muriel. "About the panel thing? I have no idea. I wouldn't call it a painting."

"So why waste money on hauling someone out here to see it?" asked Merry.

"I'll decide later," said Halsey, rousing himself. "We can stick this piece of shit in the kitchen for now," he said, gesturing to the panel painting. "Muriel goes in the dining room, across from the cabinet, so that everyone will know how lovely she was."

"What will the Rotarians think?" asked Dottie.

"They'll think I was a lucky son of a bitch."

Jules and Fred stuffed the smaller crates in the dumbwaiter and hauled them up to Jules's room, then hung the Turner and the Dixon on either side of the cabinet, which only had one coat of varnish to go. This was Fred's real baby, a twelve-by-eight cherrywood Craftsman masterpiece that would eventually hold some antiquities and other smaller pieces.

"Don't you want to be there?" said Fred, gesturing to the Turner orchard.

"Sleeping in the grass in the warm rain with a different life to go home to?" said Jules. "Sure I do."

Fred snapped out of his daydream and snorted. "Your different life would end up as bad as this one. We won't get peace until we're under the grass."

"Fred," said Jules. "Stop it. I remember what you did last time. I'm sorry. I didn't know Dottie would make the difference."

"Neither did I," said Fred, with some humor. "But don't worry, I'm not going to off myself this time. You got five minutes and I got a sweet lady."

Jules blinked. "She is," said Fred, daring him to disagree.

"Who knew?" said Jules weakly.

"You've got to talk some sense into that old asshole. He needs to sell the stuff. It's a sin, keeping it in an old hotel where no one can see it."

"No it's not," said Jules. "It's beautiful, and he loves it, and it would get lost in the shuffle at any large museum. I'm sure he'll give it away eventually."

"He'll die eventually," said Fred. "And Dottie will sell it in the end."

Jules shrugged. "Whatever happens I'm sure Merry will be fine."

"Well, she could be finer."

By now Jules was staring at him. "It's always nice to see someone change their opinion."

"What's that supposed to mean?"

A month ago Fred had called Merry a patch of bad road looking for the right car. "Nothing," said Jules.

"Screw you," said Fred.

JULES WALKED INTO the bathroom, the scene of the crime, and washed his face. He'd aged, or he was still mired in a fungal half-life: he looked gaunt, melancholy, and pale. He'd done a bad job shaving and his mouth looked crookeder than usual. He leaned forward to study his bloodshot eyes and banged a knee on the cabinet. It was ajar, and wouldn't shut, and when he opened it he saw the cord of a hair dryer. Fred was probably using it on wallpaper or the paint or the tape or all of the above. Things were grim when a contractor resorted to hairdryers on a ten-thousand-square-foot project and spent his spare time bopping a sociopath.

Upstairs, Jules started to unpack the crates. When Halsey climbed the stairs a few minutes later a half dozen objects were already unpacked, and Jules was profoundly shocked.

"Like I said, it's no hurry," said Halsey. "I don't give a damn anymore."

"What on earth?" asked Jules. "Did you know what she was sending you?"

"This stuff or the paintings?"

"Everything," said Jules. He lifted out another object, a small brass candleholder, and clapped his hand to his forehead.

"I had a good idea," said Halsey. "For the purposes of the

IRS, her will states that the crates are filled with 'lamps, returned books, and privacy screens.'"

"Maybe that explains the mess of a landscape on the back of that bar art," said Jules.

"Maybe," said Halsey, looking out the window.

"I gather you expected something else, a different canvas."

"I did," said Halsey. "Though I'm aware that it might seem spoiled to be disappointed in what I got."

True enough. One of the things that made Halsey bearable was his lack of pretense. "What about insurance?"

"What about it?"

"Does anybody know these things exist?"

"We do," said Halsey. "The rest of her collection, the stuff she left to Berkeley, is probably properly authenticated, insured, the whole bit. She said she was leaving me the fun stuff."

Jules eyed the fun stuff he'd revealed so far. A wood folder had held an Apollinaire pen and ink of two women, some illustrations for a broadsheet edition of *Fanny Hill*, and a half dozen "Wish you were here" postcards from a Belle Epoque Parisian whorehouse. The next four items out of the box were two priapric oil lamps, probably Roman, a red figure vase from approximately 475 B.C. of a woman climbing on top of an exceptionally eager man, and an Italian glass lamp designed like a mobile and on a rheostat, so that the jewel-colored dancers gradually lifted one leg higher as the light grew brighter.

Halsey tapped the lamps. "Muriel actually used these. She'd pour oil in them and light them, stick flowers in a vase like that, then invite people over and see how long it would take them to really look. She had special tastes."

She certainly did. Now Halsey was looking at two different stone nudes, both showing women whose limbs would be politely described as akimbo.

"The left is really something," said Jules. "Sixth century at least and worth a fortune."

"She's very lovely," said Halsey. "What about the one on the right?"

"Cement," said Jules. "A great job, but things like this turn up all the time. A few Turkish craftsmen probably have their work installed in most of the world's great museums."

"Muriel could never resist a good-looking salesman," said Halsey.

"Are you going to keep all of it?"

"We'll talk to Dottie and Merry about that. You sort through it and we'll go from there. But let's try to do it fast and cut down on the arguments."

"I think Dottie's right about calling in an appraiser. I might be able to figure out when and where it was made, but in this case the value is especially in the eye of the beholder." Jules rubbed his head, still embarrassed. "But nothing's going to cut down on the arguments about the Turner and the Dixon, not from what I've gathered about the terms of your will."

"I think you underestimate people," said Halsey.

"It's my profession," said Jules, reaching for his coat.

"Where are you rushing off to?" asked Halsey.

"It's Easter. I went to church as a kid. I'll look through this later," said Jules. "I have to go check on the ham before my mother kills it. She always asks me what I've been doing up here, and today it's going to be hard to explain. Do you want me to come tomorrow night?"

"Please," said Halsey. "I'll be home by seven."

Jules had never found his keys or the Yale lock, but the couch was near the furnace grate, and losing keys in such a fashion was a classic maneuver on his part: he'd once found a set in the refrigerator. He didn't mention the missing padlock to Halsey, and Halsey didn't mention the new lock or ask for a key.

Before Jules left he returned everything to the empty crate and screwed down all three lids, leaving a single hair under one screw on each. He got to his mother's ham before it was past saving, and ate a full quarter of Alice's scalloped potatoes and Olive Clement's lemon meringue pie in competition with Peter. In the spirit of the holiday, they toasted Alice's egg-shaped stomach, and Olive pulled out Jules's ugliest baby pictures.

ON MONDAY, JULES attempted to prove he still cared about his day job. This was easier than he expected. Axel was in court in a shirt and tie, quizzing Jules politely in one hearing and Harvey in another, and no one mentioned seeing each other over the weekend. Jules saw Divvy walk across the parking lot with a bandage across his nose, but when he'd leaned out the window to yell, "What happened to your face?" Divvy only smiled and waved.

So Jules got on with the mundane. He gave a talk on drugs at the high school and tried not to notice the way the older teachers smirked. He arrested a couple for abusing their three-year-old earlier that weekend; the three-year-old with a broken arm was with his grandmother, and seemed happy about the arrangement. He signed off on payroll, read the weekend's reports, had lunch at the Rotary, and gave Grace a bouquet for her birthday. And after hauling Caroline into the valley, supposedly for help with a property dispute but actually for the sheer joy of proximity, he went to find Leon Baden and ask him about petty thievery.

When they arrived at the Bachelor they simply found Merry Maier again—Leon had gone on a two-day antiques buying trip in Great Falls and Miles City.

"How sensitive of him," said Caroline. "I always feel like shopping when someone I love dies."

"He said he couldn't afford to miss the appointments," said Merry. "They hadn't exactly been getting along anyway."

"Still," said Caroline. "How long were they married?"

"I don't know," said Merry with a stony expression. "I don't care."

Caroline actually growled on her way out the door. "Any idea why he hasn't returned any messages?" asked Jules.

"I'm not his secretary," said Merry.

"I know that," said Jules. "But I've left two with you. What did he say when he got them?"

"He said he wished you'd die," said Merry primly.

Back in the car Caroline was playing with the radio, obviously trying to realign her mood. "What a cow," she said.

"That's a line you don't hear enough in this state," said Jules.

"How are you feeling, after the shindig?"

"Fine, now that I talked Harvey out of quitting. Axel hasn't brought it up."

"Did you talk to Jonathan?"

"Yeah."

"That lady's still bothering him. Does he know who it is yet?"

"He hasn't seen her face. Skinny, black hair."

Caroline flipped open his glove box and poked through. "I've been trying to think of who he's arrested or dealt with in the last few months, and I keep seeing one woman's face but I can't place her. She had dark hair, and he picked her up more than once, and she kept sticking her fingers through the grill, trying to touch his hair. At the time I thought it was funny."

"It probably was," said Jules. "Ask him. Maybe the memory was so traumatic he buried it."

"He has been a little weird lately," said Caroline. "I never used to believe that line about someone thinking too much, but I get the feeling Jonathan's on overload. You know what he just read?"

"What?"

"*As I Lay Dying.*"

"Christ," said Jules. "Couldn't she give him something upbeat to read?"

"Like what?"

"I don't know. *Tom Jones*?"

She laughed. "You're giving yourself away. But he is very confused."

"Aren't we all," muttered Jules.

WHEN JULES WALKED up the stairs to the music room that evening, he found two boxes of small frames leaning against the door with the new lock, with a note from Dottie:

> *Stuff on hotel back from framers. Do you have room for it?*
>
> *Please tell Halsey we need an appraisal, at least on the q.t. I know you can find someone who'd fly out here for cash.*
>
> *xo Dot*

Beneath, in penciled block letters, someone had written *bitch.* Jules raised his head slowly and stared at the ceiling. The majestic chords of bad eighties techno-pop filtered down the stairway. Merry was in residence.

He took off his coat and tucked the new lock into his jeans pocket. No one had touched the crates, and now he cleared papers from the long desk and gradually covered it again with every last item from Muriel's mysterious collection. Then he made a rough list.

After an hour, when Halsey still hadn't shown up, Jules took a break and looked through Dottie's boxes. Half the frames held old pages from the hotel's guest book on the left with a name circled; on the right she'd matted photos and explanations of these illustrious guests. Theodore Roosevelt (visiting Yellowstone), Sarah Bernhardt (as Candide at the Blue Deer Opera), Clarence Darrow (putting on a one-man anti-Prohibition play), Sally Rand (leading the 1934 Fourth of July parade), John Barrymore (just being John Barrymore). Dottie had also framed two small pieces of art that Jules hadn't known existed: Thomas Moran had stayed at the Sacajawea in 1893, recovering from a second trip to Yellowstone, a decade after he'd first come to the region and sold a huge canvas of the canyon to Congress for the then astronomical sum of $10,000. The canvas had been key to the park becoming a park, art forcing hardened politicians to protect wildlife for possibly the first time. Framed next to Moran's signature was a tiny watercolor of the terraces at Mammoth Hot Springs. And Charles Marion Russell had visited in 1905 and 1917 and left a pretty pastel of a little girl, labeled "Muriel." Jules began to understand how Dottie had come by her pipe dream about the goofy panel picture.

The other box was full of framed front pages from the *Blue*

Deer Bulletin, each with a banner ad at the bottom for the Sacajawea. When Halsey finally arrived Jules sorted through headlines and let him look over Muriel's things in peace. The earliest announced that the citizens of Castle, a boomtown twenty miles north of the Sacajawea, were leaving in droves, part of the panic of 1893. The Sack ad suggested Blue Deer inhabitants check in and watch the geese fly south. In 1901 a last scheduled public hanging of a murderer, one Adolph Zidmaier, was thwarted when Zidmaier took the task upon himself in the privacy of his cell, possibly with the tacit help of an officer. The Sack advertised an impromptu policeman's ball. In 1908 Sarah Bernhardt's visit made headlines, and the hotel made sure everyone knew where she was staying for most of her two-week engagement at the opera. In 1912, when there still wasn't a foot of paving in town, headlines announced the fall of the Manchu dynasty and smaller columns dealt with the impending statehood of New Mexico and Arizona. In local news, an eighteen-year-old cop named Charlie Clement, Jules's great uncle, had been hired, and the banner ad announced the birth of a daughter, Muriel, to the Sacajawea's owners.

"When were you born, Halsey?"

"Nineteen eighteen. End of the war, beginning of Prohibition. I lost my mom to influenza before I was a year, and Muriel claimed that was why I liked older women."

The 1935 front page dealt mostly with an earthquake centered in Helena, which had fatally damaged the Sacajawea's western tower and cracked one of the plunges. This advertisement—"Don't believe everything you hear! We're still open!"—was probably one of the last. "What year did you two marry?"

"Nineteen forty-four. I got lucky and was shot lame

in France. Your uncle Joseph always claimed I did it on purpose."

Jules smiled. "You don't even limp now."

"Well, I did then," said Halsey. "And I limped to get Muriel and some others to look my way. I had a field day."

He was sitting on the couch by now. "It's a little overwhelming, seeing everything at once."

"If you do decide to sell, the dirty stuff should go as a piece," said Jules. "You need to get the right dealer in the right city."

"I'm not selling," said Halsey. "I decided last night. But as a compromise I'll agree to an appraiser."

Jules wondered how this was a compromise, given that Dottie had won on both counts. "I will sell Muriel's joke after it's appraised," said Halsey, reading his mind. "I have too many nice things around to waste space on trash. We'll make Merry happy by letting her handle whoever you get to come. She'll start thinking it was all her idea."

Jules nodded; he'd used such diversionary tactics on her before. "I stuck the stuff that didn't fit in over here," said Jules. "A half dozen botanicals and this."

He handed Halsey a nineteenth-century ledger. A note in Muriel's handwriting was pinned to the front: *Little things first, love.* Older handwriting inside the cover said *the Sacajawea, August, TM.* Inside there were a dozen pencil sketches, some tinted lightly with watercolors. "It's the view from this window," Jules said. "A guest who knew what he was doing."

Halsey took the drawings and laid them out on the table. He looked at them for a long time.

"You've seen them before?" said Jules. He picked up an amber egg and twirled it like a top on a bare patch of table.

Halsey took his time answering, and Jules noticed one hand shaking for the first time in weeks. "Yes, I have," he said softly. "Damn." He covered the shaking hand with the other, then gave up and slid the drawings back into the leather pouch.

Jules watched him, worried. Halsey had skipped a physical the week before, and Dottie had asked Jules to keep an eye on him. "Whose are they?" he asked.

"More Moran," said Halsey. "Not someone I care for in every case, but I was fond of this notebook. A sketch sometimes has more heart than a finished piece. Fred really loves the man's work. I'll have to show him these."

"So what were you missing yesterday?"

Halsey started to speak, then paused and sighed. "Muriel had a still life by a man named Adolphe Monticelli, an old crank van Gogh admired. And she had a lovely Whistler watercolor of a meadow, only one I ever saw like it."

"Good to know everyone second-guesses a gift," said Jules, amused.

"I admitted as much yesterday," snapped Halsey.

Jules was turning a mysterious stone object back and forth in his hand, frowning. It was smooth, curved pink marble, two by four inches, creased down the middle, and he couldn't identify it. "What do you think this is?" he asked, holding up the translucent pink stone.

"A very private part of a woman's body," said Halsey, distracted from missing paintings. "Muriel used it for a spoon rest but I think it was meant for incense. I'm worried that you didn't recognize it. That's not a sign of a healthy private life."

"I don't have one," said Jules. "I aspire to one." He pointed to some Roman brass wind chimes shaped like phalluses that still rang melodiously against dangling bells. "Did she use this to call you in for lunch?"

Halsey's good humor began to recover. "Muriel grew up here, ran from end to end without anyone paying much attention. I often wondered if she saw or heard things here that started her on her particular enthusiasms."

He sounded like a psychiatrist discussing a favorite patient. "This might be a rude question," said Jules, "but why did you get divorced?"

"Well, we didn't get along most of the time," said Halsey. "She'd been married before, and she wanted someone obedient." He stacked a half dozen rough coins, whorehouse tokens from southern Italy stamped with naked women. "And when we did get along she wore me out. I was only twenty-five and I had trouble keeping skin on my dick."

Jules looked dubious. "Most twenty-five-year-olds would be hospitalized before they'd complain."

"True," said Halsey. "So I stuck it out for almost five years. It was a fine time, except for the in-betweens when we'd have to talk or wash the dishes."

"I bet you had a maid to do that," said Jules, reaching for the amber egg.

"You know what I mean," said Halsey.

"Yeah," said Jules. "But I'd kill to wash the dishes with someone."

"If you ever get up the nerve to get married, I'll give you that egg you like so much as a present."

"Don't be silly," said Jules, surprised that Halsey had noticed. "And it has nothing to do with nerve."

"Sure it does," said Halsey.

He was probably right. Jules rolled the translucent apricot

egg around in his hand. The naked woman carved into it was beautiful, her long hair and legs wrapped around the egg.

"Pretty biblical," said Halsey.

"Well before it," said Jules, handing it to him. "I'd say four to six hundred B.C., somewhere in North Africa."

Halsey smiled. "That one was from my uncle, the customs inspector. I gave it to Muriel, trying to goose her into a baby." He handed it back. "Don't forget the deal."

"I don't need bribery," said Jules. "I need a bride."

They covered most of the rest of the table in the next hour. Half the items had a label in Muriel's handwriting, but not all of them were accurate. According to Dottie, Muriel had been obsessed with outsmarting the government, and her Byzantine arrangements for Halsey's inheritance had given her much enjoyment when she was dying. Many of the notes were deliberately misleading—calling a gold armband of entwined lovers a fake, saying she'd bought a small emerald crocodile ring at the Metropolitan Museum of Art gift shop—and others were highly personal mash notes to her ex-husband, who spent most of the hour snickering happily over the labels, missing inheritance forgotten.

JULES MADE A few calls the next morning. Arnie Wildason, who would arrive in a few days to cook for the wedding, had lived with an art dealer for years, and fixed Jules up with some old friends. Arnie's old friends and the contacts Jules had made at Sotheby's (he wasted a considerable amount of time explaining that the art wouldn't go to them, that someone had to come to the art) came up with the same three candidates. One had just taken a job at the Getty and couldn't be bothered, another proved to be in Marrakesh, but the third candidate sounded ideal. He lived nearby (or what passed for it in Montana: Seattle); he'd been known to work swiftly and quietly for cash. And his areas of excellence were strange but perfect: he'd gone to school for ancient art, now dealt with erotica as a lucrative sideline, and through a partner he'd since become interested in American painting, what Jules's informant called "western esoterica and macabre memorabilia."

"What the hell does that mean?" asked Jules.

"What it sounds like," said Arnie's friend. "He'll ask if you have any old invites to hangings stashed in the courthouse."

"Huh." Jules was having second thoughts.

"I don't know about Altschuler's private life, but he was hot shit in school and ever since, and some of what he deals in now is American, mostly turn-of-the-century landscapes, so he should have an idea about your dirty painting, too. Maybe it is a Charlie Russell."

"It's not a Charlie Russell," said Jules patiently. He dialed Piers Michael Altschuler a few minutes later.

"This weekend? You're joking. Send Polaroids."

"No time. The man has plenty of money."

Altschuler named a figure and Jules agreed. Peace of mind was worth a lot.

"The antiquities are mostly Greek?" Altschuler had explained that he'd had a monthlong head cold, and his voice was a harsh whisper.

"Mostly. Some Roman, Egyptian, and some bone items that might be Scythian."

"Bone items." Altschuler sounded amused. "You don't sound like you need my help on these."

"I don't know the special interest market at all," said

Jules. "We don't want to sell, but we want an idea of how to handle it if we change our minds."

"Tell me about the prints and paintings."

Jules told. Over the course of two more conversations they haggled over fees and dates. Altschuler wanted to rent his own car and had no interest in actually staying at the Sacajawea. "I'll come for several days. I wanted to check out the collection at Deer Lodge. Do you know of any county collections you can recommend?"

"Collections?"

"Forensic stuff. Nooses, guns, old evidence."

"You do like variety, don't you?" said Jules. "Gallatin has a few things. We had a fire in the teens that got rid of the gory stuff. But come here first," he said.

"You'll pay for haste. I like setting my own pace."

"The money's fine," said Jules. "Call Merry Maier at the Sacajawea. She can book the flight, rent a hotel room, send you a check, whatever. She's the niece, and she'll have the most questions."

"Is that a warning?" asked Altschuler in a whisper, after trying and failing to clear his throat.

"Yes," said Jules. "But please don't quote me."

7 *April Fool, or Two Blood-Sucking Cats in a Tree*

Rough inventory, crate 3 from Muriel Z.Z.V. Meriwether Gagnaire

Two sets of phallic wind chimes, bronze, early Roman 3-200 B.C. No idea.

Copper weather vane with imaginative male and female symbols. Egyptian? Insure 10K.

Five glass perfume bottles, various female shapes. Roman, A.D. 3-400 Insure 1K.

Etruscan-style satyr. Contemporary copy.

Two chastity belts, one ivory, Flemish, prob 13th-15th c, one wood and leather, Cyrillic lettering. 17th c Russian? No idea.

Greek female nude, 6th-8th c. Insure 20-30K.

Greek-style female nude. Contemporary copy.

Greek gold amulet, poss to ward off disease. 7-500 B.C. Insure 2K.

Two small gold bowls, acrobatic engraved figures, poss. Persian. Insure 12K.

"I USED TO THINK APRIL WAS SPRING," SAID CAROline. "This is another detail that didn't come out in my job interview."

Jules turned on the wipers to ward off fat flakes. Blue Deer was covered with another foot of snow, and the whole town looked like a huge white comforter, but he might have come up with a different image if he weren't so tired. It was Saturday, and they'd both been up most of the night before to watch a barn burn—since the barn had been near two others and a house and a stand of cottonwoods, it had been one of Divvy's Invite Everyone parties. The snow had started at 4:00 a.m. and put an end to the matter, but Jules and Caroline had been on shift at eight. "Happy April Fool's Day," he said. "Just think of other fibs that might come out."

They drove on through the soundproofed streets until they came to a small house surrounded by some of the only maples in town. They got out and plowed across the yard toward the maple surrounded by people. "This has to be six inches," Caroline griped. "Maybe eight."

Jules peered up into a snow-laden tree, blinking as fresh flakes fell into his eyes. It wasn't very tall, and the two kittens weren't particularly large or fearsome-looking. They'd been chased up the maple by a neighbor's dog and belonged to an eight-year-old girl whose mother had died the year before of ovarian cancer and whose father's eyes were vacant. Jules had given Caroline the background on the way over, explaining why they couldn't just wait for the kittens to wise up.

"Why don't I go up?" she said.

"No," said Jules.

"I thought they'd be down in a few hours," said the father. "But they've been up there since last night."

Jules imagined the kittens keeling out of the tree in a week, dead of starvation because the county sheriff didn't like heights. They were too young to have the sense to retreat. He'd get them down or die, and then he would go to the little girl's neighbors' house and tell them that if they didn't keep their goddamn Jack Russell in its own allotted space he'd give the midget asshole a lobotomy.

"I don't think this is a good idea," said Caroline.

"Neither do I," said Jules, reaching for a branch. He was twelve feet up when the first healthy doubts settled in. The kittens were at least eight feet higher, swinging gently on slender branches, hissing with buttoned-down ears. Jules peered down at the watchers and the girl's teary face came in and out of focus, not a good sign. Apparently, like a bee allergy, vertigo grew worse with each episode. On the plus side, Caroline actually looked worried.

The branches were slippery, and plops of snow landed on his head as the tree protested against his weight. He was holding the rope to a net bag in his teeth, and it made him want to gag.

"Are you okay?" asked Caroline. "I thought you didn't like heights."

Don't ask, he thought, throwing the bag over a branch. "Just four feet to go," he said with false cheer. "Get ready to catch kittens."

He moved up quickly and scooped up the first, dropping it into the bag with a surprising lack of difficulty. He lowered it and pulled the empty bag back up. The second kitten, a gray ball with glittering, rabid eyes, had moved another two feet higher.

"He's a bloodsucker," said the little girl's brother.

Jules peered down at him. The kid was four, tops, but spoke with utter authority. As Jules turned back up to the kitten, it leapt down with a high-pitched hiss, latching claws into his scalp, scrabbling down his face and neck. Jules lurched backward, lost his grip, grabbed the next slippery, snowy branch and lost that, too, plummeting to earth and landing on his back with the kitten attached to his chest.

When Jules opened his eyes Caroline, white-faced, was hovering over him, touching his leg, clutching his hand, touching his stomach. "Can you feel that?" she asked.

He could and for one moment he couldn't believe his

luck. Then the rest of his body woke up in a way that had nothing to do with Caroline's prying fingers.

"Aaagh," said Jules, tears blooming, his eyes locked on her face. He inhaled and his ribs screamed. His spine felt like a traumatized violin string, and he feared this might be a high point. "Aaaaaagh."

"I'll call the ambulance," said the father.

"No," said Jules. "Just let me lie here for a minute. Aaagh."

"Move a foot," said Caroline.

"No."

She was panicked, utterly lacking any luscious nurselike empathy. "Move a foot or I'm calling Al and Bean."

Jules moved a foot, then a hand. "It's my ribs, I think."

"Call," said Caroline.

"No," said Jules, lurching up. He made it to his knees, a good position for reflection. "Aaaaaghh."

The father brought him slowly to his feet, while the little girl stared, the nice kitten on her shoulder and the killer on her head. The little boy staggered around the yard, giggling hysterically.

Caroline was furious. "Get in the car, now. We're going to the hospital."

"Okay," said Jules, shuffling in that direction.

"Thanks, mister," said the little girl.

"You're welcome," he said with dignity.

Caroline had his elbow. "You asshole," she hissed. "I can practically hear the fluid leaking out of your vertebra."

"It's screaming your name, honey."

"What?"

He really did hurt; it was making him light-headed and he needed to concentrate in order to fold into the car. "You heard me."

She slammed the door and did not take corners carefully on the way over.

JULES HAD TWO cracked ribs. Caroline insisted on sticking around to hear Horace recount two decades' worth of previous abuse from the X-rays and from memory: rodeos and construction work, bike mishaps in high school and college, a bad car accident for his thirtieth birthday, a twenty-foot fall on a dig in Turkey that had cracked his skull, the violence of various unhappy constituents, and, as Horace so succinctly put it, "years and years of fucking around."

This short course in humility kept him in a cold sweat long after the medication should have kicked in. Given that he was in too much pain to keep his muscles flexed or stomach sucked in, Jules badly wanted his shirt back on. Caroline watched with disdain and didn't say much of anything.

"You might need some antibiotic for those scratches," said Horace. "I've wiped you up but they're pretty deep. Kitten okay, or did you squish it when you came down?"

"The kitten's just fine," said Caroline. "He should go home, right?"

"Or stay here, though you might want to move him while he can still walk."

She took him as far as his couch, found a blanket and a glass of water and some magazines, and left to deal with the multicar accident the radio had been trumpeting about. On her way out she stared down at him until he found the courage to say, "What is it?"

"Were you saying it's my fault you fell out of the tree?"

"Absolutely not."

"What were you saying?"

"Nothing at all," said Jules. "You better get going."

DIVVY, WHOSE FACE was still yellow and swollen from Axel's attack, came by to see how Jules felt. He'd heard the news after he'd dropped a cross-country skier off at the hospital, a man he'd found trudging down the road with blood running over his boot, who'd somehow managed to impale his leg with his own ski pole. "You should have let my boys come by and take care of that problem," he said to Jules. "We have ladders."

Jules was drowsy from muscle relaxants, not happy about his interrupted nap. "You've fallen out of more trees than I could count."

"I'm off today. I'm the only one who falls."

"Maybe it was our early misbehavior," said Jules. "Some sort of permanent brain damage that's altered our sense of balance."

"Maybe," said Divvy, not always one for regrets.

Jules moaned. Divvy filled his water glass. "Axel finally apologized to me yesterday, after Peter got it through his thick skull that I wanted to press charges. Did you know he gave Harvey a formal apology, too?"

"No," said Jules. "I haven't wanted to bring it up."

"See, sometimes problems really do disappear. Anyway, I went to the Bat last night to celebrate and saw Fred and his new lady out drinking. He really picked the lushest lush of the bunch this time, didn't he?"

"Um," said Jules, enjoying the description.

"I guess he always used to like rich girls," said Divvy, plainly confused by Fred's taste. "She didn't seem particularly nice."

"I recall one or two earlier models," said Jules. "Nothing quite like this."

"Maybe she's really something in bed," said Divvy, his

forehead creased with effort as he tried to wrap his mind around the idea. "I mean, she has to be. Money's only good for new furniture."

Divvy had been happily married for fifteen years, and therefore imagined that others wallowed in a sexual paradise. Jules had discovered, firsthand and over and over, that this paradise didn't exist. "No one's that good," he said. "No one. What were you up to today when you found the skier?"

"Pulling people out of ditches," said Divvy, squinting to read the fine print on Jules's prescription bottle.

"I thought you said you were off."

"I am. I've just been driving around, pulling people out of ditches."

Jules pulled the pillow over his face and fell asleep.

PETER WALKED OVER in the midafternoon. Alice, he explained, needed the working car to look at wedding napkins, and after that she needed it to drive to the shower. Had Jules forgotten the Seattle appraiser was due that afternoon?

Jules had forgotten, but he was more troubled by the idea of Alice worrying about napkins. Oh, how the mighty had fallen. In her previous life, Alice had been known to forget napkins entirely.

"Why are you on your couch?"

"I fell out of a tree."

"Why were you in a tree?"

Peter's sympathy wasn't overwhelming, but by then the codeine had kicked in and Jules saw no good reason to stay on his back when he could go to the Sacajawea and earn another hundred dollars.

He made Peter drive, and while his friend rambled on about a wide variety of new worries—timetables for wedding arrivals, mystifying gifts—Jules stared out at fresh snow and warming air and had a drugged epiphany: he didn't like pain. He didn't like hangovers, or falling out of trees, or going sleepless, or seeing dead bodies. He liked food and loving people and sex and not waking in psychic torment. He liked the notion of a job that didn't deal exclusively with the grim side of human nature.

Peter was talking about wedding problems, oblivious to the fact that a small bomb had gone off in the passenger seat. Jules agreed to everything Peter wanted him to agree to without losing hold of his new resolve: he wasn't suffering through another summer as sheriff. No more speeding tickets, no more searches for firecracker-shredded fingers, no more drowners, overdoses, beaten children, bad checks. No more willingly sleeping and eating and living alone. There would be intermediate pain in pursuit of pleasure—quitting a job and disappointing people, risking disappointment himself. This last made him actually shiver in blurry, narcotic anticipation.

Peter eyed him. "You're a mess. You know that?"

"Yep," said Jules. "I'm all through with feeling this way. I'm going to start enjoying life." Now, when he worked on a staff schedule, he'd stop avoiding Caroline and start gluing himself to her until she either hated him or loved him.

"Really?" said Peter, amused.

"Really," said Jules.

MERRY ROARED UP just as Peter parked, and tried to beat them to the door without talking. Jules had lately made a habit of talking to her when she looked like she wished he wouldn't.

"Jogging?" It was a fair guess. She looked flushed and

overheated and wet, but she didn't have skis or the kayak on the Range Rover.

"Yes," she said, scurrying on ahead.

They followed her into the kitchen. "Where's your friend?" asked Jules.

She stopped in alarm next to Fred, who looked like he had a level-nine hangover. "What do you mean?"

"Dottie said someone was visiting. She wanted you to bartend the shower and you couldn't."

She looked at him coldly. "He couldn't make it."

Fred turned away. Maybe it was a bone of contention; maybe the friend was more than a friend, and Merry had opted for her carpenter.

Jules went upstairs and Peter and Halsey went to the bar to talk business. It was three o'clock. By three thirty, when P. M. Altschuler, appraiser par excellence, still hadn't shown, Halsey had run out of new bequests for Peter to fret over, and they'd eaten a good chunk of the snacks for Alice's party. Peter and Dottie had begun to trade horror stories about drunks from relative perspectives. "This week I had a client whose defense was that he was actually too drunk to move, let alone drive," said Peter. "He says he was just in the car to sleep, and since he was comatose and no one actually saw the car move, I think I might be able to wangle it. He was medically incapable of movement."

"What'd he blow?" asked Dottie.

"Point three-eight," said Peter. "That might be a record for someone who's still alive."

"Nominally alive," said Jules. "You're talking about Leonard, right?"

"Right," said Peter. "After point three-five, anyone can turn into a vegetable."

"He walked a few steps after Ed hauled him out of the car," said Jules.

"Pure reflex," said Peter. "Kind of like a headless chicken dancing. The point was that he was too drunk to actually turn a key. Hence, no DUI."

"Well," said Jules. "The engine was cold anyway."

Fred and Merry had reappeared but stuck to the far side of the kitchen, where they drank health tea and Merry looked disapproving. Fred was shaky and pink-eyed and looked longingly at Jules's coffee.

"Where's the art guy?" Merry asked.

"Probably a problem with snow, honey," said Halsey. "What time did he say his flight was getting in?"

"I think noon. He wouldn't say much."

"We should have picked him up," said Halsey. "Snow is hard on Seattle people."

"He didn't want that," she snapped. "He didn't want to be stuck here with you people."

Everyone was quiet. She marched out of the room; Fred followed, abandoning his tea.

She'd left the burner on. "Nothing personal," said Jules, turning the knob, "but are you actual blood relations?"

"She takes after her father," said Halsey. "Not my sister."

WHEN ALTSCHULER DID arrive, he had an uncomplicated white-bread handsomeness that Jules found surprising. The man who'd been described as "a good all-around strange-o for your special interest" looked like an ex-frat boy, a *Playboy* bunny fan rather than an expert on the expression of humanity's complicated loves, and now that his hoarseness was gone he even sounded like one. He rushed toward Jules to take his hand, shook violently, reawakening Jules's spine, and thanked him for the opportunity to visit "such a lovely landscape."

It came out stiffly, like a teenager trying to work a pickup line from Shakespeare into a normal sentence. Piers Altschuler didn't seem like the Ivy League art boy he'd been led to expect—something indefinable was missing in the accent and overall manner, though in terms of sheer attitude he reeked of inherited money. Jules had trouble imagining this man having a fascination for anything but beer, bonds, and real estate. Merry, who'd been herding Altschuler as if he were several sheep, looked appalled. Within a few minutes, after he whooped at the painting of Muriel and suggested a beer, saying that "the old stuff" could wait until later, Jules tried to think of how to apologize to everyone.

"I have to go," said Peter to Jules, eyeing the clock. "Any minute now we're going to be hit by a wall of estrogen."

"Take the truck," said Dottie. "Jules has to stay."

"We're having a bridal shower tonight," explained Halsey to Altschuler. "Mr. Johansen's intended. He'd rather not be here."

"Can't blame him," said Altschuler. "But it sounds like fun to me."

He winked at Jules and started asking Halsey questions about the hotel. How many did it sleep, how many did the restaurant seat, how many customers until he broke even. Merry looked like she'd eaten pickled sea urchin, and Altschuler explained that he loved the business aspect of his business, and had invested in two area restaurants. It gave him a chance to hang the stuff he liked.

Jules faded in and out of the conversation, and when Altschuler asked for a second beer—he was calming down visibly—Jules wandered off toward the kitchen to look for food, something he'd forgotten in the hubbub of falling out of a tree. He built a sandwich out of the sample wedding prosciuttos and cheeses Arnie had ordered in advance, with extra vinaigrette on top. He was only a third of the way into this thing of joy when Dottie came up from behind and slapped him on the back, once again killing his mood.

"What the hell?"

Jules shrugged. "The business is full of creeps. I'm just surprised no one warned me. It doesn't mean he won't know his stuff."

"The man's an asshole."

"You think most people are assholes. This time I tend to agree."

"Halsey seems to like him."

"Halsey's polite. You can't tell what he thinks. Merry looks like she'd like to run the guy over with her car."

"She's going to make you pay."

"For once I might not blame her."

"Can I have some of that sandwich?"

"No."

She stalked off. Jules finished and followed her. Back in the bar he remained standing and gave Halsey a pointed look.

Halsey cleared his throat. "Shall we begin?"

"I think we might as well," said Jules. "I don't think we need twenty women on this tour."

"I'll take twenty women any way I can get them," said Altschuler, winking and pulling a small leather pad and gold pen out of his pocket.

He didn't say much, and seemed embarrassed by Muriel's odder pieces. Possibly Merry and Dottie cramped his style—Merry had never seen most of them, and her face literally steamed, while Dottie kept elaborating on how strange it all was. Maybe Altschuler had been raised a Baptist, branched out in rebellion without entirely shedding shame.

"Jules," snapped Halsey. "Where are you?"

Altschuler was declaiming on a wooden couple who came apart and moved back together again. "Carpathian, fourth or fifth century?" he said, looking at Jules.

"Maybe," said Jules. He'd filled out an index card to that effect a few nights earlier for Halsey, and by now was miffed at any sign of know-how from the man.

"Another frippery for people with special tastes," said Altschuler.

Jules had tentatively valued many of the fripperies in the room at ten to twenty thousand, without accounting for special tastes. He began to hate the appraiser in a pure, clean way.

Altschuler looked at the title page of a fifteenth-century how-to manual and shrugged. Merry led him to the next exhibit, gold Ottoman harem pasties, and he shrugged again.

"What kind of appraiser doesn't even look at a five-hundred-year-old hand-painted page covered with naked women?" whispered Jules.

Fred started and turned. Drinking wasn't agreeing with his nerves.

"Just leave it," he hissed. "You found the guy. Let him work."

"He's not working," muttered Jules.

"Merry showed me the résumé. He knows his stuff. Who cares anyway? Halsey's already decided he isn't going to sell. It's not our problem."

Toward the end Altschuler seemed to relax and acquire a sense of humor. He took some Polaroids and scribbled notes, then picked up one especially optimistic alabaster phallus and waved it under Merry's nose. "Have you ever *seen* such a thing?"

Dottie loved this, and snickered. "Dining room next," she said, leading the way. "Here's one we wondered about. This looks like it could be C. M. Russell, but it's hard to know how to evaluate it." She pulled the sash.

Altschuler gave a silly little giggle, and Jules was sure his Baptist theory was correct.

"Seems like you have the piece de resistance for the dining room."

They waited for more. Altschuler pulled the sash two more times and chortled. Jules tried to imagine the first pulling away of the curtain to a bar audience, the first huge drunken guffaw. Most dirty stuff was meant for private pleasure—each man at a strip club letting his mind sneak into a private den—but this was comedy, theater, aimed for a collective snicker.

"What's your question?" asked Altschuler.

"Our question is who do you think painted it," said Dottie, annoyed.

"And what you think it's worth," said Merry. "If it's nothing, we have a local dealer who can get rid of it for us."

"I wouldn't call Leon a dealer," said Dottie. "Unless you know more than I do."

That small, acid comment landed with a thunk, but Altschuler was oblivous. "There's certainly no account of Russell doing anything like this. The man preferred horses and Indians."

"That's not true," said Dottie, who wasn't going down without a fight. "He did portraits, too."

"A fan," said Altschuler derisively. "I see. Why don't I

take it with me, show it to some people I know and see if they have a clue? If we could pin any sort of name to it you'd be better off than you are now."

"We brought you here to avoid that," said Halsey.

He hadn't said a thing for a long time. "Oh," said Altschuler, taken aback. "Well, it's probably not worth the effort. Keep it, if you like it."

Merry was staring out the window, and for a moment Jules thought she looked happy. Then the familiar wronged frown set in.

"Check out the flip side. What's the point to the double frame?" asked Jules.

"Just leave it, Jules," said Halsey. He looked tired and confused.

"No," said Dottie. "We should take advantage of Mr. Altschuler's expertise." She whistled the last *s*. "Fred, please help Jules."

They swung the heavy frame out from the wall so Altschuler could eyeball the veiled landscape, the graceful outline, theater curtains, and safari animals. "Huh," said Altschuler. "Maybe someone used this side for art class."

"It seems stranger than that," said Jules. "Look at the quality of the paint."

"Be glad the animals don't move like the people do on the other side," said Altschuler, smiling at his own joke.

Jules opened his mouth but Halsey interrupted.

"Leave it," he said sharply. "Hang it back up now. And you, don't go home."

"Why not?" said Jules.

"Because I've been thinking," said Halsey. "And we need to talk."

Merry beamed, obviously imagining a lecture. Jules and

Dottie looked at each other directly for the first time in a week, and she was just as confused as he was.

WHILE JULES WAITED for more coffee water to boil he listened to Altschuler boom on down the hall in the dining room, exclaiming over the Turner and Dixon, commenting again on the lovely Muriel. “I have several buyers in mind for the funny stuff, if you decide to sell,” said Altschuler. “One in Vienna, one in L.A. But we’ll probably end up with someone from the Far East,” he said. “That’s where I have an advantage, being in Seattle. You wouldn’t believe the things that come through Vancouver. Or maybe the Middle East. They have all the money, after all.”

“But I don’t want to sell,” said Halsey. “I want an idea of worth.”

“If you want a worth on the silly piece, I’ll have to take it with me,” said Altschuler. “Show it to some people. A photo won’t do it credit.”

“No,” said Halsey.

Jules walked up the stairs but the voices followed him. In the hall, Merry was telling Altschuler they didn’t want to take more of his time. Altschuler was saying he’d take a second look in the morning and scribble down some figures. He’d call the following week with potential buyers, if Halsey cared.

Halsey didn’t say anything.

UPSTAIRS, JULES PUSHED to one side all the things from Muriel’s crates he knew Halsey wouldn’t care about, the pieces to donate or sell. There were at least ten nude Greek gods and as many goddesses; he saved out two each. He winnowed down tiles and steles and pottery in the same way, making up new labels or adding notes to Muriel's elegant handwriting and storing anything good in an old set of sewing store drawers Fred had found at Leon's. He hung the three sets of wind chimes from the track lights so that Halsey could compare form and melody and decide which to give to Dottie and which to hang in the kitchen for orders. He suspended the Italian dancing girls from the ceiling lamp and gave them a twirl.

Through it all he heard cars pull up, more than a dozen women arriving to celebrate a pregnant bride. Jules could make out Alice's and Edie's and Caroline's voices, and once even thought he heard Merry laugh. A special uproar greeted the arrival of a core group of Aches, old hands at showers. Many of them had come to the Sacajawea for such parties in the thirties and forties, and through the open window they admired the restored pool. "Back then, of course," said Cicely Tobagga through the open window, "we'd go swimming. No such fun these days."

"When the bride's four months gone," said Indy Whitsan, "it's just as well."

"I'm not saying Alice should jump in, but there's nothing wrong with Caroline. Or Edie or Dottie or Jetta."

"I will if you will," said Caroline.

Jules peered out the window to see her standing at the deep end, waving her arms at her aunt. He knew she wouldn't strip and jump in, but he let the image of her, pale and naked in blue water, float through his mind.

Soon they came inside, and everyone clumped into the dining room, where a collective shriek (Jules could pick out his own mother's wild cackle) meant that Halsey had introduced them to his first wife. Cicely rattled on; she had known Muriel after all, he guessed.

His back ached, and they made him lonely. Halsey, who, as host, had invited himself, brayed throughout. Jules finally put on his coat and headed down the back stairs. Dottie was pulling a tray of mozzarella toasts out of the oven and spoke without turning around. "He'll be up. He was afraid you'd sneak out."

"It's nine o'clock," said Jules. "I fell out of a tree this morning and I'm done for."

"If you persist I'm supposed to haul you into the bar. Have a toast."

She popped one in his mouth. Garlicky olive oil and mozzarella burned his tongue, which made it hard to respond. He kept on toward the door.

"Stop," said Halsey. "I just looked for you upstairs."

Jules turned. Halsey was in the hall doorway, a cloud of women swarming behind him. "You're our tour guide," said Halsey, happier than he'd been in days. "You can't leave. You have to help me show the collection."

"Muriel's collection?"

"Don't you think it's in keeping with a bridal shower?"

"It may be," said Jules. "But I'm not."

"Come on, Jules," said Alice. "Don't play coy. If you stay, we'll talk about you, but if you leave the stories will be worse."

An hour later they were still poking around the workroom, hooting. The Aches were the noisiest and silliest of the bunch, and had egged Jules on throughout what passed for a tour. The younger women seemed somewhat abashed, as if they'd just found themselves in a sex shop with their grandmothers.

Halsey had told everyone to pick something small. "A party favor," said Halsey. "Just the right type of gifts for the right type of party."

Jules had retreated to the couch. "How are you feeling?"

asked Caroline. She'd picked up a box of small fragments from his desk and sat down next to him while she turned pieces over.

"Fine."

"I don't believe you."

"You never believe me."

She smiled and gestured toward the ceiling. "This is what you've been spending your days looking at?"

"When I'm not installing sinks."

"It's got to be better than looking at drunks," she said. "Of course, tonight you get to do both."

Jules looked around. Everyone seemed to be holding up pretty well, especially the juice-guzzling bride. Caroline poked through the box. "Are these pieces from Muriel, too?"

"No. They're Halsey's strays."

"What's this?"

"A piece of chalcedony, probably part of a bracelet."

"This?"

"Mosaic fragments. If you put them together they show a cluster of grapes."

Caroline rolled a carved lapis pebble through her fingers. "What's this?"

"I think it's the eye of an Egyptian cat," said Jules. "But the cat's long gone."

"Keep it," said Halsey, who'd wandered over.

"Oh no," she said.

"Keep it." He was struggling with a wine cork.

"It's not especially valuable without the cat it was made for," said Jules. "Make Halsey happy now, or he'll make you take home one of those wind chimes."

"Okay, ladies," said Halsey. "Back downstairs." He shooed them out the French doors, women from thirty to eighty all holding strange objects in one hand and wineglasses in the other. "Wait ten minutes," he said to Jules. "Just ten. It's important."

"How important?"

Halsey paused. "I need to know how to handle a problem. A bit of thievery."

"Okay," said Jules, blinking. But within five minutes of wondering who Halsey had in mind, he was asleep.

HE WOKE TO the sound of a car engine and a slamming door and opened one eye to look at his watch. It was twelve thirty. He waited a few minutes, hoping it had been the last of them. He could hear Halsey howling at someone, maybe Edie, who lived nearby with Patrick Ankeny on their new ranch, about the importance of building a house with big walls for art. Then another door and another engine, and Alice's tired voice saying goodbye. Jules limped down the stairs, making for the back door.

It was quiet in the bar now but he could hear Dottie's voice as he neared the kitchen. "It's just as well," she was saying. "You look okay, but you'd be better off staying here. We'll figure out what's wrong with the car in the morning."

"I know what's wrong with the car," said Caroline. "It's fifteen years old, and it was a piece of shit when it was born."

Dottie turned. "What are you still doing here?"

"Halsey asked me to wait. Remember?"

"Sure," said Dottie. Her eyes were a little bright, her smile lopsided. Caroline was similarly off a notch, with scattered hair and pink cheeks. They both seemed to sway, and Caroline gave him a broad, completely open smile that made his skin prickle.

"Where's Halsey?" asked Jules.

"Went off to talk to Merry. She complained about the little gifts, and he's pissed."

"What's wrong with your car?" he asked Caroline.

"I don't know," she said. "Probably the starter. Maybe I'll shoot it in the morning."

His eyes widened. "Don't worry," she said. "I left my gun at home."

"Let's go," he said. "I'll give you a ride."

It was snowing again but warmer, and flakes disappeared quickly into the puddles in the rutted gravel. Caroline looked up into the flakes and nearly walked into a puddle, and he took her arm to steer her around it.

"Did Alice have a good time?"

"Yes," she said. "And she'll be the only one having a good time tomorrow."

"What were you drinking?"

"Tequila, wine. Don't bother saying you can't tell."

"Ah," he said, tucking her into the truck. "You probably haven't had a break in a while. When was the last time you got silly?"

"Longer ago than you, I guess. At least someone's been having fun."

He pulled around the building. "You shouldn't believe everything Alice says."

"I had trouble figuring out if more of the women there had slept with you or diapered you."

Not many suitors in America had to respond to a comment like that. She was smiling with her eyes closed, head on the seat back. "If it makes a difference, I'm not having any fun anymore," he said finally.

"Why not?"

He didn't know what to say, but she didn't push the matter. A minute later he realized she was dozing.

Jules made the turn onto the interstate and Caroline tilted. "Do you mind if I lie down?" she muttered.

"No," said Jules. She already had her head on his thigh.

Grace might have described it as an interesting predicament. Caroline was out cold and Jules gave in to a fantasy of driving straight through Blue Deer and winding up in a motel somewhere—anywhere—to the west of reality. Instead, he pulled up in front of her house and said her name.

"Crap," said Caroline, before she bothered to open her eyes. She lurched up and looked at him. "I'm so sorry."

"Why?" he said, getting out. "No one got any sleep last night."

He came around, helped her out of the truck, and led her up the icy sidewalk. He slipped twice and each time she whooped and grabbed him tighter.

The temptation of St. Jules would never have rated a long biblical passage, and any second he was going to snap. He dropped her on a couch just inside the door and she immediately curled into a ball. Jules looked around. The house was spare but pleasant, with dishes piled in the sink and newspapers in random piles on the table. Past the kitchen, by the back door, a gray cat watched him. To the right he saw the bathroom, with a robe and some clothes in a pile on the floor. He peered around the corner and found the bed.

He tapped her shoulder. "Come on, Caroline. Off the couch. Get into bed."

"Whooowhooo," she said, grinning with her eyes shut. "What are you saying?"

"I'm not saying anything, just in case you have a memory tomorrow." He knelt down and started unlacing her boots.

"Well," she said, "you're a chickenshit. Did you know that?"

"Yes." He yanked off the boots and tugged her off the couch. She draped one arm around his neck and allowed herself to be led. In the bedroom she struggled with the zipper on her coat and he bent down to help. Their faces were a few inches apart.

"Thanks," said Caroline softly.

"You're welcome," said Jules. He kissed her quickly, on the lips, turned off the light, and walked out of the bedroom.

Caroline gave a wicked giggle in the dark. "Well, good night," she said. "I love you, too."

OVER BREAKFAST THE following morning he managed to turn restraint into heroism. Somehow progress had been made. He moved on to plan B and drove up to the Sacajawea.

Dottie and Halsey were eating Raisin Bran on one of the new prep tables in the kitchen. Jules wasn't usually given to arriving at nine on Sundays off.

"Christ," said Dottie. "It's Mr. Peppy."

"You look like shit, Dottie," said Jules.

"How dare you," she said pleasantly. "Any word from the art boy?"

"He's been and gone," said Halsey. "Told Merry he'd call next week."

"Did he give you anything else to go on?"

"No," said Halsey. "But he sure as hell took my money."

"I feel bad," said Jules. "Lots of people vouched for him, and there was no problem with credentials."

Halsey shrugged. "Maybe he'll come through. Most

people in that world are objectionable. No reason Mr. Altschuler should be any different."

He finished his bowl and carried it to the sink, looking older than usual. "We have to talk. When do you have time?"

Jules had had time the night before. "This afternoon?"

"My niece and I need to go on a long drive. Tomorrow morning?"

"You know I can't take off Mondays. How about tomorrow evening, after Alice and I go to the airport?"

Halsey looked miffed. "How about now?"

"I have something else I need to take care of first," said Jules. "Is Fred up?"

Dottie and Halsey both started laughing, and by the time Jules filled his coffee cup, Dottie had tears running down her face and into her cereal.

Fred was honestly talented: he could fix everything, comprehend how almost any object should work and why it might not always do so. As a kid, he'd probably been in the 99th percentile on spatial relations tests. Jules had never even understood what the phrase meant. With a different past—a competitive high school, a different genetic makeup re alcohol—Fred could have been a physicist, or at the very least a boffo engineer.

Jules climbed up to Merry's den and hammered on the door. "Go away," she said again.

"I don't want to talk to you," said Jules. "I want Fred."

"What?" asked Fred. "If something bad's happened, I need an hour."

"Nothing bad," said Jules. "Help me get this car started."

"What will you do for me?"

"Lots."

HER VOICE WAS a little creaky. “Your piece of shit car is fine, lady,” said Jules. “Would you like a ride up?”

A long pause. “I was kind of hoping to creep up there with a tow truck without having to face you for at least twenty-four hours. Are you saying it starts?”

“It starts. It’s fixed.”

“You fixed it?”

Her disbelief was palpable. “Fred fixed it,” said Jules. “He said you’ll need a new starter soon. I can’t fix anything automotive, but I’m a good bully.”

Caroline didn’t say anything. “It’s noon,” said Jules helpfully, enjoying himself. “I’ll give you a ride up.”

“I’m sure I can get up there later. You don’t have to do this.”

“I’ll get you in an hour,” said Jules. “I’ll even buy you a big coffee.”

He had to jump puddles to get to his pickup. She was sitting on her porch, very pale, and her hair was still wet from the shower. She had the ethereal look of a Victorian consumptive, not a benefit most people got from tequila.

“I’m sorry I was disgusting,” she said.

“I wouldn’t use that word,” said Jules, opening the truck door for her. What word would he use? Drunk? Edible? Just plain fuckable? “You probably just need some breakfast.”

“You’re too kind,” she said acidly. “I feel like dogshit. I bet you’re relieved you made it out alive.”

“I wouldn’t say that either,” said Jules. “I wouldn’t say that at all.”

Caroline looked at him and he smiled, some of the wolf slipping out. She turned pink.

It was a long, quiet drive, but he enjoyed it.

8 *A Thaw*

BLUE DEER BULLETIN

SHERIFF'S REPORT, WEEK OF MARCH 27–APRIL 2

March 27—Officers responded to a call from a local tavern, where two patrons had begun to fight after arguing over who would drive home. Both were driven home, and keys were held until morning.

Officers responded to another call from the same tavern, where a man claimed to be experiencing a heart attack. Paramedics determined he was very drunk and had failed to eat, then had compounded these errors by sampling several small round pickled peppers.

March 28—Reports of several houses along Cottonwood Street being egged were received by sheriff's deputies. The city-county building was also extensively egged, along with two squad cars.

March 30—Several reports have been received of a yellow motorcycle operating at high speed in the downtown area. The motorcycle could not be located.

March 31—A man was observed parked opposite a local business for three hours. He would leave his car to walk around the building, then return to the car. An officer failed to locate the man.

A woman who'd lost a license plate somewhere in Idaho came to the station for help.

April 1—A concerned citizen reported suspicious behavior at a local motel. One individual was arrested for resisting an officer.

April 2—A report was received of a woman talking to herself on the street, explaining hygienic practices to passersby. Officers were unable to locate her.

THE LADY WHO LIKED TO DISCUSS CLEANLINESS HAD been Jonathan's special visitor, and Jonathan had been one of many people who called in, concerned. Jonathan had also been the bozo who'd investigated suspicious behavior at a local motel: the man blowing smoke out of the bathroom window had merely been hiding his lack of progress in quitting cigarettes from his wife, not testing pot he intended to sell at the local grade school. The incident had been classic Jonathan: bust down the door, then arrest the person inside for getting mad. By the time Jonathan reported his stalker, Jules's sympathies were mixed, and it was too late to say "April Fool" to the poor man in the hotel. The boy needed some other outlet for his energies. Twenty-three was not an ideal age to believe in chastity.

Jules patrolled some Monday mornings, reasoning that this was the likeliest time for a motorist to shoot a deputy. This was an honest wish to protect others, rather than some like-father like-son desire; his week never ended or began, anyway, and why ruin someone's happy speeding home on a Friday? Today he drove with his window down, fifty degrees feeling like summer after the last several months.

After lunch Grace was in a bad mood, good news for

Jules as it meant she wasn't talkative. Jules eyed the folder on top of the familiar mess of paper on his desk. The file was Anne Baden's, from the state lab. Caroline's handwriting covered the note attached to the top, which told him she'd been and gone. He imagined she'd planned it that way.

> This finally arrived—body's at the hospital. Back around two.

ONLY 210 PEOPLE had been born in Absaroka County the previous year, and 162 had died. If you were a sheriff, that meant that you'd dealt with only a dozen births, either because of winter emergencies or because of parents who'd been deemed unfit even before delivery, but in the same period you'd be called on at least three dozen deaths. Paradigm America: birth was almost invariably normal (albeit often springing out of delusion), but death was often nasty and suspicious. An overweight man of seventy dies in his sleep alone of a classic heart attack or stroke (a fortunate death in the modern sense that not having time to think meant good fortune), and relatives would insist to Jules that the man had been smothered, poisoned, even hexed. And birth was only accidental at conception, whereas a good tenth of county deaths really were abrupt and surprising, at least to the people who died: falls and drowning and a failure to recognize the deadliness of weapons and vehicles and animals and lovers and the weather and drugs or alcohol. Or even that funny feeling in your head or chest.

But by the time such cases made their way to the state lab, they lacked mystery. That winter Jules had looked down on an eighty-year-old who'd known he shouldn't shovel snow and a twenty-year-old who'd thought a bumpy ice floe would hold him and two skiers who'd brought an avalanche upon themselves on Heart Creek (they'd found the couple after four hours of digging, and the man's face had been covered by a translucent bubble of ice; no one knew how long that meant he'd lasted, looking for breath in gray light). Even though the cause of death in all cases was perfectly clear—their deaths were as accidental as deaths could be—they had to be autopsied. The answers would be simple even if the medical language wasn't: lack of air, a broken neck, or crushed heart. Anne Baden's answer was a little more complicated.

> *Case 124/96, Absaroka County: attn. J. Clements, H. Meyers, C. Fair. Anne Margaret Baden: a 46-year-old woman, weight 130, height approximately 5'3", found frozen in a snowbank twelve hours after last having been seen. At autopsy, her blood alcohol concentration (BAC) was 0.26 g/dL. Hypothermia was listed as the primary cause of death, with ethanol intoxication as a contributing factor. Tests also determined the presence of fluoxetine and codeine, as well as smaller amounts of other medications.*
>
> *Observed irregularities included perimortem bruising and scraping on knuckles, fingers, and shins. The subject also had abnormalities in her ovaries and kidneys consistent with early stage carcinoma, likely undiagnosed.*
>
> *Samples taken from under the deceased's fingernails consisted primarily of potato detritus, as well as small fragments of wood. Stomach contents were consistent with a dinner of ground meat, potatoes, and Brussels sprouts.*

Jules finished the condensed version, read carefully through the details that followed, then held up the bag of fingernail scrapings and eyeballed them with the magnifying glass in his desk drawer. The mysterious spots now looked just like what they were, wood slivers with fragments of paint floating in melted ice; the brown bits were old potato. He could even tell that the paint was light blue, just the color of the chalet's window frames.

"Fuck the budget anyway," muttered Jules. It was worth having it in someone else's writing, though he doubted it would matter.

Anne Baden had had a good many options and she'd taken advantage of several, according to her autopsy. Weather, obviously, plus drugs (a muscle relaxant, a blood pressure medication, pain medication, an antidepressant, and some cough syrup), and the equivalent of six mixed drinks. People who ingested on this level needed minders, but Anne had Leon, locking his door in a blizzard after his wife set off on foot, already drunk, for a bar two hundred yards away. He'd told them he slept with pillows over his head, sometimes the comforter, too, because he couldn't abide the wind. He also did it on still nights, lest he hear his own bar customers; he couldn't abide them either. But Jules thought again of the rickety A-frame's porch, the baying dog. Snow could only muffle so much, even if visibility had been down to ten feet. He thought of how close he'd been to the house when he'd tripped over Anne Baden, and he had proof now that she had made it to her own door that night and knocked until her hands were bruised and her fingers raw and she gave up and tried to walk back to the bar. Anne hadn't frozen on her way *to* the house but on her way *back*. Jules was sure, suddenly, that Leon had heard all of it and not unlocked the door.

He'd probably heard her crying softly when she lay down in the snow, lost.

Leon said Anne had her own key, and she was the one who usually insisted on locking the door. He hadn't noticed she hadn't returned because they no longer slept together. She'd been banished to the couch, and anyway, he'd expected her to dig up a more comfortable resting place.

Jules supposed she had. At the very end, Caroline had attached another yellow sticky note, with two lines in loose scrawl:

> I think he heard her, and I think he decided not to unlock the door.
>
> Can we do anything about it?

Probably not, he thought, though it was always good to know you agreed with someone you loved. They could check the wooden windowsills and screen door for blood and bits of nail, but the bottom line was that Anne had peeled potatoes for a man who couldn't be bothered to unlock a door, who claimed he'd never heard her scratching and calling, and they wouldn't be able to do a thing past hoping he ended up in hell.

Still, Jules made a list:

- She had no keys when we found her, despite Leon's claim.
- She had no regular pill or alcohol problem but was full of virtually everything when found. She would have been confused even without alcohol. Leon said she was fine, but she was taking antidepressants. Leon claims he gave her one pain pill; autopsy shows a dosage equaling at least three. He said he made her

two drinks, and Merry said she made her two drinks, but four drinks doesn't seem like enough to get her up to .26, especially on top of those potatoes.

- Leon was in the habit of answering the phone on nights when he was off, and usually wanted the bartender to call in if there was the slightest hint of problems.
- The dog would have barked; Betty mentioned the sound of a dog barking over the wind when they went outside to look. No one could have slept through a rottweiler baying.
- Anne had some notes about the Southwest in her pocket. She's been described as quiet as a mouse, as if she simply didn't exist outside of Leon. People who don't exist don't plan to run away. Something had woken her up.
- No one knew them well, but according to the previous bartender, Leon and Anne had spent time with the people who lived in the trailer, Bob Frame and his wife. Find them.

It was one o'clock. Grace was eating an egg salad sandwich. "Do you know where Caroline went for lunch?"

"To the Chinese place with Harvey."

"No one ever asks me along."

"No one thinks you want to see them," said Grace. "You're so obvious about not wanting to be here. It's hard on people."

He snorted. "This has nothing to do with me liking my job."

"You're a real a-hole," said Grace. "I might talk to your mother after church. Somebody has to haul your head out of your whatever. Anyway, it's their award meal."

THE GEEK AWARD for March, given each month by the jail tenants from a pool of nominees submitted by the deputies, had gone to the man whose girlfriend had called him in for having relations with her dog, an obedience-trained standard poodle. Jules, though sympathetic to the dog, enjoyed any incident that caused Axel Scotti to swear and blow dust off his law books. Other contenders had been the man who'd knocked on the wrong hotel room door and insisted the woman inside was his wife, and the teenager who'd stuffed a hoagie and two apples in his jeans in the supermarket and headed for the door looking like a porn star.

Harvey, who'd answered the dog call, had selected a free lunch at the Chinese restaurant from the menu of possible rewards. Caroline, who'd delivered the poodle to foster care (a friend who ran the local humane society chapter immediately fed her a steak, sobbing), had gone along, saying she'd only have one single spring roll for her part in the drama.

"She's dieting," said Grace dryly. "She thinks she's gained weight. She says she can't afford a new dress to wear to the wedding because she has to repair her car."

Caroline was long and lithe, with nothing much extraneous about her body or manner. The thought of even a square inch disappearing into the void unseen broke Jules's heart, but he tried not to dwell on exact locations.

He went to find them and took a small rib off Caroline's plate. A test—if you'll give me your food, what will you give me next? The spring roll was long gone.

"I read the file. The three of us need to take a trip down the valley."

"Are we going to talk to Leon?" asked Caroline. She had better color today, but she didn't look at him directly.

"If he's around."

"He said she had a key. It wasn't in her pocket."

Jules reached for a last rib and said calmly, "She probably dropped it. Hard to hold on to a little piece of metal when you're drunk and your fingers have begun to freeze."

"I asked around and she didn't have much of a drinking history," said Caroline. "It's very rare for this to happen without one, hard to get that far gone if you don't have a constantly elevated blood level."

"True," said Jules, "but she was very drunk, and she was on meds, and she was upset."

Two huge plates of food arrived. "Grace said you were on a diet," said Jules, stabbing at a shrimp.

"I am," said Caroline, drizzling hot oil onto a dish already studded with hot peppers. "I've gained weight right where it matters. Not that there's anyone to notice."

"Don't be so sure," said Jules, drumming his fingers on the table.

"If they notice, what they see isn't nice enough to make them put their beer or their book down. Here, have some," she said, scraping a pound or so onto a plate.

"It's the time of year," said Harvey, between dainty bites. "Everybody'll wake up again in May or June, after a month of good weather."

This comment was out of character and unwelcome. "You wouldn't want them to put their beer down," said Jules, trying to offer a safe opinion.

"Don't be so sure," said Caroline.

He ate in lieu of responding, then chugged a glass of water.

"Sorry about the hot oil," said Caroline.

"Just right," said Jules.

"I thought it was a little far gone."

Jules dragged his hand across his forehead. The last time he'd fallen for the idiot game of trying to impress a woman with hot food he'd been in college. "Let's go down there. We probably won't be able to prove negligence, let alone murder, but we can talk to Leon again and look around."

Caroline dabbed at her mouth. "I can't find anyone who knows about a boyfriend, and since when does anyone keep a secret in this town? The whole story's bullshit."

Most were, finally. "Do you have an ax to grind here?"

"I'm getting one," she said evenly.

Jules reached for the check.

When they piled out into Leon's empty driveway, Jules muttered at the pain in his ribs and blinked at the sun and warm wind. They edged onto the icy, thawing, blustery field and within a few minutes stared down at the tiny size-six prints of thin, cheap sneakers, perfectly preserved in month-old ice. The tracks made the next day in cold fluff, after these had frozen, had simply blown away.

Harvey pulled out the camera, a notebook, and a measuring tape. "Did we check the phone records yet?" asked Caroline.

"I did last week," said Jules. "Leon picked up the phone once on a call from the bar, but only for five seconds. That was the only call that went through."

He rolled a peppermint around in his mouth, thinking it over. Merry's Range Rover was parked behind the Bachelor. She had no customers. Leon's truck was nowhere in sight, and Leon always drove. His version of exercise wasn't walking but weight lifting, and after a lifetime on steroids, the truck probably wasn't so much an extension of his prick but all he had left, his only remaining forward-moving object.

He had this on good authority from Dottie, who seemed to have the lowdown on most male details in the county.

"Merry's still working both places?" asked Caroline.

"I guess," said Jules.

"Are you going to tell her what we're up to?"

"No. Aren't you?"

"No," said Caroline firmly.

Merry could fret over it, and wonder what they were doing. Caroline was following the prints to the chalet, giving them a wide berth. Anne's tracks headed right up to the porch, then backtracked to the bedroom window and around the perimeter of the building, with extra stomp marks under every window.

"This only shows how hard she tried," said Harvey. "Do you think she dropped the key, or do you think she never had one?"

"The only way to even begin to find out would be to stake the tracks," said Jules. "All the way across the field and back, and then go over the whole route with a metal detector." Leon might fuck with them; he might drop a different key if he was as guilty as Jules wanted him to be. Leon couldn't have known she'd die; she might have made it back to the bar. But if she told the story there, drunk, Merry wouldn't have listened, and by morning Anne might not have remembered. Even if Anne persevered and told the police, there was still no way to bring charges, nothing to prove. And if Leon was completely innocent, if he was a tired, sleeping man who'd patiently put up with a drunken, unfaithful wife, he'd be entitled to raise a stink.

When Anne had given up and set off cross-country for the bar again, the tracks looped around in a far part of the field, then headed in the right direction as if there'd been a clearing in the snow and she'd seen the lights. But by then she was falling on every other step, and within twenty yards they came to the bare patch of grass where they'd chopped Anne and her ice bed free. They'd find nothing on the house without a warrant and wood samples, and even with such samples they'd never prove that he heard her.

"What do we do?" asked Harvey.

"Hold her for a while longer, just in case, see if anything else happens," said Jules. "Let's check his record, see if he had any insurance on her, see if there's someone he likes better. Let's look for the neighbors."

"You're saying we can't do anything?"

"Do you have any ideas?" asked Jules politely.

Caroline kicked at a chunk of ice. "We can rattle his cage," said Jules. "We can look for reasons. Right now we don't even have a motive, let alone evidence. But we can play with his paranoia."

"You never know how someone'll act if you corner them," said Harvey. "Leon's already a paranoid asshole."

"That's what I'm counting on," said Jules.

"I'm going back to the station," said Caroline. "I'm on until midnight, and I've got a headache."

"Still?" asked Jules.

"Still," she said.

THE FIRST TIME she saw Fred drink a beer Alice's expression liquefied, like bedrock during an earthquake. It was Monday night, and she and Jules had just picked up Arnie Wildason, the wedding chef, at the airport. After the kitchen tour they'd entered the bar through the back door and found Fred and Merry with their heads together. Fred had the half-empty beer bottle gripped in his hand, and his eyes were starry. He ran for it while Alice was still speechless, leaving Merry to fire haughty looks over her shoulder as she followed Fred.

"Hey," said Jules. "It was a beer. She's been drinking martinis. Think of how bad it could be."

Alice made a funny guttural sound and hugged her stomach, which had recently moved up and out. Jules's mother, Olive, called it "popping"; she called labor "popping," too.

Arnie was behind the bar, poking through the bottles with his customary Dakota calm, sizing up Dottie, who sized him up in turn. Jules introduced them and watched the exchange of smiles with relief—things would be far better that week if the two of them got along. Of course, there was always the danger they'd get along too well; this seemed to be going through Alice's mind, too, because she collapsed on a stool.

"Fred's getting the job done anyway," said Jules. "He'll keep it together until the wedding."

"And then what? Shoot himself?"

"Maybe," said Jules. "But at least the place will be ready."

"Hey, Jules," said Arnie. "Did anyone ever tell you were too nice for your job?"

"Yes," said Jules. "And they were wrong."

Arnie grinned and squinted at a bottle of marc. Jules had never known a more low-key cook. Arnie had no illusions about local taste buds, and on the way back from the airport had waxed poetic about a particularly fine hot dog and sauerkraut he'd downed at the Minneapolis airport. Put him in a place like Montana and he really reverted; now he sounded exactly like his mother, whose visits to New York had always been a surreal treat.

"Things are fine, Alice," said Arnie. "I've checked the

kitchen, and I checked the orders again before I even left this morning. I'll start tonight, and Jules can start helping tomorrow night. Go home and don't even look at this place until Saturday."

"What about the rehearsal dinner?" she snapped. "Last I heard that was Friday."

"Get out of here," said Arnie. "Jules can help, your friends can help, we hired people. You take care of the old ladies and the baby and Peter and sleep a little. Weddings are to enjoy."

"Let's go, darling," said Jules.

"You two wouldn't be talking to me this way if I weren't pregnant," Alice muttered. But she walked toward the kitchen and the back door, willing to go along with them.

"Where's the panel?" asked Jules. The spot where it had hung was now covered by a chalkboard. "I wanted to show it to Arnie."

Dottie was scribbling Arnie's supply requests on a pad. "Back in the crate, in the basement, so that Merry will shut up. As soon as we hear back from Altschuler, Halsey's given her the okay to take it to Leon's."

"Why does she care?"

"I don't know. She just does. She says it offends her sensibilities."

"Where's Halsey anyway? We were supposed to finally have that talk." She handed Arnie an inventory list. "He said to tell you he changed his mind."

"What's that mean?"

"I guess that he doesn't need to talk to you about whatever it was you were going to talk about anymore."

"Oh."

"What were you going to talk about?" She was suddenly

on alert, finally distracted from Arnie, who was humming and flicking burners. "He spent all morning with Merry. Was it about her?"

"I don't know," said Jules.

Dottie was smiling when she turned away.

ONE OF THE many reasons Jules preferred sorting antiques to mopping up Blue Deer was that in a cop's job shit happened and continued happening, and could only be alleviated, never cured. Good things were private, and really bad things were usually horrifically public. The bad things still happened to other people—Jules wasn't so self-absorbed to think someone else's misfortune was God spitting in his own eye—but not everyone on the planet was called upon to notice how much happened.

Several hours later, when Jules was slumped on a hospital bench in the aftermath of a bad three-car accident, he looked up to see Caroline at the far end of the hall, dragging a crumpled man through the doors of emergency. When the ambulance call had gone out she'd been dealing with a possible lost child, and later with a bar fight.

The man had a long raised welt along one cheekbone and was locked in a fetal curl on the floor, moaning. "What happened?" asked Jules.

"Pool cue at the Baird," said Caroline.

"Why?"

"He did an Iggy Pop for the wrong guy's girlfriend."

"Where's the wrong guy?"

"He left. It wasn't worth bothering you guys."

Jules started helping Caroline and Ralph, the night nurse, straighten the man out on a cart. He hadn't realized

Caroline was familiar with Iggy Pop's finer moments. "It's not just his cheekbone," said Caroline. "I hope you're not feeling queasy."

No one had bothered zipping the man's pants back up, and Jules and Ralph recoiled at the same moment. "I gather Horace will be in surgery for some time," said Caroline in a dry voice. "Maybe some ice while he waits."

Jules had recovered fairly quickly; tonight a blown scrotum didn't rate as horrific. Caroline looked him over. "Can I get you a coffee?"

"No," said Jules. "But you can buy me a beer."

OUTSIDE IT WAS warm but so windy he couldn't hear Caroline talk. They went to the Blue Bat where Delly, who'd been about to close, groused a little, then bought them each a drink. "Fred was in here."

"I guess he's branching out," said Jules.

"It's a shame," said Delly. "Has he tried to off himself yet?"

"Not yet," said Jules.

Caroline looked at him sideways. Jules explained.

"He came in with a pissed-off piece of work," said Delly. "Would that be what got him going again?"

"I don't know," said Jules.

"Leon Baden came in, too. Now you really know why I wanted to leave early. That piece of shit hasn't been in this bar for ten years."

Next to Jules, Caroline had tilted her head like a very lovely bird dog. This wasn't the sort of compliment he could ever give. "What did they talk about?" said Jules.

"Bitched about the old man," said Delly. "The old, old

man. How he doesn't care to sell anything. I could swear I heard my beloved's name taken in vain."

Delly was part of the Dottie fan club. Jules had heard a rumor they rendezvoused once a year in Butte.

More people walked in and Delly wandered down the bar. Jules had never arrested the new customers, and from the way she relaxed after she studied their faces, neither had Caroline. She looked up at him a minute later. "Are you okay?"

"More or less."

"You looked kinda chalky back at the hospital."

He thought it over for a minute. "I'm not cut out for this job."

She managed to look sympathetic and amused at the same time. "You thought you were?"

"No."

"I imagine doing work for Halsey is heaven in comparison."

"It used to be," said Jules. Then he told her about the things that had been bothering him for weeks now: the missing pieces, the war between Dottie and Merry, the chips in his friendship with Fred, the way Halsey seemed to be pulling back. The wedding was the least of it.

"I guess I'll stop envying you," said Caroline. Delly turned the channel on the television and they stared blankly at the news. "Why have you never married?" she asked suddenly.

He was startled and stared at her. "I just never made it to that point. Why haven't you?"

She shrugged. "Bad timing and bad behavior. Alice said you had a girlfriend who died."

"That was a long time ago," said Jules. "I don't know that we would have married."

Delly flicked off CNN four minutes into the headlines

and put on an Al Green CD. Delly was a walking Allman brother, and this was unprecedented. But Caroline didn't notice, and plugged on.

"What about Edie?"

"A lot of comfort but no real enthusiasm."

She had the disconcerting habit of listening, of never arbitrarily changing the subject or weighing in early with her own point of view. Now she said nothing, expecting him to continue. Jules found a drink straw and tortured it. "We might have thought we wanted to, but when she fell in love with Ankeny, she understood. She hadn't really fallen in love before, even with her first husband."

"But you had, and you knew better."

"I had. I'm not sure about knowing better."

"You don't fall in love often?"

"Not often," said Jules, "but I fall."

9 *A Little Too Dead*

Dear Dora:

Over the last year I've been increasingly attracted to a man. This should be good news: he's funny and smart, with no current girlfriend or obvious horrible habits besides a tendency toward mood swings. The bad news is that we work together, and he doesn't seem to notice my existence in a romantic context. Since I've gradually realized he's known just about everyone else in our small town in this way—the man's really gotten around—should I take his disinterest personally?

Yrs, Cora Sue

Dear Cora Sue:

Take it however you like, but take it and run for your life. There's a slight chance he's being professional, but it's likelier his friendly dim bulb will eventually turn in your direction and cause all sorts of problems. A man who's gotten to know most of a town (even a small one) needs to rent a U-Haul, go into counseling, or both!

Good luck, Dora

"HOW DO YOU LIKE THIS WEEK'S LETTER?" ASKED GRACE.

"I haven't had a chance to read it yet," said Jules. "Is it full of pleasant sexual perversions?"

"You need some time off," said Grace.

IN ABSAROKA COUNTY, people were always disappearing, freezing to death in the winter, falling and drowning in the summer, forcing others to go into inhospitable corners of God's country after them and risk their own toes and minds. Not many American sheriffs had to devote such an appreciable chunk of their budget to finding idiots with a poor sense of direction, and though not everyone who went missing deserved their fate, most did. Search and Rescue spent the season searching for lost horn hunters and other fatuous men of the woods, dug for days in avalanche areas for drunken yodelers, scraped the rivers and lakes for happy fools who died panicked, horrible deaths. A dry line in the newspaper, something about a hiker having been "partially consumed" by a grizzly, was a whisper compared to the real scream of the sight itself. When you spent an afternoon crawling around in search of bits of scalp and gristle it made no difference if the bear had killed the hiker outright or been cleaning up a mess left after an accident. It made no difference that Jules, all in all, preferred the bears. Some of the hikers probably had, too.

There were several dozen search and rescue calls a year, with a half dozen training days visited upon the sheriff's department, fire department, and volunteers. Summer brought water rescue classes, which involved bumping along the river bottom in a wetsuit; winter called for avalanche training, the reading of snow and terrain for fatal conditions. Other classes involved methods of getting in and out, snowshoeing and skiing, helicopter reconnaissances, horseback searches.

The last session had had to do with "low-angle raising," which included such skills as anchor systems, backboarding, litter packaging, and low-angle rappelling.

Truth be told, Jules was never in the mood to rappel, and he probably never would be. That autumn, after he'd had to crawl along a ledge to reach a fallen hiker, Alice had fed him a fine cioppino and then subjected him to a special showing of *Vertigo*, which only reinforced Jules's realization that he wasn't Jimmy Stewart, and that Kim Novak wasn't Grace Kelly, and that Jules preferred brunettes anyway and never intended to visit San Juan Capistrano. Because he liked his weekly meal and was by and large a polite boy, he shared a joint with Peter and the two of them slumped, slit-eyed and snickery, on the couch in front of the television while Alice, who'd once taken a class on Hitchcock, provided a voice-over.

THE NEW CALL came in a little after eight on Tuesday. A birder had seen a man float by on the far edge of the river, waving his arms for help. Then he'd followed the current around the far side of a small island and disappeared.

No one was on the island, and no one was anywhere to be found on the next half mile of banks before the river narrowed and speeded up for a canyon. It wasn't the best time of year to be wearing a rubber suit, but not the worst either, and after a season of edging around icy precipices, a boat made for a nice change.

Normally they wouldn't have bothered looking in a canyon, but this one was packed with deadfall from an earlier flood. The previous fall, Jules and Divvy had been called to pull out a whole raft full of tourists in the same area, and joked about dynamiting the logjam free to avoid future problems. The Army Corps of Engineers and most other interested parties frowned on such maneuvers, though, and now the fire chief and the sheriff were left to joke about how it was definitely too late— what if they blew the waving man in half? Because of the rapids, the choice between a boat and a rope wasn't as obvious as it might have been. Divvy quickly drove Jules batshit by muttering "rock and a hard place, rock and a hard place" like a demented parrot while they unloaded grappling hooks and nets. Neither really saw the point to bothering—in a fast-moving stretch of river, they almost never found anyone until they stopped looking, and the snags were as potentially deadly to searchers as to floaters. The body always literally popped up later, forced itself upon an unsuspecting tourist, some poor fool who'd come to the river looking for a little peace and natural beauty, only to tumble over a lifelong nightmare image. Water and rock did horrible things to soft tissue, and drowning simply wasn't an easy way to go, even if it was the way a person had chosen: the last agony when water hit lungs transfigured features.

They tried the boat in the lower canyon, and left the narrow upper reaches to the young, athletic, energetic rock climbers who'd actually volunteered. Ten minutes later they were wet and shaking and hacking on the bank, never having seen the rock that had flipped the boat. Nor did they expect to see the boat anytime soon.

"We knew better," said Jules.

"Shit," said Divvy, dumping water from his boots and stripping off his socks. His beard quivered and his toes were blue. He was missing one on his left foot. They'd been playing tomahawk together at age eight when Divvy and his toe had parted ways, and seeing Divvy's toe hop across the yard wasn't something Jules would ever forget.

"At least the air's warming up."

"What are you talking about?" shrieked Divvy. "We nearly died. Since when were you so goddamn upbeat?"

"I'm happy to be alive," said Jules, lying back on the warm gravel. "I've been falling out of trees and boats. I'm sick of it. I have things I'd like to do before I really fuck up."

"Jesus," said Divvy. "Let me guess what sort of things."

"Of course, you have kids, and that probably ups the ante on dying."

"You only know what you know," said Divvy. "But I'm glad you're going to finally try to have a life. Maybe you'll stop trying to kill me."

WESLEY WAS ARGUING with someone about loose horses when Jules first walked in and sorted through his messages. Jules didn't know him well yet, but he liked him—Wesley was very smart, and his training was thorough and current. He could be relied upon to handle a complex problem from start to finish with little need for advice, which was more than Jules could usually say for himself. Jules now had someone who could double for him in meetings with the county's various social workers, juvenile parole officers and commissioners, teachers, doctors, and welfare management. It wasn't that he was necessarily a better cop than Ed or Harvey (no one could argue for Jonathan), but he could do it all, and now when Jules looked at him he saw an out.

"Where's Grace?"

"Her daughter might be in labor."

Wesley thought this was exciting; he thought of this as news. But this was Grace's daughter's third pregnancy since Jules had become a cop, and each previous time the labor-scare stage had lasted weeks. Grace would be unofficially part-time for the next two months.

"She's a few weeks early," said Wesley. "It could be a problem."

Jules nodded sympathetically. "Would you consider picking up a couple of shifts for me this week?"

"I would have, but Caroline just asked me the same thing. I said yes."

"What's Caroline doing?"

"I don't know. I figured you were taking off together."

Wesley was digging through a desk drawer and straightened to see Jules's stricken expression. "I'm joking," he said. "Some old codger just found a body."

"Har de har har," snapped Jules. "The joke's getting worse."

"I'm not joking," said Wesley. "Do you want the body, or do you want to answer the phone? I can't find anyone to fill in for Grace for another hour."

BY NOON THAT Tuesday the temperature reached seventy-five and spring began in earnest. But it had been a locked-in winter, the kind that allowed certain deep drifts to accumulate. One such drift had begun to form back in November under a high, dark, north-facing bluff of the river only a mile east of town and had grown larger with each snowfall and each subsequent big wind. So that even though the sparse turf on the hill above was now dry and soft and beginning to sprout, the drift below was still a four-foot-deep wedge of dirty ice fringed by a few halfhearted trees.

Crocus opened in south-facing flower beds, people started taking down storm windows, and a retired insurance salesman named Trimble spent the morning scrambling up and down the banks of the Yellowstone, looking for arrowheads and other treasures that might have been dislodged by the spring thaw, and not incidentally keeping an eye out for the county's missing boat. The year before he'd found three arrowheads, some granite flecked with gold, and a rock embedded with petrified vertebra that the museum in Bozeman decided had belonged to a prehistoric lizard.

This year he only found a dead man's head. He reported this to the emergency room nurse who treated him for irregular heartbeat, and the emergency room nurse called the station.

THE OLD BLOOD had fanned out a full foot into the snow around the man's neck, giving him a rusty, glittery collar, jasper instead of garnet. His lower face, just above the barely visible wound to his throat, was pristine, but the top of the skull had emerged from the snow much earlier, and the scalp had split and the hair turned to tufts.

"Anyone who saw that poking out would have guessed a dead cat," said Caroline, circling the body and peering down. "Underneath the reds look red and the flesh looks fresh. Could be a laundry ditty."

Jules was sitting on a log, feeling woozy. He'd expected the floater from the day before, not another Popsicle. He did not appreciate Mr. Trimble's efforts—he was sick of winter and what it did to animal and vegetable matter. It seemed that he spent most days each winter walking in circles without seeing anything, and in the summer he walked the same circles but details appeared, like quartz in a gravel bed or morels in the grass. When details appeared in winter, beyond pretty window dressing like coyote tracks and frost crystals, they usually had to do with death.

Caroline was untroubled, energetic, and fully recovered from her weekend. "How do we get him out?"

"Dig, I guess. Maybe a heater." Jules roused himself.

"How many people kill themselves by slitting their throats?"

"Not many."

But several hours later, after digging around the perimeter and bringing in propane-operated heat lamps and fans, they saw that the man still had a hunting knife clutched in his right hand, which seemed consistent with the direction of the wound. He was small and wiry, no older than fifty, with mousy brown hair and patchy stubble on his cheeks. He wore good leather boots, lined Carhartt overalls, and a down coat.

As the body heated up the chemical smell became stronger, and eventually they found a rifle and a cleaning kit and bottle of Hoppe's at his side. From the stain pattern he seemed to have squirted it over his head and body.

"Keeping his options open," said Caroline. "Is that why nothing ate him? Do you think he doused himself to keep animals away, or do you think he was going to use a match?"

"I don't have a clue," said Jules. "He was definitely making sure he didn't walk away."

The coroner arrived and they hunkered down in the car together to fill out a pile of forms. Then they took samples and photos and measurements, bagged the man's weapons, and covered his hands with more plastic. Jules checked the coat, then rolled him over and aimed the heat lamp at the back pockets. They were empty.

"Maybe he threw his wallet in the river," said Caroline.

"Where's his car?"

She shrugged. "We're close to town. When do you think he came?"

"He was sitting on dry ground," said Jules. "That could have been last fall or the end of the February thaw."

"He'd be a lot uglier if he'd been here during that whole week. I was wearing shorts. He must have landed toward the end."

Dead bodies all around, and all he could think of was Caroline in shorts. All his life Jules had fallen for women who had a dry sense of humor, but Caroline was redefining dry. They searched the area again and came up with some soda cans, old cigarette packs and candy wrappers, a child's cheap ring, a hubcap, and four burned matches in a line, ten feet from the body.

"He couldn't have thrown the matches that far, let alone have them land together." Caroline placed the matches carefully in a bag.

"Especially not if he'd already cut his own throat."

"Maybe he only did that after he couldn't light himself. Maybe it was windy. Maybe he stood here and smoked and thought it over before he even sat down and doused himself."

Jules went in closer and sniffed the dead man's hands. The whole area reeked of Hoppe's, and he couldn't tell if it was on the man's hands as well as his clothing. He stood back.

"He would have caught," said Caroline. "At least for a minute, even if the wind blew each match out. We'd at least see scorching."

Jules nodded. The coroner nodded. "What do you think?" asked Jules.

"I think someone else tried to light him, and didn't want to get too close," said Caroline.

"You'd think they'd get the job done."

"Not if they were worried about someone coming. People were on the river by the end of that thaw."

They searched again. "I suppose he could still be a suicide," said Caroline. "There's an explanation for everything.

He smoked before he sat down, threw the butt in the river, got too weak to light a match at the end."

"Sure," said Jules. "But what do you think?" He somehow needed to hear it a second time before he believed it.

"I think someone killed him. What do you think?"

"I think you're right," he said, giving her a weak smile. "I think I should have quit last week. Let's send him north."

"Crap," said the coroner.

THE MAN HAD no ID on his body and no car parked nearby. He matched no missing persons report, and his prints weren't on record. No one in the department or the hospital recognized him, and a photo struck no chord at the courthouse, Job Service, supermarket, bus station, or churches.

Horace thought the wound and position were consistent with suicide but Jules sent the man to Missoula anyway, a fresh Absaroka County representative to replace the newly returned Anne Baden.

Caroline sifted through February's papers until she found what she wanted. On February 26 the temperature had reached sixty. That night it had dropped to twenty-five and they'd had ten inches of snow, which had continued through the next day. On the twenty-eighth the real cold front had arrived, with single-digit temperatures, and winter had locked in again.

Caroline went back around town with the photo and these dates, revisiting the bus station and the hospital, hitting motels and bars, but still found nothing.

JONATHAN WAS AT the station, staring blankly out the window.

"What's wrong now?" asked Jules.

"That lady showed up on my porch again. She was on the swing when I tried to go home."

Jules watched him.

"And I finally figured out why she was familiar. I drove her to Warm Springs a couple of months ago."

"Who was she, and why were you picking her up?"

"She kept starting branches and leaves on fire, and then she'd lie down next to them. It happened three times before you had me take her up. I guess she got attached to me. She had a shaved head then, but now she almost looks normal."

Jules put his pen down. "Are you talking about Lucretia Frame?"

"That's right," said Jonathan. "How'd you guess?"

"What does she want out of you?"

"She says I'm the only one who was nice to her, so she wants to be nice to me."

Jules rubbed his forehead.

"What do I do?" asked Jonathan.

"Next time she comes by, try to grab her. I want to ask her some questions about her old neighbor, Leon."

"I don't want to grab her," said Jonathan. "I don't want to go near her."

"Then call one of us."

AT FIVE ON Tuesday, despite another dead body, Jules headed up to the Sacajawea to help prepare sauces, freezable pastries, compound butters, and the like. He and Arnie roasted veal bones, chopped vegetables, made a fish fumet and trial sauces. They made four large terrines of goose liver pate and one small one, which they taste-tested with bottles of good bordeaux and some bread and roasted peppers and garlic. Jules would have been happy if this stage of preparations had gone on indefinitely.

WEDNESDAY WAS WARM again, with a soft, moist wind. It was the first morning that year that Jules could smell the earth, a lovely enough day if he hadn't been looking down at a drowned man. The man he and Divvy had searched for had surfaced on his own a mile farther downriver.

"This guy didn't die yesterday morning," said Wesley.

"No. He's a little too dead." By the time the report had come in of a drowning man waving for help, this man's arms had been rigored and broken, flopping in the current, and the open, panicked eyes that the caller had been tormented by were already cloudy, though still and eternally surprised. He was at least two or three days gone, bloodless and battered by rocks, turned to a prune by the cold water, which had at least kept him fresh. Five-eight or nine, maybe forty and slight, with light brown hair and what had been a high, pale forehead. His eyes reminded Jules of the fish heads he and Arnie used for the fumet the night before, and he intended to leave their true color to the lab.

The body had been caught in a deadfall, in chest-deep water, and sighted by a man walking a spaniel puppy. Jules and Wesley had waded out and pulled the body in with ropes and bungees, which dented the dead man's flesh in an unpleasant way. Jules hoped the next time he jumped into water fully dressed he'd be after a fish.

"No shoes, no clothes, no wallet," said Jules. He hadn't been planning a full day off, but two bodies in two days seemed frankly unfair. "The man wanted to sink. It's a disease lately, this dying with no identity."

"He had to really want to," said Wesley. "The water's about forty degrees."

"I noticed that yesterday, too," said Jules. "Good luck finding your dick."

Wesley glanced down, frowning. "Why do people think it's easy to drown?"

"I don't know," said Jules. "I haven't heard yet of a really easy way to die. We'll send him to Missoula."

The coroner, a happy man in his former life, pulled up slowly and climbed out of his car. They waved.

AT THE HOTEL a triage policy kicked in, with Halsey speeding up the process by handing out envelopes of cash to Fred's growing crew. Even Fred was drinking water, and he snapped at Merry when she dawdled while helping him. Arnie's small kitchen staff had creaked into action that morning and he'd begun to train the wait staff in the afternoon. By Wednesday night, sixteen of the twenty rooms needed for family guests were ready, though the paint was too wet to hang pictures or curtains. Jules finished two pâtés while Arnie worked on the components of the cake, muttering that he wasn't a dessert chef. The seafood wasn't due in until Friday morning, but the walk-in was packed with cheeses and salamis, produce and cream, pastry dough, peeled garlic, and stocks.

Wednesday night at nine, while Jules was pureeing roasted tomatoes and Arnie was running the new dishwasher, the kitchen went dark with a crackle and a poof.

"Fuck me," said Arnie in the dark.

Jules thought he could hear more crackles. "This could be bad," he said, ricocheting to the wall and feeling for the fuse box.

"What do you mean, could be?"

But Jules was running up the stairs, relying on memory and the moonlight that came through the tall windows on each end of the hall. The crew had gone home, but down the wing he could hear Alice and Caroline and Dottie, who'd been making beds, calling to each other.

"Where's Halsey?" he yelled.

"In town," came Dottie's voice. "Someone's birthday party."

"What's going on?" Alice asked.

"Just a short," yelled Jules. "Where's Fred?"

"He and Merry ran to town for some stain."

Jules felt along the wall across from the music room for heat, or more bad crackles, and found both near Dottie's door. He started to yell for her key when he realized the doorknob turned.

Inside, the tall paned windows were open, letting in real moonlight, and Dottie had a battery flashlight plugged into one outlet, the one on the newer line, connected to the guest rooms. On the far side of the room Jules saw smoke coming out from behind the bed, which was against the wall above the kitchen.

He jerked the bed out, smooshed together the smoking blankets and tossed them out the window. Small flames licked out of the plate and the wall looked ominous. He ran across the hall for his claw hammer, grabbed the very ancient-looking fire extinguisher, and ran into Caroline, almost knocking her down.

"Sorry," he said. "Could you get Dottie to get Alice out of the building?"

By the time she got back he'd smashed a hole in the wall and covered the wiring with foam. She helped him pull the bed out farther, then ran downstairs to the kitchen with the extinguisher while he ran upstairs, rattled Merry's locked door, and opened it with one good kick. Her wall was cold to the touch and he shot back down the stairs with only a brief look around her room. Even a glance was interesting. Outside, Arnie had tossed the burning blankets in the small pool and was smoking a cigar, something Jules had never seen him do. Jules turned all the breakers back on but one, and heard Alice shriek with relief at the sight of lights. The whole incident had taken no more than five minutes.

Jules, exhausted, found two more flashlights in Fred's workroom and walked upstairs slowly. In Dottie's room, Caroline was scooping up papers and boxes that had been under the bed, trying to keep them from touching the foam. Jules looked around: Dottie's hideout was spare and almost monkish, with some odd touches. One of them was Arnie's T-shirt and jeans, lying across the hamper. Another, on a spool table under the window, was a missing Etruscan horse centered on a missing block of obsidian.

"Oh dear," said Caroline, following his gaze.

Jules helped her carry the boxes from under the bed across the hall, trying to hide his rage.

A leather folder was dry, but the open cardboard box had been flecked with spray. It held smaller folders, pouches, and tissue-wrapped objects. Jules unwrapped one and found a lapis box he'd never seen before. A small folder was filled with illuminated capital letters on vellum and some Dutch studies of poppies and pepper plants that had to be hundreds of years old.

He went through it all slowly and carefully. Most of the objects were entirely new to him, and two folders had notes reading "Hold on to these. H."

"Was she taking them, or holding them for Halsey?"

"Maybe both. I think they're both playing with me."

One paper-wrapped packet said "Muriel."

"She really doesn't look like a Muriel," said Caroline a moment later, amused.

"Halsey probably knew she had these. I think he was imitating some Courbet nudes," said Jules. "Nothing you'd see in most books."

"Still," she said.

Halsey's love of his first wife's body was palpable, a little too palpable for present company. Jules rewrapped the drawings. Alice was calling for him somewhere in the building, but neither of them answered.

"These are all the things you thought Merry and Fred had taken?" asked Caroline, holding the flashlight for him.

"A few of them. Dottie could have simply told me," said Jules. "It'll all be hers anyway. But she let me think they'd taken everything."

"Maybe they didn't take anything," said Caroline.

"Nah," said Jules. "Come upstairs with me."

Merry's already cluttered space was now packed with Fred's stuff, books and tools and clothes. Jules picked his way through and pulled a handful of Egyptian glass necklaces off a lampshade. He nodded to a bronze hand on top of the stereo. "Grab that, will you?"

Caroline reached for it tentatively. "Do you want her to know we've been in here?"

"I want her to wonder who's been in here. I've been looking for all these things, wondering if I was losing my mind. Everyone in this goddamn building's so arrogant that I'd like them to have a little doubt."

Under the window, they saw a small stone nude of a

woman and a foot-high bronze griffin. "They're beautiful," said Caroline. "Should I take them?"

"Nah," he said. "I think the griffin is a fairly modern copy, and the nude is a fake, but she doesn't know the difference. I've been locking up most of the real stuff. I like the idea of her lugging it to a gallery and finding out it's polished cement." He looked at Merry's lock. None of the wood had splintered when he'd kicked it open, and he simply slammed it shut again.

"Where the hell are you?" yelled Dottie up the stairs.

"Down in a bit," yelled Jules.

Back in the music room, Caroline looked for a clean surface for the bronze hand, and put it next to the Moran ledger.

"What's with the mattress?" she asked.

"Dottie miscounted and I asked her to throw it in here. Do you like those sketches?" he asked. "It's the view from this room."

Caroline studied the drawings, then sat on the mattress. "I've never seen the view," she said. "I've never been in this room in the daytime." She reached over to plump the pillows. "Last night was my last late shift in a week. I'd give anything to just go to sleep now."

Jules turned slowly. "Whose drawings are they?" asked Caroline, lying back with her eyes closed.

"Thomas Moran," he said. "Halsey's sitting on another fortune." He walked closer and looked down at her.

"Jules." It was Alice, calling up the stairs. "Are you up there? Arnie wants to know if he can turn the dishwasher back on."

Caroline opened her eyes and they looked at each other for a long moment. Then she rolled slowly upright, looking wearier than ever.

"What's he doing?" answered Dottie, from somewhere in the stairwell.

"How the hell should I know?" answered Alice, closer.

"Come on," Jules said, reaching down and taking Caroline's hand. "I'll make you some dinner."

JULES WAS A good cook, mostly thanks to Alice back in the years when they'd lived in New York, and in the past he'd used this talent—at first without realizing what he was doing—to seduce. Food almost always worked, and failure meant that it shouldn't work anyway. He did not persist with women who insisted on fat-free dinners, or women who wouldn't try strange shellfish, or women who liked to skip dinner in favor of dessert. Alice maintained he was looking for the female equivalent of lamb couscous with seven vegetables, boeuf bourguignonne with roasted potatoes and a salad of fennel and apples, followed by crème caramel; a full Batard Montrachet or Grands Echezeaux of a woman.

And she was right. So though he hadn't necessarily planned to do this with Caroline that night, he bore down on the snack he'd intended to prepare for him and Arnie with extra vigor, while Arnie worked on the rehearsal dinner tarts and Alice and Caroline made Xs on a ragged master list. Jules thawed some crab legs under running water and made cakes with scallions, some of the roasted pepper puree, and garlicky mayonnaise. He'd put aside some of the best veal liver when he'd made the pâté, and sauteed it until it was crisp on the outside and pink and juicy inside, covered with mounds of caramelized onions and soft, chewy fried currants for the pregnant woman with strange mineral desires, and served it with a fast slaw of celeriac, apple, and cabbage.

Watching Caroline mow through it was both amusing

and enlightening. She didn't roll her eyes or camp it up, but she didn't at any point forget to taste. Nor did she leave a token pile on her plate.

"I heard a rumor," said Caroline, when Arnie, Alice, and Dottie had faded into other corners of the kitchen.

Jules gave her a reproachful look.

"About Anne Baden," she said, amused. "Not about you. Though I can't blame you for being paranoid."

"Enough about me," he said. "And we have other problems now. I'm not sure I care whether Leon gets away with murder anymore."

Caroline raised an eyebrow and located the only remaining fragment of crab on her plate.

"Okay," said Jules. "Tell the story."

"I was helping Marge at the Frost Motel get an old pickle to the hospital last night, and she told me she'd found him in a snowdrift by the steps a week earlier." She took a bite of coleslaw.

"I get the parallels," said Jules.

"I'm chewing," said Caroline. "I'm being polite."

"You're playing with me. In a manner of speaking."

She smiled. He smiled. A little blast of honesty came and went. "Anyway," said Caroline, "Marge said it reminded her of 'that poor frozen woman,' and I asked if she meant Anne Baden, and she said yes, and added that at least Anne had had a little fun before she died."

She swabbed some bread through leftover sauce. Jules watched her eat it, content to have an excuse to watch her mouth. "It turns out 'before' meant this winter. Anne checked into the Frost on a half dozen afternoons with a man, slight build, mousy brown hair, mid-forties."

"Any name?"

"She called him something like 'Rafe.' Marge remembered the name because it was odd."

Jules thought it over. "How does she remember that it was winter?"

"Because the Christmas lights were up," said Caroline. "That was the only reason she saw them leave."

"Rafe as in Raphael?"

"Maybe," said Caroline. "We had a missing person we decided was a runaway with that name in February."

She was running her index finger through the butter and kosher salt and onion fragments left on the plate. "Give me another hint," said Jules.

"Leon's tenant, the man who lived in the trailer that burned, was named Robert Raphael Frame," said Caroline. "Leon just calls him Bob, but his loony wife called him Rafe when she told us he was missing."

Jules rubbed his eyes and tried to remember exactly what he'd seen months earlier. He hoped Anne Baden's affair had been a true gust, a blast of love or sensual pleasure that made up for some of the rest of her life. "Did we ever find him?"

"I think he turned up back in the south, the Carolinas or wherever he'd come from," said Caroline. "Otherwise we'd really have something to worry about. But it always seems a little squirrelly when two people have an affair and both disappear, in a manner of speaking. Especially if one of them had a possessive husband."

Jules actually moaned.

"I'm sorry," said Caroline. "I thought we'd have a few days without seeing Leon. I'd like to enjoy this wedding."

Jules filled her wineglass. "Anne's been dead for a while. She can stay dead until next week."

VIA FAX, 4/6, MISSOULA MEDICAL EXAMINER'S OFFICE TO BLUE DEER SHERIFF'S DEPARTMENT

Hey, Jules: what's with the die-off in your neck of the woods? Stop sending us your mangy, middle-aged suicides. —Barry

ABSAROKA JOHN DOE #1—SUMMARY: The body of a man, found frozen in situ on April 4 (see attached A.C.S. report). Approximate age 45–55, height 5'6", hair color light brown, eye color light brown, one small tattoo "L" with roses just above navel. The exposed portion of the head shows considerable weathering, consistent with death having occurred some weeks previous.

The individual was in generally good health at the time of death. The individual had not eaten or drunk for several hours before death. The wound, though of some force, is consistent with the motion of a fit right-handed man inflicting damage upon himself. The individual was liberally soaked in Hoppe's #9 Solvent, though this has no apparent relation to his manner of death.

ABSAROKA JOHN DOE #2—SUMMARY: The body of a man, found partly submerged on April 5 (see attached A.C.S. report). Approximate age 35–45, height 5'11", hair color mid-brown, eye color light gray. One 2 cm burn scar on left inner thigh, a large mole on his left buttock, and an appendectomy scar. Rigor and decay indicate that the individual died 48 to 96 hours prior to discovery, with the preservative effects of river water (42F when the body was found) making a more specific recommendation impossible.

The individual was in generally good health at the time of death. Toxicology pending. He had ingested a light meal (a salad and souplike broth) within two hours of death. Water was present in the lungs, consistent with death by drowning, though the skull was also bruised in three places, consistent with the impact of river stones. Some peri-mortem bruising of the small of the back; a lack of bruising on the fingers and hands may indicate that the individual was unconscious before or soon after entering the river. The only other physical anomalies discovered were the presence of severe ligament damage in the right elbow and a dislocated shoulder.

THESE TREATS WERE WAITING FOR JULES WHEN HE checked in at the station on Thursday afternoon. He'd asked for fast this time, and fast had gotten him nowhere. He stared at the bruises on the man's back, linked and matching three-quarter-inch semicircles, and drove back to the station without a glimmer of understanding.

The nitty-gritty wedding attendees had begun arriving Wednesday night, most planning to spend a full week. Many had wanted to come earlier to help; the bride and groom had begged them not to. Peter drove to the airport for his parents, who were smug at his nervousness; his younger brother Hannes, who planned to stay in town where no one would see him misbehave; his older brother Tommy, whose second divorce had just been finalized and whose sexual morals made all other attendees look saintly; and his grandmother Marie, who was eighty, had lived in Stockholm until she was sixty, and wanted to know how that darling boy Jules was doing.

Alice drove to the airport with Caroline in tow, having

bullied her three oldest friends onto the same flight. The first, Elsa Gresko, was in a depression so profound that every step, every movement of hand or eye was halting. This had been the case since she was twenty, and she confessed to Alice and Caroline at the baggage carousel that she'd left for the airport from an institution, and intended to return posthaste. But they weren't to worry, and how, by the way, was Jules? The other two, both old roommates who'd stayed on in New York after Alice left, rolled their eyes and during dinner in Bozeman, with lots of wine, picked apart the menu and each other. It became clear to Caroline that the other four women at the table—every single one of them, including the bride—had slept with her boss, and still regarded him with great fondness.

Only the pregnant bride blushed as the deputy's eyes widened. "This is just the tip of the iceberg," said Alice. "Or whatever."

"Well," said Irene, a flower arranger who'd been raised as an army brat, "it's not that surprising. I've always said plain boys are the ones with the imagination and energy. They have to *try*. What's that skinny dog up to these days anyway?"

"You're married," snapped the third friend, Tammy, a curator for MOMA. "Herb will find out. Jules has been calling me lately, lots of questions. Perks up my day."

On Thursday and Friday, the skinny dog himself made three trips to the airport. He picked up:

Alice's two red-haired great-aunts, Peach and Ginger. Peach was tiny and spry, Ginger phlegmatic, with a dangerous cane. They insisted on having two drinks apiece at the airport bar after Jules loaded their luggage.

Simon and Ambrose, old coworkers from a New York gourmet store, who'd traveled together to the wilds of

Montana despite a deep and abiding dislike for each other. Simon, now a fashion photographer, looked like a standard-issue barrel-chested Aussie and spent much of the drive in a snit after Jules pointed out that everyone would assume he and Ambrose were lovers: if two gay men came to a town like Blue Deer, surely they were together in every respect. Ambrose, six feet, five inches, reed-thin and black, was used to all manner of assumptions, and beamed at Simon's angst.

Three guests who'd rendezvoused from Chicago. One was Peter's cousin Mike, a conservation officer from Ishpeming, Michigan; another was Alice's old schoolmate Doug, a writer; and the last was an Ann Arbor roommate of Jules and Peter's, once an eye-popping imbiber of every known illegal drug, now a Republican heart surgeon who commented happily on the all-white airport crowd. Mike wore a T-shirt, Doug wore a flannel shirt, and Mark the surgeon wore a polo with little golf clubs on the pocket. Jules hoped the Baird would find him a room next door to Ambrose, one of the old ones with a shared bath.

The Baird and Sacajawea lobbies were minefields. Though Jules had been to many weddings, he'd never had to deal with one where he knew virtually everyone, and knew them as well as he knew the bride and groom. It was at once enervating and terrifying. When he dropped off Simon and Ambrose, Peter's grandmother made him sit down for a vodka and a talk in German, their common language. When he dropped off Mike and Mark and Doug he nearly tripped over Elsa, who was slumped in a chair and burst into tears of happiness when she saw him. And when Jules deposited Peach and Ginger, late Thursday night, he was assaulted by the rest of Alice's drunken cronies, who'd added enough stories after dinner for Caroline to burst into wicked laughter at the sight of him. He ran for it after Irene, the floral arranger, bounced out of her chair and onto his lap a second time and licked his ear.

WHEN JULES ARRIVED at Peter and Alice's house at eight Friday morning, he found Edie on her hands and knees just inside the front door, cleaning up dog vomit. Peter was in his underwear in the back room, chasing the dogs with a flyswatter while Alice, still in a bathrobe, covered her eyes with one hand and reached for her small allocation of coffee with the other. Pearl and Earl, unaware that Peter had other things on his mind and had forgotten his blood pressure medication for three days in a row, had eaten two bags of last-minute wedding supplies, including two pounds of English butter and a small fortune in aged Spanish ham.

While Peter told Jules the story, Pearl tried to ooze out of the back room on her elbows. Peter leaned down and hissed, "In your dreams, cur." Pearl moved backward, one with the crumb-laden carpeting.

Jules stayed long enough to watch Peter swallow a blood pressure pill, then took the dogs to his mother's house for babysitting a day earlier than anticipated. Olive, whom he'd awakened, joked about needing to buy them diapers, given the morning's high-fat diet. Jules reminded her that Marv the Airedale had once survived devouring a half-gallon of duck fat from a smoker. He was back at his car when he realized the strange background sound he'd heard had been snoring from Olive's bedroom. He spied a pickup in the alley; it belonged to John Dribnitz, a retired high school principal who'd apparently survived Divvy and Jules's class and waited twenty years to take revenge or simply forgot that Olive was related to one of them.

Olive was watching him take it all in through her screen door. Jules waved and she flapped her hand, then shut the door firmly. Everyone else on earth had a love life.

MOST OF THE people coming to Peter and Alice's wedding believed the adage that food is love, and shipped or brought gifts of copper and Paderno instead of silver candlesticks and picture frames. Their parents had gotten together and bought a six-burner Thermador, and their siblings had pooled money for a vent system. Alice staggered around for days, humming about BTUs and venting systems, no longer caring that both their cars had more than a hundred thousand miles, that they'd found their couch in an alley, that her annual historical society salary was $14,000. Jules had never seen her like this; if she could only make a third of the guests vanish, he thought she'd float off into pure bliss. Nothing, aside from a live, healthy baby, could have made her happier.

"What'd you get them?" asked Caroline. It was Friday, and she'd come to the Sacajawea to help hang the last pictures and move the last beds and chairs into the last guest rooms, where the paint was still tacky and aromatic. A half dozen fans worked overtime. Caroline was drinking coffee and standing by the front window in Jules's workroom while he wrestled with pliers and wire and tiny nails and antique frames. Halsey hadn't made his final picks until the night before, and some had taken Jules by surprise.

"A case of good pasta, a case of industrial-grade, dishwasher-approved wineglasses, a big Provencal bowl, and a wicker bassinet."

"Good lord," said Caroline.

"I owe them at least a hundred dinners," said Jules. "Plus some."

THE PHONE RANG off and on all day, though this was usually Dottie's problem. Just after lunch, while Caroline was perched on top of Fred's cherrywood cabinet and Jules was on the ladder handing her some of Muriel's finest items, an especially relentless barrage began, and no one answered.

Caroline was crouched on all fours, bracing delicate pottery with shims and small tacks. "I thought this was going to be a hotel," she grumbled. "Some poor sap thinks it should be run like one."

Jules, just inches from the primary object of his affection, handed her another tack. He was beginning to sink into a sort of predatory anticipation, a single-mindedness that he hadn't felt in years. "It's probably just the florist."

"Well, Christ," said Caroline. "I think I'm in charge of flowers. Can you try to get it?"

He tried and got a hang-up. Later, when they were trying to work the coffee machine in the bar, the phone started again and Caroline snapped it up. "Sacajawea," she said. "No. Do you want me—"

She made a face and hung up. "No, he didn't want me to get her."

"I found filters," said Jules.

"I think that was Leon Baden," said Caroline suddenly.

Jules looked up. "What did he say?"

"He said 'Dot.'"

Jules went back to the coffee machine, wishing this didn't make him feel unhappy. Caroline watched him. "But it was 'Dot' like he thought I might be her, not necessarily that she was the person he was calling for. And I'm sure there are all sorts of reasons for him to call here, all the time."

"I'm sure," said Jules.

AT SIX JULES showered and headed to the Baird to find Peter's brothers and shepherd them north. They were in the bar, flanking Caroline and Alice's New York friends. Jules told Hannes and Tom it was time to go and glowered until they left their stools and scurried off to find stray aunts.

Caroline looked embarrassed. "I picked up the flowers at the airport and stopped in to see if anyone needed a ride up."

Jules didn't believe her, despite the fact that she was drinking a soda. "That's why I stopped, too."

"They wanted a ride," she said defensively.

"And I could take Peach and Ginger, right?"

"Right," she said.

They eyed each other. Jules thought he could see just a hint of a smile as Hannes and Tom showed up, and he handed his keys to them. "You can follow us. That way you won't get lost in the next forty-eight hours."

They climbed into her aunt Cicely's minivan, which was packed with several thousand dollars' worth of wholesale roses, tulips, and lilacs. Jules liked it for the first two miles, then rolled down the window. Caroline gave him sidelong glances on the way north. "Are you going to give a toast?"

"I think I have to."

"Tonight and tomorrow?"

"Yeah."

"Do you like doing that?"

"No."

They drove another five miles. Hannes was caroming around behind them. Peach, a birdwatcher, was probably shrieking about goshawks on fence posts. "Are you going to sit down or hide in the greenhouse?" Jules asked.

"Both. I'm going to make sure I'm on hand for the first course and your comments on marriage."

Jules slumped a little and covered his face. "Caroline—"

She reached over and patted the back of his head. "I'm just joking." Then she laughed.

THE LONG WALL facing the plunge was lined with potted spruce and budding fruit trees, and the whole was wound with lights. At night the water steamed, making the lights shimmer and the tall, graceful windows of the main building and the conservatory glitter. Plenty of L.A. hoteliers would have killed for the effect, though it was marred by the presence of Merry, out cold in a lawn chair at the deep end, two empty margarita glasses on their sides underneath her, and her bottom bulging through the plastic straps of the chair. Somewhere in the background, Fred was still hammering.

Jules and Caroline didn't want to wake her, and unloaded the flowers into the greenhouse in near silence. Jules then walked slowly down the hall into the dining room, where he noticed that one of Halsey's pretty Japanese screens shielded the anxious pre-event crowd from the highlights of Muriel's collection. Everyone was shooting down their cocktails but the bride and groom, whom Jules expected were simply relieved that all the guests had arrived and events were finally under way. The families had known each other for a decade, which made it far more relaxing than the last wedding he'd attended, where a man from a family of Southern Baptists had married a woman from a family of strangely dogmatic Zen Buddhists. It had been ugly, scary enough for Jules to indulge once again in his escapist habit of sleeping with a bridesmaid. He hoped devoutly that no one thought to tell stories about this habit to Caroline.

The meal for twenty was insanely rich, an overflow of the desires no one could afford for a hundred. It began with fritters, some made of sweetbreads and others actually whole soft-shelled crabs. Jules watched as Peach and Ginger wrinkled their brows, probably wondering if they should pursue identification. Caroline, who slid into a chair far down the table, tucked in with a vengeance. Arnie followed this up with a fennel, arugula, and pear salad; then a bourride of sea bass, scallops, and spot prawns topped with chives, threads of lemon peel, and blobs of butter. The last salvo was an Alice favorite, tart tatin with big bowls of clotted cream.

There was too much wine but Jules was careful. Alice, possibly the only other sober person at the table, stared at him in curiosity when he passed up a glass of very good Sancerre. Jules got the toast out of the way between the fritters and the salad. He left the ribald bullshit to Peter's brothers and said simply that he loved both Peter and Alice, that they'd already made it through ten years with a sense of humor and he expected another forty out of them, despite their advanced age.

He slipped out while the tart was being served, snagging a bottle of the neglected Sancerre on his way, and found Caroline prepping delphinium. When she saw the wine she gave another happy, dirty laugh, a sound that filled him with an almost unbearable wave of anticipation.

She still intended to finish prepping the flowers, and Jules stripped leaves and wired rose stems, telling her stories about almost everyone who was coming to the wedding.

"I'm going to have trouble talking to anyone, knowing all this," said Caroline as they finished. She'd put all the broken, flawed roses into a huge bowl, and told him he needed them in his room. “Not that I’d do much talking anyway.”

“What will you do then?”

“Pretend like I know what I’m doing. Want to dance and avoid dancing. Do you know how to dance?”

They were passing the door to the dining room, a matter of feet from the stairs; Jules could hear Alice shrieking with laughter. “A little.”

“If I start looking wall-eyed, will you save me?”

“Absolutely.” He touched her shoulder to hustle her along, holding his breath until they were out of sight. Caroline turned and smiled.

“Are you sure you don’t want to go back to the party?”

He shook his head and opened the music room door. They’d barely made it inside when Fred marched up the stairs. He was followed a minute later by Merry, absurdly arrogant for someone who was staggering about in a bikini. She was carrying something that looked like hot cocoa when she passed the open French doors, and her backside was striped from her nap in the lawn chair. Jules swung both doors shut.

“I can’t believe she’s still walking.”

“She’d walk if you cut her head off,” said Caroline, going through a stack of botanicals, mostly watercolors of gallica roses and pear varieties from around 1830, more presents from Muriel to Halsey. A familiar rhythm began on the floor above them and she looked up.

“Figures,” said Caroline. “Great timing for the furnace to go out.”

“That’s not the furnace,” said Jules calmly. “It comes from Merry’s room.”

The old wood creaked in pain and Caroline gave up on the botanicals and looked for her glass of wine.

"Four times a day, according to Dottie."

"I would have thought he was drinking too much," said Caroline. She slumped on the couch, still looking for her glass. "It sounds a little repetitive."

"Quantity, not quality."

"Assholes unite," she muttered.

He found her glass and handed it to her, then pulled off his tie and coat and flopped at the other end of the couch. After a moment of thought he bent forward and took off his dress shoes. They reminded him of funerals and he wasn't feeling at all funereal.

"Still," she said. "They're happy, even if they don't deserve it."

"I wouldn't call them happy," said Jules. "They won't remember it. They've pickled too many nerve endings to really enjoy it."

"Mindlessness isn't always a bad thing," said Caroline. "It's good for awkward moments."

"I don't know," said Jules. "A little guilt and frustration and doubt add something. If you're completely mindless it wouldn't seem like such a prize to stop having to talk."

In the bar, people were shrieking with laughter. The thumps stopped upstairs a moment before what sounded like a tray's worth of glasses broke somewhere downstairs.

"How much guilt and frustration and doubt do you think a person needs?" asked Caroline, eyeing the floor.

"We have plenty," said Jules.

They were approximately a foot apart on the couch. Caroline flushed and stared at the pattern in the Persian carpet. Jules shut his eyes for a moment, drained his wine, and brought the glass down emphatically on the side table.

She jumped and stared at him.

"Got you to look at me," said Jules. He leaned forward, put one hand behind her head, and kissed her. Then he pulled back.

"I can't wait any longer," said Jules.

"Well," said Caroline, putting down her glass a little shakily. "Don't then."

"That's it?"

A big, slow grin started to cover her face. "That's it."

"I don't believe you," said Jules. "I can't believe it would be this easy. Prove it."

She climbed onto his lap.

11 *The Main Event*

Wedding Menu,
April 8,
Alice Wahlgren and Peter Johansen

salmon tartare, Belon oysters, spot prawns with remoulade
terrine de foie gras, prosciutto, rosette de Lyon
assorted cheeses

salade Niçoise

quail with grapes, standing rib roast, roast sea bass
with pommes Anna, peas and carrots, asparagus vinaigrette,
and celeri rave au jus

chocolate ganache with crème fraîche

JULES FINALLY LOOKED OUT THE WINDOW WHEN the sun had been up for several hours and the commotion downstairs had become a quiet din. He was naked, in the music room. “Lots and lots of people,” he said. “The linen van is here and the cake just arrived.”

Caroline was facedown on the mattress, the finest sight of his life. "Don't let them see you," she said. "We should try for a little more sleep."

"No rest for the wicked," said Jules, heading back to the bed.

AT NOON THEY took the back stairs. He dropped her off, drove home, and fell into bed like a happy dead man. At three he woke to find Peter staring down at him. "What have you done to yourself?"

"Nothing," said Jules, lurching out of bed. "I need fifteen minutes and I'm all yours."

"I'm getting married in a couple of hours, and you haven't answered the phone all day," said Peter. "All day."

"I didn't get a chance to look at the machine," said Jules, plunging down the stairs.

Peter was hot behind him. "I did. You turned the volume off."

"Oh," said Jules. "That was yesterday."

"Jesus. Have you been drinking since the party last night?"

"Nothing like it," said Jules, turning the shower on full blast. "What did you need me to do?"

"Tell me I'm doing the right thing."

"You're doing the right thing," said Jules. "Now piss off and get some coffee and I'll make it all up to you."

IN MONTANA IT was still possible to have a party for the sake of celebrating a marriage without having that marriage ceremony actually performed by a licensed holy man or justice of the peace. If you knew why you were there, and your guests knew why they were there, then the state was sanguine: file the appropriate affidavits declaring the fact and it was a done deal.

Peter had often pointed out this frontier hangover during the weeks he and Alice had wrangled over ministers, religion, and guest lists. They'd asked Jules and he'd said no. Then they'd asked Divvy, who'd said yes after Jules promised to help him "come up with something convincing." An hour before the ceremony, Divvy was already pacing around the pool, beginning to sweat despite perfect weather and a pleasant breeze.

One of Peter's brothers, both of them walking pharmacies, rustled up a beta blocker, and while Jules lectured the ushers through their paces the groom watched from the window above the pool to see if it had taken effect. "Divvy's slowing down," said Peter.

Jules plucked an olive from a bowl and looked out the window at the assembling crowd, pretty dresses and dark suits and fine moods making everyone someone else for a day. The weather was beautiful, seventy and sunny, and the ceremony would be along the plunge. He didn't see Caroline, and made himself stop looking at his watch. Divvy was still pacing, but he wondered if he wasn't slowing down a little too much.

"How much time now?" asked Peter.

"Forty minutes. In an hour life will be wonderful."

JULES MADE A perfect best man, beaming like a fiend at everyone, spreading a pure, goofy happiness. The ceremony was short and simple and to the point, just resonant enough so that most of the crowd mopped at their faces. A bee flew in and out of Alice and Edie's bouquets. Edie and Peter both wept. All the Aches cried; off to one side he watched

Caroline help Cicely with a handkerchief. The fathers both cried but the mothers were dry-eyed and beaming, having survived a ten-year courtship along with their children.

Hardened yuppies who'd been snide the evening before in the Baird bar sobbed like small children. Jules couldn't fathom why anyone would be sarcastic about the drive to love and marry. Pessimistic, yes, but why be mean-spirited about such a dire, vulnerable, starry-eyed undertaking? Why shoot arrows at humans who were at least momentarily showing their best side? There were exceptions, certainly, and he'd attended most of them. One college friend had married for money and another for breasts; both had earned the outcome and in the process clarified their characters. Jules hadn't bothered calling either since the weddings, but he'd heard the fools golfed together. His sister had married once for wildness and once for stability, only recently realizing she wanted the in-between. When he'd seen her in January, Louise had been dragging her current stockbroker to a psychotherapist and a hotel room on alternate Fridays, still not quite leaving behind the schedule.

But Alice and Peter had had some serious problems: old wrongs and disappointments and misunderstandings, alcohol, and the fact that their first flush of love, of real excitement, had almost been forgotten. That said, they had honorable intentions. They weren't terminally bored after a decade of nattering at each other about a host of common interests. They liked as well as loved; they trusted, had compassion, tried hard not to be pissy-minded and vengeful. They were still silly sometimes, and they had no second thoughts.

Jules might have cried if he hadn't been desperate to lift Caroline's dress. He wasn't in the least nostalgic, and flung himself into the rounds of kisses and hugs and shrieks of happiness.

He circled as she finished her first glass of champagne, then broke into the conversation she was having with Peter's brother Tommy and said he needed her help with something.

He felt better after a few minutes in the linen closet. An hour later, while people gobbled appetizers, they parked the elevator in the basement. Caroline, who'd talked the night before about wanting privacy, wanting to have a secret for even a few weeks, was beginning to resign herself to being caught in the first twenty-four hours.

Caroline's aunt Cicely took Jules's arm when he came back upstairs, asking him to hold her glass while she filled a plate with shrimp and oysters. "I stopped to see Caroline early this morning," she said. "Had some earrings for her to wear. And she wasn't *there*."

"Oh," said Jules. What else could he say?

"I made an educated guess, but that person didn't seem to be home either."

This time he didn't bother saying anything. She ate three shrimp fast.

"Halsey said you never left last night. He didn't know about my niece. What do you have to say for yourself?"

"I'm happy," said Jules. "Happy, happy, happy. Is that good enough?"

"That's fine," said Cicely. "That's progress."

SIMON HAD VOLUNTEERED to be the wedding photographer, asking Alice rhetorically how a wedding could possibly be more difficult than a fashion shoot. His own family in Sydney was small and rarely seen, and most parties he'd been to in the past decade were homogeneous—no old people, no children, no poor people, no fat people, no churchgoers, no women in comfortable shoes and funny hats, no humans who hadn't somehow been paid to be abused. This wedding was different. As people milled in and out of his frames he came unstrung and began to resemble a stubby helicopter, striving for polite language with Peach and Ginger and Peter's oblivious grandmother, trying to avoid direct eye contact with the jolly but uncomfortable fathers-in-law. The mothers-in-law kept retreating to the bar area together for vodka refills, giggling in sheer relief. They'd always gotten along too well.

Simon tried to use Jules as a go-between. "If you don't get that old biddy in line for me"—Peach kept wandering after Halsey—"I'll tell your pretty lady cop about the two girls in Greece."

Simon was the only person who'd noticed. "She already knows."

"Bullshit."

"Alice told her. You've got to give these people time to eat or it's going to get ugly."

Simon turned pinker. "I'll show you bloody cock-sucking ugly."

Jules sighed and walked slowly toward the herd of Wahlgrens and Johansens. Too many Swedes, unstrung with happiness by a fine ritual and alcohol and the beginning of another spring. "Against the fence, all of you. Now."

PEOPLE ATE TOO much, once again. Even the cake was good, and Arnie never once lost his temper.

Late in the evening, Jules and Halsey ran into each other in the kitchen, both of them trolling for stray oysters. "You haven't seen Dottie, have you?" asked Halsey.

"No," said Jules. "I haven't seen Arnie lately either."

"It's been my experience that when you can't find Dottie easily, she doesn't want to be found," said Halsey.

"Mine, too."

"Not only that, but she might not be amused if we persevered."

"It's possible."

"I'd like her to be happy."

Jules nodded. He'd just noticed that the bathroom door was shut.

"It's nothing I can pretend to do anymore."

Jules nodded again, but slowly. Halsey smiled.

"I feel some satisfaction with having gotten away with one last good secret. I may be Dottie's *only* secret, but it's been years."

"Jesus," said Jules. "I had no idea."

"Come upstairs for a minute," said Halsey. "I'd like to give you my present for Alice and Peter. I'd like you to hang it in their house, just have it there for a surprise."

In his room, Halsey knelt by his bedstead, slid out a drawer, and pulled out a large portfolio.

Jules had a funny look on his face. "You're thinking 'what if the old fuck died and we had no idea?'" said Halsey. "Dottie knows all my hiding places."

"She has some of her own," said Jules. "I'm afraid they turned up during the electrical fire."

Halsey shook his head. "I wanted her to keep things safe."

"Why not tell me?"

Halsey shrugged. When the answer hit Jules he flushed. Halsey stood up stiffly and waved his hand back and forth. "Please don't be upset," he said. "I trust Dottie. No one else, not entirely. I'm sorry."

Jules rubbed his head.

"The last time I poked around your room I noticed you were taking certain safeguards as well," said Halsey. "There's a certain pattern to what you've been putting away and leaving out."

Jules smiled and nodded to the large, empty frame. "You should get rid of that. It's turning you into an asshole."

Halsey smiled. "Fifty years later? It's nothing for anyone else to look at today. It's been with me for all five wives."

"Couldn't you just put a stone in your pocket?"

"Every woman who came to my room asked about why I had it, and if they still climbed in bed after the explanation I considered them forewarned."

He flipped open the folder, pulled out an envelope, and reached inside. "I think this one. Would they like it?"

It was a Delacroix watercolor, a garden in Tangier circa 1832, one of the most beautiful things Jules had ever seen. "Of course they'd like it," said Jules. "But maybe you should think it over."

"I have," said Halsey.

"They're not going to know how to thank you."

"I've thought it over," Halsey repeated. He nodded toward the window, and Jules looked out to see Merry pulling Fred toward the small pool at the back of the hotel. She'd been in already, and her pink cocktail dress was wet.

Fred ripped his hand free and took a step backward. Merry rocked on her heels.

"Sissy shit," she said sweetly.

Halsey walked out of the room.

JULES DANCED FOR what felt like hours, with Alice, Peter's grandmother, the great-aunts and mothers and old college friends, but mostly with Caroline. A modified tango led them upstairs at midnight, and afterward Caroline dozed and Jules wandered around the room, looking at the ancient statues, the four-hundred-year-old indigos and corals of the botanicals, the Moran landscapes. Nothing was prettier than the view out the window on a night with such a huge moon, clouds whirling over the silhouette of the Absarokas. It was his favorite view in his favorite place on earth.

He looked at the Moran sketches again, then at the sweep of low hills beyond the river, leading up to the Absarokas. Not many artists had painted a nighttime like this, almost no one besides Turner, but Jules now remembered the same dark outline. He started to trace the whole mess back, looking for the moment when everyone at the Sacajawea had stopped even pretending to like each other. He dated it from the arrival of Muriel's things and the argument over the double-sided frame, one side of which had this same basic line, tricked out with a curtain, dark, thick colors and silly animals. Both sides were questionable works no one would normally have given a rat's ass about. The person who'd cared the most about both at the time had been Dottie, who also happened to be the person who liked Merry the least. Merry had been in the biggest hurry to get rid of the thing. Maybe she already had.

He crouched down next to Caroline. "Let's go down and say good night to people, get a last glass of wine."

She moaned.

"I'll carry you," said Jules fondly.

"That would be wonderful."

"After we say good night I'll get you a little cake, and then we'll go down to the basement."

"But we're so comfortable here."

"No," he said, "not that. I want to look at something."

Alice and Peter were inching for the door, surrounded by

at least fifty diehards, all of them oblivious to the sound of Caroline's heels clicking down the basement stairs.

The big crate was in the center of the wine cellar. Half an hour later they were crouched near it, surrounded by a pocketknife, a wet soapy cloth, and two flashlights. Jules had unscrewed the crate by hand to avoid noise and now the frame was unwrapped, with the blobby Sunday school landscape facing up. Jules was going over it, inch by inch, with a flashlight.

When he picked up the pocketknife Caroline was appalled. He scraped off the paw a small lion, turning it into pile of powdery acrylic paint. Then he held the wet rag to a two-inch-square section of the bottom corner, softening the papier-mache and wiping away goop. When he stopped coming away with goop they saw a polished background, dark and mottled green, rather than bare canvas.

"What's that?" asked Caroline.

"Oil paint and varnish."

"What is it?"

"I'm not sure," said Jules. "But someone cared enough about it to make it look different."

12 *Springing Eternal*

BLUE DEER BULLETIN

SHERIFF'S REPORT, WEEK OF APRIL 3–9

April 3—A man who was intoxicated sat on a curb and a car ran over his feet. An officer took him to the hospital.

April 4—Several area mailboxes were reported vaporized.

April 6—Complaints were received from several neighbors about noisy, unsupervised children. Officers investigated to discover a birthday party in progress.

April 7—Officers responded to a report of a gas leak and took an elderly couple in for a physical evaluation.

A teacher called from the middle school to say he'd discovered some suspicious chemicals hidden in the boys' bathroom.

April 8—Several stolen shopping carts were discovered in the lagoon.

A report was received of an individual removing license plates from a vehicle parked on the street and placing them on an unlicensed vehicle. An officer determined that the individual owned both cars.

April 9—A Blue Deer citizen stopped at the

station to present officers with a log of his neighbor's dog's barking habits. Officers followed up with the dog's owner, who had to admit the dog barked a lot.

SPRING SPRUNG ETERNAL: PEEPING TOM SEASON, usually the May special following April's suicide season, had arrived several weeks early. Southwestern Montana was cluttered with men beset by the urge to expose themselves to the first warm nighttime breeze that would have them. Most stuck to Bozeman, which had a college and thus a higher rate of errancy and testosterone, but that Monday after the wedding, Jonathan informed Jules that Blue Deer had two distinct operatives with very different m.o.s. One liked trees, even trees without leaves, wore conveniently elasticized shorts, and was young and limber; the other was entirely naked under a duster or a raincoat, preferred back porches, and at least two women claimed both his pubic hair and a fringe around his pate were gray.

"Of course," said Jonathan, "he could have dyed it."

There was no use joking with Jonathan about dye jobs or flashers, especially given the attentions of Lucretia Frame; soon he'd come up with a conspiracy theory to apply to everyone. He'd been morose and pale for days.

"What are you up to tomorrow?"

"Taking Alan around to the schools."

Jules liked dogs, but wasn't fond of this one's job. Alan, a low-key German shepherd, was a drug dog, on loan from Gallatin County, that traveled more than most vacuum-cleaner salesmen. The mayor loved his semiannual visits and always arranged for a reporter and photographer to travel along; he liked Jonathan because Jonathan was gung ho and photogenic.

"Don't look too hard, Jonathan."

"What do you mean?"

"Prompt Alan for meth, but try not to bother with joints."

"A drug's a drug," said Jonathan, with great seriousness. "And a dog's a dog."

Jules headed to the kitchen for another cup of coffee and stared at the calendar, weighing retirement dates.

ON MONDAY AFTERNOON, down by the Paris boat access, an old man out for a walk with his fat collie found some neatly folded clothes on a river boulder, with an empty wallet tucked into the left shoe and a tie in the right. The wallet and the shoes both had Neiman Marcus labels, and a few calls determined the wallet, old but good, could only have been sold in one of the original Texas stores. The probable suicide they'd pulled out of the river the previous Wednesday now had a likely entry point and state of origin, but the world was filled with five-foot, eleven inch men with brown hair. This one happened to have a birthmark and a burn mark in funny places, but neither would be helpful to the average newspaper reader.

"But how did he get to Paris?" said Wesley. "Where's his car?"

"He was pretty well groomed for a hitchhiker," conceded Jules. "But that only means he might not have had trouble with a ride."

They checked Greyhound and asked at the local hotels, using a photo of the dead man as judiciously as possible. A waitress at the Baird thought she recognized him as a man who'd sat at the bar for an hour nursing a single soda a week or so earlier, waiting for someone who'd never shown up. She couldn't remember the night or anything else about him—his behavior had been as unmemorable as his build.

Evidently the disappointment of being stood up had been enough to make the man hitchhike twenty miles south and wade into a cold river naked, which didn't quite make sense. Jules and Harvey and Wesley made a quick trip back to the Paris boat launch and scoured the area near the boulder and downriver for credit cards or other scraps of ID.

"A man with clothes that nice would have had plenty of stuff in his wallet," said Wesley. "Someone will turn something in."

Jules didn't think so. If someone wanted to stay lost for eternity, there were all sorts of ways of going about it. He imagined the dead man slicing the wallet's contents and tossing them into a Dumpster, letting a handful of credit and personal history blow out a car window while a driver speeded on, oblivious to where his ride really wanted to go.

"Why'd he bother keeping the wallet?" asked Wesley.

Jules wanted done with the matter. Wesley was a little too businesslike, a little too in the here and now. At least 90 percent of Jules's mind was stuck in or on Caroline, and he wanted it to stay there. "Maybe he wanted the Salvation Army to have it," he said. "Maybe you should stop expecting people who are crazed enough to kill themselves to make sense."

FOR A FULL thirty-six hours Jules didn't talk to anyone affiliated with the Sacajawea. He'd hoped for longer, but on Monday Dottie walked into the station, a first. Did Jules know if Fred ever sold Leon a bronze sculpture? Halsey couldn't find it and he wanted to mount it on the base of the stairs, on the newel.

"I don't remember seeing one, but you'd have to ask Fred. Maybe I didn't know what it was for. What is it of?"

"Some fake creature, and Fred can't remember. He barely comes down the stairs anymore."

"Was it a griffin?"

"What's a griffin?"

"Half bird, half lion," said Jules. "Ask Merry about it."

She snorted. "The last time I asked her where something was she started screaming that I thought she was a thief."

"Well, you do think she's a thief. I think she's a thief."

Dottie smiled. Grace was watching them, undoubtedly imagining the worst. "The night of the fire I found some things in your room," said Jules.

He'd blindsided her. "Say something," said Jules.

"Halsey gave me some of those things for safekeeping. He told me you'd been asking around. That's how this sculpture came up."

"What's 'some' mean?"

"None of your business," said Dottie. "Jules, I love that man dearly. Don't sweat the small stuff."

"Drop it," said Jules. "Where did Halsey have this object tucked away?"

"In his room, unlocked as usual."

"So why nail Fred with it?"

"Fred might have found it while he was renovating, and assumed it was worthless and went with everything else."

"That would have been before Fred was drinking, back when he would have remembered. Pre-Tinkerbell."

"Jules, Jules, Jules." She sighed to buy time. "At first Fred said he put everything he found in the closet in the hall outside your room and Halsey's. Then he changed his tune and said he couldn't remember."

"Huh," said Jules. "Was it about ten inches high? Looked like a classical copy?"

"Yes."

"It was in Merry's room the night of the fire, along with some other stuff that had been in the music room."

"Damn," said Dottie. "I hope it's still there. I'll try to look before she gets back from Leon's."

"What's the big deal?"

"It's an early Rodin."

"Oh, for Christ's sake," said Jules. "You all make me sick."

"If it's gone, can you find out on the q.t. if Leon has it?"

"Why would you use a Rodin for a newel? Why would Fred have even hauled a Rodin to Leon?"

"Back when you started in February, Leon had a friend who was good for mid-priced stuff."

"Who?"

"Bob Frame, the guy who rented the trailer. He sold to galleries over the internet, same as you but for a profit."

The phone had been ringing for some time, and Grace was making rude gestures in his direction. "Ask Leon yourself."

"Oh, I can't talk to Leon," said Dottie. "I used to work for him, remember?"

AT THE CLYDE City high school, Alan the drug dog found two cow vaccine syringes. Jonathan was disconsolate, insisting they actually contained heroin even after two separate veterinarians had reassured him and the parents had threatened a lawsuit for harassment.

"Drop it, Jonathan," said Jules. "Take the poor mutt home. You can't expect him to split hairs."

"We still have to go to Gardiner."

"Take him tomorrow. I don't think they'll care if you cancel."

"I'll care," said Jonathan, chin trembling.

Jules drummed his pencil on his thigh. "Fine. On your way down or back, would you mind stopping at Leon Baden's? You can let Alan out of the car there and give him some fresh air, and you can ask Leon whether Fred Bottomore or Merry Maier ever sold him a bronze sculpture. They can't remember up at the Sacajawea, and they can't find it."

Jonathan wrinkled his smooth, untouched forehead. "Run that by me again?"

"A small statue of a funny animal with a bird head."

Jonathan looked worried. Jules wrote it down.

LATE THAT AFTERNOON, Jules was the only one at the station. It was a quiet day, and he'd crept down the hall, muttering about records but actually to nap in the battered kitchen La-Z-Boy Ed had retrieved from an alley. He'd been asleep for ten minutes when Grace slammed the door open.

"You have a call."

"Take a message."

"No."

Jules gritted his teeth on the way down the hall. "Are you closing in on retirement age?"

"Maybe," said Grace. "Maybe not."

He managed to sound cheerful on the phone. "My name's Jules Clement. Can I help you?"

"I don't know," said a man. "My name is Moss Jackson. I'm a detective with the Seattle Police Department and I'm calling about a Mr. P. M. Altschuler."

Jules waited, wondering if Moss as a name was some sort of Seattle weather joke.

"Do you know a Mr. P. M. Altschuler?" asked Moss Jackson.

Did he?

"Mr. Altschuler apparently traveled to Montana at your request," said Jackson. "We found a fax in his trash showing directions with your name on it."

"The appraiser," said Jules suddenly. "Sorry. I had trouble placing the name. What happened to him?"

"We don't know."

"What do you mean?"

"He apparently never returned to his office or his apartment, and his parents filed a missing persons report last Friday. We got down to his trash yesterday, and that's why I'm taking up your time. Your name featured prominently on his notepad."

"He left here a week ago," said Jules. "Showed up Saturday afternoon and drove off into the sunset the next morning."

"Seemed like a normal human being?"

"More or less," said Jules. "I can't say I liked him, but I did get the impression that he was turning the job into a vacation. The client paid him in cash. Maybe he headed for the Dakotas. Maybe he ran away."

"Nothing to run away from," said the cop in Seattle. "No wife, no money problems we can discover."

"Everyone has something worth running from," said Jules. "Especially someone in his line of work."

"Well," said Jackson. "Most of the time I'd agree with you, but right now the most suspicious thing about Mr. Altschuler, beyond the fact that we can't find him, is that he went to Montana to talk to a cop about art. Have you had a theft out there?"

"Oh no," said Jules. "It's just some work I do part-time. A mutual friend recommended Altschuler, so I called him. This has nothing to do with my day job."

"Oh," said Jackson, sounding confused. "Since it is your day job, would you mind digging into Mr. Altschuler's vacation? Or does someone else deal with missing persons?"

"We're not big on separate departments," said Jules. "I'll ask around." But not right now, he thought, standing up and slamming his chair under the desk. It was 4:55 and time to run, especially now that he had something to run for. He picked up a change of clothes at home and walked through alleys until he reached Caroline's back porch. She was already home, grinning at him through the kitchen window.

ALL WEEK JULES dodged wedding guests, the two dozen or so people who'd stayed for a real holiday and were just hitting their stride. They wanted everyone to get together every night, go everywhere together. Alice and Peter hid on Sunday and Monday night, then rallied. Jules steered clear of the fray for two more days, claiming to be tired and behind at work. Caroline used roughly the same excuse, and neither of them was lying.

On the first two nights after the wedding he walked to Caroline's house and found her waiting. On the third night he picked her up and brought her home. On the fourth night they both went to a party at Peter and Alice's for the out-of-towners, and he found it so intolerable to pretend that he and Caroline were merely friends and coworkers that they ended up together on a table in the basement, ostensibly in search of a bottle of wine. On the fifth night they called a truce, and Jules was so exhausted that he slept without moving for ten hours. On the sixth night he was sitting on the edge of his bed at eleven o'clock, wrestling with questions of character and obsession, when she appeared in the doorway. And on the seventh night, the final Saturday hurrah for most of the vacationers at Blue Deer's only good restaurant, everyone, Jules and Caroline included, drank enough wine to not notice much at all.

After that they would go back and forth, house to house, with the tacit agreement that there was no point to talking about things in a daylight sense until they'd gotten the night out of their systems. Jules was in a state of mindless rut, and though at night this made him the happiest hamster on the planet, he spent the days making absent-minded errors, while Caroline fell asleep at her desk.

No one noticed that anything was going on because they only seemed a little quieter and crankier than usual.

ON THE TUESDAY after Moss Jackson's call, Jules snuck away for lunch. When he wandered back in with a dopey expression and mussed hair, Jonathan and Alan the drug dog nearly knocked him to the floor. Jonathan was breathless, but Alan looked vaguely embarrassed.

"Alan went wild down at the Bachelor," said Jonathan. "Just wild."

"What do you mean?"

"He went nuts where that trailer used to be, and he went nuts again by the back door."

"Was Leon there?"

"Nah. Some lady was, so I asked her the question you gave me about the statue. That was before Alan went nuts."

"Was she a tall, bumpy-looking blonde? Fortyish?"

"She said her name was Merry," said Jonathan, confused. "Maybe thirty."

Jules whacked his head. Dottie, who'd used her favorite phrase, "on the q.t.," was going to eviscerate him. "What did she say?"

"She was very rude, but she said she'd ask Leon."

"How'd she act when the dog went nuts?"

"I don't know. She'd already closed the door by then, and she wouldn't open up again."

"Do you think she noticed Alan's behavior?"

"I dunno," said Jonathan. "Not too many windows in that building. It would make a perfect meth factory."

"Slow down, big boy," said Jules.

"Alan was really crazy. Really, really crazy."

"Did you check him on the flammable samples?"

Jonathan looked stricken. "No. I was so surprised."

"Okay, Jonathan. Before you return Alan, we'll pay a visit to Leon's place."

"This afternoon?"

"Sure," said Jules. "This afternoon."

"THIS IS A waste of our time," said Harvey. "I've said it before: you can't prove he heard her."

"I'm not trying to prove that anymore. I'm not trying to prove anything," said Jules. "We're just double-checking on this very expensive dog."

Jonathan and Alan were in the backseat, both in a fine mood. A dozen scent samples were in the trunk, a doggy maze.

"Humph," said Harvey.

"Married people do kill each other every day in America," said Jules. "Leon was a very possessive man. Caroline heard a rumor that the guy who lived in the trailer had an affair with Leon's wife, and now they're both gone. That kind of coincidence makes me feel squirrelly."

"You've been squirrelly all week," muttered Harvey.

Jules actually laughed.

"I'm sure it's a meth factory," said Jonathan. Jonathan and

Wesley had both gone to a meth task force meeting, and since then Jonathan had imagined meth labs in every garage in town. This had replaced his previous fixation on grow lights: Jonathan didn't believe in innocent winter gardeners.

"Nah," said Jules. "The man refinishes furniture. He's got plenty of excuses for having solvents. He just doesn't have an excuse for pouring solvents over a trailer and lighting it."

"I get the drift," said Harvey. "You can't get him for killing his wife, you sure as hell are going to get him for something else."

"That's right," said Jules, beaming. "If it works on mobsters, it can work on Leon."

Merry's car was parked behind the bar again, with a kayak strapped to the roof, and after Alan had once again done his job and foamed at the mouth over the scent of solvents (he reacted as well to a spot on the ground near the foundation of Leon's A-frame), Jules walked over to say hello.

This time she made no pretense of working, and barely deigned to look up from her book. "Where's Leon off to?" he asked.

"A big auction in Denver."

"When's he get back?"

"Sometime today."

Jules swiveled his head to catch the book title: *Better Body, Better Soul.* "I got a call from a cop in Seattle who says Mr. Altschuler still isn't home. He wants to know if any of us heard anything about the man taking an extended trip."

Merry glared at Jules. "I barely talked to him."

"You talked to him more than anyone else. He didn't mention anything to you about a vacation?"

"He tried to get into my pants that night. Maybe he was already in runaway mode."

"What did he say?"

"When I said no?"

"In general," said Jules. "At any point. Did he say 'I'm a rich man and I've embezzled two million dollars and I'm headed for Toronto, come along'?"

She stared. "What do you mean? Are you trying to say he wouldn't have found me attractive?"

He hated her, but he'd begun to think that her stupidity stemmed from self-absorption rather than ill will. Or maybe it was a combination of both. The only time he'd dealt with such a person before had been when he'd had an affair with an actress in New York for two long months, a very pretty woman who'd raged against that large part of the world that hadn't yet noticed her existence. Ten years later some of the moviegoing population had noticed, but he doubted she'd pulled her head out of her own lovely ass.

"Did he say anything that might have had anything to do with not going back to Seattle?"

"No."

Her face was impassive. Closer up, she smelled sour. Her blond kinky hair had a rat's nest on one side, her lips were chapped, and one eye was bloodshot. Just looking at her made Jules want an aspirin. He wandered across the room toward the door of Leon's shop.

"What do you think you're doing?"

"It's a store, and it's open. I'm looking."

She was right behind him, close enough to make him uncomfortable. "Hey, there's the big crate," said Jules. He looked around the room and focused on the top of Leon's desk. "He's messy, isn't he?"

"Get out of here."

He ignored her and pushed the papers back and forth,

then slid a drawer open. Inside he saw a pile of Polaroids, half of them ones he'd taken himself. He had a glimpse of the top of the head of an Etruscan woman before she grabbed his arm and slammed the door shut.

"Now go away."

"Did you actually graduate from nursery school?" asked Jules. "Ask Leon to call, all right?"

She glowered. Jules smiled. "You going kayaking after work?"

"That would be one reason to have a kayak on my car," she snapped.

"Did you ever take Fred in that thing?"

"Fred has enough trouble in a boat."

"Well," said Jules. "Don't drown. I'd have a problem fishing you out." She threw the book.

JULES AND ED finally cornered Leon that evening. It was not a friendly conversation. "You've already brutalized me about my wife's death," said Leon. "I told you I didn't hear her. Imagine what the guilt is doing to me. Imagine what it's like, wondering if she'd be alive if I'd answered the phone."

"You did answer the phone," said Jules stubbornly. "Then you hung it up again. You heard it ring, though you say you couldn't hear her."

"I want my lawyer."

"Call one," said Jules. "Go for it. But I'm not here to argue about whether or not you heard Anne. I'm here to ask how well the two of you knew your neighbors."

"Neighbors?" said Leon.

"The people in the trailer," said Jules. "Bob and Lucretia Frame."

"Not well," said Leon. "You remember how fruity she

was when the place burned down. Didn't you guys take her up to Warm Springs?"

"We did," said Jules. "And now she's out."

"What, you got her on medication or something?" asked Leon.

"No," said Jules. He had no intention of telling Leon they couldn't catch her. "It's a little hard to know what to make of her, but now we've had independent confirmation that Bob Frame and your wife knew each other quite well."

He watched Leon, but nothing moved on the man's face. "I imagine you knew that."

"No," said Leon, still expressionless.

"I've also heard from several sources that Bob Frame helped you find buyers for some of your stuff, especially the nicer stuff you got from the Sacajawea. He ran a little mail-order business and you guys did a fair amount of work together."

"So?" said Leon.

"You hadn't mentioned it."

"I didn't tell you what time I took a dump this morning either, did I?"

"Nope," said Jules. "But I'm happy to hear you're regular. Maybe you didn't want to bring it up because of some tax problem, something like that. The thing is, we now have evidence that someone burned the trailer down."

"The trailer was an accident."

"No it wasn't," said Jules. "Someone soaked the thing in some sort of solvent. We just didn't pick up on it the first time around."

"Talk to his crazy wife. I didn't even have insurance on that piece of crap."

"I'm not saying you were thinking straight. The guy was bopping your wife."

Leon was breathing heavily. “I forgave my wife. That’s why I want to pay to cremate her and have her at peace.”

“That’s great,” said Jules. “Very generous of you. Especially since we already found the wood under her nails.”

Leon hopped up and down three times. Jules knew from past experience that he desperately wanted to start hitting someone. “I want my lawyer.”

“Call someone. I already suggested it.” Jules looked around. “Gotten anything from the Sacajawea lately?”

Leon glowered at him. “Seriously,” said Jules.

“Some crappy chairs and a coupla paintings.”

“What’d the paintings look like?”

“They’re in a crate. I’m just holding them for now.”

“Dottie’s asking about some little bronze monster with wings and claws. Did Fred ever give you something like that to sell?”

Leon’s eyes darted about; he looked like a crazed iguana. “What’s that supposed to mean? No, he didn’t give me a fucking bronze sculpture. He didn’t give me anything he shouldn’t have given me. No one has.”

“Not even your bartender?”

Leon sputtered. Jules couldn’t tell if he was appalled or enraged.

“What’s the split again?”

“Forty-sixty and none of your goddamn business anyway.”

“How you doing on the deal?”

“It’s worth it. Not much more. Now get out of here. I don’t feel like small talk.”

Ed was already at the door. “Why do you think Bob Frame left?” asked Jules.

“I’ll say it again,” said Leon heavily. “Talk to his crazy wife. Anyone would have run away from her.”

"Where was Frame from?"

"South Carolina, I think. Call him and ask him. Get out of here."

"If you guys were on good terms and he left before you burned down his place, why didn't he take his computer? We found some plastic blobs that used to be an Apple in the shell of the trailer."

"Get the fuck out of here, you prick!" screamed Leon.

"Hey," said Jules, as Ed pulled him out. "At least I've got one."

JULES DIDN'T FOLLOW up on the wayward Mr. Altschuler until Wednesday, before the staff meeting and after Moss Jackson had left two more messages. This time Wesley, coming off the night shift, had forgotten the doughnuts, so there was a slight delay. Jules called the Sack, told Dottie that Leon categorically denied ever receiving a bronze from Fred or anyone else, and asked if they'd heard from P. M. Altschuler. No, they hadn't, and no, the man hadn't mentioned specific travel plans other than alluding to bullshit clients in faraway places. He'd said he'd call back in a week, and the week was up. Really, Jules should not torment himself over Halsey's wasted thousands. Did he want to ask Merry about the prick?

"I already had that honor," said Jules.

"She drank so much last night she got sick," said Dottie. "I'm trying to talk Halsey into putting her away."

Jules was surprised she hadn't said "putting her down."

"Is Halsey around?"

"Nope. He's seeing his lawyer."

Dottie was actually speaking in a melody, coming up with a little singsong; her good mood was positively indecent, and likely based on indecency as well as Merry's downward spiral. Dottie was setting a record with Arnie, over a week, and in close quarters at that.

"How about Fred?"

She whispered into the phone. "He's doing a little better."

"Will you have him call?"

"He's right here, having coffee. Hang on."

Jules practically dropped the phone in shock. Fred hadn't seen 8:00 a.m. in weeks, and it took him a minute to explain and to phrase a question. "Did you get a chance to talk to Altschuler later, or in the bar at all?"

"You're saying he's gone?"

"I only know that people expected him back, and his parents were worried enough to pester the Seattle police."

"What does that mean?" Fred's voice had an edge, and Jules decided he wasn't in such good shape after all.

"I don't know, and I'm glad I don't have to know. He probably ran away. Maybe he went off driving, had an accident, and landed in a gully. Maybe he got too friendly in a bar."

Fred didn't say anything. "I asked Merry yesterday. I gather she's under the weather."

"Don't pretend to be sympathetic," snapped Fred.

"I'm not sympathetic," said Jules icily. "I'm trying to speak politely."

"As opposed to saying what you really want to say?"

"Stop it, Fred."

"Really. Speak frankly."

"I gather that vicious, small-minded slut you've been wasting your time on got so puking drunk last night that she can't drag her sorry ass downstairs. And she probably tells you it's your fault."

"Fuck you!" yelled Fred.

"Fuck you!" yelled Jules.

Jules slammed the phone down, then slammed it again in a surge of self-hatred. He turned to see Grace and all the deputies watching him, Caroline, Jonathan, Ed, Harvey, and Wesley ready in a semicircle for the monthly bullshit called a meeting, most of them too shocked to wipe the powdered sugar from their mouths.

"I'm thinking of giving notice soon," he said.

Caroline, the only one who'd really known, watched him gravely.

"You should all think about what you'll want to do. Maybe someone actually wants this job."

JONATHAN HAD GOTTEN tears in his eyes, and after the meeting Jules took him out on the next call, which ended up involving an ambulance. A woman had phoned, hysterical, to say that her wealthy rancher husband had fired his overseer, then set off to check some fence on horseback and disappeared.

"How long has he been gone?" Grace had asked.

"He never misses his lunch," said the woman. "Never."

In the man's living room, while his wife ranted about her husband's stupidity and they tried to figure out where to begin looking, Jules stared at the fine etchings and paintings, the burled walnut bookshelves loaded with first editions and small sculptures.

It turned out that the man was a retired cable station magnate, and might not have known where to look for the fence. They found him half a mile from the house, flat on his back, sobbing, the horse grazing nearby. Once he saw them he heaved himself up onto tiny feet, and they led him home. Jules told the man a tactful story about Charles Remington, who'd also been too fat to get on a horse. "I think I had a heart attack," the rich man said. "I thought it would be better not to move, but I thought I'd die out here."

He was very nice, but immense for a man who was only five-foot-eight or so, well over two-fifty; he had no business inflicting himself upon a horse. He insisted on giving them a piece of his wife's freshly baked apple tart, and while Jules ate he looked around the kitchen. "Those cabinets are wonderful," he said. "Did Fred Bottomore do those for you?"

"Oh yes," said the fat man. "We want him to do more work but he's been tied up with a hotel restoration."

Jules nodded.

"The Sacajawea," said the woman. "We can't wait to see the place when it opens. I think there was some sort of wedding there last weekend, so they must be getting close."

"They must," said Jules. "Did Fred sell you those nice prints in the hall?"

"The Australian animals? Those came from a man named Frame who Fred suggested. Do you collect?" she asked politely.

"I aspire to collect," said Jules. "How'd you hear about Fred to begin with?"

The woman turned away abruptly, and her large husband gave her a sidelong look of fear. "A woman named Dottie Cope," he said. "An old friend. I believe she and Fred are quite close."

It was no great mystery: everyone was stealing from Halsey. Jules was beginning to wonder if he was missing a very big boat.

"I had a dream I fell," said Jonathan in the car, on their way back to town.

"I didn't know you rode," said Jules.

"I don't," said Jonathan. "I fell off a mountain, not a horse. I died."

"Oh."

"It was awful."

"What have you been reading lately?"

"Nothing about falling," said Jonathan sullenly. "Something by a guy named Grass, called *The Tin Drum*. It's about a little kid."

Jules wasn't sure if Jonathan's girlfriend should be shot or applauded. But it wasn't a good thing to have death dreams on a nearly constant basis.

"When I fell, I was heading for a big rock, and it opened and swallowed me."

Jules felt his neck prickle. "That's it," he said. "Time for comedy or adventure. Let's stop at the bookstore. We'll pick up *The Ginger Man,* or maybe an Ian Fleming."

"While we're on duty?"

They sure as hell weren't going to spend off-duty hours together. "Yep," said Jules. "My treat."

BACK IN TOWN, he checked at the Baird hotel, and discovered that Mr. Altschuler had actually stayed two nights, Friday, March 31, and Saturday, April 1. No one at the desk remembered seeing him past check-in on Friday. On Saturday he'd eaten in the dining room and flirted memorably with both waitresses. He was one of only four customers that night. Blue Deer in the off-season was a heartbreaker for restaurateurs.

But no one had seen him leave or asked where he was going next. He'd actually checked out Saturday night, saying he intended to leave early Sunday morning. One guest, Ambrose, had used the room since. Jules asked to see it anyway.

On one of the two memo pads he found the indentation of Ambrose's distinctive scribble, New York phone numbers and garbled directions to the Sacajawea. On the other he found nothing but the indentation of the word *Paris*. An art dealer's word, like a priest scribbling "Rome" or Jules writing "gun."

He called Moss Jackson in Seattle at the end of the day, and Jackson admitted that Altschuler's rental car had turned up in northern Utah that morning. "See," Jules said to Jackson. "The guy left. He isn't my problem. I have other problems and I bet you're not interested. I have dead men all over the place, but none of them is your guy."

"Could you please look into it one more time?" said Jackson. "His parents are breathing down my neck. He's an only child, a rich kid from Maryland. They don't have a clue about his personal life. They don't claim he had bad habits, no habits at all."

Jules had assumed Altschuler was rich, but Maryland was surprising. He'd have guessed Oklahoma, St. Louis. "Everybody's got a wrinkle somewhere," he said. The comment was becoming a convention of their conversations, a way of digging. "Parents don't know about wrinkles."

"You met the man," grumbled Jackson. "What did you think?"

"The man I met was so boring I was shocked. Have you dug up anything?"

"Maybe a little kinkiness. Just a whisper from a friend in college who hadn't kept up."

"What kind of whisper?"

"Bondage stuff. Men. Why would you find someone boring shocking?"

"Because of his line of work. I don't know his personal

tastes," said Jules, "but the guy came out here as something of an expert in erotica. And he seemed straight."

"Erotica."

"Very valuable and mostly ancient stuff. The man I work for part time inherited a collection. It was supposed to be one of Altschuler's specialties."

Jackson didn't say anything.

"You didn't know that?"

"No, I didn't fucking know that," screamed Jackson. "I thought he dealt in landscapes. I thought I was calling goddamn Montana."

"Well," said Jules. "You are, and he had a sideline in plein air and western stuff, plus forensic weirdness."

"How's that all go together?"

"I haven't noticed that things go together most of the time," said Jules. "Think about it."

"Erotica," muttered Moss Jackson. "Montana."

"You know," said Jules, "we have a lot of livestock out here. Things do get strange. They call Montana the land where men are men and sheep run scared."

Jackson hung up and Jules walked home to a warm bed. Caroline had left him a note telling him she'd slept until two that afternoon, and eaten most of the leftover wedding cake in the refrigerator, and avoided a dozen phone messages. She'd also rifled his music, started and forgotten a load of mutual laundry, and piled books and magazines on the left side of the bed. He liked tracking her wayward progress around the house.

13 *Gravity: It's the Law*

Dear Dora:

I am in love with someone. We have finally had relations, and I think that we should get married. She says that because this is my first time with someone I should be patient. This sounds like she doesn't care enough to even think of marriage, but she says she loves me, and she says it's important to wait. What do I do? I was raised to believe that we're doing things in the wrong order.

Yours, Blake

Dear Blake:

If she won't marry you yet, you don't have much choice, do you? Go easy on yourself and avoid bringing it up with your parents. Stick with her, have fun, and keep asking (but not too often).

Best, Dora

"NICE OF YOU TO HELP HIM WITH HIS GRAMMAR AND spelling," said Grace.

"He wouldn't let me change much," said Jules. "The light of his life just had him read William Blake, and he loved it, and he assumed that that was why everyone in high school was named Blake."

"Poor kid," said Grace. "He's behind his time. I worry about him."

Jules did, too, but the letter was a relief.

THE SECOND WEEK after the wedding, Jules and Caroline only had the same shift twice, and didn't spend more than an hour together during any given daylight. This was just as well, as long as sleep no longer mattered; it would be a fine thing to show up or have someone show up at midnight, and slide down the length of your body in a warm bed. Being together in a car, actually working together and concentrating on even a traffic violation, was hard to imagine.

But they were both off Thursday until five, which was why Caroline was sitting naked at Jules's kitchen table at noon, eating warmed-up puttanesca while he dozed upstairs, when Alice came over to steal some daffodils and let herself into the house for a bucket.

"Oh, my God," said Alice.

"Damn," said Caroline.

"Oh, my God," said Alice. "I'll come back later."

"No, no," said Caroline. "I'll just get a robe on. Are you hungry?"

JULES AND DIVVY met for lunch and planned the spring's first fishing expedition.

"Have you seen the weather forecast?"

"More rain. Don't get started. It's not going to flood."

"No, for next winter. Have you seen it?"

Jules stared. "No," he said softly. "It's still April."

Divvy ignored him. "It'll be a winter like the ones we grew up with. No thaws, and they're forecasting three big arctic air masses. Hundreds of inches of snow, and we'll be getting two, three weeks of those Alaska temperatures at a time."

Something snapped in Jules's brain. Much as he loved Divvy's dark enthusiasm, this was no place to live.

"You okay?" Divvy was shoveling chili into his mouth at an astounding rate.

"I'm fine."

"You look a little tired."

"I'm fine," said Jules again.

"You can't just work," said Divvy. "There's more to life. You said you were ready. You said you were sick of feeling like shit. You need to meet someone, make some whoopee. When's the last time you thought your weenie might fall off from overuse?"

Jules smiled slowly. "About 6:00 this morning."

Divvy put his spoon down and started to giggle, saltine crumbs exploding out of one corner of his mouth.

"While you're in a weakened condition," said Jules, "I have some questions."

"Who is it?"

"When the trailer on Leon Baden's property burned down, did you check it for chemicals? Did you run Alan over it, or smell anything, or do any tests?"

"Tell me," said Divvy. "Was it one of those women at the wedding? You dirty, dirty dog. Or did you talk Dottie into something again?"

"You know Dottie doesn't usually like anyone close to home," said Jules. "She's giving Arnie a working over."

Divvy wiped cracker crumbs off his shirt. "Since when have we had secrets?"

"There's a lot riding on this."

"Meaning you're actually serious about it?"

"That, and there are complications."

"She's married." Divvy slapped the table and pushed his bowl to one side.

"No. Please answer me. Think back to February."

Divvy was staring at him intently. "The librarian."

"No."

Divvy sighed and crinkled his forehead and worked on his sandwich with a crushed expression. "If I recall, we were worried about a body for about five minutes. Then we figured out the wife was loony."

"Right," said Jules.

"I can't remember going out there more than twice. I think that was about when we lost those skiers in the avalanche."

Divvy looked up at the ceiling and down at the floor. He chewed, took another bite, and stared at their waitress's butt. Jules, who could have been napping in the station kitchen, dragged his hand down his face.

"It looked electrical," said Divvy suddenly. "We looked for the renter, figured out he'd run off to Hawaii or whatever, then we dealt with the skiers. And when we got back from the skiers we found out the renter wasn't missing after all, and that Leon hadn't even insured the thing, and why else would someone burn something down? No motive, no arson. The place was past saving by the time we got there, so we weren't out anything."

"Do you remember if we ever knew where the renter had gone? His wife is turning into a problem."

Divvy concentrated on the waitress again, and lifted his soda glass as if he needed a refill when she caught him looking. "I just remember Leon saying someplace warm. We had a cold snap about then."

"Did we talk to anyone but Leon?"

Divvy watched Jules, the waitress forgotten. "Nope. Anne was sick or something."

"Leon said someplace warm, and Leon said the wife was crazy to say her husband was dead, and Leon said the wife probably lit the place on fire. Last week Alan picked up a solvent smell near Leon's storeroom and by the trailer and the house."

Divvy looked dubious. "Leon has a shop, refurbishes all sorts of junk. He'd have a lot of likely chemicals no matter what."

"True," said Jules. "But maybe you could look through it again."

"For a body?"

"Nah, just arson. I'll figure out why after the fact."

"We can just stop by there tomorrow," said Divvy. "I'll give it fifteen minutes. Do you want some carrot cake?"

"Nah," said Jules. "I've got to get back, act like I know what I'm doing."

"Oh, my God," shrieked Divvy. "I know who it is. I know, I know, I know. I saw you dancing and I didn't even think twice."

Most of the restaurant turned to watch.

"I mean, I'm happy for you, but this'll land you in shit with the commissioners."

Jules grinned. "By the time the commissioners know about it, we'll be gone."

DIVVY TESTED THE remains of Leon's trailer for chemicals, and came up with all-American charcoal lighter fluid. But Leon now admitted he'd poured the liquid over what was left of the trailer, in hopes of getting rid of the trash, but then the wind came up and he thought it unwise. He intended to bulldoze the site when the ground thawed and dried.

Jules and Harvey had gone down together to watch, and they were quiet on the way back. "That's that," said Harvey finally.

"Yeah," said Jules. "But do me a favor and check out the file, track the renter down and just ask him what the hell was going on back in February. Caroline said there was a note in there that Frame called in from South Carolina. Let's finish up right."

ON SATURDAY JULES and Divvy and Peter fished a tiny stream north of the Crazies. They ate too many sandwiches while they basked in the sun, then drove around and fished some more. Peter wanted Jules to come back home with him for dinner, but Jules said he had to go to the Sacajawea.

"Why?" asked Peter. "Everyone left this morning."

"That's the point."

"You work too hard."

Jules had no intention of working: he and Caroline were going to the Sack that night for the sake of privacy. It wasn't just Alice—Ed didn't usually wait for an answer when he knocked either, and earlier that week Jules and Caroline had been forced to abbreviate a perfectly pleasant shower. Jules had spent an hour one evening hiding in Caroline's bedroom when Jonathan had shown up at her door to ask for romantic advice. No one just dropped in at the Sack, which wasn't due to open until Memorial Day. Halsey and Dottie and Arnie would keep their mouths shut; Fred and Merry might not even notice they were there.

Caroline was waiting on her back stoop and actually ran to the car.

"Quite a night off," said Caroline. "What are we celebrating?"

"The usual," he said, kissing her.

Nothing was as he'd hoped. The only car in the lot was Dottie's Volkswagen, but Merry was sitting in the bar working on a beer and a ledger, while Dottie drummed her fingers on the woodwork.

Caroline's expression was stricken, and Jules held on to her arm.

"Surprise," said Dottie. "Merry put her car in the ditch at lunchtime, and Fred's truck's in town, and Halsey ran away. He was invited for dinner at your uncle Joseph's. Arnie's hiding in the kitchen."

Merry glared at them. Jules patted Caroline lightly on the back, trying to reassure. "Do you still want a martini?"

"No," she said bitterly.

"Why the hell not?" asked Merry.

"That's enough," said Fred.

He was standing in the doorway, and he was looking at the light of his life with utter disgust.

"Let's go upstairs," said Caroline, pulling Jules's arm.

"Stay for a minute," said Fred pleasantly, taking Merry's arm and pulling her off the stool. "She won't bother you. Go upstairs, Merry, or I'll call the little men in white coats. I need to talk to Jules."

"Not yet!"

"We'll see," he said. "Bye."

Jules saw Dottie smile into her dishrag. She poured Fred a glass of grapefruit juice and he sat on Merry's stool.

"What's new, Fred?" asked Jules.

"Have you found Altschuler yet? Do you still think he ran away out here?"

"He hasn't gone home, but I bet he found a better place to run away than Blue Deer."

"Anywhere but here," said Fred, looking out the window. "Have you been fishing yet this year?"

"Once," said Jules, mystified. "Do you want to go?"

"Yes."

"Tomorrow afternoon?"

"Fine." Fred smiled. "It'll be my first day off."

UPSTAIRS, THEY SLEPT for a long time, long enough for it to be almost dusk when Jules woke up. He could hear Merry and Fred arguing upstairs. "What's she saying?" he asked Caroline.

"That she wants more of something. Big surprise," she muttered, with her face in the pillow.

"You think?"

"She just said 'more and more and more' and something like 'you asshole, Fred.' Some little endearment."

Jules snickered. "I've known women like her," said Caroline. "Men, too. She deserves whatever she wants, and everyone else is out to fuck her if they don't agree one hundred percent. The world owes her, especially if the world is related."

"We've all met them," said Jules.

"You know more of them if you grow up on the East Coast. It's not just meeting them at parties or working with them, it's logging all those school hours."

"Don't be a bigot," said Jules, stretching and wiggling his toes.

"I'm not. Stupid people always feel entitled because they don't understand that other people truly exist. But if you grow up with a trust fund, you actually have something to ground that entitlement on, so it's harder for them to resist whining."

"You speak from experience."

"I lived with one."

"Ah," said Jules. He was quiet for a minute. "Is that why you have some things but not others? You have lots of glasses, lots of pots, but no silverware or plates."

"We split things up in a hurry," said Caroline. "I didn't try for the family silver or porcelain."

"You and Chauncy."

She grinned in the dusky room. "Me and Charles."

Jules had met Charles the fall before, and had contrived to have him leave town after a DUI. He'd only confessed to this recently. Caroline had been immensely pleased, and said she had wished she'd known it then.

They heard a loud clunk, Merry throwing things. "I wish they'd leave," said Caroline. "I like this room. I like being with you in this room. I like not being in town, surrounded by snoopy school board members and Rotary dweebs, waiting for the bad jokes to start. I just don't like our company upstairs."

A few minutes later they did leave, Fred first and Merry after him, calling his name and saying she was sorry, to wait up. Jules and Caroline heard them run down the stairs, and a few minutes later he heard a door slam far down the wing near the conservatory, which Fred had almost finished repairing. They crept down the stairs, and Caroline finally had her martini.

It was Arnie's last night in town, and Jules helped him

make shrimp with lemongrass, some simple chicken-filled dumplings with a pungent dipping sauce, vinegared cucumbers that seemed cool but were laced with pepper flakes, and a pork taipan with chard. Dottie looked weepy, and Caroline kept filling her wineglass.

They were washing up when Fred reeled into the room.

"What happened?" asked Jules, amazed.

"I don't know," said Fred, moving on through.

Dottie's eyes widened. "I thought he was having grapefruit juice," said Caroline.

"He was."

Caroline grabbed Jules's arm. "Let's leave."

"Let's get naked and hide in the room," said Jules.

ANOTHER ARGUMENT WAS in full swing above their heads, this time louder. Across the hall, Dottie fought back by playing jazz, but by the time Halsey came in at ten and put on a classical album things were much quieter upstairs, just murmured conversation and footsteps. Caroline had wanted to dedicate as much time as possible to sleep but now they talked, and soft gusts from the open window touched them on the mattress. Jules leaned out the window and looked up.

"Their light's out. Let's go down."

A few minutes later they sat by the pool, leaning back to watch stars.

"It's so warm," Caroline said. "It's usually only fifty or so by midnight. This is almost like being back East."

"No stars back East."

"No," she said. "Not like this." She smiled at him. "Fred's not going to want to go fishing tomorrow."

"Sure he will," said Jules. "Fred's a tank. That's the problem. If he felt normal pain, he'd have quit years ago."

"What do you think he wants to talk about?"

"He wants to tell me that he helped Merry steal a painting," said Jules. He pulled off one of her sandals. "Let's swim."

She looked nervously at the hotel. "Are you crazy?"

"Everyone's asleep or blind drunk. We can turn out half the lights."

She made him turn out all of them, but the moon was so bright that once the lights were off it was hard to believe they'd made a difference. They floated, climbed out to roll about on a towel on the grass, slid back into the water again afterward. "It's hard to remember winter," said Caroline, as Jules towed her around slowly by one hand.

"That's why people stay."

"Will you stay?"

"I might leave for a while, but I'll always come back," he said. "It depends."

"On what?"

"On you."

She was quiet. "Say something," said Jules.

Caroline smiled, still floating on her back. "You can depend on me."

Back upstairs in Jules's room, they heard Fred's voice droning on and the sound of Merry crying. But they fell asleep anyway.

THE SCREAMS WERE abrupt and mind-boggling; there was no possibility they'd slept through any of them. There was another, stranger noise, like doves cooing in an airshaft or a gibbering madman locked in an attic. Jules was off the mattress and on his feet before he'd fully realized what he'd heard. He was in his jeans and out the door while Caroline still groped for her dress.

Halsey was outside by the pool, on his hands and knees on the tile, and Dottie, the woman who'd screamed, stood behind him with Arnie. But Halsey wasn't hurt or dead—Jules ran right up and stared at him hard, then looked at Dottie's face. Both of them were looking into the long plunge, which now looked more violet than blue. Twenty feet away a naked man was doing the dead man's float, and Jules once again ran, this time along the edge of the pool.

The warm water was almost a shock when he jumped in; it must take a lifetime to retrain expectations if you'd spent a childhood traumatized by cold water. Jules opened his eyes when he was still underwater and took in certain things: the thin dark spool of blood from the man's hair, the broken glass on the tile at the edge and on the bottom of the pool, the fact that his own haste was pointless. Then his head popped up in the chilly air and he paused, treading water, before tugging gently on the closest arm and towing the man to shore.

Caroline and Arnie were at the edge, and they pulled while he pushed, then followed the body out. Jules turned Fred over slowly on the hard tile, flinching at rubbery, broken arms and the wound on his head. He felt Fred's throat and torso. The body was warm from the water and nothing else.

It was 4:00 a.m. Jules looked up at the open balcony window, the swaying curtains, then down at the body again. He walked to the far side of the pool. Fred had missed the pool by only six inches or so, and a little creek of blood dripped into the water close to where he'd hit; he'd apparently slid in after impact. The blood was still liquid but cool and coagulating. Fred's skin looked soaked and rubbery, circulation a memory. The water had kept him limber, but Jules was sure he'd been dead for at least an hour, maybe two.

He walked back toward Halsey and Dottie, who stood in

the doorway to the bar. Caroline and Arnie stuck to the far side of the pool, next to Fred.

"I heard Halsey," said Dottie. "I think it took me awhile. I'm sorry about screaming."

"How long had you been here, Halsey?"

Halsey shook his head back and forth and Jules's worries multiplied.

Caroline suddenly came to life. "I'll go call Harvey and Wesley."

"Wait," said Arnie. "Think about what you're going to say first." She didn't get it at first, then nodded and ran into the bar to call, barefoot in her dress and moving gingerly on the tile, trying not to step on anything that might matter later. When she came back out, Jules asked her to stay with Fred while he went to look for Merry.

"Okay," she said, looking into the water. "I told them you called me. I didn't tell them I was here."

He took the stairs a few at a time. Merry was facedown in her bed, not hard to find at all. He called her name, prodded her, checked her breathing and her pulse. She reeked of booze, and he screamed directly into her ear with no response. Fred's clothes were in a pile in the center of the floor.

Downstairs, Halsey was propped in a bar chair while Arnie wiped his face with a warm cloth. Jules grabbed the phone and headed outside. "We need an ambulance."

Dottie was wide-eyed. "For Fred?"

"For Merry and for Halsey. She's out cold, needs her stomach pumped. You have any idea what they drank?"

"None," said Dottie, looking up at the stars, into the water, anywhere but at Fred. "I can't believe it. I kept my eye on him for so long."

"What do you want to do?" Jules asked Caroline.

"Does it matter?" she asked.

"Not to me."

"We've only had a couple of weeks to ourselves," she said. "I don't want to have to talk about it. I don't want people talking about it."

"Then go upstairs," said Jules. "Lie down and don't come to the door." He turned to Dottie and Halsey and Arnie. "Is that okay?"

"Yes," said Halsey. It was the first word he'd spoken. "I could have stopped this."

Jules, who was simply happy that the old man could still talk, didn't ask how. Dottie nodded absentmindedly. She was finally really looking at Fred and she started to cry, the awkward, ugly tears of someone long out of practice.

"I'll go sit with Merry until I hear the cars," said Caroline.

JONATHAN CAME UP with Harvey, and Al and Bean followed close behind. Jonathan looked older, blue water reflecting up on his face when he looked from the tower window to Fred's body. They photographed the window and pediment, the room and the body, bagged the empty bottle of scotch they found in the sink and searched the trash for other empties.

"I wouldn't have pegged Fred as a diver," said Caroline, after everyone had left and they were driving back to Blue Deer. "He wouldn't walk within five feet of that pool even when Merry was swimming."

"He wasn't a diver," said Jules.

"I know he hated it, but anyone would have jumped to make her shut up."

"Not the way he felt. Not from up there."

"What do you think then? That he got drunk and fell?"

"I can't even see that. He wouldn't get that close to the window, not even drunk."

"What the hell," said Caroline. "You saw her. She couldn't walk, let alone throw a man. She's going to have brain damage."

"I know," said Jules. "But he wasn't a diver."

"You can't argue with failure," said Caroline.

But Fred had been a drunk. It wasn't until after Merry had her stomach pumped and Jules walked into the hospital basement to look at Fred that it all truly kicked in. A dead, naked, middle-aged man lay on the table, the body entirely sad now that it had lost the pride and power of movement. His head was broken but still the right shape, like a hard-boiled egg ready to be peeled. Jules asked if he could have moved after he fell.

"Guess what," said Horace. "People don't bounce. They change shape. They go splat. Sometimes there's a last jerk of surprise, but that's all she wrote."

"He bled for a long time," said Jules.

"He didn't feel anything after he landed," said Horace. "Don't fret over it. Even if Missoula finds water in his lungs, it won't really mean anything."

"How'd he slide into the pool?"

"Entropy." Horace scowled. "By the way, I've been asked to ask you to get rid of these other bodies."

"What am I supposed to do with them?"

"I don't know," said Horace. "Bury them?"

FRED'S BLOOD ALCOHOL, determined before they sent him north to Missoula, was .35. Never in all the years Jules had known him had Fred done anything but sleep when he reached a similar state. The last time he'd tested Fred during an ugly stage he'd been below .3, and his suicide attempts had always come soon after he'd begun a binge. This time he'd been drinking for weeks.

"There's such a thing as cumulative disgust," said Caroline quietly, late the next night. "He was trying to handle it and couldn't. Maybe he saw how drunk she was and either felt guilty or revolted. How many times did he try to kill himself before?"

"Three or four."

"I don't know why you're questioning it. You're that way about everything lately. You've got people killing themselves right and left. Even if I want to see Leon nailed for something, too, the fact is his wife drank too much to make it back to the bar, and the man in the river wanted to be in the river, and the little guy wanted to bleed to death."

She was right on most things; how depressed had he been, that winter? Enough to empathize too much with a troop of suicides?

"Fred wouldn't have jumped off a step stool," said Jules stubbornly. "He wouldn't have gone near that window."

She stared at him.

Neuroticisms didn't just disappear when you were puking drunk; if anything, they got stronger. He hoped Fred had been too drunk to think in midair. "He had real vertigo," said Jules. "Are you scared of anything?"

"I don't like snakes."

"You don't like them, but could you pick one up if you had to?"

"I suppose," said Caroline. "It'd take a lot of money."

"Then you're not in that league," said Jules, "the 'not for love or money' league."

"And you do understand it?"

"Yes."

"What are you scared of?"

"I don't want to talk about it right now," he said, with a very small smile. "Fred wouldn't have gone near the window."

"If he was staggering, he might have. If she was near the window and saying she was going to dive into the pool, he might have tried to haul her away. Maybe one of them was going to be sick and tried to do it over the edge. That would explain the broken stonework."

The ledge had lost a brick or two, and the double windows were broken. The glass had fallen more or less straight down, as if someone had slammed them hard enough to break them, rather than Fred carrying along bits with his flying body.

Jules came up with a final quibble a few minutes later, when they were both nearly asleep. Two seasoned drunks wouldn't, simultaneously, accidentally drink enough to kill themselves. Without having her stomach pumped, it wouldn't have been a sure bet that Merry would have woken up.

"That's true," she admitted, cradling his head. "That's strange. When Merry can talk we can ask her."

THE NEXT AFTERNOON Jules went back up to the Sacajawea and walked straight up to Merry's room. There was no way of knowing if she'd even noticed that Jules had seized some items ten days earlier. The cement sculpture was gone, but he'd already known that.

Halsey wasn't playing music on the floor below today—Dottie had given him sleeping pills. Jules threaded his way around exercise equipment to reach the sink. Two glasses lay on the drainboard, rinsed but unwashed. The sink still smelled of scotch, all that the lab had found in the bottle.

Jules turned slowly, looking for every other receptacle in the room. It took awhile, and the two clear bottles on the windowsill, one with dried flowers in it, were only suspicious because so many petals lay on the sill underneath. The rest of the room was spic and span despite the surfeit of belongings, practically licked clean. He found some paper towels and picked up the bottle without flowers first, staring at the inch of scummy liquid inside. It smelled of a dead bouquet. The real moment of truth came when he pulled the dusty strawflowers out of the other bottle, swirling the eighth of an inch of clear liquid that was still in the bottom, and smelled laboratory alcohol.

MERRY HADN'T REGAINED consciousness on Sunday, and when Jules tried the next morning she was still asleep, still on an IV, being pumped with liquids to rehydrate a brain that had wizened with a blood alcohol of .42. Halsey was sitting in her room, reading *Reader's Digest* with little expression; Dottie was wandering outside every fifteen minutes to smoke. She told Jules she felt guilty for having disliked the woman.

"I still dislike her," said Jules. "I can't see any reason to change my opinion because she helped Fred die."

She shook her head. "Don't blame her. She didn't get him started again. I did. You did."

"Bullshit," snapped Jules.

"Did you ever tell Caroline about that?" asked Dottie.

BLUE DEER BULLETIN

SHERIFF'S REPORT, WEEK OF APRIL 17–25

April 17—A man reported that a chunk of ice or rock fell off the back of an excavation truck and punctured his radiator. Deputies were unable to track down the truck.

April 18—A loose pig was reported on the corner of Park and Tintern. Its owners were located.

A citizen reported that a large garbage can was blowing back and forth under the overpass and causing traffic problems. Deputies removed the can.

April 20—A local restaurant reported a drunken man who refused to leave their drive-through and demanded free food. Deputies were unable to respond immediately and suggested the restaurant give the man some food and ask him to be on his way.

An individual reported a damaged fence on the East River Road, apparently caused by a car. No accident had been reported in that area.

April 21—A Ford Explorer was discovered stuck in the mud on Big Hill. The owner had not noticed it was missing.

April 22—A visiting individual reported a

downed power line on the road near Big Creek. A deputy determined that it was baling twine.

April 23—A nine-year-old boy called dispatch at midnight to say that his three-year-old brother had been crying and their mother could not be found. An eight-year-old was also upset. One deputy stayed with the children while another found the mother downtown. She returned home immediately.

THE BLUE DEER PUBLIC LIBRARY HAD FINITE RE-sources, and on Monday its single volume on Thomas Moran was checked out.

Jules drummed his fingers on the counter. “When’s it due back?”

The librarian peered in the computer. “Yesterday.”

“Hummph,” said Jules. “Does my friend Fred Bottomore still have it?”

She looked surprised, stared into the computer again, and laughed. “Yes. Just tell him to call in a renewal and give it to you.”

He wondered if she’d notice the obituary in the *Bulletin* that afternoon. Two years earlier, niggling things like this would have bothered him, but now he drove to Fred’s little house on Tintern Street, using the excuse of a welfare check on the same block, an old woman named Mrs. Mayall who hadn’t made bingo the previous week. Jules used Fred’s own keys to let himself in with a mixture of curiosity and guilt. It was one of the few times he’d used being a cop for no obvious good reason, and once he arrived the sadness of the filthy, abandoned kitchen made him regret this license. He tried to imagine living as Fred had and couldn’t, even though in many ways the difference between them had been very slight.

The sink was filled with dishes, and a hamper laden with dirty clothes sat on the kitchen table. Lining the dusty mantel, the shelves and tops of the television, the refrigerator, the windowsills were painstaking models of houses and furniture in shoe boxes. A roof with an interesting dormer in the dish drain, a stairway in a mixing bowl.

In the bedroom, Jules stopped in surprise. Shirts lay on the bed and a suitcase was half filled with pants and socks. A cardboard box was heaped with books, not the kind anyone got rid of. Fred was going somewhere, or had been in the midst of changing houses. Maybe he'd intended to move in with Merry, take up permanent residence in the tower of the Sack.

Jules searched the house from the basement up—closets, cupboards, drawers. He'd almost given up when he took a second look at a stack of wood samples wrapped with a rubber band and noticed a wisp of fine stationery between layers. He pulled the paper out expecting a price list and instead saw fine, old-fashioned feminine writing:

> *Surprise, darling. Don't you remember how that hill used to watch us?*

He recognized the writing; he'd seen it dozens of times on labels taped to erotic oddities. Muriel Zilpha Zirn Vinnecombe Meriwether Gagnaire, but Muriel out of context. Why would Fred bring a note home and hide it? He'd expected one of her belongings, not a message.

Jules put the paper in his pocket and headed out the front door. The mailman was walking toward him, the same one who worked Jules's block. "What's up?" he asked, pausing. "Is this why Fred didn't pick up his package?"

Jules nodded.

"He wasn't that poor drunk who fell?"

"Sorry," said Jules. "He was."

"Damn," said the mailman. "Poor son-of-a-bitch. What should I do with this?"

"I'll take it inside," said Jules, reaching for the mail.

"While you're here, you might want to check on Mrs. Mayall, two houses down. She hasn't emptied her box in a while."

"We got a call," said Jules. "How long?"

"I'm not sure," said the postman. "I was out last week. Too long to feel good about it."

"Jesus," muttered Jules to himself as he walked inside with Fred's mail. A bad feeling started wiggling in his stomach, the certainty that things would get worse before they got better. Fred's mail consisted of bills, a postcard from a brother in Tacoma, a receipt for a package, catalogs.

Jules tossed the lot on the table and searched the place in vain for the book on Thomas Moran. Then he locked up, and walked slowly down the sidewalk.

Five minutes later he sat stiffly in the parlor of the old house next door, as far away as he could be from the old woman in the upstairs bedroom. Smells like that clung to your skin, or possibly your brain; looking around, he saw more evidence that she'd gone unmissed for days or weeks. The African violets on the dusty piano back had collapsed over the edge of their pot, and the Swedish ivy was dry, translucent lace. Some of the mail he'd slid on when he'd opened the unlocked door had already faded slightly in the sunlight from the south window, which now warmed his legs. The loaf of bread open on the kitchen counter was hard as a rock, mold not being much of a problem in Montana, and dust covered the water in the cat's bowl. The cat itself had survived because of the small pet door. Maybe neighbors were feeding it; possibly it would watch the upcoming commotion from another yard.

He heard footsteps on the front porch and walked to the door, expecting Ed. But when he swung it open he discovered two young men in smooth black suits, each with a briefcase and an equally smooth Bible tucked under an arm.

"Is Mrs. Mayall available?"

"No," said Jules. "She's not."

They sized each other up. "When can we stop back?" asked the shorter kid. "We visited with her two weeks ago, and promised we'd come by again."

"I wouldn't bother," said Jules. "How'd she look when you saw her last?"

They pursed their lips and eyed each other. "She looked elderly," said the taller one finally. "When can we talk to her?"

"I'm afraid the best you could do would be to talk at her, but I don't recommend it," said Jules. "She's dead."

They took this in without retreating. It gave Jules time to think over more points for his letter of resignation, more complaints. One: people kept dying alone, which somehow seemed worse than having company. Two: the ones who didn't die whined, not realizing their good fortune. Three: no one ever apologized for this unbearable self-pity. Four: those who claimed to want to help society were often the most insufferable. Jules recognized that he might be included in the last category.

Jules only sought a middle ground in life, and it was not forthcoming. The young men shuffled nervously on the porch, not knowing what to make of his expression.

The tall one had paled, but the short one was stubborn. "Have you been saved?"

"Do I look saved?" asked Jules. He was enjoying the cool unscented air on the porch.

"This is no joking matter."

The county van pulled up. "Sorry, no, I haven't, and it isn't in the cards today. Hop along now." He made a swatting gesture with his hands.

The short one gave him an ugly look. "This town's filled with jerks and you're the biggest one yet to joke like that. This block was just as bad last time. This old biddy wasn't up to seeing us, two other people slammed doors, and next door a lady threw books at us and swore."

"That house?" asked Jules, pointing toward Fred's.

"Yeah," said the kid. "That house. She was having a fight with some guy and she took it out on us."

Jules filled his lungs again, dreading the next thirty minutes. "What'd she look like?"

"Tall and blond. Built." A little spasm at his mouth told Jules he regretted the slip. "They were big fat art books, and she threw them hard enough to ruin them."

"That's interesting," said Jules. "What'd she say?"

"She said 'fuck off.'" He smirked.

"You sure you don't want to talk about God?" asked the tall boy apologetically.

"I'm sure," said Jules. "Don't fret. I've been baptized." He loomed over the other missionary. "That's it?"

"She said we were all a waste of her time."

"Including the man she was arguing with?"

"Mostly him."

"Thanks," said Jules. He inclined his head toward Ed, who was in uniform and carrying a stretcher up the walk. "Now scram, and good luck with the rest of humanity."

They left.

HE DROVE TO the bookstore in Bozeman, paid $80 for a coffee table book he didn't particularly care for, and spent more hours looking up images on the computer. He was still at it when Caroline let herself through the back door at 1:00 a.m.

"How could any human being not take advantage of a chance to sleep?" she said, making directly for the stairs. "I'm offended you didn't warm the bed up for me. The bloom must be off the damn rose."

"Wait," said Jules. "Listen to this. Thomas Moran spent six weeks recovering from pneumonia at a hotel on the Yellowstone River in 1893."

"You knew he was at the Sack. I remember seeing the drawings."

"I knew he'd stayed, but I didn't realize he'd practically lived in the place. That's long enough to get a lot of work done."

"Did he bring home many paintings?"

"Just some small ones and studies for larger pieces he ended up finishing in his studio. Look at this watercolor. It's like the two Halsey had, and here it's called *Study for Shell Mountain.*"

She looked, then shut her eyes again.

"There's nothing on record that's simply called *Shell Mountain,*" said Jules. "I think it's sitting in a crate at Leon's. I think the big gift Halsey was expecting from Muriel was a Thomas Moran canvas she left with in 1952."

Fred must have opened the crate when it first came in, before anyone else saw the painting or the note. Jules remembered the hairdryer they'd used on the wallpaper; he remembered the slightly used-looking screws in the top of the crate. Halsey had been abusing Fred's patience and affection for weeks, and both Halsey and Jules had finished the job off the night of the bachelor party, primed him for Merry's various encouragements and a return to alcohol. It wouldn't have taken more than a few hours for a man that adept, someone who'd once dreamed of being an artist, who knew paint on a practical level of opacity and drying time, to turn a masterpiece into a convincing temporary joke.

ON TUESDAY MORNING, Merry's skin was yellow and her face was swollen and bumpy like a melon. Halsey walked out of the room when Jules came in.

"Feel free to shoot her," he said.

Jules watched him lumber off down the hallway.

Merry kept her eyes shut and simply lifted a finger when Jules said hello. Before he asked a single question she told him she didn't remember much, and the doctors told her that this was to be expected. Jules didn't even try to sound sympathetic.

"What were you arguing about?"

"Were we arguing?"

"Yes," he said. "You were screaming earlier that night, and that evening Fred seemed annoyed. At four o'clock he was sober. What happened?"

Her face was swollen like a pumpkin, and her skin was yellow. She rambled, and Jules doodled on his pad to keep from losing his temper, drawing trees while she patched together what she claimed was memory. She and Fred had been arguing all day between Fred running errands to Leon's; after Jules had seen them at the bar, Fred had come upstairs with the bottle of scotch and poured them each a scotch and soda.

"Where'd he get the bottle?"

"Dottie gave it to him."

"Dottie usually refused to serve him."

"You'd believe anything she told you. Maybe Leon gave it to him. I don't think it was full."

Jules tapped his pen on the paper. "So you drank while you continued the argument."

"I guess. I can't imagine how else I got this way."

To say nothing of Fred, thought Jules. "What were you arguing about?"

"He was going to move in, but then he decided we needed our own place. I thought we should stay at the hotel so we could help Halsey."

"Did he want you to move to his place in town?"

"Oh no," she said. "He wanted to get a *real* house, but in the end he agreed to stay at the hotel."

This was plainly bullshit: a shack was real to Fred, as long as it had a little woodwork.

"I tried to get him to slow down on the drinks," said Merry.

"You didn't exactly slow down yourself."

"Just a few drinks," she said.

"Your blood alcohol was point four-two. Fred's just came back at point three-five. Try twelve drinks."

"I can't explain," she said. "I thought we were fine."

"You'll have to explain," said Jules.

She started to cry, and she was remarkably noisy for someone so weak. A nurse stuck her head in the door and Jules waved. When he turned back he caught Merry watching him with a yellow, bloodshot eye, just for a split second. Then she shut the swollen lid again.

Jules watched her, feeling unkind. "I'm not sure there's enough alcohol in a bottle of scotch to do that to two people."

She squeezed out some tears. "Maybe someone added something to it. I know there wasn't anything else in the room. I'd been trying to help him."

"What was Fred dropping off at Leon's?"

"I don't remember," she said. "Something big I couldn't handle on my own."

"Something like a crate?" asked Jules.

"I think that's what it was."

She squinted her eyes, a miserable actress.

"Did you finish the argument?"

Now she smiled. "We must have. I remember being in bed. That's the last thing I remember."

"So you flopped around for a while, fell asleep, and when you woke up you were having your stomach pumped?"

"If I hadn't fallen asleep he wouldn't have jumped," said Merry, an IVed arm draped over her face. "I would have reminded him of everything he had to live for."

Jules was tempted to see if she had this schmaltz written on her palm. "Ah," he said.

"He seemed fine after the argument. Happy, even."

"You had your usual good time," said Jules.

"Of course." She missed his sarcasm but her voice was defiant; Fred had been happy because he was with her, presumably pancaked himself as an act of joy and devotion.

"But you're not surprised he jumped."

"Sometimes his mood changed terribly quickly."

"True," he said in a neutral voice. "But why then, and why jump?"

She started crying again, and Jules once more turned to face the nurse. She didn't seem amused. "Two more minutes."

He edged closer to Merry, just a foot from her ear, and spoke softly. "Fred wasn't a very likely jumper."

"He wasn't so afraid of heights anymore," said Merry. "I even got him to go into the pool once."

"Are you sure there hadn't been anything lately to make him especially unhappy? Something that made him uncomfortable, or made him hate himself more than usual?"

Her face didn't move.

"What were you really talking about that night?"

"Just about where to live."

"You're lying," he said. "I'll be back."

JULES HAD PUSHED Missoula to check out Fred as quickly as possible, and when he got to work the next morning the report was waiting on his desk. Fred had been alive for up to an hour before he'd slipped into the pool and actually drowned. His brain had had plenty of time to swell and seep. The answer to how long he'd been in the pool was also up to an hour, but the two totaled were painfully inexact: Fred had fallen forty minutes to two hours before Jules had pulled him out of the water.

Jules didn't find black and white satisfying this time, and called the lab. "Could you tell what kind of booze he drank? Scotch, or grain alcohol, or wine?"

"Nah."

"What about mixers? Can you tell if he had a lot of soda water or juice?"

There was a pause, a rustle of paper. "Not much salt. Couldn't tell you about juice."

"Was he capable of movement?"

The examiner snorted. "Hell no. I can't even account for how he kept breathing."

"Then how did he end up in the pool?"

"I don't know. Is there a slight slope? Has your wind been bad lately?"

JULES DROVE DOWN the valley.

The cottonwoods along the river bottom had a bug-green furze, tiny leaves that would be full size in a week if the weather stayed warm. Leon's truck was gone and the bar was locked up. Through the small window in the back of the Quonset hut, he could still make out the large crate from the Sacajawea basement. He was in the process of trying to boost himself higher by balancing on some firewood when his old friend, Leon's rottweiler, hit the other side of the glass, foaming at the mouth. Jules shrieked and fell backward, waving his arms as if he could fly. He lay on the ground for some seconds, rediscovering his kitten-rescue injuries, before he trudged to his car.

He decided to take it out on Merry, but found the hospital room empty and every nurse occupied. His mother was behind the front desk, humming and reading a book called *Adam, Eve, and the Serpent*.

"She's been released to her uncle's care, and right now she should be en route to a fancy clinic, along with a nurse." Olive looked grim. "At least I hope so. Poor Halsey. Looking at that woman made me want to give up gimlets."

"Someone could have called," said Jules.

Olive tilted her head. "You're surprised they didn't?"

Jules didn't say anything.

"What have you been up to since the wedding anyway?"

Olive was grinning. The hospital supervisor walked past the doorway, saw Jules, stopped in his tracks and crooked a finger. Jules followed him downstairs.

For a very small town where everyone seemed to know

each other, Blue Deer had produced a surreal number of dead strangers lately. In the basement of the hospital, only a thirty-bed facility for the living, bodies were piling up: the river Texan, the snowbank man, now Mrs. Mayall and Fred, just back from Missoula. That weekend had also produced an itinerant named Rex Jones who'd suffered a fatal heart attack. A name like Rex Jones didn't get them far, and Jules assumed he'd end up in the county plot at county expense.

At least Leon had finally retrieved his wife. Jules could send Mrs. Mayall to her daughter in Denver, and Fred, now that all the tests were complete, to his parents in Vera, Montana. Jules had already set things up: a train to Miles City and the mortuary van for the last hundred miles. Or maybe the Bottomore seniors would use their own pickup. Imagining something as old-fashioned as loading a casket on a train made it seem like a movie, but really loading the casket at a dingy siding would turn it into bad truth, sad and mundane. Jules had suggested cremation, but Fred's mom wanted to see him one last time.

Jules dug in on the question of the two John Does, remembering what had happened a year earlier in Sweetgrass County, when they'd buried a similar John Doe after a week, only to discover he was a kidnapped rich man. Jules didn't want to pay burial and exhumation costs, and he didn't want to be sued for negligence. If either man hadn't died alone, he wanted to find out who deserved Hell.

Jules and the hospital supervisor wrangled in the presence of all these bodies, and compromised on the county paying for funeral home storage beginning the following Monday. When the supervisor left, Jules made himself look at them, one after another, one woman and four men. The only conceivable perk about the bodies he'd seen lately was that none of them were as young as usual, not sixteen or twenty, dead in the first long spasm of stupidity. Most of these people had won second chances and pissed them away in direct and indirect suicides, all quite elemental: temperature, water, gravity. No modern niceties, no pills involved, nor cars or guns. Alcohol had been around for a long, long time, and Jules never bothered to argue with the fact that drinking lowered life expectancy. Though it made it possible for Jules to proceed with life, the one or two glasses they'd found in river man had presumably given him the edge to dive in. Anne Baden had been too drunk to find shelter, and Fred had been too drunk to keep his balance, leaving behind a woman who'd been too drunk to push him. Rex had spent every available dime on Mogen David 20/20. Only Mrs. Mayall and the man in the snowbank had been sober for the big moment.

WHEN JULES GOT to the Sacajawea, Dottie served him a soda pop and rambled on about the new prospective chef, due the week before Memorial Day, and his impossible demands; about how Arnie had flown away the day before, and what a tragedy it was that he wouldn't lower his going salary from $140,000 to $30,000 for the sake of love, quiet companionship, and mind-boggling sex; about how nice it was to not have Merry around (though this tangent petered out, because Fred was gone, too).

But the fact that Fred was gone prompted some requests. Could Jules finish off two pieces of trim Fred hadn't gotten around to, stuff Dottie didn't want to entrust to the Nitwits? And could he hang the rest of the prints in the dining room, put out the last few of Muriel's things?

"Where does Halsey want them?"

"Halsey doesn't give a damn right now. I'm hoping he'll feel better now that she's in the bin."

"Meaning that she's less likely to kill someone under lock and key?"

She shrugged. "He feels responsible."

"For what? For Fred?"

"I don't fucking know, Jules." Dottie suddenly looked vicious. "I don't want to know."

"Toward the end, I was getting the impression that you and Fred were closer than I'd realized."

Dottie's face was still.

"You'd known each other a long time," said Jules, chickening out.

"That's true," said Dottie, still without expression.

As he walked upstairs, he tried to pinpoint what she wanted, what she was trying to wangle, and why. Something was up, and something had been up for a long time. He was no longer sure that Merry actually knew what was in the crate, and wondered now if Fred and Dottie had rigged an elaborate hoodle, a scam that had gone horribly wrong. As a bartender, drunks disgusted her; as Halsey's lady, dealers, critics, heirs, and their creatures disgusted her. Dottie didn't give anyone points for money, breeding, education, looks. She either liked someone or she didn't, and once she didn't, there was no saving the situation. In this sense she was a bad bartender and hotelier. Absaroka was a small county, and the list of people she'd booted from one establishment or another was long.

But for Fred she'd cried, hard; her face was still puffy, and her calm seemed contrived. If Jules had found himself in a room with her and with Merry, and been asked who was the widow, he would have picked Dottie. But that didn't mean that Dottie couldn't want someone she'd cared for dead. She was righteous, thought she was smarter than most, and had a very selective honesty.

Halsey was reading by the window in pajamas. In the absence of the pre-wedding hysteria and in the wake of Fred's death, his vitality and curiosity had vanished.

"Did you know that when Merry took the big crate to Leon's, she told him she'd be buying that ugly landscape herself?"

"I didn't know," said Halsey. "And I don't care. I would have been happy to give it to her."

"It does seem a little silly that she'd actually want to pay for something, after taking so much."

Halsey still looked good-natured. "I've tried to make it clear that that was nothing for you to worry about."

"I know," said Jules. "And mostly I haven't. But things are a little different now that Fred's dead. Did you notice that that ugly landscape had the same silhouette as your Thomas Moran sketch?"

"That would be the view from the window upstairs," said Halsey. "Anyone working from that window would come up with the same silhouette. I did it myself, back when I still thought I might paint."

"But the painting isn't one of yours?"

"No."

"Why don't you tell Leon you've decided not to sell it? Take a look at it, think about it first."

Halsey shook his head. "Why buy something I don't like? Why make an unhappy girl unhappier?"

"I can think of several reasons," said Jules. "But I don't want to be rude about your flesh and blood."

"Good," said Halsey wearily. "Neither do I, and it's been a struggle."

Jules nodded to the large, ornate, empty frame on the wall. "You told me that frame was your symbol of marriage gone wrong."

Halsey tilted his head to look and smiled.

"Are you sure Muriel didn't try to make it up to you?"

"I'm sure she wanted to," said Halsey. "But I think it backfired. The last thing I want now is to fill that frame. I want to pretend the canvas never existed."

"Do you mind if I don't pretend?"

"Do what you have to do. Take the frame with you."

"When does Merry get out?"

"You have two weeks. But I'll be surprised if she sticks it out."

ON THE DRIVE back to town, Jules tried to come up with a variety of bearable maneuvers. Nothing ethical occurred to him, and he had to remind himself to care. Unethical maneuver number one promised to be expensive, which was a problem. He had a single $5,000 twelve-month CD, an almost paid-off house (which wasn't saying much, since he'd bought it for $42,000), and his newest vehicle ever, a truck with only 84,000 miles and a taxable value, according to the state of Montana, of almost $3,000. Relative to his sorry past, he was sitting pretty, but he still only had $400 until his next payday. One of Fred's last sensate acts before they'd argued about Merry had been to borrow $200, and Jules was damned if he'd bring it up with the bereaved parents.

He parked his truck on the side street, the better to make a quick getaway. Caroline was only a few yards away, waving her wonderful butt in the air while she looked for something in her backseat, then slamming the door.

"Hey, lady," he said, following her across the cold, windy parking lot. "Sweet girl, wait up."

Caroline whipped around, owl-eyed and pissed off. When she saw him she grinned tiredly. "You shouldn't say things like that to a coworker."

"I don't care."

She'd just arrested an unhappily married couple who'd begun hitting each other in the hardware store in a disagreement over faucets. One of them claimed to have lost a checkbook in the patrol car, and both suggested Caroline had lifted it. "I just want to kill," she said. "It's a blanket desire. The next poor shit I deal with is going to get it."

"Let's go for a drive," said Jules. "Do you have any money?"

"What kind of money?"

"Money to burn." He goosed her across the lot, steering her toward his car.

"I burned my money on my idiot car," said Caroline. "I'm down to $80 after the trip to the grocery last night. What do you need it for?"

"Something pretty for our wall."

"GET OUT OF here," yelled Leon when they walked through the back door. His sole customer put down money, drained bad coffee, and left through the front.

"We're not here to harass you about Anne or the trailer," said Jules. "I wanted to check out something you got from Halsey."

"No, you're just here to tell me I'm a thief all over again," roared Leon. "You're not looking at a fucking thing!"

"We're not here to look," said Jules. "We're here to buy the painting in the big crate."

"Merry's buying it."

"How much?"

"She's paying $300, and my commission is $100," said Leon. "Setting her own price. For that profit I should charge rent."

"Why didn't she just buy it from her uncle?"

"She said it was only worth a couple of hundred, but he'd charge her a grand, just on principle." He lit a second cigarette and after he shook the match out, he held it high above the bar and let go. It fell next to the first match, landing in a perfect line.

"Doesn't sound like Halsey, does it?" said Jules.

"People are weird with family," said Leon.

This begged for a smartass comment, but Jules managed to keep his mouth shut, and gave Caroline a dirty look when he saw the corner of her mouth twitch. "Merry give you any money yet?"

"No. When's she getting out anyway?"

"Not for a while," said Jules.

"It's not just a question of drying out," said Caroline. "She has some brain damage. She needs physical rehab, drug therapy—"

Leon was impressed. "She doesn't remember a whole hell of a lot," said Jules. "She might even forget her deal with you. I'll take it off your hands for $400."

"What's so special about this piece of shit?" asked Leon. "Even I can tell it's crap. What are you going to do with a porno painting and a bad landscape?"

"I have a friend who has a bar and could use the panel

painting, and I like the view in the landscape even if it is weird."

Leon shook his head. "She'll make my life hell."

"Tell her you'll tell her uncle she's cheating him, and she'll shut up," said Jules. "She's going to have her tail so far between her legs you won't know she has one."

Caroline grimaced.

"One grand," said Leon. He lit a third cigarette and dropped that match, too. It fell in line next to the first two.

"Five hundred," said Jules.

"Nine hundred," said Leon. "Period."

Jules pulled out his checkbook.

"Cash," said Leon.

"You prick, you honestly think I'd bounce a check?"

"I like cash," said Leon. "Period. Or blow it out your ass."

"Jesus," said Jules. "I'm already playing hooky here. It'll take me an hour to get to town and back."

"Tough," said Leon. "I'll be here till four."

THEY DROVE TO town. Caroline stayed in the truck while Jules butted in on Peter's conference with a client. "I need money," he said. "I need $450 in cash right now."

Peter peered through the window at Caroline. "Are you running away?"

"No."

"Don't I usually borrow money from you?"

"I know you got wads of it for wedding presents."

"Tell me what it's for," said Peter. "You and Caroline aren't in trouble, are you?"

Jules hit his forehead with his hand. "Think of it as an investment. We're buying art and splitting the proceeds."

"We're buying something from Halsey?"

"Halsey doesn't want it. He's already sold it."
"Explain," said Peter.
"No," said Jules. "Trust me."

CAROLINE GOT THE giggles on the way north the second time, with the crate rattling in the bed of the pickup. Jules had radioed in to say she'd come down with stomach flu while they were moving loose cows. Grace wasn't there to find holes in this story: her daughter had finally given birth.

"I thought you said it was worthless."

"I never said that. Some other people did, though."

"What do you think she paid that man in Seattle to lie?"

"A lot, if that's why he's not showing up."

"Where are you going to put it?"

"I don't know. I might clean it off and hang it until we figure out what to do."

"Aren't you worried about damaging it?"

"No. I'll double-check with a couple of friends, but that top layer of acrylic should come off with a sponge. Fred would have been careful."

"What's Merry going to do when she gets home and it's gone?"

"I don't know," said Jules honestly. "Pretty scary, huh? I'm hoping they'll keep her at least a month."

"I'll give you $175 out of the next paycheck, but I won't want to die for you for at least another two weeks," said Caroline.

"I know you care," he said.

She grinned and leaned her head against the window, watching the greening landscape speed by.

"Jules?"

"Yeah."

“That was quite a trick with the matches, wasn’t it?”

It took him awhile to get the point.

JULES HEADED IN as soon as he unloaded the crate. Harvey was just coming on the evening shift. “Did you find that man Frame?”

“Nope.”

Harvey was sorting paperwork and looked pissed off. Grace had probably chided him again about illegible reports. “Did you look?”

Harvey dropped a pile into a drawer and slammed it shut. “Robert Raphael Frame moved here from Beaufort. His father, known as Robert Rufus Frame, was not at home last night. I asked Wesley to call today, and Wesley left me a note saying that Robert Rufus Frame says he hasn’t talked to his son since Christmas, but that this isn’t rare, and he doesn’t much want to talk to his son anyway.”

In hindsight, Jules wasn’t sure what he’d wanted to hear. “Why did we think he’d gone to the Carolinas anyway?”

“There was a note in the file saying that Frame had checked in with someone and said he was visiting his parents.” Harvey gave a skinny little smile. “Mrs. Robert Rufus died in 1988, by the way.”

“Who left the note?”

“Jonathan, and it doesn’t say who told him, and he can’t remember for sure.”

“He can goddamn well try,” said Jules.

“Good luck,” said Harvey. “You might as well ask him if he remembers geometry class. But the note was dated March 4, and I looked on his duty sheet, and he happened to answer a call at the Bachelor that night.”

DOTTIE WASN'T IN the mood for a talk, but then again Jules hadn't been in the mood to drive back to the Sacajawea. Caroline opted for simply going back to work, and told Wesley the flu Jules had mentioned had been a passing thing.

"What's that guy Frame look like?"

Dottie was doing a crossword. "Haven't you talked to his loony wife?"

"It's hard to keep her on the subject, Dot. You'll do."

She pursed her lips. "I didn't see much of him. A little guy, but a real charmer. Completely ordinary when he keeps his mouth shut or his pants up."

Jules was beginning to feel something like awe. "What does he *look* like?"

"Mousy brown hair, wiry, shorter than me."

"What's he like when he doesn't keep his mouth shut or his pants up?"

She smiled gently. "Here's the thing, Jules. I get curious, and I get a little burst of energy, and that's all she wrote. If my parents had raised me right, I might have been curious about outer space instead of men. I'm trying to retrain myself to notice other things."

"Like art and old men and chefs."

"Exactly."

Jules tapped his fingers on the bar, trying not to lead her. "So what's so special about Robert R. Frame, besides the obvious?"

"Oh no," she said. "The obvious is ordinary. But he has one of the prettiest tattoos I've ever seen."

"What kind of tattoo?" asked Jules, in a flat voice.

"A rose tattoo with an initial."

Dottie persisted in thinking, for half the drive to Blue Deer, that Jules was arresting her for pilfering art. There were, as she pointed out, so many better people to pick on. When she finally understood that he wanted her to look at a dead man, her protests were still strong.

"Find someone else who knew the poor son of a bitch," she said. "Find his wife. Make Leon do it. He probably killed him."

Jules turned into the hospital parking lot. "Now why would you say that?"

"Because Rafe and Anne had a thing."

"And why didn't you tell me that a month ago, before we had to waste time digging it up somewhere else?"

"Because you'd ask how I knew."

"But now you don't mind?"

"I didn't want Fred to know," said Dottie. "Every time it came up, Fred was around."

"Dottie—"

"No."

"Just tell me what mood you thought Fred was in the night he died."

The look she gave him was utterly stern. "His mood was drunk. Period."

The big subject—what had Dottie felt for Fred?—once again went untouched. Jules led her to the basement and made her turn around while he draped a cloth over the throat of the man in the snowbank, and another over his tattered scalp and forehead. Dottie peered at the face for some time, then shook her head.

"I better see the tattoo," she said.

Jules drew the cloth aside. This would be another moment to enjoy forgetting when he and Caroline were five thousand miles away.

"Oh poop," said Dottie. "That's him."

JULES WALKED HOME and found Caroline in a bathrobe, heating up leftovers while Fred the cat watched her expectantly. Edie had never gotten used to the way Jules was desperate to make love after looking at dead people, but with Caroline he didn't have to explain. "How'd it go at the hospital?" she asked eventually, reaching down to help him off the kitchen floor.

Jules told her, and spelled out his guesses. "I think Anne told Merry that she suspected Leon of killing Frame. And I think Merry's holding both deaths over Leon's head."

"To keep him quiet about the stuff she takes from Halsey?"

"Or more."

"Like what?"

"I don't know."

"Leon wasn't in the Sack the night Fred died," said Caroline.

"Leon didn't know about the painting. I'm sure of it."

"Then what?"

"I don't know," said Jules again.

15 *The Good Boy*

clement@blue.net

Dear Jules:

Talking to our mutual friend Henry about lovely Montana and told him you were thinking of a career change. He's been working south of Kiev, wants you on a dig there in late June, says it's up your alley, something about kurgans. Solid money but Chernobyl-sized mosquitoes.

I've been back at work a week, still having strange dreams about that strange bartender. One thing's been bothering me since Fred, and I should have told you sooner. Dot should have told you, but I bet she hasn't. She caught Merry Xeroxing one of your crate inventories. Merry told Dot she owed Leon money, and she'd taken something to give him in payment, and he wanted proof it was real. She said she was scared of him, and she actually begged Dottie not to let Halsey know. (This was a first, I think.) So Dottie typed up a note for her saying whatever Merry had stolen was a Greek nude worth $20,000 to $30,000. Dot thought doing this was harmless, since she doesn't like either Leon or Merry, and since it turns out this particular statue is a fake, but last night we talked and she said that

Leon might have killed some guy you asked her to identify. So I've started to worry about what Leon might do if he finds out he's been cheated on a debt. Why would Merry owe Leon anyway?

I realize by doing this I may be screwing my visiting privileges, and it breaks my heart. I've almost been talked into coming back for an extended stay, would be especially eager to do so if you can promise me Dot or her boss didn't kill anyone. Is it possible that you could keep an eye on everything without letting her know I tattled?

Also: I heard Halsey leave his room twice that night. Dot only heard and followed him the second time, which is when we all heard her.

Working on some duck thighs in cider. Hope I can make them for you soon. Would Caroline go to Russia with you?

Arnie

USUALLY CHECKING E-MAIL WAS A RELAXING EXPErience, something safe to do after a maudlin late shift and before bed. Jules printed it out and carried the sheet into the bedroom, where Caroline was already dozing.

"Arnie sent me a note."

"Um."

"He thinks Halsey pushed Fred in the water."

Her breathing stopped being even. "Um."

"He's afraid Leon's going to kill someone."

"Who?"

"Merry."

She snorted. "We should be so lucky. Get in bed."

FRIDAY WAS A night-shift day. At 11:00 a.m. the phone rang twice, and the muted answering machine handled it. Ten minutes later it rang two more times, and when it started for a third, Jules reached for it without sitting up.

"I'm aware that this is your day off," said Grace, "but we've got a problem, and I had Ed drive by to see if your car was at home."

"Just tell me," said Jules.

"A lunatic on a log grapple at the mill."

"Say it again," said Jules.

"You know, one of those funny-looking things with claws. They use it for lifting logs."

"What's the lunatic doing with it?"

"Chasing a coworker. The coworker's hiding in the mechanic's shed and the lunatic is ramming it. By the way, I think you might have gone to school with him. His boss says he's thirty-seven, raised locally."

"What's his name?"

"Byron Maggles. Recently divorced, or in the process, or something. They think that's the problem. Might be worth a call to Peter."

Jules couldn't remember the name offhand, and wasn't sure he wanted to try harder. "Who's down there?"

"Jonathan. Remember? You wanted him on days so he wouldn't run into that crazy lady."

"Son of a bitch," said Jules, finally sitting up and lifting Caroline's head from his thigh. "Damn."

"I don't want to know," said Caroline, rolling over.

"What was that?" said Grace.

"Nothing," said Jules. "Is Ed keeping an eye on him?"

"More or less. You entertaining?"

"I'll go down there," said Jules. "Everything else is my business."

The job was filled with strange requests. The day before a man had wanted an officer to tell his son to rake the lawn, and had become abusive with Grace when she told him to do it himself. That afternoon a caller complained of youths shooting arrows at gophers. This was, as Jules happened to know, perfectly legal within the city limits.

Now the lumber mill had called them about a maniac behind a ten-ton machine, a maniac who'd been given the keys by the company. Somehow it didn't seem fair that such dramatic stupidity should be the Absaroka Sheriff Department's problem. When Jules asked the mill manager to block access to the highway with some of their other large equipment, the man said no; if Byron Maggles rammed a dump truck or a backhoe or log cutter with the grapple, he'd cause tens of thousands of dollars worth of damage.

"Tough shit," said Jules succinctly. "You have any better ideas?"

The manager sulked, still crushed because he'd had to send most of the employees home. Jules and Ed and Jonathan killed time watching the grapple ram the machine shed over and over again. It was gradually folding and slicing the buckling metal wall despite reinforced steel and a cement floor, and the man inside, one Bill Koslowski, had to be having a problem with sphincter control. Byron didn't like Bill for the oldest reason on the planet: Bill was sleeping with Byron's almost-divorced wife.

"What kind of insurance you got on that thing?"

"The building?"

"No, you asshole," snapped Jules. "Can you imagine what

it will cost the company if he makes it onto the highway and takes out a few cars?"

The manager had the exits blocked by two very nervous employees, one of whom was stupid enough to sprint to the mill office where they watched rather than to the McDonald's across the road after parking an ancient bulldozer. Byron Maggles made a run for him, which was exciting for everyone, then turned from the manager's building at the last minute. Jules was sure he saw the door on the shed wiggle, Bill Koslowski considering a run for it, but by now it was too bent to open.

"How fast does that thing go?" asked Jules.

"About twenty."

"How much gas do you think he has?"

"Plenty. The tanks are designed for off-premise work."

"Fucking lingo," muttered Ed.

"Are you really sure the glass is bulletproof, not just shatterproof?"

"That's what the company promised. It's built to withstand falling tree branches and suchlike."

"But it's a grapple, not a cutter. It's for dealing with downed trees, right?"

The manager curled a lip. "Accidents happen."

Jules stared at the machine. Shooting tires was not an option, and there was no easy-to-toss stick dynamite lying around. He'd brought the .223 but knew he didn't have a chance with it.

He walked out with the bullhorn. "Byron, please tell us what we can do to make you happy."

The answer was a muffled shriek. "Kill that son of a bitch for me."

"Would it help to talk to your wife?"

Byron made another run at the building. When he'd backed up again Jules tried a second time. "Maybe we could bring someone else down here for you to talk to. A counselor, or a minister, or a priest!"

Byron screamed in rage and put on the gas. This time he came away with a piece of corrugated aluminum. Jules walked back inside, picked up the phone, and dialed Peter. "You know who might be dealing with a divorce client named Byron Maggles?"

"Ho ho ho," said Peter. "I could use a good joke on that one."

"Give me some background."

"There's that pesky confidentiality problem, you pig."

He was in a wonderful mood and Jules found this annoying. How could anyone be at work and in a wonderful mood at the same time? Peter should be on a honeymoon, which was what Jules wished he was doing.

"Byron's trying to kill a man and we're having trouble stopping him."

"He's trying to kill Father Mark?"

That explained a lot. "He's trying to kill a guy named Bill."

"Oh," said Peter. "Bill. He's old news. She's boffing Father Mark now. I heard through the grapevine Byron found out yesterday. Sorry I didn't warn you."

It seemed Bill Koslowski's romance had ended when Byron Maggles and his wife had gone into counseling with Father Mark, the stunningly stupid priest at St. Anne's, a man who had a rep for ruining half of Blue Deer's Catholic funerals and weddings. Divvy, who was on the school board and petitioned the diocese on a weekly basis for the priest's removal, would be thrilled to learn that Father Mark (a) had been having an affair and (b) had been outed by an enraged husband with heavy machinery.

"Ick," said Jules.

"Takes all types," said Peter. "If I was Byron I'd say good riddance. Too bad he found Bill first."

The mess was insoluble. Ed had managed to calm Byron down a little by suggesting he rest up, think about his children, but it was only a matter of time before he set in on the buildings again.

"How many of those wires would we have to shoot to stop the thing?"

"Most of them," said the manager. "Isn't there some way not to damage the machinery?"

"Does that thing have vent holes on all three sides?"

"I don't know," said the manager.

"Have you ever driven it?"

"No."

Jules thought it over. "You sure he doesn't have a gun?"

"Sure. Doesn't need one in that thing, does he?"

Jules walked outside again and lifted his binoculars, then the megaphone. "Byron, we're going to have to shoot you if you won't stop."

"I want to die," screamed Byron.

Back inside, Ed shook his head. "You thinking a bullet can fit through those holes?"

"I was hoping to hit him low," said Jules. "We have try for the hydraulics first."

"I can't take a shot like that. Can you?"

"Are you kidding?" said Jules. "Not a chance. We'll use the eagle scout."

By now Harvey had arrived with a Highway Patrol cop. Jonathan stared at everyone, the news dawning slowly, pleasure spreading over his features. Jules wanted to think that most people wouldn't be so happy to learn they might have to kill someone, but he put the thought aside to trouble him later. "Do you think you can do it?"

"Yes, sir. What rifle?"

"The .223's in my trunk."

Jules had parked his car behind the headquarters, tucked away from Mr. Maggles. Jonathan pulled on a bulletproof vest. Jules held up the shoulder harness. "What about the tripod?"

"No time. He could turn that thing around and run you over before you were set up."

"I thought he wanted to die."

"He might change his mind," said Jules patiently. "And obviously he has things he wants to do first."

Jonathan frowned. "Just try," said Jules. "I'll go out there with you. Count and aim between each shot, and if he turns around toward us, try to pop through one of those vent holes and hit him low. Then we'll run, because he'll probably ram the building and we'll want to be at the back wall."

By now Maggles had ripped another hole in the corrugated wall, and was swinging back and forth to free the grapple. "Okay," said Jules.

When they walked out together Jonathan kept the rifle along his thigh until they were thirty feet from the grapple, then went down on one knee, leveled the .223, and fired. He hit one wire and made sparks, missed on his next, and hit with the third. They heard the hiss of escaping air. Byron redoubled his efforts.

Jonathan took out two more wires and the engine cut out. Byron shrieked and wrestled with the door, and Jules, seeing what he had in his hand, felt ice move up his neck.

"Shit!" yelled Jules. "He's going to blow his head off or shoot us."

Jonathan froze. "Shoot him in the knee," said Jules. "Anything."

Byron Maggles finally managed to fling open the door to the grapple and by the time it was open he had the gun to his head. His eyes were squinted shut, his teeth gritted, and Jules stopped worrying about his own skin and fought the urge to shut his own eyes. Then Byron's hand became a pink puff, and his gun fell, bouncing off the side of the grapple.

Jonathan lowered the rifle. "Oh God. Look at him bleed. I shoulda tried for his leg after all."

"Just your basic arterial bleeding," said Jules, running forward. "It's fine. You did great."

A minute later, as they pulled Maggles off the grapple and put a tourniquet on his wrist, the mechanic's shed finally collapsed. They found Bill Koslowski under a table, physically untouched and psychically ruined.

"Old Bill won't be playing hide the wrench with Mrs. Maggles tonight," said Ed, as the manager led the man away and Al and Bean loaded Byron in the ambulance.

"Shut up, Ed," said Jules. "I'm going back home. This is supposed to be my day off."

ON BAD DAYS, the idea of how little he knew about people often buried him. The assumption that everyone at least meant to behave reasonably had always been ludicrous, but even the worst maniacs had to start somewhere. Most mass murderers started by torturing animals; most embezzlers started with a pack of cigarettes at a convenience store.

Jules knew very little about Leon, given that he suspected he'd killed two people, but it only took him a few hours to find out a lot. Leon Miller Baden, age fifty-eight, had been born in Nepheris, Utah. His parents were dead, and he had no siblings. He'd gone to a community college, served stateside during Vietnam, and afterward gotten his teaching certificate in Bozeman.

It was during this period that Jules found the only wrinkle in the record: a child endangerment charge, subsequently dropped, that had been brought before Leon had even begun his thirty-year career teaching chemistry and history and wrestling.

Harvey, whose wife taught typing and accounting at the school, shook his head; he'd never heard a thing. The Gallatin officer who'd signed off on Leon's 1967 report was Hank Merrault, who could only be a few years older than Leon. He'd only retired the year before, and phoning him would be far pleasanter than slogging through the records. If he remembered.

Jules called, and after a lengthy discussion of how horrible the spring had been for gardeners, they got down to business. Hank remembered quite well, which he admitted was surprising. He put it down to the fact that he'd only been a cop for a few years at the time, and that the incident had bothered him.

"Weirdness," he said. "I've seen worse things, but they've been real obvious. This was something else."

Leon, it seemed, had married young, and when his first wife had to drive to Wyoming to see family, she'd left their infant daughter with Leon for a week. She'd returned early, having tried to phone without luck, to find the baby alone and dehydrated, alive but no longer screaming in her crib. The wife was distraught, assumed someone had murdered Leon, that he'd somehow been forced to leave the house or had some horrible accident.

Jules had called Hank from home, and paused now in the middle of assembling a sandwich. "What had happened?"

"He'd gone on a canoeing trip in Idaho. He'd planned the trip, told his wife he'd canceled it but lined up a sitter instead. Then the sitter wasn't able to take the baby at the last minute, and he left anyway."

"The county didn't bring charges?"

"The wife dropped hers for the sake of a speedy divorce and sole custody, no visitation. Leon had gone canoeing alone, and the doctor who examined the baby couldn't give a firm estimate on how long she'd been without food or water. The child was out the next day after they rehydrated her."

Jules was quiet for a few moments. "Where do the wife and daughter live now?"

"They moved to Georgia, I think. The girl would be thirty or so now. Last I heard she was sweet and happy, but then I recall the wife was a fine person. It's rough, marrying someone and then realizing you never knew him."

THERE WAS ABSOLUTELY no evidence to tie Leon to the gory scene of Robert Raphael Frame's death in the snowbank. Jules couldn't even prove that it wasn't suicide, any more than he could prove the same about Anne or Fred. The only satisfying maneuver he could come up with was to ask Leon to come identify his old business partner.

Jules didn't bother with politely draped cloths, but Leon was cocky about the whole thing. "Yep, that's him. Poor asshole. I thought he'd run away."

"Pretty deep cut on the throat there for a suicide," said Jules. "I think you made sure he couldn't run away."

"What's that supposed to mean?"

“What the hell you think it’s supposed to mean?” asked Jules. “I think you killed him, and I think we have a better chance of proving that than we ever did of proving Anne. You told Jonathan he called you from South Carolina.”

“He said that’s where he was,” said Leon.

“What was he calling to say? ‘I’m fine, even though you want me dead?’ “

“He was calling to see if his old lady had been around.”

“You make me sick,” said Jules. “You’re a fucking monster.”

Leon started to walk away. Jules kept up with him. “We just sent a few more things up to the lab, sloppy shit you probably didn’t notice.” He held the morgue doors open politely. “We’ll be watching you, and you’ll fuck up.”

“Piss off.”

“What’s the favor Merry Maier owes you for?”

Leon stopped in his tracks.

“She doesn’t owe me, and I don’t owe her. She works for me, period.”

“That’s good,” said Jules. “I’d keep it on a professional basis. She’s a scary lady.”

Leon got into his truck and left.

“I WANT TO dog him until he loses his mind,” said Jules. “But we can’t really afford to spare that many hours.”

“I’m not spending any part of my last year following that asshole,” said Ed.

“Maybe I could give him to Jonathan,” said Jules. “The kid needs a reward, and it’ll sound like a reward, saying I want him to tail a man who might have killed two people. It’ll keep him away from Frame’s wife, too.”

They still hadn’t tracked down Lucretia, though Jonathan

glimpsed her on a daily basis. "It'll keep him away from all sorts of things," said Ed, perking up. "But don't let him talk to Leon."

Jonathan was thrilled. "I don't like Leon Baden one bit," he said. "I still think he was up to more than burning down the trailer and killing that poor man."

"Isn't that enough?" said Jules. "Don't forget his wife."

"Right," said Jonathan. "I won't."

"It's a lot of time in the car," said Jules. "It's going to be boring. I want him to be able to see you, but I don't want you close enough for him to approach."

"Why?"

"Leon's got a bad temper."

"Can I read while I'm on stakeout? I mean, he's a murderer, but what if he just works for eight hours?"

Jonathan had probably been aching to say "stakeout" and "murderer" for most of the last two years. "If you promise not to lose him," said Jules.

JULES WENT TO see Peter. "I need a phone number," he said. "I need to talk to that expert you used in Leonard's trial. You know, the 'too drunk to even start the car' defense."

"Sure," said Peter. He looked like a new man, or at least a man who'd begun to sleep again. "But if you want to use him, I need to warn you that he has all the court presence of a one-celled organism."

"Yeah, well, maybe we'll get to that. Can I call from here?"

"I'll dial for you and go make copies."

Jules asked several things. Was there enough alcohol in your average bottle of Wild Grouse to put such a high percentage of poison into two good-sized humans? How likely was it that anyone could even walk with a blood alcohol of

.35 or .42? How much high-voltage grain alcohol could a human ingest without dying, and how quickly would it hit the bloodstream? Jules had in mind someone who assumed she'd be found within four or five hours.

While the man hemmed and hawed, Jules studied the Lamaze schedule tucked under the desk phone. Peter and Alice were due to see a birth on video that weekend and Jules would have to try to take Peter fishing afterward, smooth over the trauma. Peter was in the next room now, probably listening to all of the current discussion. Jules didn't care a bit, thanked the expert, and hung up.

"What did he say?" asked Peter, not bothering to pretend.

"He says she couldn't have thrown a Ping-Pong ball, let alone Fred, if she'd hit that point before Fred fell."

"What do you mean, if?"

"She could have finished drinking after. I pulled some dead flowers out of a bottle in her room and the clear stuff in there wasn't water. The lab says it was grain alcohol."

"Did anyone hear anything?" asked Peter, looking out the window.

"They were arguing earlier in the evening."

"Does she have a motive?"

"Not offhand," said Jules. "But I'm looking. You know she inherits plenty, but I'm getting the feeling she wanted more, sooner rather than later. That's the only explanation for talking Fred into disguising the painting."

"Shouldn't the appraiser have caught that?"

"He never really looked at any of the stuff. I think she paid him off."

"Quite a risk."

"Yes." Jules wondered if this was what had upset Fred that last day. But why be upset over bribery when you're already a counterfeiter? Why would that tilt the balance among thieves?

"You'll never prove it."

"Probably not, but I can let her know that I know, and I can make her life miserable."

"I'm a little surprised she didn't just try to kill Halsey and collect."

"She might still," said Jules. "I'd be a little nervous if I was Leon, too."

"ANY WORD ON Mr. Altschuler?"

It was the next morning and Moss Jackson was making his ritual twice-weekly call.

"I don't have anyone else to ask," said Jules. "There won't be any word. But if he turns up, I'd like to talk to him myself. I think someone might have bribed him to mislead a client."

"How about this body I read you fished out of the river?" asked Jackson. "I was sitting on a comfortable toilet this morning, catching up on the file shorts from a couple weeks back, and there I find you have a naked male floater, thirties or forties, dark hair, approximately Mr. Altschuler's height and weight, lungs filled with water. Imagine my surprise, especially when I discovered you'd found the guy weeks ago."

"It wasn't Altschuler," said Jules, watching Caroline and Ed reason with a dark-haired woman across the room. "I met the man. I met both of them, one alive and one dead."

"Ah," said Jackson. "That's true."

"The dead man s face was untouched. They're both five feet, eleven inches, brown hair, clean-shaven, but with totally different features, skull shape, the works. Altschuler's hair was dark brown and this guy's is mousy. And we have reason to believe our man started out in Texas. So there's no point in bothering me."

"I'm bothering you?"

"I'd rather have someone missing than a waterlogged body any day," said Jules.

"Couldn't have been too messy if his face was untouched," said Jackson. "You should see what I have to see everyday."

"Dead people are always messy," said Jules. "I'm wading through them. And you're the sucker on a city force."

"I'm sending the file," said Jackson. "His parents finally came up with a few particulars that might be helpful if you find another dead man you don't know."

Jules was beginning to look forward to these conversations. He would have liked to have had a drink with Jackson, talk over the man in the river, the lovers left to freeze, the drunk in the pool, the vagrant, and the poor old lady nobody had missed. He might even have told Jackson he was in love despite all this death, something he hadn't told anyone, including the woman in question. The calls perked him up, and he imagined Jackson made them partly because he was bored and heckling Jules was the most pleasant option in a sea of dead ends. Jackson had admitted that Altschuler's wealthy family had given their attorney standing orders to call the cop every morning for an update.

"Jules," said Caroline. "We need a little help here."

Jules stood up and Ed crossed the room toward him, rolling his eyes. "We picked her up setting fires under cars. She says she'll only talk to Jonathan."

Jules and the woman looked at each other. She had light gray eyes and long, thick black hair, small features, and brown skin. She was lovely but something was obviously off;

when Jules walked into the room she was rubbing her nose dreamily, turning it into a pig snout, and when she turned toward him the movement was overly rapid. She twitched away just as quickly and balled her hands up on her lap.

"You don't happen to be Lucretia Frame, do you?"

She smiled. "Not if you're not Jonathan, I don't."

LUCRETIA ULTIMATELY AGREED to talk to Caroline, after Caroline promised her a meal, specifically a Caesar salad. "I haven't had one in so long," said Lucretia.

The whole thing flummoxed Caroline. "It's hard to follow her train of thought."

"I bet," said Jules.

"She says someone burned up her husband. She says 'he' burned up her husband, but when I mention Leon's name she just rubs her nose."

They were talking while Jules cleaned the painting, working inch by inch, and Caroline made a stew. Peter and Alice were coming to dinner that night, a coming-out party of sorts. Jules had found a signature, and though he'd found no mention of the canvas existing in any of the books about Moran, this didn't trouble him. If Moran had painted it when he was ill at the Sacajawea, and left it with his hosts, few people would have ever seen it. According to roundabout conversations with Halsey, Muriel's parents hadn't much liked it, and kept it in the music room; Muriel hadn't cared for it either, and had taken it from the frame out of pure spite when she left. Jules had found a mention of another painting that Moran had done on the same trip and brought home with him: when he searched out the image he recognized the Sacajawea's mostly defunct orchard and part of the small pool on the other side of the hotel. The colors and the styles were similar, the subject unmistakable even a hundred years later.

Alice, after taking a very long time to understand what Jules was saying, was the first to really come to the point.

"So how much is it worth?"

"I have to ask Halsey again. I have to give him another chance to take it back."

"You said that. How much is it worth?"

"A hundred grand. Two hundred. Maybe more, because of the size and the fact that it's western."

"What about the thing on the back?"

"I don't know about that. I'll have to send it to someone for a real going over."

Peter was rolling his eyes in the general direction of the ceiling, probably imagining a car that worked and a paid-off mortgage.

"I'm so confused," said Alice. "Is this some sort of bizarre wedding present? You already gave us the bassinet and the pasta."

"You invested," said Jules. "I'm still not sure that it's going to work."

HE WENT UP to talk to Halsey the next morning, and found him outside, gesturing to a high school dropout with a shovel. Halsey had color in his cheeks and was wearing his hightops. Once again, he was a man with a project, no longer weighed down by troublesome family.

"I've officially hired Alice to do the garden," he said. "I gather she and Caroline may be in business together. Nice for you, heh?"

It would have been very nice if Jules had wanted to stay.

"I think they might do just a few jobs before the baby," he said. "Maybe more next year."

"I'm getting six different kinds of apple trees," said Halsey. "Twelve in all to start with. Four varieties of plums, four pear. Gooseberries, black currants, roses—"

"I went to see Leon," said Jules. "I bought Muriel's jokes. Merry hadn't actually given him a deposit, and she only planned to give him three hundred."

Halsey seemed nettled to have been pulled out of gardening dreams and took a moment to respond. "How much had she charged him?"

"Two hundred."

Halsey snickered, then feigned disinterest.

"I started to clean it up, enough to make sure it's what I thought it was."

Halsey shook his head. "Sell it and keep the money. It'll change your lives. It's nearly ruined mine."

Jules was stubborn. "Would you like to have the money go to Dottie?"

"No. She'll have plenty, and she hasn't exactly kept her nose clean. No one has."

"This isn't right," said Jules. "And why didn't you tell me what you suspected? You were going to, the week before the wedding, and then you clammed up."

"I wasn't sure who to suspect," said Halsey. "And then I didn't want to make a fuss. It seemed easier to let it go. If you don't sell the thing and split the profit with your cronies, I'll leave it to you in my will. Then there'll be less."

"Thanks," said Jules stiffly.

"I don't want to hang anything that someone's died for," said Halsey. "Period. I don't need it and I don't want it."

"Can you prove someone died for it?" asked Jules.

"No. And if I could, I wouldn't. Family's family."

"Did you hear anything that night?"

Halsey sat wearily on the old stone wall. "Just the usual endearments. They won't get you anywhere."

"What else?"

"Nothing. When I got back I read, played something on the stereo. I went to sleep early."

Jules remembered the music, a Telemann piece that had sounded like tree frogs. He could imagine running his hand along Caroline's hip while he listened to it. Halsey watched him, then turned away.

"Merry added grain alcohol to Fred's scotch and threw him out the window when it kicked in. If you didn't hear anything, then why did you go downstairs twice?"

"Checking to see if the stoves were off."

"You didn't see Fred lying there the first time?"

"No."

Dottie slammed out the back door and shook a rug, sending a cloud of dust into the sunlight. Halsey waved. "How can you bear having your niece come back here, knowing all this?" asked Jules.

"I can't," said Halsey brusquely. "I talked to Peter this morning. He's sending her a letter saying that she is no longer welcome here, and that her things will be packed up and sent to the destination of her choice. I'll handle her medical bills, and I've placed a sum of money in trust for her, but she'll have nothing more coming from the estate."

Jules stared at him.

"I'll sign off on these changes tomorrow," said Halsey. "And I'll make sure she knows it's a done deal, so that she doesn't come up with some new plan. I'd like to live another ten years."

Jules had a sudden, violent desire for a drink. "What if she comes back for something that wasn't in her room?"

"That's your problem," said Halsey, smiling for the first time since he'd told Jules about the apple trees. "Or maybe it's Leon's."

Jules started back toward the hotel.

"Tell Alice she still has to pay the wedding bill, but I insist on paying her for the garden work. And I don't want her touching a shovel."

"Okay," said Jules. "Okay."

"And you have to finish in the workroom."

"Right."

"And don't forget the deal with that egg. If you do the right thing."

"I'm getting closer," said Jules.

He'd parked in the front lot and headed back through the building. Dottie snagged him in the hall. It was almost like old times.

"Could you also put away Merry's bicycle? She left it by the back door."

"In the basement?"

"Upstairs," said Dottie.

"Does the elevator work?"

"It's light," she said blithely. "I'd do it myself if Arnie hadn't put my back out. Did you hear he's coming back?"

"I heard he was thinking about it. Congratulations."

She beamed. "Thanks. Don't go telling any stories."

"I'm the last person who'd think of it," said Jules, lifting the bike.

Jules was beginning to enjoy invading Merry's privacy, even if she wasn't there to appreciate the gesture. This time he dumped the bike on the pile in the middle of the room and looked around, knowing nil about the woman. How could you understand someone who had no personality? The mounds of creepy collectibles, piles of magazines but only a half dozen books, touchy-feely crap. Lots of fancy candlesticks and fussy pottery. The *TV Guide* and remote control had their own wicker basket, which Jules, whose intellectual snobbery occasionally burbled up, found telling. On the shelves he found two photo albums, one with baby pictures of Merry and one that seemed to cover the last ten years or so, an endless selection of party shots, six or ten people huddled together with creepy grins in affluent settings, leaning in to the camera with beers and wineglasses outstretched, dressed in bathing suits, ski gear, evening dresses. Jules flipped through quickly and slid it back on the shelf in disgust and in haste, but a second later he'd reached for it again in a panic. In the last several pages he found him three times, cheek pressed against Merry's, arms flung around other, saner blondes. It was Piers M. Altschuler, the runaway art expert.

Dottie stood in the open door, poised on her tiny, quiet feet. How someone so top heavy could move so quietly was beyond him, and Jules wasn't sure how he'd even realized she was in the room. "What are you doing?"

"Looking," he said.

"For what?"

"I don't know."

"Try."

"Looking for why Fred died."

"I bet no matter how hard you look you're going to come down to one answer," she said.

"What?"

"Fred was a bad drunk."

They eyed each other. "Did you come up just to tell me that, or to check on me?"

"I came up to throw some more of her junk on the pile and because I wanted you to check the sink trap," said Dottie. "The usual exciting reason."

"Can I ask you something?"

"You're going to anyway."

"Did you know that Merry and Altschuler were friends?"

"Before or after I saw him sticking his tongue down her throat?"

Jules stared at her. "By the back door," said Dottie. "When she was seeing him out. Nobody seems to hear me."

"I didn't mean that kind of friend. I was under the impression that Altschuler was gay."

"That guy wasn't gay. Period. He didn't have the imagination." She grinned at Jules. "You boys never have a clue."

But now Jules was looking at the middle distance. Being this stupid didn't come naturally; it took real effort. He wondered what else had passed him by in the weeks when his mind had been addled by Caroline and anticipation.

Dottie tossed a bag onto the pile and left. Jules knew he'd missed something without having a clue where to start. It was a given, after all, that he'd missed a lot. Had Merry actually known Altschuler in advance, or had she paid the real thing off and put a friend in his place? The latter, clearly. The man hadn't seemed like an expert in antiquities and erotica, and he hadn't been one.

JULES BEAT BACK a sense of doom on the drive to town. He brought the photo albums with him and called Moss Jackson immediately. "You said you were sending a photo and a few other things on Altschuler. When will they come?"

"You have them already. I e-mailed a photo and some physical particulars and a handwriting sample. Why?"

"Just cleaning up," said Jules, trying to sound happy.

"Just because it's spring?" asked Jackson sarcastically.

"I don't know," said Jules. "I don't know. I'll call back in a bit."

He hung up and logged on to the computer, watching through fingers as the screen resolved to the file of Piers Michael Altschuler, forty-two.

His distinguishing marks included a cowlick at the base of his skull, an appendectomy scar, the possession of only one of his original wisdom teeth, an inch-long burn mark on his left inner thigh, and a dime-sized beauty mark centered on his left buttock.

Jules read these last two items twice. He started to get out of his chair, then saw that Wesley, the only other human in the room, was on the phone. He sat back down slowly and with some dread scrolled down to the still-loading photo.

The truth was out: Jules had never met P. M. Altschuler alive, but he'd definitely dragged him out of the river. Altschuler had not been the man who'd come to the Sacajawea; Altschuler had probably been dead before Merry's friend had eyed Halsey's paintings and drunk the old man's beer. Which meant that instead of a lonely suicide from out of town, Jules was dealing with a three-week-old murder on his own turf, a murder that had almost certainly been premeditated and deliberate.

Now Jules knew what Fred had been upset about, and he was beginning to think he understood the little favor Merry owed Leon for.

He bit the bullet and hit redial. "Got a minute?" he asked Jackson.

THE RIVER MAN, P. M. Altschuler, had been moved to a corner drawer at the funeral home. Jules took some Polaroids, then stared down at Altschuler. The thin face had probably once been tremendously arrogant, but now it simply looked frail, tallow yellow and gray, a bad wax job with fatal dents. "Let's roll him over."

"I don't really need to see this guy's ass again," said Wesley. "I don't like the burn scar. I don't want to think about it."

"Come on," said Jules.

They flipped the slender man and Jules stared down at the twin semicircles above the tailbone. "It's a shotgun," he said. "Someone pushed a double-barreled shotgun in his back. He didn't want to go into the river, and they had to really push. He didn't want to jump either."

"Either?"

AT THE BAIRD, Jules and Caroline determined that the real P. M. Altschuler had checked in on Friday night but the man who the waitresses had remembered Saturday night was Merry's boy.

Merry's friend Betty Dillinger was skiing in Red Lodge until the following night. Halsey recognized one person in the picture, a girl named Connie, but it took until the next morning to find an old boyfriend of Merry's in L.A., the only man whose last name Halsey could remember.

"Connie's last name is Bones," he said. "Sounds weird but she's from some sort of tissue paper money. They knew each other in Austin."

"When did Merry live in Austin?"

"I have no idea," said the man. "By the time I met Connie I didn't really want to know. She was there with a recording crew, before she got fired from the last job."

According to Social Security and the state's driver's license database, no one named Constance Bones lived in the state of Texas.

"You know," said Halsey that afternoon, "you could simply phone my niece. She called me this morning."

"How was she doing?" asked Jules politely. Arnie had gotten in the night before, and he and the plumber were a few feet away, arguing about the faulty garbage disposal.

"She wasn't very happy. I believe she'll try to leave early. And she wanted to know why you were talking to her friends."

"Where did she want her stuff shipped?"

"She didn't say yet."

Dottie was almost too happy about Arnie to notice when Wesley and Ed sorted Merry's belongings methodically, piling items into waiting boxes as they finished. No one deigned to explain, but Jules knew she'd get it out of Halsey later. They didn't find a thing.

Late that afternoon the whole department met by the Yellowstone. They started where the body had washed up, then walked upstream to the rock where Altschuler's clothes and wallet had been neatly piled.

"Maybe that lady was with him and promised sex," said Harvey. "Maybe he thought he was getting nookie and she pushed him in the river."

"No one's going to get completely naked outside in Montana in April," said Wesley.

Jules avoided looking at Caroline.

"I used to," said Harvey.

"That was high school, Harvey," said Jules. "And I don't think she came near here. She worked the bar that night, and Dottie and Halsey told me they heard her walking around and playing music. Fred was with her, and at midnight or after they came downstairs for snacks. She was trying to make it very obvious that she was home."

"She could have left," said Harvey.

"She could have," Jules agreed. "But why bother if Leon would do it all for her. And anyway, this is plainly bullshit. Altschuler went off the bridge."

They could see a corner of it from where they stood, a few hundred yards farther up. "That's pretty risky," said Wesley. "Someone might have seen him do it."

"There's not much traffic at night. Leon's got a pickup. He would have kept the guy behind it if he heard a car coming."

"Why are you so sure it was Leon?" asked Caroline. "Why not Fred?"

"Fred wasn't good at fibs."

"He was about the painting."

"What painting?" asked Harvey.

"A little hoodle Ms. Maier and Mr. Bottomore were pulling on Halsey Meriwether," said Jules. "Fred wasn't up to wrapping someone's arm behind them so tightly it popped out at the shoulder, or pushing a shotgun into a back hard enough to cause a bruise. Leon coached wrestling. He'd know how to make someone hurt. He probably didn't mean to leave any sign at all."

"This guy really didn't want to jump, did he?" said Wesley. "Even in the dark he knew it would kill him."

They walked back to their cars. Ed was never good with open-ended things. "Could we search Leon's place with Halsey's permission, and without a warrant?"

"I don't want to do that yet," said Jules. "Jonathan, keep an eye on him, but don't breathe down his neck tomorrow."

"Should we watch him at night, too?"

"We probably don't need to if we don't scare him," said Caroline.

"Do you really think it might have been Fred?" asked Jules.

"Nah," said Caroline. "I bet this is what he wanted to talk about, that day you were going to fish."

JULES ASKED WESLEY to track down the current wrestling coach at the high school and ask about ligament damage and wrestling holds.

And then there was the problem of Merry. He phoned the clinic staff, who brought up privacy issues. Broaching the patient's potential involvement in a capital crime only brought alarm and questions, and Jules settled for trading assurances: they promised that Merry wasn't going anywhere soon, and he promised that she was unlikely to cause harm to herself or others.

For years, Leon had used secondary dealers for smaller items that had no place in his store, things like belt buckles, cuff links, watches—the sorts of things that Altschuler had been wearing, according to the night clerk at the Baird, but that hadn't been left on the boulder or found on his body.

Jules believed that dogs loved to chase men in uniform because men in uniform were seemingly in endless retreat. Such men persisted in approaching week after week, but they ran when threatened, a dog's version of a feel-good video game. United Parcel Service workers seemed to have more humor about this than U.S. Postal Service employees, who were probably exhausted by forever being on the lookout for coworkers with automatics.

At any rate, Jules wore his uniform only when he had to patrol or appear in court, and on this day he walked untouched past two German shepherds to knock on Frank Purvis's door. Purvis actually trained his shepherds to bark at uniforms, and he was deeply annoyed to see Jules.

"I might be here as a customer," said Jules. "Relax."

"You might be here to give me a backrub," said Purvis.

"I'm looking for accessories. Belt buckles, that sort of thing. Maybe a watch."

Purvis was succinct. "I don't believe you."

"You don't have to. I'm just trying to be pleasant about something that might come out in the wash anyway."

"Jesus, Jules. I've kept my nose so clean I don't even sneeze anymore."

"It's not you, Frank. It's whoever sold it to you."

"Promise?"

"I promise."

He came out of the back room with two boxes. Jules didn't want to think about where the things inside came from. He had a description of the watch, an older Elgin pocketwatch, and according to Altschuler's parents virtually everything their boy had possessed was initialed. Within five minutes Jules had a buckle, a money clip, and the watch, all of them beautifully engraved with P.M.A.

"Is Leon Baden just about the greediest, stupidest man you know?"

Frank's eyes widened. "Jeez, I don't know. There's so much competition."

"Just tell me who sold you this stuff, Frank."

"Leon Baden."

"Thanks," said Jules, sliding them into an envelope and pulling out a department notepad. "I'll give you a receipt, so you know I'm not grabbing these for graduation presents."

"Who'd they belong to?"

"A dead guy. Mention this to Leon and I'll come back."

They almost had enough now.

WHEN HE GOT back to the station, Caroline was just heading out. "Are you going to the store?" asked Jules.

"Betty Dillinger called. I'm going to Bozeman to talk to her."

"I'll go with you," said Jules.

Betty naturally had a very nice house, the kind of house that Jules was reasonably sure he'd never live in. Which was okay—the carpets were too white, and what did one woman do with four bathrooms? He'd expected more out of her, but she did offer them a very good glass of merlot.

Betty couldn't remember the man's name—that was a different crowd, people Merry had known during a short stint in Austin a few years earlier. It had started as a job, but become an engagement, and the engagement had fallen apart when Merry had started drinking again and slept with one of her fiancé's friends. Betty had the vague sense that the man Jules was pointing to was the friend in question, and that he hadn't lived in Austin, but she'd frankly tried not to really listen to the mudbath. She'd heard plenty of similar renditions over the years. She'd look around in the morning, make some calls.

Jules was as pleasant as possible when he told her that she needed to look now, rather than later. He didn't think Betty would call the clinic to warn Merry, but he wasn't going to risk giving her the chance. When Betty simply refused to jump he spelled it out, even pulled a photo of the man fished out of the river from a manila folder. Caroline gave him a disgusted look, but the cheap shot brought results: Betty searched through a stash of letters.

"Gerry," she said, waving Merry's handwriting in front of Jules.

"That's it?"

"That's it. She wasn't much of a correspondent."

THE NEXT MORNING the telephone rang early, but Jules was awake, staring at the ceiling. Halsey sounded like he'd been up for hours.

"My niece called with an address and a care-of name for her belongings."

Jules scribbled. "Thanks. Did she sound happier?"

"Yes," said Halsey. "I didn't take it as a good sign."

He rolled over, flipped through the phone book, and called Betty Dillinger. "Sorry if I woke you up."

"I always get up early."

Probably because she didn't have to. Meanwhile, Caroline had a pillow pulled over her head. "How does Gerald Bach sound?"

"Perfect," she said. "That would explain why I kept thinking of Italian last names like Vivaldi."

Jules got a copy of Gerald Bach's driver's license photo e-mailed up from Texas, and this time, while the image downloaded, he shut his eyes. When he opened them he saw the glad-handing idiot who'd kept using the same stupid catchphrases and doled out business advice to Halsey. The idea that Merry had actually provided her uncle with this man's name astounded Jules. Apparently her ego hadn't shrunk along with the rest of her brain under the assault of the grain alcohol.

Gerald Bach lived in Fort Worth, where he worked for his father's investment company. It was almost five o'clock in east Texas when Jules was told that Mr. Bach had left just that morning to attend a funeral.

"When will he be back?"

"Well, he's driving," said the secretary. "I'd guess it'll take a week. I can have him call."

"Where was the funeral?"

"Montana."

"WHAT ARE YOU going to do?"

"I'm thinking of planting the crate back at Leon's."

The next morning Leon quite conveniently headed up to Helena for an antiques fair. Jonathan followed him as far as Townsend, and a half hour later Jules and Ed were using Halsey's keys to open the back door of the Bachelor. Wesley helped them pull the empty crate out of Jules's truck but wouldn't go near the building. "This is crap," he said. "Entrapment. It won't prove a thing, and none of it is admissible, and all of it will get you in trouble."

"You're right," said Jules. "Nothing's going to get us anywhere in a legal sense, as far as Merry Maier goes. I'm just looking for a little personal satisfaction."

THE NEXT NIGHT Jules and Caroline planned to have dinner and spend the night at the Sack. The day in between was endless—two fender benders, a fight at the high school, and a power line blown down in a sudden out-of-season wind. When Jules checked in at the station he found a note from Merry's clinic and an urgent message to call Dottie.

He called the clinic first, but the woman he usually talked to had left for the day. "She said to tell you Ms. Maier has checked out."

"Did she say when Ms. Maier left?"

"No. She's not on the morning census. I don't have access to yesterday's records."

Minnesota was a long way away. Jules phoned Dottie. "I can't talk now," she whispered.

"What's going on?"

"I grabbed Merry's vitamins a week ago, before your boys searched the room, when Halsey was coming down with a cold. And I found something in one of the bottles."

"What?"

She went back to whispering. "I don't want to upset Halsey. Arnie's taking him out in a bit. Aren't you coming to dinner later?"

"We'll be up in about an hour."

He was preoccupied when he pulled out of the lot, and didn't notice Ed behind him until he was almost to Caroline's. He pulled over, feeling shifty, and walked over to Ed's car.

"Jonathan wanted you to know Leon got back this morning. All he's done so far is unload stuff."

"He might not even notice the crate," said Jules. "Whose car does Jonathan have today?"

"He's got the patrol. His has some sort of brake problem, and Harvey's wife needs their extra."

"I don't want Leon seeing a cop car," said Jules. "That might be too much."

Ed looked him over. "Where are you off to?"

"Errands."

He nodded. "Keep your nose clean."

Jules watched him drive away, and circled two blocks out of his way before he came down Caroline's alley. It was eighty degrees, and she was wearing a peach-colored sundress that slid up her tan legs when she climbed in, carrying a bag with clothes for both of them. She pulled out a bikini and waved it in the air.

"It's almost May Day, and I'm going to celebrate."

"I think Ed's figuring things out," said Jules, already caring a little less.

JULES PARKED IN front, by the long pool, and Caroline ran straight upstairs. Jules walked through the bar and into the kitchen, calling "Dottie, where are you?" in a joking singsong. He was heading toward the back door when he heard a funny sound from somewhere above him, a sound like a box being dropped. He looked up.

"Caroline?"

No one answered. Jules had started to push open the kitchen screen door when he saw Leon's truck, with the engine still ticking.

Jules stood still for a long moment. He heard a knocking sound, again deep inside the building, and crossed the room in a few steps to the dumbwaiter. He flung the door open and saw just a sliver of the bottom, with Dottie's red-painted toes sticking out.

"He stuffed me in here," she hissed. "He says he wants to kill himself."

Jules ran back through the hotel to his car, moving as quietly as possible and leaving doors open behind him as he pulled his gun out of the glove box, ignoring the wild static of the radio, and tucked it into his jeans waistband under his T-shirt.

He rounded the first two flights and heard a moan. Caroline was in her underwear on the third landing, where Leon had thrown her. She had blood running down the side of her head but she was alive. He bent to pick her up and the plaster exploded above his head, the shot echoing up and down the old stairwell.

"Stop," said Leon. "Straighten up and walk toward me or I'll shoot both of you."

He had a rifle trained on Caroline. Jules looked back down at her. Her eyes were open, and she nodded.

He walked up the stairs. "I gotta talk to you," said Leon. "Get in that room. She'll keep."

He gestured Jules into the music room, then pushed the rifle into the small of his back. Jules thought of the marks on Altschuler's frail body, but wasn't eager to point out the parallels.

"Stand there by the window," said Leon. "You set me up with that bitch. She's going to make sure I pay, and she won't get nailed for a damn thing. She even cheated me on art, and she's got something here that'll finish me off."

Leon was a weepy mess, visibly shaking, though his vibrations didn't make the rifle look any less harmless. "It's all of a sudden a moot point, Leon."

"I wasn't expecting you or that girl. It's not *my fucking fault*!"

The last two words were a scream. "Don't give me that bullshit," said Jules.

"Why do you have that little shit following me?"

"Because you killed a few people. We all know it, and this isn't going to help."

"You tell him to stop following me."

"I can't," said Jules. "I left my phone in the car."

Leon backed up a step. Jules turned slowly to watch him. Leon was crying. "I'm fucked," he said. "Completely fucked. Aren't I?"

"Yes."

"I want to kill you."

He was holding the rifle on his hip. Jules's heart was pounding hard enough to make him dizzy. "Can I patch her up first? Don't make it worse for yourself."

Leon was still crying but he didn't move. "This isn't my fault. This wouldn't have happened if Anne hadn't fucked that little asshole. That little asshole." He was still crying. "Some things make you feel better. Do you know what I mean?"

"Cutting someone's throat?"

"Maybe." He stopped crying abruptly. "I want some privacy. You get your girl, and you go down to your car, and you call that little prick deputy and tell him to lay off. I need some time."

"What about Dottie?"

"I won't hurt Dottie. You've got a minute. Go."

Jules went. Caroline had dragged herself a few feet and he scooped her onto his shoulder and moved quickly down the stairs, hoping he wasn't making Caroline worse but knowing they'd both be worse if he didn't take the risk. Leon followed him halfway down, and bellowed as Jules crossed the lobby. "Move it!"

Jules lowered her into the car, started it, and punched the radio as he accelerated out of the driveway before he saw a plume of dust approaching them.

"Christ," he said. "Christ."

He threw the handset down and slid to a stop across the road, blocking it, jumping out as Jonathan stopped, too, a few feet away. Jules waved his hands as the boy pulled up and stared confused through the windshield. "No," he screamed. "Stay down."

Jonathan opened the car door and stood up. "What?"

The top of his head disappeared. Jules, ten feet away, stopped in his tracks and howled. Another shot ripped through Jonathan's chest as he fell, and a third dusted the ground by Jules's right foot. He stared down at his foot, at Jonathan soaking into the dirt, and heard Caroline screaming his name. Then he jumped into the car and threw it into reverse, speeding backward toward the hotel while she scrabbled for the radio and shots dusted the dirt around them.

He jumped out of the car, ran back inside with his gun out and up the stairs. Leon was still in the music room, trying to point the rifle at his forehead, shaking even harder.

"I can't do it," said Leon. "I can't do it."

Jules shot him twice in the chest and Leon folded slowly, slipped down the wall. Jules crossed the room and bent down to take Leon's rifle away.

"Did you hear Anne crying in the snow?"

Leon nodded weakly.

"Did you make the man jump off the bridge?"

Leon sighed. Jules put his own gun on the floor next to Leon's and sat on a crate. They watched each other.

"What are you doing?" whispered Leon.

Jules could see the blood move under Leon's clothes in a slow wave; it dripped out from his pant legs and flowed over his shoes.

"I'm watching you die," said Jules.

JULES CALLED JONATHAN'S parents from the hospital, where Caroline eventually had her spleen removed and her leg splinted. Then he walked down to the basement where he watched Horace perform a rudimentary examination of Jonathan, looking at the young strong body, the ruin of the skull. Jonathan's face was untouched, perplexed, covered with soft blond furze. Jules tried to imagine what he would have looked like in twenty years, but all he could see when he closed his eyes was grave rot. He did not look at Leon's sheet-covered gurney at the far end of the room.

Ed and Harvey came down and burst into simultaneous

tears. "I don't need to tell you he couldn't have felt a thing," said Horace, fretful and pissy.

"Oh, screw you," said Jules wearily.

"Please go away," said Horace. "None of you should be in here until the state boys arrive."

They sat in the hall during Caroline's operation. Wesley had finished up at the Sack and took a chair next to Jules. No one was working, and it didn't matter a bit. "Let me get this straight. He threw her down the stairs?"

"Yes," said Jules. "Hit her with the rifle and tossed her."

"Her head's okay?"

"Seems fine."

"Must have tried to rape her and gotten pissed off."

Across the hall, Ed and Harvey twitched and looked miserable. "What do you mean?" asked Jules.

Wesley peered at him. "The nurses said she came in with no clothes on, so we assumed the asshole had given it a try and she'd fought him off. Dottie Cope wouldn't even talk about it."

Jules looked at Wesley, and Ed and Harvey, worried and curious. "No," he said. "Her clothes were off because she was waiting for me. She was waiting for me to come up the stairs. We met there sometimes. That's why he's dead."

No one said anything, no one moved. "I should have kept an eye on Jonathan," said Jules. "It's my fault."

CAROLINE WENT IN for a second surgery the next day, to bolster her tibia with some pins. By then her parents had flown in, and it became quickly apparent that neither Caroline nor Cicely had told them the truth about the sheriff. This somehow tripled Jules's misery.

"It would be very selfish of you to bring this up today,"

said Cicely. "Act like a grown-up and give them a little time to be sure she's fine."

In the end it didn't matter because Caroline asked for him while she was still groggy. Five minutes later, Jules was outside with her father.

"Is this your fault?"

"I think so," said Jules. "It certainly isn't hers."

THE ATTORNEY GENERAL came down to sort out the mess. Jules did not volunteer an excess of information, and they didn't care to pry too deeply. Leon had killed a cop, and Leon had been a killer—the note Dottie had found hidden in Merry's vitamin C was helpful on this point. The writing was loopy, stylized without style and a little shaky:

> *To whom it may concern: If anything happens to me, I would like it known that I suspect my husband, Leon Miller Baden, of murdering Robert Raphael Frame on the night of February 26. R. R. Frame and my husband left together for a night out approximately a week after my husband may have seen Mr. Frame and myself in a compromising position. (I cannot prove that he saw us.) Mr. Frame did not return. The next night his trailer burned. I am not aware of my husband's whereabouts before this fire.*
>
> *Sincerely,*
> *Anne Baden, 3/19*

THE STATE BOYS clung to several other points: Jonathan had talked to both Wesley and Ed on the radio as he headed north, and both of them had told him to stay away from the Sack as soon as it had become clear that Leon was headed there. It was Jules's day off; it was bad luck that he'd chosen that day to finish up his part-time job. It was Caroline's day off, too; Jules told them that she'd been up there with him. Period.

No one mentioned the empty crate at Leon's. When Ed and Harvey searched the Bachelor the next day, looking for anything to tie Leon to Frame or Altschuler's deaths, there was no crate in sight, though they'd noticed a sledgehammer tossed on top of a crushed cement woman, Leon's last constructive criticism. A neighbor mentioned that a Suburban with Texas plates and two passengers had pulled in the previous evening and left with a large, boxlike item. The bar had been closed during their stop, Leon at that very moment being occupied with blowing the top of Jonathan's head off.

DOTTIE HAD TOLD Jules once that when Halsey died he wanted to be launched down the river because he'd always loved looking up at trees and sky, like a kid daydreaming, an infant on a blanket; he liked the way the sun and the wind warmed and cooled the top of his body. That evening Jules lay in his hammock staring at the undersides of leaves and scudding clouds and could only remember the view from childhood, if he discounted certain altered moments. Jonathan hadn't been much beyond that stage. Jules wished he'd never left it, and made up his mind.

He went to see Caroline late, after her parents had left for their room at the Baird and visiting hours were over. They were already weaning her off painkillers, and she managed a few very feeble jokes while she jabbed at the button that regulated the morphine drip, suggesting that Jules could partially redeem himself by raiding the evidence locker for some good narcotics.

They talked for a long time, Jules unstrung by Jonathan but Caroline drugged and dispassionate. "I think you're right," she said. "I think you should go. Quit and take the dig you've been talking about, the one near Kiev."

He had his hands over his face. "For a long time, if we're together, we'll think of Jonathan," said Caroline. "It's nothing we can help each other with."

"Why not?"

"Are you worried that you won't come back?"

He finally took his hands away from his swollen eyes. "I'm worried that I'll come back and you'll be gone."

"No," she said. "I'll wait for you."

"BUT IT'S ALMOST summer," said Alice. "How can you leave when it's finally summer?"

"It'll be summer near the Black Sea, too," said Jules. "Imagine my wanting to miss a Fourth of July on duty. It just wouldn't be a holiday if someone didn't puke on my shoes."

"You wouldn't have to work it. Go ahead and quit the job and take a break, go fishing, just live here."

"I need to leave. I'd like to go someplace where people don't look at me cross-eyed and I don't know all their dirty secrets."

"What about Caroline?"

"She told me to go away. I'll be back in early September, before you have the baby."

Peter determined that in the absence of a mayor (in Las Vegas for a last vacation before the summer wave of tourists) or even a single county commissioner (one in the hospital following a mastectomy, the other two in Helena for a probably fictitious seminar), Jules needed to see the county attorney, his cousin-in-law, Axel Scotti.

Things did not go well.

"What the fuck do you mean, 'you're leaving'?"

"Well, at least I want to. By the time it's all over I'm not sure I'd have a choice. You need an inquest into Jonathan's death, and Leon's death, and one big question will be how Caroline and I happened to be up there together to begin with, and why Jonathan was chasing after someone who hadn't been charged with anything. What does it matter to you? There's nothing to give you a headache, and next election you might end up with a conservative son-of-a-bitch you can bond with."

"I am not a conservative." Scotti stamped his foot, then pawed through a box, looking for a cigar. It was an old argument; his wife joked that he felt this way because he was to the right of Attila the Hun.

"I don't care anymore," said Jules.

Scotti stared at him, stunned by his indifference to a political argument, suddenly understanding that this wasn't simply a threat to get a certain plea. "Who'll take over until the election?"

"Wesley," said Jules. "We all decided this morning. Ed wants to retire, Harvey doesn't want to make decisions, and Caroline doesn't anticipate sticking with the job past the summer."

"Oh, well," said Axel, his face gradually filling with pleasure. "Wesley's great. Do you think he'd agree to run?"

"I don't know," said Jules. "But at least for the tourist season almost everyone can be happy."

JONATHAN'S FUNERAL MARKED the first time that Jules and Caroline were together in public, and a photo of him pushing her wheelchair made the front page of the *Bulletin* along with the news that he was resigning. The cause and effect were clear.

Jules spent the funeral thinking of how little the etiquette of such a ceremony had changed since his father had died. The same guns and flag and a similar marker in the cemetery, even though Jonathan's parents were taking him home to North Dakota, twenty-five and dead.

THERE WAS NOTHING to be done about Merry, no real proof for any of it. Jules's favorite interviewer from the Attorney General's Office was succinct.

"You shouldn't have killed Leon Baden."

No, he shouldn't have. But he wouldn't admit to anyone, ever, how much pleasure doing so had given him. If Leon had lived, he might never have been charged with anything beyond Jonathan's murder. There would probably never be enough evidence to put him on a bridge with Altschuler or a riverbank with Rafe Frame and a knife, and certainly not enough to prove that he'd heard his wife scratching her fingers bloody on their door. One crumbled cement sculpture wouldn't get them anywhere—Leon had a perfect right to take a sledgehammer to lawn art, especially after a snotty Manhattan gallery had told him it was worth $30, not $30,000. And there would never be enough evidence that Fred had done anything but fall, drunk. Leon wouldn't have helped with whether or not Merry really pumped her lover up with grain alcohol before she gave him the heave-ho, then retired to the bed to dose herself.

Jules tried to think of it as a wash. Maybe he shouldn't have killed Leon, but on the other hand at least Leon was dead.

He was officially on leave, but he started cleaning up at work anyway, passing files on to Wesley and tying up loose ends with Grace, who could barely speak. He finished removing Fred's layer from the Moran landscape, took the panel painting off the back, and sent each of them to a different auction house. He did not go back up to the Sacajawea to work, but left things where they lay. The inventory was almost finished, and it would do Halsey good to have to record a few of his own possessions. Jules explained to Dottie that almost everything he'd left out in the weeks before Fred's death had been a copy, there for Merry's benefit, and he told her where to find the originals, especially Muriel's beautiful female acrobat.

"That's a dirty trick," she said.

"It wasn't meant for you."

Halsey resumed landscaping and dithered over what to do about the all-important first impression—he couldn't quite remove the stain of Jonathan's blood from the driveway with a hose, as he'd sluiced Fred's blood off the tile. He didn't feel right having bloodstained gravel shoveled into the field, but he didn't want his guests to see or drive over something so human either. Jules preferred the field, and suggested Jonathan would, too. A few days after Caroline came out of the hospital they took her parents out for dinner, and at the end of the evening everyone seemed tremendously relieved.

Jules left a week later, the day after the inquest and just before Memorial Day weekend.

16 *Labor Day*

JULES SPENT THE SUMMER EXCAVATING BURIAL mounds seventy miles south of Kiev. The largest mound, opened the summer before, had produced the undisturbed fifth-century grave of a Scythian prince, a forty-year-old buried with beans and meat and fifty gallons of wine, gold and jewels and silk, his decapitated horse, a garroted servant, and a dress and some necklaces that apparently served as a proxy for his lucky wife.

The smaller surrounding kurgans that Jules worked on had been plowed over and eroded, and nothing quite so wonderful was discovered. Bits of several skeletons, many Greek and Roman coins, four rings and some bracelets trickled in over the course of a summer spent working under shade tarps in humid, eighty-five-degree weather. In one mound they found a horse with a gold bridle and inlaid saddle, but no evidence that a human had shared the chamber. In another they found a woman with little finery but the distinctive bowed legs of a rider and the flattened cheekbone of someone who had used a bow and arrow for decades.

He called Caroline several times from the best phone in the nearby town, but these conversations were of necessity brief and cramped. He sent her a letter every week or so, and got six long ones back over the course of the summer.

Letters from Peter and Alice and his mother and Harvey, of all people, told him more: Alice persisted in gardening all summer, and she and Caroline were talking about starting a nursery and landscaping business; Peter and Divvy fished almost every weekend; Merry had never reappeared; Wesley liked the job and wanted to run in the fall elections.

Alice was due September 29, and Jules flew back to New York on September 11, almost four months after he'd left. He spent three days in the city taking care of loose ends and overeating with Ambrose and Simon, who'd finally made contact sheets of the wedding photos and gave them to Jules to carry back. "Alice *hates* me," he said. "But it was so much work."

They watched Jules blink when he hit the first photo of Caroline, then politely averted their eyes.

HALSEY DIED IN his sleep two nights before Jules finished driving home, a peaceful, painless exit. Caroline told him about it when he called late in the afternoon from Moorcroft, Wyoming. "You should talk to Peter," she said. "There's a problem."

"He had a stroke, right? Didn't you just say he had a stroke?"

"It was perfectly natural," she said. "But after Horace left, Dottie dressed Halsey up and got Arnie to help her put him in a boat instead of calling the mortuary."

"A boat."

"A johnboat. She says it's what he wanted, but someone in Honeywater saw them slide Halsey in, and called Wesley, and Wesley's really pissed off."

Jules was standing at a gas station pay phone, trying to take it all in. "I'm sure Halsey's in the next county by now."

She snickered. "Aren't you practical."

"Did you quit yet?" He hadn't been brave enough to ask before now.

There was a long pause. "As a matter of fact I did, last Monday. Two more weeks and I'm done. That isn't helping Wesley's mood."

"It's helping mine," said Jules.

"Where are you staying tonight? Sheridan?"

"I don't know yet."

But he'd just decided to drive all the way home. He got in at 2:00 a.m., parked in front of her house, and threw pebbles at her bedroom window until the light came on.

CAROLINE HAD TO work the next morning on virtually no sleep, and Jules made her coffee, helped her through a shower, and boosted her down the walk before he went back to bed. At lunchtime he drove to Alice and Peter's, where he and Alice gaped at each other until Peter got home from the office. Jules was brown enough to make a dermatologist cry, and Alice was massive. Jules imagined twins and asked how many sonograms she'd had. Alice, who now existed at a perpetual tilt, tried not to be offended. She was very quiet and mostly sat, looking expectant in a variety of ways, with her hands on top of her belly. When she moved it was with a lurch and astonishing speed, but her stops were awkward because her midsection tended to lend momentum.

"Are you always this calm?"

She smiled. "No. I'm actually feeling a little funny. I think things are starting."

It made Jules a nervous wreck, and soon after Peter showed up he drove on to the station. Wesley wasn't doing badly. He was a little skinny, a little shaky, but that was to be expected after a summer of tourists. "I don't want to bring charges," he said. "I just want to know what Dottie had in mind. I want to be sure that she's not going to do it again."

Jules nodded, ready for a nap. "Could you talk to her?" asked Wesley. "She makes me nervous."

"If you let Caroline go early today," said Jules.

"I gather I'll have to let Caroline go for longer than today."

DOTTIE CLAIMED TO have followed Halsey's instructions by launching him dead down the river like Ophelia, or the Lady of Shalott. The johnboat had proved an extraordinarily tough bier: Halsey had circumnavigated snags, snaked under at least a dozen bridges, and bounced off banks for nearly a hundred miles with nary a speck on his black suit, before being dumped unceremoniously when a Jet Skier hit him outside of Billings. The Jet Skier reportedly inhaled a good deal of water, screaming about what he'd seen as he headed under. He intended to sue Dottie for emotional distress. Dottie had plenty of wherewithal to fight him, and had naturally retained Peter.

"He wanted to float down the river," said Dottie calmly. "And I wanted him to have that. It's even in his will. Ask Peter."

"Peter's got a few other things going on right now."

"Is Alice finally kicking in?"

"She thinks so. Look, Wesley doesn't care. He'll have to charge you with something, maybe disposing of a body in an improper manner, just because it made the paper. But you might be in trouble downstream. I don't know if Sheriff Callum, in Laurel, will have such a fine sense of humor."

She had a far-off look. "Is his first name Benjamin?"

"I think so."

Dottie smiled.

"Do you specialize in cops?" asked Jules. "Should I give Wesley a clue about the future?"

"You weren't a cop when I specialized in you," she pointed out. "Bennie used to moonlight selling pool tables to bars, so we naturally ran into each other from time to time."

"Well," said Jules, irked. "Why don't you rob a goddamn bank, if you're so well connected?"

She flicked some lint off her black skirt. "Anyway, Arnie's here now. When will I get Halsey back?"

"You want him back?"

She nodded. "If anyone pulled him out of the river, he wanted to be cremated and thrown back in. And we need to have a funeral."

They were sitting on his porch swing late in the afternoon and Dottie swirled the ice cubes in her drink. Caroline was inside taking a shower; she and Jules were taking Peter and Alice out. The plan was to feed Alice crab, which everyone claimed on good authority would speed up labor. Jules thought that Alice and Caroline simply wanted an excuse to eat crab. "Did he ever confess?"

"To what?" asked Dottie, snapping out of a trance.

"To pushing Fred into the pool."

She looked down. "He started to talk about it. I told him I didn't want to know."

Jules couldn't quite leave it alone. "Why do you think he did it?"

Dottie finished her drink. "He said it was like dropping a rock on a dying baby bird, but I think he did it for Merry. I think he was worried Fred would wake up enough to talk."

ALICE DIDN'T HAVE the baby, a little girl named Clare, until late the next day. She was skinny and long, born two weeks early, possibly because her mother had been unwilling to forgo one more flower bed, and had spent the day before she went into labor slicing out sod. All that exercise and a crab meal didn't seem to make things any easier or faster or quieter. Toward the end, when Jules and Caroline stopped in at the hospital, the sounds coming out of the labor room metamorphosed to those of a dying moose.

"Get out of here," said Olive Clement cheerily. "This is nothing you want to hear until you want to hear it, if you get my drift."

"I feel *great*," said Alice, shortly before she passed out. "Look at her!"

Clare was a red, pointy-headed mess, who only opened one eye at a time. Jules was worried. "It takes a while," whispered Caroline. "She'll be beautiful. Just agree with everything they say."

They had a celebratory bottle of wine by the river that evening. It was still eighty, and the leaves hadn't yet begun to change.

"So how has work really been?" asked Jules.

"Boring, stupid, painful. Things that never used to bother me do now. It's hard to really look forward to seeing Harvey, and Ed's sad, and Wesley's buried in stuff, and the new guy mostly talks about hunting and movies I don't like and his kids' Little League careers. And everybody's pissed at me for quitting."

Jules was lying back in the sand. "Are you going to stay?" asked Caroline.

He shook his head. "Probably just a few weeks. I was offered a nice, relaxing dig down in the Pimeria Alta, on an old church, and Sonora seems like a nice place to spend the winter. But that depends."

Caroline was looking in the other direction. "On what?"

"On how hard it is to talk you into coming along."

"Oh, come on, Jules," she snapped. "Just like that. Drop your life, travel with your former boss, just throw it all up in the air."

"The former boss part is one of the reasons I think we'd be better off somewhere else. If I were planning to stay, would you want to see me again?"

"Of course I would."

"We talked about leaving for a while before I left."

"That was months ago. My pissy little savings account went out the window while I was recovering, and I don't want you volunteering your savings. If Alice and I are going to try some sort of business I'll need to work this winter."

"I'm not volunteering my savings. I don't have any. Remember trying to drum up the money for the painting?"

Caroline was confused enough to finally meet his eye. "So?"

"If you could, would you want to go? Or at least want me to stay?"

They watched each other. "Of course I would," she said softly. "You were gone a long time. But you'd have to promise we could come back."

Jules sat up and slid next to her. "I just got word this morning that the painting sold."

She shook her head, not getting it. "The Moran. The after-commission price was $170,000, which means that we each get $42,500, and Peter and Alice can pay their hospital bill."

Caroline grinned. "That buys some time."

"Aren't you curious about the other painting?"

"What other painting?"

"The silly panel thing."

Caroline stared at him. "Dottie was right," said Jules. "It was a Charles Russell, so we should probably give her half. Which still leaves us with $242,000 to split four ways."

Caroline started to laugh and Jules kissed her. "Let's go see the world."

They left when Clare Johansen was four weeks old. On the way south they took a detour through Vail. Caroline thought it was an awful idea, and only agreed when Jules promised it would be one of the shortest bad ideas of his life. One glimpse, one real goose.

Halsey had paid a detective to keep an eye on Merry, without explaining if this was for his welfare or hers, and Dottie had passed on her location. The restaurant was supposed to be good, anyway, and Jules and Caroline showed up for an early dinner, six thirty. They didn't see her until their appetizers had arrived, and she didn't see them until the main course. She was on the far side of the room behind some potted ferns, facing them as she smiled sweetly at an elderly couple who dithered between pork and veal. She didn't push them, hid her exasperation by scanning the restaurant, and that was when she met Jules's eyes.

After a long look, Merry walked over to the table. "Are you here for me?"

"No," said Jules. "We wouldn't ruin a perfectly good vacation that way. Are you enjoying waitressing?"

She hissed and went back to her table.

They walked out to the car. "You're not being straight about something," said Caroline. "Why's she working if she took all that art?"

"Halsey disinherited her, and everything she took was worthless."

"Everything?"

"Everything she took after I knew what was going on. I only left the forgeries and copies out for her to grab, and I took photos of those. She tried to sell them all summer."

"You checked up on her?"

"I passed it on to Halsey's detective and Dottie, so that if Merry ever contests the will they'll have plenty to fight her."

They climbed in the car. "Do you want to stay near here, look around in the morning?"

"Nah," said Jules. "Let's try to make New Mexico. She scares me."

Acknowledgments

THANKS ARE DUE to Stephen Potenberg and Leslie Wells, the most patient people in my corner of the world. I'd also like to thank Anne Baden for the use of her name, and I wish I could have given her a more interesting character.

© John Potenberg

JAMIE HARRISON has lived in Montana for more than thirty years. She is the author of the Jules Clement novels as well as the novels *The Center of Everything* and *The Widow Nash*, the winner of a Reading the West Book Award and a finalist for the High Plains Book Award. Find out more at jamieharrisonbooks.com.